The Mysterious Death of an Illuminator

The Mysterious Death of an Illuminator

a steampunk murder mystery

Harrie Blake

SHB Books

Published by:
SHB Books
Brisbane, Australia
First Published 2023

ISBN: 978-0-6453929-5-1

A catalogue record for this book is available from the National Library of Australia

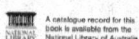

A catalogue record for this book is available from the National Library of Australia

Contents

Tick, Tick, Tick 1

1 What a Difference a Day Makes 4

2 The Usual Suspects 17

3 Keeping It In the Family 42

4 Every Family Has One 64

5 The Walstrand's Reside 88

6 The Diary of Ancilla Walstrand 105

7 Death of the Day 119

8 Pick Me, Pick Me 131

9 Ancilla Illuminates 145

10 A Cake of Lies 163

11 One Tentacle at a Time 191

Contents

12   Pinning It Down 206

13   Family Closes In 230

14   Beaumont Gambles 241

15   Ancilla Investigates 259

16   Hoadley Takes All 268

17   Breaking or Breaking Free? 290

18   Beaumont wakes up 302

19   Ancilla Fights 333

20   Death's Confusion 339

21   Trapped 356

22   One Clue at a Time 361

23   Frying Pan, Fire 373

24   Hoadley's Clue 381

25   Ancilla's Freedom 395

26   Beaumont Brings It Home 405

27   Ancilla's Haze 422

28   The End of the Matter 425

Contents

29 Family's End **436**

30 Epilogue **448**

Tick, Tick, Tick

A dark chasm yawned between her and the safety of the street.

Tick

The front door's bar dropped. She froze, breath scraping at the back of her throat.

Tick

Her gaze scurried around the room, twitching at any movement on the other side of the glass, searching for a hiding place.

Tick

An ancient prototype of a mechanical timekeeper dominating a wall, its internal clockwork exposed, flashing bronze.

Tick

She reached for a jug covered in miniature pipes but drew her arm back. Without a lid, it would be easily found.

Tick

The clock drew her gaze again, but she dismissed it. Too big, too obvious.

Tick

Another device caught her eye. She had seen its compartments a hundred times. A click, then a small tray slid out.
Tick

Her fingers spasmed, crumpling the letter in them.

Tick

She hissed, frantically smoothing it, her hands trembling.
Tick

Click, thump, click, thump, each sound louder, echoing through the glass wall.

Tick

She forced herself to breathe. To slow down. Make it fit.
Tick

She was a fool. To tip her hand like this, to risk everything, for what? A moment of glory?

Tick

But it wasn't over yet. The compartment with its precious cargo clicked closed.
Tick

She paused, listening for a whisper of the threat.

Tick

It was time, to be somewhere other than here.
Tick

She slipped out the door leading to the Garden of Devices, leaving the clock and her hard-won proof behind her. Her hatless head naked in the icy night air. Another thing to come back for.

A trellis, full of metal vines, forced her to traverse a

mechanical pathway, designed to carry visitors through the creative delights of the garden. Tonight, still. After all, she was no guest. The scrape of her uneven footsteps echoed.

A rift in the treillage promised escape into a grove of sculptures. She left its shelter, stepping into a gust of wind. A scratch on her head shook her and she spun to find a lifelike kraken, thankfully not to scale, bobbing at her. She swatted its tentacles away, battling to bring her heart rate down.

She focused on the gate now visible in the fortification surrounding the property, and the semblance of protection it promised. But her stride faulted. Sweat stung her eyes and her unresponsive legs sent her stumbling. She crashed to her knees. Cheekbone striking the ground. Her arm stretched forward, her fingers scrambling in the gravel.

Nails burrowed into her shoulder and jerked her, now useless, body onto its back. She glared at the figure, cowled by the dark, looming over her. Teeth flashed and hard fingers struck out, clamping over her nose and mouth.

Her lungs screamed with rage and her mind with one last thought.

Killing her was their second mistake.

What a Difference a Day Makes

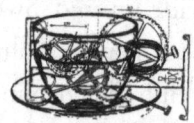

Barnaby Beaumont leapt backward. A steamer screamed past, the edge of his heavy coat slapping against the metal. He peered after it, his hand instinctively reaching for his jotter.

Think of the paperwork.

He shifted deeper onto the footpath, contemplating the Way, with its over-the-top turrets and high stone walls. Despite being so early that the use of the word morning was misleading, people flowed in and out of the gendarmerie's headquarters. Their only thing in common, the life choices that had led to them being here.

He should have let the steamer take him out. Let the world and its problems be someone else's responsibility. Icy-cold tendrils tapped his neck, and he pulled his scarf tighter, shifting it up over his nose to protect it from the cold damp odour of the street, and its bitter aftertaste.

Lamps flickered, struggling to remain alight as their night's reserves ran low and highlighted the chilly mist swirling around the Way like a moat, parting as he shuffled forward.

A guard standing near the front desk glanced up as he entered.

"Morning, Prime Inspector."

The guard, their night supervisor, was coming to the end of his shift but didn't show it. Impeccably dressed, his waistcoat pulsed its navy and emerald official pattern, telling anyone he was on the clock.

"Alfred." He let his eyes crinkle at their edges and strode deeper into the building, removing his top hat, scarf, and heavy coat.

Alfred's concerned stare followed him. He hated it. If he had been going to break, it would have been a long time ago. He forced himself to smile and nod to those that he met along the corridor and was grateful to escape into the stale air of the investigators' pen, away from the well-meaning, grating, sympathy of others.

The Way might never sleep, but the Gendarmerie's inspectors did. An empty room, its dark woods and murky rugs barely visible in the light of a stuttering streetlamp, greeted him.

He shambled through the chaotic mill of desks and chairs towards his own den in the back corner, with only the over-loud swoosh of his shoes against the rugs to accompany him.

He paused next to a pristine desk with its quills and jotters at attention. He had tasked Inspector Hoadley with capturing the events of the night before and, to give her credit, she was reliable. Most of the time. More importantly, it was against the rules to take an official jotter home, and Hoadley had never met a rule she was willing to break.

He dragged her chair, squawking against the floor, out of the way. His head jerked up, his gaze darting to the entrance. *Still alone.*

He opened the drawers, shaking his head. Who needed three quill wipers? Maybe it was an age thing. Despite the fact she was probably a few years older than him, he didn't really think of her as old. But the number of quill wipers was concerning.

He picked up one. It was a fine fabric with embroidered spots for placing one's fingers, presumably to keep them clean? Surely people knew how to use a piece of cloth.

There must be notes.

He continued to rummage through her drawers, sharp edges of quills and the soft fabric of the wipers batting his fingers. He almost missed it, blending into the wood of the desk and buried under a variety of other paraphernalia. Her familiar brown leather satchel, sealed by two straps with tight buckles. The metal of the clasps, small pops of cold against his skin, stubbornly refused to release. He fumbled with his oversized fingers, trying to get a grip and release the tension. He flipped through the pages and groaned. A gasser of a manuscript.

Instead of the summary he expected, Hoadley had taken

the time to note down meticulously everything, including every thought she had about it. His gut tightened. Something else to be added to the list of things she would never forgive him for.

He shoved the jotter back in the satchel, tucking it under his arm and slammed the drawers shut. The chair screeched back into position. The desk once more, to the casual eye, in order.

He opened the door to his windowless den, one of the few privileges of rank. A waft of dead air hit his nose, causing him to sneeze.

The door shut behind him. Click. The wall lamps ignited. Click. The hum of a small brass fan filled the space. His usual routine complete he shuffled forward with one last click sending a small brass fan humming, shifting the stale air around.

His chair dominated the space. A modern tentacle design with bronze hinges and velvet padding. It groaned and squeaked shifting to support his slumped back. He dropped the satchel with a thump on the desk in front of him.

It had all started with such a nice evening. Home alone, a pleasant dinner prepared, a book to read, and no pressure of having an early night. A fleck of unexpected optimism seeped into his soul, allowing him to celebrate several months free from death.

And now, twenty-nine hours, fifteen minutes, and forty-five seconds later, here he was, sitting at his desk, begging his brain to fire up.

Beaumont fiddled with the satchel, triple-checking it was

centred on his desk before opening it. The jotter was thick and heavy. He weighed it in his hands wondering how long it was going to take him to get through it.

Pushing the satchel to the side he placed the jotter in front of him. A couple of torn pages peeked out the side. His fingertips stroked the ripped edges of ornate thick cotton paper. Using his nails, he drew them free of the jotter, tracing the slight lines woven in, some sort of delicate mechanism embedded in the paper itself.

He scanned the markings on the pages. A scramble of incomprehensible gibberish. A new type of cryptography?

He pulled a small lamp kept for close work near him, clicking its inbuilt flame starter. It burned clear white. A reminder that he should be grateful the Gendarmerie paid the bill for the high-quality gas.

Eyebrows pinched together, he squinted at some faint letters across the top of the page.

From the desk of Ancilla Walstrand.

The weight of his body hit him. He stared down at the paper for a while, finally forcing himself to lift his head.

Tick. The hand of the clock on the wall, a gift from an old friend, shifted. Wilhelmina had given it to him to remind him of the passing of time. That nothing they did mattered. Wilhelmina, now on the mainland building a following as a writer. She even made the newspaper here a few weeks ago.

He occasionally got a postcard, and its inevitable offer to join her if he ever woke up from the waste that his life had become. Though it had been a while since he received one. She'd given up on him.

The clock also told him it was too early to send out enquiries.

The scramble of letters on the page stared back at him. Hoadley wasn't one to leave a puzzle unsolved. He put Ancilla's pages on top of the empty satchel.

The energy his entrance brought to the room faded, folding into the pale sounds of his breathing, the tick of a clock, the hum of a fan and the rustle of paper turning.

Lavina Hoadley, Inspector
Noxrath Gendarmerie
Great Espya

It was the murder I had been waiting for.

After a month of handling petty crimes, my move to Noxrath has paid off. I was called into duty at twelve fifteen in the morning by a knock on my door. A death had been reported at one of the Families' houses. I was always ready to be called in, and following the instructions given to me, I met Prime Inspector Beaumont outside Atwater Place, the Atwater Family's principal residence, at forty-two minutes after midnight. So far Beaumont has been something of a disappointment.

High walls protected the grounds, but steps, made of a pale stone and wider than my entire flat, led up from the street. The large wooden doors, reinforced with enough metal to hold back a floating armada, opened onto one of the most spectacular foyers I had ever seen in my life.

Lit by a seemingly infinite number of gas lamps, we found ourselves in a room with a two-storey high ceiling. The only art, a masterpiece depicting a singer in full song, presided over one wall, but it was the glass atrium in the middle of the house framed by two spiral staircases, with its captive moonlit olive tree, that grabbed a visitor's attention.

The door to my right was closed, but the one to the left was open with gendarmerie guards standing in front of it. We handed our hats to one of the guards. My top hat fine in my hometown of Solverde, seemed squat next to Noxrath's, as did my drab clothes compared to the Noxrath's inspectors' flair.

I followed Beaumont into the room, admiring the silver pattern woven through his waistcoat. Beaumont was renowned for only having his clockwork buttons showing any movement. His high-low waterfall was tied with an elegant wide ribbon across his hips, the fabric a dark silver, dropping to his upper thighs at the front and flowing down to the back of his knees, highlighting the black and silver stripes in his britches.

Made of a durable fabric with a minimalistic pattern and limited movement, my waterfall wrap, tied with a double knot at my waist to avoid any embarrassing moments, was more mid-calf at the back and knee-length at the front. A side effect of being shorter than the average person, and I suspected the result was dreary.

He strolled into the room, and I jerked to a halt. The scent of whisky hit my nose. I shuffled backward, ensuring I stayed appropriately back from the armchair with the dead body draped across it.

"What have we here..." asked Beaumont, stepping forward and peering down. He went way too close considering the forensic technicians had not yet been.

A glimpse of the face on the body, once a strong and very attractive man, caused me to gasp out loud. A guard flicked a glance my way before turning back to Beaumont.

"Looks like a suspicious death, Prime Inspector."

Beaumont grunted, running his fingers through his hair, ruffling it. I struggled to hold back my frown. Technically, it wasn't against the rules for a Prime Inspector to have long curly blond hair. But perhaps if he pulled it back, it would lessen the dissonance between it and his station.

Every wall in the room was covered in shelves of books, each with its own rolling ladder. The armchair would have been the ideal reading spot, and the room had little nooks in each corner for those who wanted to escape from it all. Two other doors led from the room. One was covered by a curtain, hiding the room from outside gazes, and the other had the muffled chatter of a crowd filtered through.

"Has the doctor," Beaumont said, gazing around the room, "seen the body?"

The guard shook his head. "Not yet, zer. We've sent for her."

Beaumont grumbled, "Forensics..." He shuffled around the chair, getting even closer to a glass on the rug with a wet patch in front of it. I held my breath.

"Should be here any moment, zer."

The dark red rug had a golden thread woven into a

pattern that shifted, like waves in red sand. The chair, with the dead body in it, was upholstered with a padded purple velvet and placed in a prime position in the room, giving its resident a perfect view out the bay window at the front of the house. A stoppered crystal decanter half filled with amber liquid sat on a brass table, painting a scene of a man enjoying a quiet drink alone.

"Why Hoadley..." he stared at me, mournfully, "...aren't dead bodies discovered at a reasonable hour?"

"Err, I'm not sure, zer."

Was any hour a reasonable hour for death?

"Not much chance of tea..." Beaumont ran a hand over his mouth.

Everyone stared at him, and his lips drooped. A clatter of footsteps heralded the arrival of the forensic team and the doctor.

"Barnaby, you're looking well." Doctor Morten smiled. She was old, even older than me, vintage almost. "What do you have for me today?"

White hair pulled back in a firm twist behind her head, highlighted well-cared-for skin that couldn't quite hide the lines and discolouration that age brought.

"A death..." Beaumont contemplated the body, "Which for now at least, we're treating as suspicious..." Beaumont turned to the forensic team and gestured in the general direction of the floor. "Best test that."

Despite Beaumont's cavalier attitude, there was a flurry, resulting in pieces of the rug being cut out and the whole pattern freezing, its waves interrupted.

"He's dead," said Doctor Morten.

I tried not to roll my eyes at the obviousness of the statement.

"Do we know who he...is?" asked Beaumont.

I stared at him in shock. But I wasn't the only one. Some of the other guards even exchanged disbelieving looks with me.

"Marcellus Overton, one of, if not the, most talented illuminators of our time, zer," I said. "His control of essence, his ability to channel pneuma was unsurpassed..."

"Are you..." Beaumont trailed off as he glanced at me. "Sure?"

I nodded, but then shook my head, struck by the fear of being wrong, having never seen him in real life.

"Humph." Beaumont turned to a guard near the door. "Best bring the host...Zer Felicia Atwater, in here. Can you..."

The guard nodded and exited the room.

"Who discovered the body?" I asked.

The remaining guards glanced at each other.

"Come on..." said Beaumont, frowning at them. "Someone must have, or otherwise we wouldn't be here."

A guard pulled out his notes. "It was a Cuthbert Walstrand, zer."

"What's his relationship with Zer Marcellus Overton?" I asked.

They shrugged.

"What's a...Cuthbert Walstrand?" asked Beaumont.

One of the guards cleared his throat. "Apparently a poet, zer, or aspirations of being one."

The other guard snickered. "From what I heard he's a pretty bad one," she said.

The forensic team packed up the glass with the stained rug, but the whisky odour lingered.

"Is he..." Beaumont appeared vaguely interested, "What brings him here tonight?"

"Something to do with his family, zer. They're all on the guest list."

"Hoadley..." Beaumont stared at the ceiling, "Make a note to get a copy of the message sent notifying the gendarmerie."

"Yes, zer." I wasn't sure why a guard couldn't do it, but I made a note to myself to carry out the menial task.

The doctor sidled up to the body and she prodded it with metal devices.

"What killed him?" I asked.

Beaumont flicked me a glance mingled with amusement and resignation.

The doctor glanced up from the body. "Excuse me?" she said, staring at me.

I didn't step back.

"Inspector Hoadley..." Beaumont waved at me. "New to the area."

"Inspector Hoadley." The doctor's lips thinned. "I can't determine what killed the man until I've done my examination."

Her waistcoat was distracting. Layered with different shades of brown, and muddy pool clockwork buttons, with brown lines swirling around a black centre. I found it impressive that despite the latest trends in colour and clockwork fabrics, the doctor had taken those modern fashions and reduced them to grimy.

"What, not even if he was poisoned-"

The doctor's mouth thinned even more. "No."

"Hoadley," Beaumont ran a hand across his eyes, "let the doctor do her work." He glanced at Doctor Morten. "If we're lucky, it'll be natural causes, but until then...but until then..."

"Yes, zer," I said dutifully, knowing he was deluding himself.

I admit to being disappointed at the time that Beaumont would be so unrealistic, but since it didn't change the fact that this was murder and how I would be approaching our investigation, I allowed him his optimism.

The guard appeared in the doorway with a tall, elegant woman, a silver walking stick matching her steel grey hair, clutched in her hand. She might be a similar age to the doctor and wasn't classically handsome, but her power was clear for all to see.

"I understand you need me to identify, Marcellus?" Her eyes glinted with traces of liquid and a tight high twist pulled her hair back, leaving the starkness in her cheekbones exposed.

After a couple of quick adjustments to the body's clothes, the doctor stepped back, observing Felicia. The whole room held its breath.

"Zer Atwater..." Beaumont tilted his head, his voice gentle. "I'm sorry for your loss." He examined her face. "It'd be appreciated if you could assist—"

Felicia waved her free hand the gripping her stick, her

knuckle bones pushing against her skin. "Yes, yes, I want to...understand this as much as you do." She took a few steps into the room and glanced down at the body. She patted her hair, its soft twist showing signs of wear from the night. "This is, was, Marcellus Overton." Her mouth pinched, and she swallowed. "Tonight, someone has made this world a little darker." She spun and her vest, now inappropriately, swirled with blooming flowers. Her green and silver waterfall flared from her waist as she strode from the room, her stick making short sharp raps on the floor.

Beaumont blinked.

"Zer?" I asked.

"I had more questions..." He exhaled. "I need to talk to..." He closed his eyes. "Right...Hoadley—"

"Yes, zer."

"Best..." he rubbed his jaw. "Yes, best see if we can identify who can help us work out his movements for the night." He paced, adjusting his cravat and collar.

"Yes, zer," I repeated.

His shoulders slumped. "I'm going to need tea."

Everyone just stood around, watching the doctor finish her examination. Like there wasn't other work to be done.

Cool, clean air in the foyer provided a refreshing contrast from a room with too many bodies and stale whisky. I paused, but the buzz of people talking drew me deeper into the house.

2

The Usual Suspects

Lavina Hoadley, Inspector
Noxrath Gendarmerie
Great Espya

I rested my hand against the chilled dark metal frame of the atrium, my gaze following the two storeys of glass above me. The frame flowed up to the stars, supporting a complex system of glass wings, suggesting it was capable of opening up and letting the outside world in.

Magnificent.

The tree must have been in the family for generations. Dozens of thick branches had woven together to form an abundant trunk before striking up to the sky. The silvery green leaves of the tree, the perfect foil to the soft moonlight reflecting off the glass surrounding it, gave an otherworldly contrast to the artificial light of the gas lamps inside. In summer, with the softer nighttime breezes and the subtle woody scent of the tree, it would be the perfect space to take a moment. To breathe.

To be.

My gaze dropped to the smooth cobblestone paths flowing around it, carrying the visitor through to other parts of the house. The transparent wall running down the side displayed a gallery full of inventions. Not wanting to smear against the glass, I kept a breath between us as I peered in. The gallery's open doors exposed the guests in the ballroom beyond as they milled, their hum of nervous conversation spilling out through the house.

I moved through the atrium, leaving the glass structure behind and entering the ballroom through its wide entrance. How the whole building was still standing with this amount of glass and doorways, I didn't know.

The liberal use of competing perfumes smacked me across the face, destroying not only my memory of the soft woody scent just moments before, but potentially my ability, or desire, to smell again.

The guards, easy to locate by the pools of space surrounding them, observed the guests. One guard turned towards me; I recognised her, Guard Mabel Dalley. I headed in her direction, breathing in through my mouth while I waited for my nose to go into shock.

"Prime Inspector Beaumont wants to talk to anyone who can give an insight into the victim's movements," I said.

Guard Dalley stared at me for a moment before giving me a sharp nod. "Yes, zer."

"Have statements been collected from everyone?"

"Not yet, zer." Dalley gawked at me.

Like pulling teeth.

"Do we at least have an idea of the guests' movements?"

I wasn't sure if Dalley would answer for a minute. She was tall, taller than me, not that that was hard. Her waistcoat, lit up with the gendarmerie's official signal, gave her authority, diminished by the wilting points on the collar of her shirt.

She took a deep breath. "It looks like most of the guests and domestics have been in the ballroom all night. Even the food was served here," she pointed to some tables against a wall, "rather than the dining room across the hall."

"No reason to leave this area then? What about the washrooms?"

"No, zer, the washrooms are behind the stage."

A large platform, raised by a series of mechanical legs, currently squatting low, was positioned at one end of the ballroom. Musicians, on display, sat on it, a variety of the more modern instruments resting next to them, watched by a guard. The wall on one side of the stage had a set of double doors. It didn't have any markings on it, but I assumed the guests knew what it was for.

"Very well. I've been told that Cuthbert Walstrand discovered the body. We're going to need to talk to him."

Dalley shifted her weight. "And the rest of the family, zer?"

Another guard gave her a sharp glance. Hopperton was his name. And if I remembered correctly, he was less competent than most.

She shrugged back.

"How are they relevant?" I asked.

Dalley's lips tightened. "Apparently one of the sisters was with the victim most of the night, zer."

"Do you know why?"

I observed the room, which was a sea of colour and questionable fashion choices.

Dalley exhaled and straightened her shoulders. "Zer Ancilla Walstrand is employed as Overton's assistant, zer."

That information could have been offered a lot earlier. Hopperton wandered closer. He was a bit shorter than Dalley, but solid, useful for crowd control.

"The party was a demonstration of the Atwater's latest prototype, they call it the illuminier," he said, his gaze unfocused. "Apparently, you could walk through it."

"Through what?" I asked.

"The illusion. The guest said it was like you were in it." He gazed at the wall.

I followed his gaze to some pretty wallpaper, nothing worthy of the attention he was giving it. It appeared he had a problem with focus. I glanced around in case I missed the device but if it was in the room it was concealed.

Of course, there was always another explanation. "Have they been drinking...something?"

Hopperton's eyes focused on me, widening. "No, well yes, but no they weren't hallucinating."

Perhaps I should have the drinks tested. I cleared my throat. "We'll need to talk to this Ancilla, and Cuthbert." The murmur of the room had faded, the weight of its gaze on me. "I'll let you know when. Don't let them out of your sight."

Dalley and Hopperton stared at me blankly.

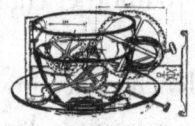

If Beaumont remembered correctly, around that time he had gone in search of tea.

Instead, he had found a drawing room with a rather disappointing drink station.

Centre stage, four elegant chaise longues fitted with mechanical legs, gathered in a square, facing each other, plotting.

This would do.

He needed somewhere to conduct the interviews after all.

The absence of dust gave the room a clean crisp feel, a sharp contrast to the air in his own flat. He shuffled around the room, enjoying the slight aroma of polish.

His fingers ran across the velvet of the chairs. Pretty, but thin, typical in a prominent family's house. Beyond a few more chairs and the tealess drink station, there wasn't much of interest.

He approached, with care, one of the chaises and lowered himself into the corner with the high curved arm. Similar to his office chair they adjusted, using their six jointed legs, and some sort of system he didn't understand, to manoeuvre their positions for optimal conversation.

He was trying to find a comfortable position when the door to the drawing room crashed back. Hoadley entered, no doubt leaving a swath of chaos in her wake.

Beaumont gestured to another chaise next to him. "What do we have?" he asked.

She peered at it, clenched her jaw and took a seat. He smothered a smile as the chaises' legs engaged and slowly shifted for a better angle for conversation, two unused chaises moving subtly out of the way. Or as subtly as scampering metal feet on a stone floor could.

"Not much, but besides the Atwaters, there's the Walstrand family who might be of interest. I've asked the guards to keep a close eye on them." She sat straight, avoiding letting the chaise have full control of her posture.

"No one else?" He shifted in his seat, his back aching. Why did furniture at the height of fashion, have to be overstuffed and uncomfortable? Intentional? To avoid visitors overstaying their welcome?

"No, it seems like everyone was well-behaved."

"Except for the dead body of course."

She appeared to be in pain until he realised that she was trying to humour him with a slight smile.

He should have known better.

"I've asked Felicia Atwater to meet with us." He shifted again. "She needed time to change."

"I suppose her festive gear became uncomfortable." Hoadley pulled out her jotter and quill, pausing to gaze at the quill. One thing he was learning about Hoadley is that she did like her stationery. "Especially considering who Overton was to her."

"Quite right," said Felicia. Her steel grey hair was tightly pulled back now and she had changed into dark orange mourning clothes and placed an orange stripe down the length of her walking stick.

Beaumont rose to his feet, noticing that Hoadley's cheeks darkened. He was just glad she hadn't said anything inappropriate. Not that Hoadley was wrong.

"Thank you for joining us, I'm Prime Inspector Beaumont and this is my colleague Inspector Hoadley. I'm sorry that we must do this now, but we need to find out what happened to your..." It was Beaumont's turn to feel uncomfortable.

"Lover, no need to be bashful Prime Inspector. Marcellus has been my lover for over a decade. We might not have registered the relationship, but it was established as any that are."

"Yes." Beaumont resumed his seat. "Of course." He cleared his throat. "Zer Atwater, would you mind, in your own words, sharing with me what happened tonight?"

Felicia lay her walking stick on the end of a chaise and took a seat, draping sideways on it, letting the curved end support her body and the chaise position itself so she didn't have to turn her head to converse with them. Her face was calm but he imagined the lines in it were deeper.

Beaumont wished he could follow her lead to get back support but with Hoadley sitting rigidly upright he suspected he would never be forgiven if he did.

Felicia's eyes took on a sheen. "Yes, yes I can do that." She blinked, taking a couple of breaths until her body settled a bit further back on the chaise. She focused on Beaumont. "After months, years, of work we were ready to launch the first real innovation that had been seen in the light-imaging industry in over a decade. The patents are lodged and approved of course, with a special showcase scheduled with parliament next week. Tonight's preview was for everyone who'd been involved, to acknowledge the work that had gone into it." Felicia swallowed.

Beaumont examined her with concern. His gaze darted back to the small drink station. He rose, heading towards it. If he wanted to get out of this without a flood of formal complaints a bit of finesse was going to be needed.

Not that he really cared about formal complaints, not anymore, but he certainly didn't want to lose any more of his life to them. He ignored Hoadley's look of disgust—maybe he could send her to a poker playing course—and poured Felicia a glass of plain water.

"Thank you." She accepted the glass, taking a sip.

"Perhaps." Beaumont resumed his seat. "Perhaps, you could walk us through the evening?" he asked, trying to exude a concerned, empathic expression.

Felicia drank another mouthful and nodded. She straightened her shoulders and took a deep breath. "Necket, our butler, had organised for the guests to arrive at nine…"

Who starts a party at nine? By nine he was already in bed with a book.

"That's late," said Hoadley.

Felicia raised an eyebrow. "No, not really," her voice had a drawl to it. "Everyone was on time and by about half past we were ready to commence."

The glass was placed on a small table at the end of her chaise, and she rose, wandering over, without her walking stick, to the bay window. The sheer curtains provided privacy, with the pale blue velvet layer tied back, allowing the light of the streetlamp in.

"Nine-thirty?" prompted Beaumont. What distance could she travel without her walking stick?

"It was a marvel. Marcellus cast an almost lifelike setting, a table, and a chair."

"A table and chair made of light?" Beaumont was slightly confused. It didn't seem to be that impressive. Perhaps from an engineering front, but hardly on an artistic one.

"You had to see it to understand, it is a major breakthrough."

A breakthrough that happened just when the pattern inheritance laws changed. A potential new art form could be a motive for murder.

Felicia stared down at the street below. Her clenched hand rested on the glass, and she leant forward as if she was willing herself from the room.

Beaumont tried to focus, he needed to lock down Marcellus Overton's movements, then work out motives, all the while waiting for the death report, and missing out on being in his nice warm bed.

"And after the presentation?" asked Beaumont.

"After?" Felicia turned towards them, her smile bitter. "For something so amazing to be dismissed so quickly..." Her mouth tightened. "I suppose understandable from those who aren't artists." She peered down her nose at him. "I'm not sure which Marcellus would be most upset about, his death or the fact it overshadowed one of the highlights of his career."

"My guess it'd be his death," murmured Hoadley.

Beaumont flicked her a sharp glare.

Unhelpful.

Felicia turned towards her for the first time.

"Potentially," she said, transferring her disdain to Hoadley. "Though if you understood what it meant to him..." she cleared her throat, "but you're not capable. Not your fault."

Insult?

She glided back, picking up her glass and taking her seat.

"And what happened after the presentation?" Hoadley asked.

"How's this important?" she asked.

Beaumont captured her attention by leaning forward and smiling at her. He put a bit of effort into it, making it one of his nicer smiles.

"We just need to understand Zer Overton's movements over the night."

Felicia slumped a little. "Yes, yes of course." She took another drink and then, putting the glass down, gave Beaumont her attention, eyes shiny but face otherwise composed.

"Do you remember the last time you saw him?" asked Beaumont, his voice soft.

She closed her eyes for a moment and swallowed.

"The presentation was at nine-thirty and lasted an hour. He was working. He, Ancilla, his assistant, and Necket set up on the stage."

"Necket?" Hoadley asked.

She glanced at me. "My butler, Florence Necket. I had

asked her to take personal responsibility for the prototype, the illuminier, for the night."

"And she was with it all night?" asked Beaumont.

"Yes, she takes her duties very seriously."

How seriously? It would not be the first time he had dealt with an over zealous employee.

"And Overton? Did he stay with the illuminier as well?"

"For the demonstration, yes. Then the speeches, thirty minutes? So that means around eleven the music started playing and a late supper was served. Busy with people, I'm not sure what happened after that."

"You don't remember him leaving?" asked Beaumont, leaning forward slightly. Surely she would have kept an eye on him. He was the star of the night.

"No, no he was usually exhausted after a performance. Even for someone as skilled as him...to use that much pneuma...it was no small feat. He would've needed a moment to recover."

"It was normal for him to go to the library?" Hoadley asked.

He had to admit Hoadley had a natural flair for being the hard-nosed inspector, while he usually erred on the side of diplomacy. Perhaps they could make this partnership work after all.

She blinked at Hoadley, and her eyebrows drew together. "The library, his workshop upstairs..."

"He has rooms here?" Hoadley straightened.

Beaumont kept his face smooth, but inside he grimaced.

He was pretty sure the guards hadn't conducted any investigations upstairs.

"Room, his own space when he's here."

A room they had given her time to interfere with.

Pipe it. Too late to fix now.

Beaumont nodded. "Understandable. So, at eleven the official part of the evening is over. You're circulating and don't remember seeing him? Across the room talking to someone?"

"I saw him standing next to the device and Ancilla for a while but then it was just Ancilla. I don't know exactly when he..." Felicia cleared her throat again, her gaze on the empty glass in her hand.

Beaumont refilled it.

"Thank you, Zer Atwater." Beaumont settled across from her, leaning forwards. "I know this is probably the last thing you want to do right now, but it's important we find out what happened."

"You think...you think someone killed him?" She gazed at him intently.

"To die so unexpectedly? We must assume...until we've a reason not to." He pulled out his jotter and quill. "Can you think of anyone who might have wished him harm?"

She finished her water.

"He was the best in his field and of course that gave rise to jealousies. But I can't think of specific people or incidents right now."

"Any threats received?"

"No, nothing like that." She exhaled heavily, placing the

empty glass on the table next to her. "I want all the guests out of my house."

"Of course, of course." Beaumont shifted in his seat. His back was caning now. If he didn't get up and start moving around soon it would become unbearable. He cleared his throat. "Once the guards have verified their contact details." Beaumont put down his unused jotter and cleared his throat again. "But first we will need to talk to Cuthbert and Ancilla Walstrand, and your son Alistair tonight."

"Alistair? What for?" Frown lines deepened in her forehead.

"He was also a host of this evening's events..." He leaned forward. "And he assists Overton with the production of devices, am I correct?"

"Yes, he works closely with our manufacturing side." Her shoulders tensed. "An artist in his own right of course."

"Of course," Beaumont raised his hands palm out. "I believe it's his work in the foyer?"

It hadn't taken him long to realise that she was the singer depicted in the painting and that the AA signature in the corner was Alistair Atwater. She wouldn't have another family's artwork displayed in her home.

If his parents had a son with that kind of talent, every wall in the house would have been covered in his art.

Felicia straightened even further. "Yes."

"A master artist in his own right." Beaumont tilted his head. "Was he involved in the presentation tonight?"

Felicia studied Beaumont. "Not really. He has a stronger

affinity with materials like paint than light." She shook her head. "Certainly nothing to the level of Marcellus."

She rose from the chaise, grasping her walking stick and leaning on it heavily.

Beaumont gratefully clambered to his feet, almost groaning with relief as his back stretched. His chaise skurried out of his way.

"And you could see him the whole time?" asked Hoadley. She stood too, but her posture was combative. Future paperwork loomed.

"What are you implying Inspector...?" Felicia's mouth was tight and her fist clenched the handle.

"Hoadley, Inspector Hoadley. I'm merely trying to establish everyone's movements, zer."

Beaumont stifled a wince. He had not deliberately forgotten to introduce her.

Felicia's fingers on her other hand shifted her waterfall to be centred on her stomach and smoothed out the fabric at the back, so it fell straight to her heels, glaring at Hoadley and turning her attention back to him. "I can assure you that Alistair had no reason to want him dead. Quite the opposite. Their work together had only benefited the family and Marcellus."

"Thank you, Zer Atwater." Beaumont gave her a little bow. It usually worked a treat. "I appreciate you meeting with us at this difficult time."

He wasn't finished with her yet but couldn't see any benefit in keeping her here. Better to bring her down to the Way at a later time, out of her own environment.

Some of the fire drained out of her and she gave him a short nod.

The guard on the door scrambled to open it as she approached, her stride never missing a beat.

Lavina Hoadley, Inspector
Noxrath Gendarmerie
Great Espya

"What do you think Hoadley?"

He did remember I was here after all.

"A possible suspect, zer. Registered or unregistered, it's usually the partner who does it."

"She's also..." Beaumont tilted his head back, gazing up at the ceiling, "the head of the Atwater family."

"Doesn't mean she didn't kill him."

He turned toward me, frowning. "At her own party?"

I was surprised at his optimism. "These types..."

"Types of...what?"

"Types with power, influence, sometimes they think they can get away with anything."

He shook his head, making a few more notes and stared at them glumly. "This is going to be a nightmare of a case."

He appeared tired, like he wished the whole thing was over already.

Typical. A rare case with plenty of witnesses, a physical scene to process and a puzzle to solve; everything needed to make the work interesting and here he was moping around wishing for tea and home.

Beaumont lumbered to his feet. "You wouldn't happen to know where the washrooms are?"

I hated that this was the first question today I knew the answer to.

"Yes, zer."

After Beaumont left for another one of his *breaks*, unsurprising considering the amount of tea he consumed, I examined the room. It was clean. Well well-maintained and thankfully, perfume free. If there were any subtle odours my olfactory senses were still too traumatized to make them out.

If I had been running this investigation, I would have declared the entire house a crime scene and locked it down. Instead, everyone was trampling everywhere, with the owner of the house free to wander around, doing goodness knows what upstairs.

One wall was empty—no cabinets, no chairs up against it, nothing. I strode over to examine it more closely, dragging my fingers over the panelling. Even so, I almost missed it. I stepped back to take in the shape cut into the wall. It was low, lower than I was expecting, too low for a door, maybe a cabinet?

There were three chairs in this corner of the room. Two of them occasional chairs, presumably for people to rest in while they had a drink before returning to the fray of conversation. But one was higher, with proper back support. Still pretty and covered in the same pale blue velvet as the chaises. An office chair designed to blend in. I took a seat.

The hidden cuts in the wall matched the level I would expect a desk to be at and the space in front of it was rug-free. Rising I stepped forward, pressing into the wall, searching for the release.

Click.

I spun, to find Beaumont lurking in the doorway, morose, as usual.

"Best..." He flicked a glance at me. "Get on with it." He ran his fingers through his hair, and his shoulders slumped. "Bring Alistair Atwater in." He collapsed back onto the chaise, his blond curls falling over his forehead, the light reflecting off a small cluster of grey.

I glanced at the wall. It would have to wait.

I think it fair to say Alistair was everything an heir of a leading family should be. Tall, with a full head of dark hair, beautiful brown eyes and a smile that lit up the room as he entered it.

"Inspectors, a horrible business. My mother is quite done over."

It was hard not to warm to him, but I had to remind myself that he was a suspect.

"I imagine it's all a bit of a shock," I said.

He even smelt nice. My nose had recovered enough to make out a soft spicy scent mingled with the clean scent of polish. Did he wear perfume? Or was it something he bathed in?

"Zer Atwater…" Beaumont rose. "Allow me to introduce myself. I'm Prime Inspector Beaumont and this is my colleague Inspector Hoadley." He gestured, somewhat, in my direction. "I'm sorry to have to question you at this time of the night but considering Marcellus Overton's unexpected death…"

How much did the scent cost? Did he have a favourite scent?

"Yes, of course." Alistair moved deeper into the room, slumping onto a chaise. My jaw tightened while the seats scampered into position, I gave him a half smile. If making the suspects comfortable was beneficial then I would do my best to give it a go.

"I'd value your input into what happened tonight…" Beaumont examined him. "I understand that you were overseeing it all?"

"It was a team effort and," he flashed me a rueful smile, "most of my involvement was undertaking the testing earlier in the day. Checking no pipes were blocked. I am sure you can understand, in a device that complicated all it takes is one small pipe to break and the whole thing stops working."

Which basically meant he was free to kill. It made sense that the first nice person I had met in this city was a murderer.

"Is your registered partner…" Beaumont glanced at his jotter. "Vivian Payne-Atwater of the Payne Family, here tonight?"

I blinked, trying to keep my face smooth. Of course he was in a registered relationship. That made sense. And to one of the heirs of a powerful family not only in Noxrath, but Espya.

At least Beaumont had done some research. Maybe he was only pretending to not care.

"No, Viv's on the mainland." He slumped further into his chaise. "Payne Family are not supportive of the bill; they are exploring relocating."

Viv had probably created the scent for him. I heard that she was a special kind of artist, one that did an all-round sensory experience in her art from scent, taste, sound and touch. Immersive.

"Strange..." Beaumont stared at him intently. "To not be here on your big night."

And the illuminier? An opportunity or a threat?

"She'll be back for the parliament presentation." He gave a rueful smile.

Answering the questions, but not offering too much detail. Smart. Not very useful to us though. Time to get this moving.

I leaned forward. "What exactly—"

"Did you..." Beaumont glanced at me for a second but refocused on Alistair. "Did you see Overton after the speeches were finished?"

Alistair flicked me a smile but turned his head, giving him his attention. I struggled to keep the heat out of my cheeks and kept my focus on the jotter in my hand.

"Umm, not sure to be honest. Whenever I glanced over Necket was watching the device like a hawk and Ancilla, dealing with the guests."

"Hmm..." Beaumont stared blankly at his jotter. "And what can you tell me about Ancilla Walstrand and Overton's relationship?"

"Oh, it was very amicable. Ancilla, well she's not one to make waves. An excellent assistant."

I revised my estimate of him. In *my* experience, it took a lot of skill and effort for people to find you *amicable*.

"Would you say..." Beaumont tilted his head. "...that their relationship...was purely professional?"

Ah, a solid question, the first one he had asked all evening.

"I would say that they were work colleagues nothing more." Alistair's eyebrows rose. "Marcellus was faithful to my mother if that's what you're asking."

"A standard question..." said Beaumont.

Alistair's gaze followed the movement of Beaumont's quill across the jotter, his eyebrows drawing together.

"When did you last see Marcellus?" I asked, trying to bring the conversation back on track.

"Standing next to Ancilla at the illuminier—"

"Did you see when Overton left?" I asked.

Alistair blinked. "Well...er...they had finished their presentation, Melody had finished... singing. There was quite a crowd around Marcellus and Ancilla, and the next time I glanced over, it was just Ancilla. I assumed he'd gone to find some peace and quiet. The illuminier needs an extremely high level of pneuma control and he was always a bit frazzled after using it."

"Was that normal?"

Alistair sat back, playing with the buttons on his vest.

They reflected the light in a way that made me think of diamonds.

"It wasn't guaranteed, but yes it was likely."

"Thank you…" Beaumont put his quill, and barely touched jotter, down. "Zer Atwater…what was *your* relationship with the deceased? Was he a father figure for you?"

Alistair snorted. "He'd no desire for that role."

"What role did he…play?" Beaumont scrutinized him.

"He was an artist, an inventor." He shrugged. "A brilliant one. The way his mind worked was inspiring to watch. He was fearless." Alistair shifted his gaze to me. "He could also be arrogant, opinionated and extremely cutting, especially when he'd been drinking."

"And had he been drinking tonight?" I asked, maintaining eye contact.

"Not that I saw. He'd been too focused on the presentation," Alistair, gazed at both of us and gave a shrug. "But he might have had some afterwards."

"Would he…" Beaumont shifted forward in his seat. "How likely would it have been for him to…take…something…other than alcohol? To calm his nerves?"

Alistair shook his head sharply. "No, he refused to take anything else for fear of hurting his ability to channel pneuma, though that didn't slow down his whisky intake. He was a strange and contradictory man at times."

"He's not…" Beaumont glanced down at his jotter. "…not registered as your mother's partner…"

"That's correct." Alistair's back was ramrod straight.

"Which meant..." Beaumont's gaze was unusually alert. "He wasn't given access to the family intellectual property..."

Another decent question. I had been afraid that Beaumont had been too afraid of the Atwaters to ask the real ones. That he was afraid of Zer Felicia.

"He was part of the team, contributing to some of our major inventions, and was remunerated generously." Alistair's gaze flicked between us. "But all patents are lodged in Mother's name."

"Was he financially independent?" I asked.

Alistair stared at his glass, his hair flopping down to obscure his face. "He could've been, but...he lived for the moment." He rotated the drink in his hand. "Besides, Mother was more than happy to fill in the gaps."

"Did that cause any issues between you?" I asked.

The interview guides said to let the silence do the work, but I had found throughout my life that a few well-placed questions sped things along.

Alistair shook his head, putting down his glass and settling into the chaise. "No, that's between them, and she's more than capable of taking care of herself, and the family. To be honest Marcellus and I argued more about the design of the prototype than anything else."

"The design?"

"Just a squabble and hardly relevant to this—"

"I choose what is and isn't relevant." Beaumont picked up his jotter.

Alistair's eyebrows drew together, and I suppressed my grin. Now this was proper investigation work.

"He wanted to change something."

"Change...what...exactly?" asked Beaumont, his face expectant.

"On the illuminier. We'd finished a successful testing round, and it was only three days before the presentation. He wanted to take it apart and examine it, said he thought something wasn't working. A ridiculous suggestion."

Beaumont shifted forward. "And were there any witnesses to this argument?"

I was pleased with his line of questioning but the eagerness for an easy answer was, to my mind, clearly written on his face.

"Yes, Ancilla was there of course."

Beaumont nodded, a pleased expression on his face.

Seriously, one argument does not a murderer make.

"And... did she agree with the change?" asked Beaumont.

"Ancilla doesn't say much, but no, she didn't. In fact, I remember feeling grateful to her for helping Marcellus see that it was unreasonable."

"What about any..." Beaumont glanced up from his notes, peering at Alistair, "enemies?"

"Marcellus?" Alistair sat back, his body relaxing. "A few bruised egos, but I can't think of anyone who'd want to kill him. If people went around killing others because they were annoying," he paused to flash a charming smile at me, "none of us would be able to sleep safely."

And we would have a lot more murders to solve. Though I couldn't imagine anyone finding Alistair Atwater annoying.

"Any professional...jealousies? Other artists...envious of his talent...or connection with the Atwaters?"

"A rival for my mother's favour you mean?" Alistair shook his head. "As far as I'm aware they've been faithful for over a decade." Alistair slumped. "This is a loss for my mother as well as the Atwater Family's ventures."

I examined him. His form was right, the sloped shoulders, the droop around the mouth. But something was off. They talk about a smile not reaching the eyes, but sadness can miss them as well.

"And... you didn't see or hear him arguing with anyone at the party tonight?" asked Beaumont.

He needed to work on his intimidating glare.

Alistair lifted his head, staring at the Prime Inspector for a few moments. "No..."

"Thank you for your time..." Beaumont rose to his feet. "Hopefully we can let you and your mother rest soon."

Alistair mirrored him. "Did you want me to get anyone else for you?"

I could not believe it. Beaumont was ending the interview. We had nothing. We should have taken them all back to the station and let them stew before starting the next round of interviews.

"The guards..." Beaumont gave him a smile.

Alistair stood there. His brow furrowed, glancing between Beaumont and the door.

"Right then." He shook his head and left. Only the scraping of the chaises shifting, and the scratch of my quill sounded as I made my notes.

Beaumont glanced down at me, his eyes dropping to my quill.

"What'd you think of him?" asked Beaumont.

"Charming, but oblivious. I suspect he's more upset about the loss of Overton's skill than him as a person."

"An interesting response...when I asked him about possible arguments."

I examined Beaumont, he was frowning at the door.

"You think he heard something?" I asked.

"Yes..."

"Then why not just tell us?" I followed his gaze to the door. "It would be to his benefit. He was upfront about his own argument."

"Yes indeed...why not?" Beaumont wandered over to the drinks station, picking up several of the infusions but, in the end, pouring himself some water. "I could really do with a cup of tea..."

I certainly wasn't getting it for him.

3

Keeping It In the Family

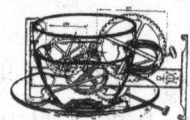

Beaumont's stomach clenched.

Her notes painted a picture of an intelligent, and angry, person.

Perhaps if she was a little less angry.

Was it helpful to know her opinion of him? He pressed against the stiff muscles in his jaw. The cogs loitered in the clock, an eternity between ticks. Thirty hours, five minutes, and twenty-three seconds since this case began.

Never enough time.

He should have left after the last case. He had never wanted anything more than to avoid being a painter, and to pay for food and shelter. Instead, he had gotten caught up in it all and started caring about the work. A mistake.

Prime Inspector Wilhelmina Beard had realised she was wasting her life and chucked it in for poetry. Now she was earning twice as much as him, but working three times as hard, physically fit, channelling pneuma, chasing the perfect word and giving his partner Gordon an early promotion.

Beaumont reached out, picking up Ancilla Walstrand's diary pages. The paper was complex, with an inlaid mechanism. He traced it, his gaze jumping from scrambled word to scrambled word, lingering on the torn edges.

Thump. Thump.

He froze, staring at the incriminating jotter and pages in front of him.

His doorknob rattled.

"Come in," he said, wishing the words go away passed his lips instead. He breathed in, leaning forward, casually resting his arms across other's private thoughts.

The door creaked open, revealing Alfred, awkwardly juggling Beaumont's favourite perpetual teacup and a plate. "Prime Inspector."

Beaumont forced his lips to curve up in a smile. "Alfred, I might be presumptuous, but it appears you've brought me tea and food, so I think we can ditch the title."

Alfred moved into the room, setting down the plate, which had a hot pastry filled with cheese on it, on the edge of his desk.

"Thought you might be hungry." Alfred tilted his head, examining Beaumont.

Beaumont kept his arms relaxed on the table in front of him. And if his arms happened to obscure a visitor's view of a certain jotter and pages? That was completely coincidental.

"You know me too well Alfred." He had to move. Weird if

he didn't. Making a decision, he swept everything into a pile, shoving it under the satchel to the far side, and pulling the plate closer to him.

Smooth.

His eyes closed briefly as he inhaled the aroma of butter and melted cheese infusing the air. "Thank you."

"Figured you'd need something to get you through this morning."

"Err...yes." He gazed up at Alfred, standing there, full of energy and spotless. "Have you finished for the day?"

"Just about to head home for some sleep," Alfred examined Beaumont. "Which is where you should be..."

"I would if I could..."

"Hmmph." Alfred held out the cup. "Tea?"

Beaumont took it with both hands. Its weight, fully loaded with tea and water, comforting. His fingers followed their routine brushing the intricate gas lines mapping the outside of the cup and clicking open each of the small compartments. Alfred had filled it with fresh tea leaves. He swivelled a small lever on one, allowing it to move into the infuser. Near the handle, he adjusted a dial and the gas lines hummed, heating the water as it filled the cup. He closed his eyes as a waft of infused steam warmed his face and admired the dial designed to hold it there for the perfect amount of time. A thing of beauty.

Alfred stared at him, a deep vertical crease in his brow. Nothing was free.

Careful not to spill his tea, Beaumont slumped in his chair.

"Don't give me that." Alfred frowned at him. "The others

might be fine with letting you flash your smile and give an okay but you and I both know that you're on the edge."

Wet heat pushed at the corner of Beaumont's eyes, but he breathed in, relaxing his body.

"It's been a rough year." Beaumont cradled his cup, its warmth comforting.

"A rough few years," said Alfred, settling into the visitor's chair.

"Okay, a rough few years, but the truth is I don't have time to deal with it all right now."

"You're not alone." Alfred shifted to the edge of his chair, leaning forward. "You're not the only one who can solve crimes. Gordon—"

"I'll see this through."

It was the least he could do.

Alfred shook his head. "Just don't be so arrogant that you think you're the only one who can solve this." He narrowed his eyes. "And if you report me for insubordination to a senior officer I'll remind them of the time—"

Beaumont gave a weak chuckle. "I'm fully aware of how many stories you can tell, about me, about all of us." He gazed at the older man fondly. "Though I will say that most of those nights of too much food and liquor were entirely your fault."

Alfred gave a quick smile. "It's healthy for you to loosen up." He stared at him. "When this case is over, it's time for another."

Whether Alfred meant a night out or another case, he wasn't going to be around either way.

Alfred stood and moved to the door.

"Sounds like a plan." Beaumont smiled, relieved.

"Don't let the cheese get cold."

Beaumont threw him a salute and Alfred left, shutting the door behind him.

First things first.

He wiped the pastry grease off his hands, finishing a cup of tea and setting it to start another infusion.

His mind whirling in a tired eddy of pastry, tea and death.

A glance down showed that he was once more holding the torn-out diary pages. He blinked, his hand flexing. He didn't remember picking them up.

Ancilla Walstrand.

Beaumont tried to remember the first interview with her. A blur of conversation was all that came to him. A woman, similar in age to him, maybe a bit older. Simple clothes, average features, mousy brown hair.

There had been nothing remarkable about her, but Hoadley had been suspicious of her from the start.

Hoadley always interpreted things in the worst possible way, assuming everyone was either lazy or incompetent.

Except for Ancilla Walstrand. Instinct? Or did she know something he didn't?

The Mysterious Death of an Illuminator

Lavina Hoadley, Inspector
Noxrath Gendarmerie
Great Espya

I heard that when Marcellus entered a room his energy ran before him, causing everyone to stop and look. Felicia exuded strength and Alistair, well, he was captivating. But Zer Ancilla Walstrand, of average height, her features, when not twisted in worry, pleasant but not striking, faded into the background.

She was dressed simply, her waterfall a dark purple with scalloped edges touched with hints of silver, shivering under the gas lamps of the room. I liked that she had gone with one leg of her britches purple and the other leg black. It was probably the most unique thing about her.

Beaumont rose to his feet. "Zer Walstrand, thank you for seeing us. I'm sorry to have to keep you and your family here after what must have been a long and shocking night."

Ancilla blinked at him. "It's tragic." She stood there staring at them, her expression blank. Normal? Or just not firing all cylinders right now.

"I'm Prime Inspector Beaumont and this is Inspector Hoadley, please..." He gestured to the chaise in front of him and she inclined her head, moving to take a seat, unknowingly following Alistair and choosing the one opposite me. I was pleased as it gave me a better angle to study her. This efficient and amicable assistant. I didn't care what the others said. She was a suspect until we had proven she wasn't.

{ 47 }

Beaumont smiled at her. A little too sympathetically.

She gave a small smile back.

It was the perfect amount of smile too, like she was too overwhelmed to give a real smile but was making an effort, just for him.

Nicely played.

"If you don't mind, Zer Walstrand," Beaumont shifted so he was at an angle, facing her, then reversing the move when the chaise adjusted under him, "we're particularly interested in Marcellus' movements. I understand he was with you most of the night?"

"Yes, such a... tragedy." Ancilla's fingers picked at the edging on her waterfall. "Do you know how he died? Did he suffer..."

"I'm afraid..." Beaumont shook his head. "I'm sorry but I can't say at this time."

"And it was definitely Marcellus...?" She leaned forward. "There hasn't been some dreadful mistake?"

Beaumont shook his head. "I'm sorry, Zer Felicia Atwater identified the body herself."

"I can't believe it. Not really." Ancilla patted her tightly pulled-back hair. "Can I see..."

"He's already been removed," I said.

"Right of course." Her fingers twisted in her waterfall's knot at her hip, her gaze down.

Why wouldn't she trust Zer Atwater to identify her lover of a decade?

"However, it would be helpful to understand his movements." Beaumont gave her another sympathetic smile. "I understand he was with you most of the night, until after the speeches?"

The palm of her hand smoothed out the fabric across her lap. No lines marked its abuse. A strong, sensible fabric. Like its wearer?

"My main responsibility tonight was to ensure the device was cared for and provide Marcellus whatever support he needed." Her gaze flicked up for a second and she gave a weak smile and then returned to contemplating her lap.

Was she normally so physically weak?

"And after the demonstration, after the speeches?" I asked, making her gaze flick to me. I tried to find evidence of calculation in her eyes, but I couldn't. The worry had settled like a fog obscuring everything else.

"It had been a long three days." Ancilla swallowed, her eyes glistening.

"Inspector Hoadley...perhaps some water?"

Great, now I was playing servant to the suspects. I rose and went over to the drinks station. The soft perfume of the infusions signalled a variety of options, but I ignored them, grabbing a glass and hefted a tall, narrow jug full of water, thrown off balance when the jug moved under its own power. I smothered a snort. Two legs had extended down, pushing off the table, helping me lift it high and stabilising it while I poured it into the glass

At Atwater Place, even water jugs were devices. What would happen if I just let go? Probably nothing. No spilling here. A crime considered worthy of a death sentence.

I plonked the glass down in front of Ancilla.

"Do you know what time he left your side?" I asked.

"I'm sorry it was all a bit of a blur." Ancilla picked it up, taking a sip.

At least my effort wasn't wasted.

"What about a particular song?" I asked.

I resumed my seat, leaning forward, staring at her. Beaumont blinked but kept his attention on Ancilla.

"A song? Yes, of course, Melody." The colour in Ancilla's cheeks darkened.

Why would she be embarrassed by having a singer in the family? Next to light, they were currently the most popular artists. Felicia Atwater being an example, though she only sang for the higher echelons of society.

"Your sister..." Beaumont tilted his head.

Her eyes dropped to the glass in her hands. "Yes."

"And Marcellus left during her song?" I asked.

"After." She gulped some water, shifting in her seat, keeping her eyes down.

Beaumont and I exchanged a glance. I wasn't sure how this was relevant.

"Thank you, Zer Walstrand..." Beaumont took out his jotter and made a few scratches on it. "That was very helpful."

Was it? She was quite masterful, giving just enough that the listener would fill in the blanks. And there he was writing it down.

Ancilla examined the top of his head and glanced at me.

"Does that mean we can go home now?" Her eyes, vacant.

No. We had a thousand more questions for her. Or I did anyway.

"Unfortunately..." Beaumont gazed up at her, a soft frown on his face. "We still need to talk to other guests...perhaps we can organise for you to have a private space to rest?"

And keep an eye on her. I didn't know why Beaumont was letting her go with so little interrogation. She hadn't said much at all, and I wanted to know if it was evasion or exhaustion.

"Thank you that's very considerate of you." Ancilla pushed herself to her feet.

It took a long time.

Beaumont glanced up. "We may need to talk to you again..."

"Yes of course."

She didn't move, seemingly waiting for direction.

"Hoadley..." Beaumont glanced around the room. "A room for Zer Walstrand?" He clambered to his feet, not letting his hand leave the back of the chaise until he was fully upright. "I'll talk to the guard about our next..."

"Yes, zer." I strode towards the entrance to the foyer.

"Actually..." said Ancilla, her voice was soft but she raised her gaze. "Perhaps I could wait in the lounge?"

My eyebrows rose and I swung back around. "The lounge?"

Ancilla pointed at another exit. Like the library, the drawing room had a second internal door.

"It has the most comfortable chairs, well except those in the library of course."

"Familiar with all seats in the house?" I asked.

"Hoadley..." Beaumont's voice was soft and deep, disappointed.

It was my turn for my cheeks to darken. I mumbled something.

"I have been here a lot over the last few weeks assisting with preparing for this evening," said Ancilla, she blinked but otherwise her expression didn't change.

"Very understandable, Zer Walstrand." Beaumont nodded, giving her another smile. "The lounge sounds perfect. Hoadley?"

I will admit I grunted my yes, zer, but I obeyed, proceeding Ancilla into the room.

She had to wait for me to take a breath. I noticed the glass roof along the side of the house as we arrived, but I wouldn't have been able to imagine this.

Glass accordion doors, folded back revealed a mystical setting of wrought iron and greenery, emphasised by the soft green of the gas lamps, and broken up with the occasional burst of colour from imported flowers. In the middle, a large collection of copper and brass pipes intertwined around a sphere of glass. It took every bit of willpower for me not to ask Ancilla to activate it. Or to take advantage of the small garden benches scattered throughout, inviting visitors to stop for a moment and immerse themselves in its beauty.

Ancilla lowered herself into a huge armchair with a back that was so high and a series of levers decorating the sides. All the levers suggested it could be modified to any angle its resident required, but some of them were out of reach for the person sitting. A design flaw? Or an assumption that the sitter would know what they wanted before they sat? I coveted the soft velvet covering, a beautiful emerald green, matching the greenery it faced. Not that I could afford one, or even fit it in my small rented flat.

"Stunning, isn't it?" she asked. "Felicia's sanctuary."

I nodded my gaze drawn back to the enchanting conservatory.

"This is my favourite part of the house, though Felicia doesn't usually allow visitors in it." Ancilla let the high-backed armchair take the weight of her head, her eyes closing. Too relaxed to my mind.

"Where's Marcellus' room?"

She opened her eyes as if a great weight or glue held them down. "Upstairs towards the back of the house."

The emerald green of the chair only highlighted the dark grooves under her eyes. Her skin was so dry I was almost tempted to get her another glass of water. Instead, I studied her, and she studied me back. Perhaps it would be better to say we studied each other.

What are you hiding?

"What do *you* think happened to Overton?" I asked.

She exhaled heavily. "Honestly, I've no idea."

Cuthbert Walstrand needed to cut back on something.

"Zer Cuthbert Walstrand..." Beaumont, standing at the window gazing down at the street outside, straightened. He glanced at the colourful gentleman in the doorway and took in my return. "Thank you for taking the time to speak with us at this late hour."

I was right to assume Beaumont would not wait for me.

"To be honest, Inspector—" Rail thin, with a slight tremor in his hands, his words fell over each other.

"Prime Inspector Beaumont," I said, my tone clipped. Considering how the gossip's feet would have wings tonight. Deliberately rude? Or self-involved and oblivious?

"Prime Inspector..." Cuthbert chuckled and gave a small bow. "I wasn't aware I had a choice."

His clothes, at a height of fashion that I could only dream of, abounded with striking colours and lace, dripping from anything it could attach to. The moving patterns in his waistcoat somehow brought the lace and bold colours together. Any envy I might have had about his fabric choices was lessened by the overall effect of fragility. His thin body, lost in his sea of style.

"We..." Beaumont moved over to the chaise which had been my seat earlier. "Inspector Hoadley and I have some questions, about your, and Overton's movements, after the demonstration."

It was nothing. What difference did it make? How quickly we attach ownership to arbitrary things. As Beaumont had taken my seat, I took his, which foolishly made me feel better.

Cuthbert flopped down on a chaise, blinking as it shifted its position. Not a regular visitor then.

"Ah, the demonstration, and what a demonstration it was. Quite the masterpiece."

I snorted. "We heard—"

"Have you seen it work?" Cuthbert's hand stuttered

through the air. "No of course not, they probably wouldn't let you. When you do…" Cuthbert raised both his hands to his head and expanded them out.

"What we're interested in—"

"Old Marcellus' movements. Understandable, his dying has certainly put a bit of a pall on the evening." Cuthbert's leg bounced.

"How did you discover his body?" asked Beaumont, he had pulled out his jotter again, I wasn't sure why, so far his jotter was mostly blank.

"I walked into the library and there he was." Cuthbert's shoulders relaxed and his leg stilled. "Didn't take much skill at all." He flicked me a grin.

My lips turned downward, despite my effort to keep them neutral. From the corner of my eye, I could see Beaumont's doing the same.

"Zer Walstrand," Beaumont's voice was dry, "it's late and a lot of people would like to go home. In the interests of brevity could you tell us what brought you to the library?"

Cuthbert crossed his legs and let the top one swing, his heel tapping one of the legs under him on every return swing. "Nothing spectacular I'm afraid Prime Inspector." He smirked. "No dramatic love scenes or dark dirty secrets." His shoulders shifted, their full movement muffled by his clothes. "I'd a question for Marcellus and when I couldn't see him in the ballroom, guessed he might be in the library."

Beaumont glanced down at the loose pages from someone else's jotter in his hand.

"Perhaps you could clarify the topic of conversation?"

Beaumont glanced up. "In the shared interest of succinct-
ness, I can inform you that we've multiple reports from the
guests saying they overhead you and Overton in a heated
argument."

Cuthbert grimaced. "Heard, did they? As much as I would
like to think that my voice is distinctive, I find it hard to
believe that—"

*"There's no point being a sook about it, Marcellus, these things
happen and if you report it as fraud, you'll ruin it for everyone.
It needs time. Even if the bill passes, we'll be sitting pretty, or my
name isn't Cuthbert—"*

Cuthbert raised his hand and Beaumont put the note he
was reading from down beside him. My fingers tightened
around my quill, but the hard metal resisted the pressure. I
would need a copy of that full transcript.

"It seems I'm once more to be struck down by the burden
of a memorable name." Cuthbert chuckled and adjusted the
cuffs on his shirt. "Yes, we may have had a disagreement. But
it wasn't serious."

"The threat of reporting you for fraud, which can carry a
death sentence if convicted, isn't serious?"

Cuthbert's leg jittered. "He was mouthing off." He peered
at me, inviting me to share the joke, demonstrating his in-
ability to read a room. "You know, as people do."

"What was the fraud he was...mouthing off...about?"
asked Beaumont, his gaze steady. Awake even.

If only Beaumont had been this direct with the other
suspects.

"It was a business venture. All above board, I promise

you. I've his signed papers and the details of the agreement at home—"

"We'll need a copy," I stated.

Beaumont cleared his throat. "Yes indeed." He gazed at Cuthbert, his brow creased. "Zer Walstrand, please know that I've asked for authority to gather any documentation related to Marcellus Overton. Hoadley will collect them when we escort you, and your family, home."

"Where are they?" I asked.

Cuthbert's colour was high, and his lips struggled to move. "In the top drawer of the desk in my rooms." He shook his head. "There's nothing to worry about. We would've still made a profit, which was very important to Marcellus." He shifted. "But you know what the delays have been like at the patent office since the bill was announced..."

Beaumont nodded. "Why was Overton so interested in making a profit?"

"He wanted out from under Felicia's thumb..." A small smirk lifted the edge of his lips.

"Under her thumb?"

"Leave her of course, but still live the life to which he'd become accustomed." He stared down at his wrists, once more adjusting his cuffs. "Not here. Back on the mainland, before they change the laws there as well." His eyes narrowed and he smirked. "The only thing I wasn't sure of was whether he wanted to take little sis with him or not."

Beaumont's eyes widened, and I am sorry to say that mine did too.

"Ancilla or Melody?" I asked.

Cuthbert's gaze slashed towards me, and he leered.

"Like a bit of gossip, do you? If that got your attention, I've more." He sat back, resting his arm across the back of the chaise. "The real question is how much did Alistair want to be rid of Marcellus?"

Beaumont's forehead now had some serious lines in it. "Why would Zer Alistair Atwater want to be rid of Overton?" he asked.

"A bit of family intellectual property shared to fix a rocky relationship." Cuthbert smirked probably thinking he had the Prime Inspector on the hook. "She never registered it you know. Always kept Overton out of the family fortune. He spread his hands out in front of him. "But if she decided to share some family secrets, well...it could affect Alistair's rights, couldn't it?"

I had studied patent law, as did every child, but I needed to brush up on the ins and outs of sharing with partners, especially unregistered ones.

Beaumont made a few marks in his jotter, probably to remind himself to ask me to undertake the research. He certainly wasn't going to do it.

"And Overton shared all this with you?" asked Beaumont, an eyebrow raised.

He somehow managed to infuse it with the right amount of doubt without it being insulting.

"Obvious to anyone watching what was going on." Cuthbert relaxed further into the chaise. "I know what jealousy looks like. Felicia had her butler Necket watch Melody and Marcellus like a hawk."

"A hawk..." Beaumont tilted his head.

Melody must be an extremely talented singer if he chose her over an intelligent woman like Ancilla.

"Especially Marcellus, though he managed to hide his little whisky habit from her to a degree..."

"Do you really think so?" Beaumont regarded Cuthbert with a raised brow.

Cuthbert snorted. "That house manager, he made a pretty penny working to keep it hidden."

"Overton paid..." Beaumont checked his notes, "Franklin Vyner...to what? Buy the whisky? Or not tell Zer Atwater about it?"

"A bit of both, I'd imagine. It certainly explains his new waistcoat selection."

"Thank you for sharing your observations." Beaumont nodded and made some more marks. "Now the guests who heard you arguing with Overton were standing in the gallery. Can I confirm where you and Overton were when this argument took place?"

Cuthbert's forehead creased. "It was out on the veranda that runs down the side of the house and leads out into the garden."

"Was this before or after your sister's performance?" I asked.

"Poor Melody doesn't have the breath for it." Cuthbert's leg started twitching, but he caught it, uncrossing his legs, sitting up straighter.

My forehead creased. If she wasn't a talented singer, what appeal could she have for Overton? He was a master in his craft. Surely he wouldn't respect any artist who didn't take the time to build her skill in her essence, her pneuma, control?

"Zer Walstrand..." Beaumont's voice was tired, probably dreaming of tea and a biscuit.

"Yes, right. It was near the end of Melody's performance. Marcellus slipped out onto the veranda to hide in the library."

"You were already outside?"

He sneered. "Oh yes, living with Melody, I knew what to expect."

"Err...the veranda..." Beaumont cleared his throat. "Were you by yourself? Before Overton joined you?"

Cuthbert's fingers tapped the chaise. "A gentleman never—"

"Zer Walstrand..." Beaumont exhaled. "While I appreciate your...discretion...now is not the time." He sat back, his jotter now sitting forgotten next to him.

"Alistair had joined me after Melody started her performance."

"Alistair Atwater?" I asked, not wanting to assume.

Cuthbert was fidgeting, he would catch himself adjusting his cuffs, and relax, putting one arm across the back of the chaise until he forgot and started playing with his cuffs again.

"While there might be other Alistairs, there is only one worth mentioning."

Beaumont picked up his jotter again, Cuthbert's gaze tracking his every movement.

"Was he still out there with you when Overton came out?" asked Beaumont.

"No, he had returned to the ballroom. It was a cold night."

What would a Cuthbert Walstrand and an Alistair Atwater have to talk about? Perhaps it was the conversation that drove him back inside.

"What happened then?"

"Marcellus appeared, he saw me, and I'm afraid to say glared at me quite fiercely before he stormed off in the direction of the library." Cuthbert gazed around the room and rose, heading to the drink cart. "Felicia and her waters and infusions." He grumbled, picking up and pressing a lever on one of the containers. Gas hissed, a carbonator.

He stood there, taking a sip, before turning back to us.

"What did you do?" I asked.

"I knew he was being melodramatic." Cuthbert shrugged as he moved back to his seat. "I followed him to the door to the library and I clarified the situation for him. He continued into the library, and I went back to the ballroom, joining my father."

"How did you end up back in the library with his dead body?" I asked.

"I waited for him to come back to the party." Cuthbert attempted to savour his drink. "I had planned to continue our conversation, but when he didn't..."

"How did you access the library?" I asked.

Cuthbert tilted his head, expression quizzical.

"What door did you use?" asked Beaumont.

"Oh," Cuthbert blinked. "The one through the gallery."

Beaumont nodded and jotted down a note. "And did you speak with him?"

"He was very dead. I knew..." Cuthbert tried to swallow and took another sip of his water. "His pneuma was gone." He stared down at the glass in his hand, frowning. "It really is most inconvenient."

He couldn't quite hide his relief.

We went over the details of his movements a few more times but couldn't extract anything else useful from him. Beaumont eventually sent him away. I organised for him to be taken by a guard to a separate room.

"Full of spite and greed that one," I said.

Beaumont rubbed his chin. "Frustrated at life definitely."

"You believe him then?"

"There's some truth in there, but whether the conclusions he drew are true..." It was Beaumont's turn to shrug. "Vyner...maybe...Felicia Atwater sharing intellectual property..." Beaumont gazed through the sheer curtains to the gaslit street beyond. "Seems less likely."

"Do you want me to organise Vyner to come in?"

"No, one of the guards has already taken his statement and I want a bit more information before I question him. Let's talk to Melody Walstrand and the father, verify some of these timings." He rubbed his jaw. "Then everyone can go home, and we can get some rest before hitting this all again tomorrow...is forensics still here?"

"I'll check, zer."

Beaumont nodded. "And bring Zer Melody Walstrand in, will you?"

"Yes, zer." I paused at the door. "I admit to some curiosity."

Beaumont smiled. "You and me both."

A burst of warmth at the camaraderie rushed through me.

Every Family Has One

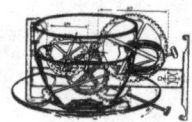

Camaraderie?

How was he ever going to...

She didn't help herself. With a lens of perpetual dissatisfaction with the world, judging it and everyone in it.

A cup of tea was the only thing that should be perpetual.

The back of Beaumont's throat hurt. Was he meant to be the one to help her see? He had enough going on without having to mentor someone else.

He glanced at the clock. Thirty hours, forty minutes and fifty-five seconds wasted.

It would all be over soon.

This would be his last case. Time to move on. Make his parents proud.

His neck muscles lessened their grip. Even the anxiety of meeting with the High Protector lessened, after all, what was the worst that could happen? The case was handed over to Gordon and he joined his old friend Wilhelmina on the mainland, dedicating himself to painting. Just the thought of the amount of effort required was daunting, but he couldn't bring back the dead, or even heal his back, but maybe he could reverse his youthful mistake.

Two short, sharp taps, reverberated through his door.

He slumped in his chair, staring at his desk.

Two, louder, raps followed.

He forced himself to straighten and face the door.

"Come in."

His former partner materialized, decked out in all the latest trends of lime greens and electric blues, even managing to find a waistcoat with a polka dot pattern that combined the two. It should have been ridiculous.

"How you holding up?" she asked, the door bouncing as she threw it open, striding into the room, and flopped down into the guest chair opposite him. "This room smells like ass."

"Gordon." Beaumont settled back deep into his chair.

"Beaumont." Gordon smiled at him.

Noxrath's newest Prime Inspector, Hortense Gordon, was, as always, very awake for this time of morning. Her bright green eyes examined him from the top of his head to the notes in his hands. The first few days after her promotion he had enjoyed the quiet slow mornings a great deal.

"How many coffees have you had?"

She shrugged. "Enough to get the engine running. Have you had your morning tea?"

He frowned. "Yes."

Her head tilted. "Then some more food might help." She pursed her lips. "Don't worry, I have it covered."

He did miss other things about her though.

Footsteps heralded the arrival of a guard with a tray.

"Prime Inspectors."

The guard put the tray between them. Sweet and dark roasted aromas battled with the musty air in the room. Beaumont could make out a plate of sweet biscuits and a cup filled with coffee.

"Thanks, you're a saviour." Gordon flashed him a broad smile. The guard blushed and backed out of the room.

Beaumont frowned at her. "Do you have to do that?"

"Do what?" She picked up her coffee cup, then took a sip.

He touched the dial to heat up his cup, cradling it in his hands. Despite its mechanics being insulated from the hot liquid inside there was just enough warmth to lend some to his icy fingers.

He examined Gordon. "Can I help you with something?"

"That's what I was going to ask you."

He reached forward and took a biscuit. Small enough to be eaten in one bite, it melted in his mouth. A heady mix of peanut and blackberry flavours hit his tongue and, for a moment, dominated his thoughts.

"You okay?" she asked, even as she picked up her own.

He gave a tight smile, trying to force it to reach his eyes. "Of course."

The bergamot of his tea mingled and lightened the flavours in his mouth.

She shoved a biscuit in her mouth and knocked it back

with a gulp of tar. "Heard the High Protector wants to talk to you." Her cup clinked as it landed back on the tray. Break time was over.

"Yes."

"Anything to report?" she asked.

He stared at her. "It'd help if I could review my notes."

"I imagine it would." Gordon drawled. "Can't say I didn't try." She rose and reached for the plate, but his arm snapped out, catching her wrist. They stared off.

"Leave them." He kept his expression serious.

She raised an eyebrow but withdrew her arm. "You aren't the boss of me anymore..." She tilted her head, contemplating the plate and then him. "But because we're mates..."

He snorted but let a small smile show. "Let me finish this then..."

She spun towards the door, pausing in its frame.

"You're not on your own."

He let his hand rest against the satchel. "Inspector Hoadley..."

Gordon exhaled. "She's..."

"Don't..." He stared at her, tilting his head. "There is one thing you could do for me." He shifted forward, the chair's tentacles adjusted, cradling his back. Bronze tipped with dark green velvet cushioning, the chair was something of an office legend. The rumour mill had him earning it as a reward. Truth was, he had hurt his back chasing after a suspect a few years ago and needed the extra support to reduce the pain of sitting. Though the velvet did imply some measure of thanks from the High Protector.

She leaned against the doorframe. "Name it," she said, smiling.

Beaumont glanced at the clock and then down at the jotter in front of him. "Warn me when she's in?"

Gordon's eyes, bright with curiosity, examined the jotter. Beaumont shifted his hands, obscuring her view.

She sniffed. "Fine, but you'd better be quick." She gave the door frame a quick tap before letting the door smash shut behind her.

With Gordon, and the coffee gone, the sourness of the air, now with a sugary tinge, pressed down on him.

He dug into the muscles of his face and opened his jaw wide. This, his last case, was not one he could leave unsolved. Focus.

Hoadley's notes had been helpful, even putting aside her criticism of his techniques. Cuthbert, jittery like a live wire, with guilt written all over him.

But was it impulse? Or was there a mastermind behind it all?

Hoadley fixated on Ancilla, but even if Ancilla was more intelligent than she appeared, that didn't make her a murderer. Perhaps the encrypted pages were from a prototype she was working on. Or stole.

His fingertips scraped the thick edge of Hoadley's jotter. She did like her puzzles.

The Mysterious Death of an Illuminator

Lavina Hoadley, Inspector
Noxrath Gendarmerie
Great Espya

The hum of the guests had died to a whisper. Cold exuded from the stone and glass, the early hour of the morning leaching away what little warmth remained. I paused, letting my gaze rest on the moonlit atrium. But I had work to do and with a deep breath, I headed into the drawing room.

"Zer, forensics have sealed the library." I didn't like telling my prime what to do, but we still had all the other guests in the house. "I think we should send the rest of the guests home. Statements are captured and details verified."

Beaumont, slumped on the chaise with his eyes closed, straightened quickly, blinking at me. What if I had been bringing Zer Melody Walstrand back with me, how would that have looked?

"Yes, yes," Beaumont yawned. "Fine. Everyone but the Walstrands."

"Yes, zer." I smothered my snort, closing the door behind me and making a mental note to knock when I came back.

I found Dalley and Hopperton, bedraggled, but standing. A layer of staleness joined the perfume cocktail of the ballroom but this time my nose was ready for it and shut down on entry.

"Prime Inspector Beaumont said that all guests, bar the Walstrands, who have given statements and had their ID verified, can go."

"They can go?" Dalley asked.

"All of them?" asked Hopperton.

"Except the Walstrands." It was important to be clear.

"Thank the Prime Inspector. Things were getting ugly," said Hopperton.

I wanted to roll my eyes but let it go and scrutinized the crowd. It was no longer moving and every chair, and sometimes even the floor had been claimed by tired, and grumpy, guests.

"He wants to interview Zer Melody first and then the father, but they are to be escorted home, by me. We need to collect some documents."

They gave short sharp nods.

I stared at them, waiting for one of them to offer an introduction to Melody Walstrand but they just stared back at me.

"Melody Walstrand?" I asked.

They both blinked but Dalley tilted her head towards two people. I examined the woman adorned in clashing colours and too many feathers. The electric blue sleeves of her shirt against the moving fuchsia of her waistcoat and the red and lime green of her waterfall made my eyes want to take a nap. I was right, this was going to be interesting. I headed in their direction.

"Zer Walstrand?"

They turned towards me with identical frowns.

The man rose to his feet, towering over me. He was tall, like his son, but whether from muscle or fat was hidden by his dark purple outfit.

A starry night motif on dark purple connected his waist-coat, to the edge of his knee-length waterfall. Despite the limited use of colour, the unified pattern, the glints as it moved, matching his own grey-silver eyes, made it powerful. Intentionally? Something to consider for my own outfits.

"And you are?"

"Inspector Hoadley, Zer Melody—"

"Can't this wait until tomorrow?" He shifted, turning his back on the other guests casting glances in his direction as they left the ballroom. "It's been a long night."

I tilted my head, examining him.

"Zer Melody directly interacted with Marcellus Overton tonight, we need to speak with her before that happens."

"Fine," He flicked Melody a glance. "Then I'll head home, and you can bring her—"

"We'll need to speak with you too, zer."

His lips tightened. "I barely spoke with the man—"

"You're not leaving me behind," said Melody, rising from her chair. "The only thing that I'm surprised about is that they chose to speak to Cuthbert first." She flicked out her crimson waterfall, with its flecked green pattern that dropped past her ankles, dragging against the floor. Highly impractical.

"We'll escort you all home," I said.

He glowered. "I hope we aren't suspects in this unfortunate event Inspector."

"Wait here, zer." I turned towards Melody. "Follow me."

I knocked before entering the drawing room and opened the door to find Beaumont sitting back on his original chaise sipping a cup of tea, its steam adding a pleasing layer to the increasingly stale air in the room. Not that I would reward his behaviour with that information.

"Zer Melody Walstrand," Beaumont stood. "Thank you for your time. We have some questions about Marcellus Overton's movements tonight that we think you can help with."

It was hard to imagine that Meldoy was Ancilla's sister. Not only was Melody's waterfall overly long, but it was also overly puffy, with several extra layers sticking out from the back of her waist. She had to lean against the rolled arm of the chaise to avoid squashing it and keep it from under the feet of the chaise as they shuffled. I hadn't been as careful of mine, but considering the rough quality of my fabric, the only thing going to put a dent in it was fire.

"You should've come to me instantly," said Melody, her voice strong and clear.

"I understand..." Beaumont gave her a small smile, "that he was in the ballroom during your performance this evening."

"To be expected." She was relaxed with a slight smile. "It was the most fabulous evening, and to be able to share my song with such a crowd..."

"Did you speak to him after your performance?" I asked, taking a seat, lifting my feet off the floor as the chaises adjusted. I missed my solid, unmoving, furniture, even if it was old fashioned.

"I suppose it isn't any secret. I hope..." She winced. "I had hoped he'd sponsor me. After all, it was clear that he thought well of me. Of course, he said he was happy to, but as he hadn't yet had a chance to hear me perform..." Melody shrugged. "So, I made it happen..."

I kept my gaze lowered and focused on taking my notes. More likely he hoped to avoid it completely.

"Where," Beaumont began, his jotter lay on the chaise beside him. "Where in the ballroom were you when you talked to him?"

"Technically it wasn't the ballroom."

"Not the ballroom?" Beaumont blinked and I straightened.

"No." She shifted, draping herself over the end of the chaise a bit more. She was trying to be calm and confident, but tension gathered around her eyes.

Beaumont cleared his throat. "You wanted a private word with him then?"

"Yes exactly. I saw him leave the ballroom and thought wonderful, we can talk in private."

"Where?" I asked.

Melody was silent, her fingers picking where the fabric of the chaise met the wooden curl of its frame.

"Zer Walstrand..." Beaumont folded his hands over his unused jotter. "Marcellus Overton is dead. Any information you can give could be critical in finding out what happened."

Her lips thinned and her chin rose. "In the library."

Beaumont nodded. "And what time was this?"

"I don't remember exactly. I finished singing. Saw him say a couple of words to Ancilla. I wanted to know what he'd said. The band started playing again and he left the room."

"Where'd you think he was heading?"

"Oh, I knew he was getting away from the crowds." Her

eyes gleamed and she gave a small knowing smile, "and when he headed through the atrium to the library. The perfect opportunity..."

I forced myself not to frown. How could he have gone through the atrium if Cuthbert saw him on the veranda? And how had no one noticed the man of the hour through the glass walls?

"He left the ballroom...entered the hallway and turned left...heading through the atrium to the library..." asked Beaumont.

"Yes." Melody picked at the seam again. She glanced at her hands, and they stilled.

"You followed him through the atrium..." asked Beaumont.

Melody gazed directly at him, her eyebrows raised. "Yes, I'm not sure why that's so hard to understand. Obviously, I wished I hadn't, but at the time I didn't know he was going to die, did I?"

"Walk me..." Beaumont sat back. "...Through what happened when you got to the library?"

Melody adjusted in her seat, relaxing.

"He sat there with a bottle of whisky next to him and a glass in his hand."

"On his own?" I asked.

"Yes, I know Zer Felicia doesn't approve of drinking. Ancilla says she doesn't even have wine with dinner. I imagined she'd not be pleased if she knew he kept whisky in the book room."

"What did he say?" I asked.

Melody's colour deepened. "He...indicated he wasn't happy about me being there."

"What did you do then?"

"I said I wouldn't say anything and whether now...whether he would introduce me next week..." Melody pushed herself to her feet, gliding to the front bay window. Putting a knee up on the bench she peered out at the street. With the fabric draped in a train behind her, she did present a pretty, if slightly garish, picture.

Beaumont's voice filled the room. "Zer Walstrand, I need you to tell me what happened."

Melody turned her back on the window and crossed her arms. "It's so sad." She stared down at her hands but her voice lacked the emotion to match it.

"What's so sad, Zer Walstrand?" asked Beaumont, his voice sharpening.

"When someone so talented starts to fall behind the times."

"And in what way was Overton falling behind the times?" Beaumont definitely had a bit of tone in his voice now.

"He didn't get it."

"Zer Walstrand..."

"My performance, he didn't get it. I know it was wonderful. I had a lot of compliments afterward. Necket, the Atwater's butler, a refined woman of taste said I was sensational. And Alastair himself said he had never heard anything like it." Melody adjusted the cuffs on her shirt and flashed me a smile.

Alastair the diplomat.

"What next?" I asked.

"I told Marcellus..." she cleared her throat. "That he was old fashioned and that the only reason he was anything was because of the Atwaters and that let's see how great he was once Felicia kicked him out for drinking." Melody moved back toward the chaise and lowered herself carefully on it. The crimson and green of her waterfall clashed with the soft blue velvet on the chaise, but I didn't let myself get distracted.

"And what did you do then?"

Melody frowned at Beaumont. "I left of course."

"By which door?"

"I went through the gallery. I'd seen it was open to the ballroom and thought that Felicia might be near it."

"The gallery?" I asked.

Melody peered down her nose at me. "Of their greatest inventions. It's between the library and the ballroom."

"If the gallery was open and connecting the ballroom, why do you think Marcellus went out through the atrium?"

Melody tried to shift her waterfall so she could sit up straighter with mixed success. "Marcellus' thought processes are beyond me." She sniffed.

"Thank you," Beaumont said, closing his unused jotter. "You've been very helpful."

She nodded and rose, gathering her train behind her.

"One more question if you don't mind..." Beaumont smiled politely at her.

She scrutinized him. "And what would that be?"

"Did you speak to Felicia about his drinking?"

She rose, taking a moment to adjust the fabric flowing behind her. "No, I couldn't find her, so I ended up joining my father. I did however share everything that happened with him." She peered down at Beaumont. "I trust that sharing my feelings with my father is considered acceptable in the eyes of the Inspectors?"

Beaumont smiled and rose. "Yes of course. Thank you for your time I know it's late—"

Melody laughed. "Not for me, I much prefer night to day. The day is so...bright." She swept out of the room. But the guard on the door hadn't gotten his cue, so she had to wait for him to open it. She kept her back straight not looking back at us.

"Could Zer Melody Walstrand be escorted to somewhere she could rest privately?" Beaumont peered at the guard over her shoulder. "We've one more interview before we can let the family go home." The guard nodded and followed her out.

The door clicked shut.

"Wouldn't want it to be bright, would we?" I said.

Beaumont snorted. "Don't get distracted by the dressing, at this point, she's the last person to see our victim alive."

"Do you think she did it?" I hadn't really seen this death as a crime of passion, and how was she to know that he wouldn't like her performance?

"Too early to tell but she has to stay a suspect for now."

"And Ancilla Walstrand?"

Beaumont frowned. "I can't see a motive, and she was never alone the whole night."

"And if it was a poisoning?"

The creases in his forehead deepened. "What has she to gain?"

I shrugged. "I don't know yet, but she is up to something."

Beaumont scraped his hand across his face. "I'm going to the washroom, and then we'll talk to Zer Ernest Walstrand. Hopefully, then we can send everyone home and catch some rest."

He laboured to his feet, wincing as he straightened. Sometimes I forgot about his back. Despite being a few years younger than me, being in constant pain aged him. I could only hope it was just physically not mentally as well.

Meanwhile, I was feeling fine. I grinned and returned to the puzzle of the hidden desk. After pressing on every edge to no avail I forced myself to step back. It was a desk. Something used every day. No one would want it to be difficult. Where would I put it?

Near the chair.

I trod back over to the chair and moved it to where I found it. Standing behind the chair, I scanned for what was within reach.

The drinks station, attached to the wall, had a small lever on the side. I reached towards it.

The doorknob rattled and I turned to see Beaumont had returned.

"Zer, before we—"

"I will say their washrooms are nice." Beaumont shuffled with his usual lack of enthusiasm to his seat. "Best bring in Ernest Walstrand, Hoadley."

"Yes, zer, but before we do—"

"Appreciate you have a lot to offer Hoadley," He gave me a half smile, "But it's late. Let's get this over with and we can talk more back at the Way."

He could find time to find a cup of tea but not to search the house where a murder took place? Fool!

I marched out of the room.

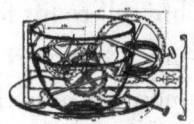

She had been right. He had been a fool.

Beaumont lifted his cup, but the perfumed steam turned his stomach.

Pipe it, even tea was ruined.

A hidden desk. He tried to recall if any of the guards had mentioned it, he was almost sure he would have remembered if they did.

Beaumont added it to the list of things he needed to follow up on.

The only thing he remembered about that night was how tired he was. His back had been screaming at him and everything took forever.

After Melody, Hoadley had brought in the father, Ernest Walstrand, whose temper had not been improved by waiting.

Ernest, a big man, though Beaumont suspected he had

gone to fat which he hid with some clever tailoring, paced the room, waving his arms.

"It is time for us to go home. It's been a tragic and exhausting night and my family has been kept here unnecessarily." Ernest took a deep breath, exhaling heavily.

"Zer Walstrand, I'm Prime Inspector Beaumont. I can assure you that once we're finished here, you, and your family, will be escorted home."

Beaumont dragged himself to his feet.

"Do you know how much I've on right now?"

He didn't, but Beaumont suspected that Ernest was more than ready to tell him all about it. What Ernest failed to appreciate was how little he cared.

"Zer Walstrand, please take a seat." Beaumont gestured downward.

Ernest stood there rigid but in the end, he lowered himself onto the chaise, his lips pinched tight.

"I've been tasked with working on implementing the whole patent legislation mess, created by others who don't know what they are doing. The amount of paperwork alone—"

"I understand, Zer." Beaumont tried to convey all the sympathy he didn't feel. "But I also understand that Marcellus Overton was in the ballroom up until your daughter Melody's performance?"

Ernest, taking a seat, sat back, one arm across the back of the chaise and his legs crossed. Mirroring the same stance as his son earlier and adding the weight of experience to the move.

"Yes, he didn't leave the side of that device." Ernest peered down his nose at Beaumont. Which was impressive, considering seated, Beaumont was slightly taller.

Beaumont blinked. "You're not a fan of the device, Zer Walstrand?" he asked.

"I am of course a lover of all art. But this new light art. It doesn't create anything tangible." He shrugged. "Of course, Melody's performance was the real highlight of the night."

Beaumont was curious about what exactly was more tangible about sound than light. But that was not a philosophical discussion he wanted to have right now.

Beaumont cleared his throat. "When did—"

"Alistair came all the way over to her after the performance to congratulate her you know. He has been very attentive to her of late."

"Where did this conversation take place?" Hoadley snapped.

He turned his stare on her. She sat, ramrod straight on her chaise, her feet slightly off the floor. What would it take to get her to relax?

There would always be more cases and she was going to kill herself if she ran at each one with this level of intensity.

"I suppose those who aren't capable of creating it have less appreciation." Ernest sniffed. "Near the entrance to the hall, if that is at all relevant."

A bit rich, considering as far as Beaumont was aware Ernest had even less artistic ability than he did.

"And what did Melody and Alistair do after that conversation?" asked Hoadley, her voice flicking out.

Ernest's eyes narrowed.

Beaumont reached up, rubbing at the tight muscles in his jaw. Bristles he hadn't had time to shave were now long enough to scrape at the skin of his fingers. He also had forgotten to tie his hair. He hated to think how dishevelled he looked.

"Zer Walstrand." Beaumont dropped his hands into his lap and tried to look alert. "If you could share with us your memory of everyone's movements it would be greatly appreciated."

Ernest grunted. "Melody left the ballroom and Alistair walked over to talk to Ancilla." He kept his stare on Beaumont. "I'm not sure why, she hadn't done much more than stand next to the device all night."

Beaumont wanted to pursue what was a strange comment for a father to make, but he needed to get this interview finished as soon as possible. Hoadley was practically vibrating where she sat, prepped and ready to fire.

"Did you see Marcellus leave the ballroom?" he asked.

"No, he wasn't next to Ancilla when Alistair joined her."

"What about Melody and Cuthbert?" Beaumont's back twinged. He adjusted, wedging into the corner with the most support. "After Melody's performance was over, did you see either of them come back into the ballroom?"

"I don't like what you're implying with the 'come back' part Prime Inspector..." Ernest's already pinched face almost caved in on itself. "Children." He snorted. "More trouble than they are worth I can tell you."

"And what trouble did they cause tonight?" asked Beaumont, picking up his jotter. He didn't really have any intention to write in it, but he had found over the years it made people feel that what they had to say was important.

Ernest's eyes narrowed. "None that I am aware of," his fingers drumming against the back of the chaise.

"I understand both Melody and Cuthbert had hopes of Overton's favour?" Hoadley, leaned forward, her tone still strong, but with a little less bite.

They just might get through this.

Ernest glared at her. "Yes, though I am not sure why. He wasn't much without the Atwaters."

"How long was Melody out of the room?" Beaumont asked, keeping his voice soft and low.

Ernest gave his attention to Beaumont.

"Not long. She was upset. But I told her not to worry. It would have damaged her career to be sponsored by him anyway."

"And what about Cuthbert..." Beaumont peered down at his jotter, "what do you remember of his movements?"

He scowled. "I'm not happy about this targeting of my children."

"Cuthbert's movements," barked Hoadley.

Ernest's eyes disappeared behind eyelids and lashes. "He spent most of his time on the veranda smoking." His lips pursed. "A terrible habit, but Alistair was kind enough to keep him company for a while. A wasted opportunity, he could've made several beneficial connections tonight if he had made the effort."

"And do you remember when you saw him in the ball-room?"

"No not really, sometime after Melody came back."

"Thank you, Zer Walstrand..." Beaumont closed his jotter, with no visible notes. "You and your family are free to return to your home."

Hoadley kept her eyes down, examining her jotter.

"Indeed." Ernest Walstrand stood.

"Hoadley..." Beaumont gazed in my direction. "I want you to escort them."

Ernest's eyebrows ran upwards. "I hardly think that's necessary."

"Your safety is a priority, zer," Hoadley said, rising, tucking her jotter away, ready for the next task handed to her.

"Guard, if you could..." Beaumont asked.

The guard on the door nodded. "Of course, Prime Inspector..." he turned his attention to Ernest. "This way, Zer Walstrand."

Ernest sniffed and followed.

Beaumont groaned as he pushed himself to standing. "Hoadley...we'll need a few steamers."

"Yes, zer." She rose as well, glancing around the room. "Zer, there is one thing-"

"At least three I suspect, and let's leave a couple of guards to keep an eye on the Walstrand residence, tonight at least.

Her lips were thin, and she was glaring at him. Again.

"Yes, zer. The thing is-"

"I appreciate they are suspects Hoadley, but it is important that we don't put the High Inspector in hot water with all of this."

Her face tightened even more.

"Yes, zer. The w-"

She turned toward the drink station.

He wanted to shout that was the wrong direction but controlled himself. "Best not keep them waiting." He pointed towards the foyer. "I'll get Ancilla for you."

She jerked her head and headed out to the foyer.

Everything was a battle. He hadn't been sure if he had it in him to deal with this as well as another murder investigation.

He kept reminding himself. One step at a time. After this, it was over.

A risk sending Hoadley with the Walstrands by herself. But she was an Inspector after all. Conducting a search for some papers was hardly something that needed his attention. And right now, he needed to head home, get a few more hours of rest and some pain relief.

The door gave a solid thump as it closed behind her. He wouldn't call it a slam, but it was close.

He stretched up his arms, leaning back slightly and feeling his muscles unclench infinitesimally.

The door to the lounge was a simple wooden door, but well maintained and the hinges moved smoothly, without any creaks or clicks as he opened it.

On entering the adjacent room, he found Ancilla curled up in an oversized recliner, sipping a drink and chatting with Alistair who was perched on the edge of an adjacent chair next to her. Leaning into her space.

A bit too close. Exactly which of the Walstrand siblings was he interested in?

Her innocuous countenance turned towards him.

"Ah, it seems we are worthy of the Prime Inspector's attention," said Alistair, rising. He, like his mother had changed into clothes of mourning. But his demeanour, still the host of a party.

Beaumont suspected he was only a little younger than him, but wealth and all its privileges had him in good health. Beaumont doubted that he had to deal with a broken back.

"Prime Inspector." Ancilla leaned further back in her chair. "Good news I hope?"

All very civilised. No tears. No fuss. At the time he had considered her a very calm and sensible person.

"We're escorting you, and your family, home, but of course, we may have more questions tomorrow."

Ancilla didn't appear to be overly thrilled at either prospect, but she knocked back her drink, hints of vinegar and sweetness suggesting something other than water, and dragged herself out of the chair.

"Excellent," her voice was dry. "Alistair, thanks for keeping me company." She winced as she straightened.

"Ancilla..." Alistair stepped forward, his hand outstretched. "Are you alright?" he asked.

"Yes. It will be helpful to have a rest though." She smiled at him. "Thank you for your kindness. I'm not sure when..." She shrugged.

Alistair glared at Beaumont. Like somehow, he was to blame for the state Ancilla was in.

"I know mother is keen to have this demonstrated at the

next sitting of parliament." he stared at a wall. "Without Marcellus though...we'll have to find another illuminator."

So, the assistant wasn't strong enough to run it on her own. Not unexpected.

Ancilla nodded at Alistair and shuffled towards Beaumont, her expression empty.

5

The Walstrand's Reside

Lavina Hoadley, Inspector
Noxrath Gendarmerie
Great Espya

I arranged for myself and Ancilla to be driven together in a gendarmerie steamer, forcing her to sit facing me.

Cuthbert, Melody, and Ernest followed in another, along with a third steamer full of guards. I wasn't leaving the Walstrands unwatched.

Our menagerie set off. I scanned the street we were leaving. The weight of someone watching made me twitchy. Shadows pooled behind fading streetlamps, easy for someone to stay hidden.

The gendarmerie steamers, distinct with their built-in hard tops, stood out. We just had to hope that the reporters were busy with the protests about the patent bill. Still, it would only take one scout to spot them.

I pulled down the privacy veil, trapping in the coppery tang of the steamer.

"Can I help you, Inspector?" She examined me, tilting her head and focusing on me with unexpected intensity.

Her plain clothing, now completed with an unadorned top hat, had stood up to the long evening better than her brother and sister's more extravagant outfits.

"I'm curious, Zer Walstrand—"

"Ancilla, please." She smiled at me. No doubt attempting to manipulate me, as I suspect she did everyone else.

"Ancilla." I touched the rim of my hat, a guard had finally returned to me after searching for ages, and I dipped my head slightly, willing to play the game. "I'm curious what an assistant does for someone like Marcellus Overton?"

She blinked, her brows furrowing.

She inhaled, releasing a breath, and settled back into the seat. "Marcellus didn't like to worry about things that he considered boring. I took care of them."

"What things did he consider boring?"

"Anything he didn't feel like doing."

I stared at her, making no attempt to fill the silence. It was a gamble. With little traffic, the drive wouldn't take long.

She shrugged. "Responding to invitations, final testing of devices—"

"He didn't care about his art?"

"If he was satisfied the device worked...he didn't appreciate multiple rounds of testing at the end."

I considered her. "And how exactly do you test an illumination device without the artist?"

She just stared back at me.

"My understanding...Ancilla," I said, leaning forward, "is that it takes a lot of pneuma control, time and skill to utilise one of those devices."

She blinked. "Even the smallest amount of pneuma can turn one on," she said, adjusting her hat slightly. "It just won't do much."

"Testing...just making sure it could produce..."

"A faint light, from a lowly assistant...ready for the real artist."

I wasn't sure I believed her, but why would she lie?

"I understand it's a strain on the body."

"What is?" she asked.

"Using large amounts of pneuma."

She shrugged. "Yes, it was important for Marcellus to keep physically fit and practice every day."

"You seem a bit stiff tonight, yourself."

Her skin, her muscles, the slowness of her movement. Something had taken a lot out of her physically tonight.

"Ahh...yes, well, it is all relative. Even a small use of pneuma can affect its user when they aren't used to it."

"A lot of testing, then?"

"Yes." Ancilla studied me. "Yes, a lot of testing."

The steamer jerked to a halt.

The icy metal of the steamer door stung my hand, reminding me I needed to invest in gloves for the winter. I unlatched it from the inside and pushed it open. There was a small step, but I ignored it, jumping down onto the street.

A narrow three-storey tenement wedged between its neighbours loomed before us. Its dark grey stone and black iron gates and barred windows created a myriad of shadows illuminated by sparsely positioned gas lamps. Hazy in the icy morning fog.

The Walstrands' residence, while grand by most standards, was significantly smaller than the Atwaters. An interesting choice for a man like Ernest Walstrand. His position usually brought to mind more grandiose lodgings.

A rattle caused me to turn, and Ancilla clambered out holding onto the frame and inching her foot down slowly until it hit the pavement before letting go. Her whole body moving in slow motion.

She glanced at me and smiled. A genuine smile, full of humour.

"What?" I asked.

"I think I'm going to enjoy working with you, Inspector."

"What work?" I frowned at her.

We stood on the street waiting for the others to exit their steamers. Between Melody's waterfall and Cuthbert's overly feathery hat, it was like watching a humorous play. So far he had stepped on her train, she had tried to squash his hat down and Ernest's voice echoing out from the steamer, added the background music to the scene.

"Investigating what happened to Marcellus, of course," said Ancilla.

My frown deepened. Calling her Ancilla had given her

ideas. "Just to be clear, Zer Walstrand, the gendarmerie will run the investigation and you're, at best, a witness, at worst, a suspect."

"A suspect?" She glanced to the side, and her smile disappeared. I followed her gaze to see her father finally escaping his steamer.

A couple of short words to Melody and Cuthbert and Ernest strode over.

Ancilla's distant, and amicable, expression returned.

"I'll have you know I have a full day tomorrow." Ernest walked up to me. He was too close and trying to use his height to intimidate.

I gave a short sharp nod. I could practically hear Beaumont telling me to be respectful. I was surprised he let me come here without supervision. Or intentional? Hoping I would fail, and he would be rid of me.

The Walstrands might have lacked the magnificence of Atwater Place, but Ernest used his position at the patent office to some effect. A fence with a metal thorn-covered vine in constant motion protected the property. The absence of front stairs was also a barrier to the casual visitor.

He pulled a recessed lever on the fence and a series of clanks heralded a set of steps unrolling from the landing above, like a rug across the floor. It was only three steps high off the ground. There was no practical reason for the floating steps' existence. Metal grated on metal as it locked in place with handrails and a small welcome mat. I glanced over to share the ridiculousness of it with the guards, but their impressed expressions made me roll my eyes instead.

I turned to see Ancilla watching me with a smirk. My eyes narrowed, and I kept close, forcing her to keep behind the others.

"You don't seem too broken up by your boss's death," I whispered.

Upon navigating the steps, we found ourselves at the door of a vault. We waited while Ernest tapped a series of patterns into its smooth metal facade. Guests by invitation only.

The guards all shuffled forward watching. Melody and Cuthbert draped themselves over the railings, probably too bored to hold their own body weight.

"Marcellus..." Ancilla's voice matched mine, a soft whisper between unmoving lips. "His talent's a loss to the world."

"But not the man?"

"Isn't all death tragic?" The corner of Ancilla's mouth twitched upward.

"Sometimes I think life's the genuine tragedy."

"Surely you must be enjoying yourself Inspector?" she said. "It's rare you get a murder, let alone one with players like these."

I ignored the flush in my cheeks. "Murder is not something to be enjoyed, Zer Walstrand."

Ernest eventually managed to pull back the bolts and the procession of Walstrands and guards entered the house.

I stationed two guards just inside the door so they didn't freeze, and ordered Cuthbert to show me his business papers with Overton. A death in the Atwater residence trumped the Walstrands' right to privacy.

The floor of the entryway rolled forward, carrying the

guests so they didn't need to take the four or five steps needed into a well-maintained living room. Dark furniture, fabrics rich in colour. Underneath them, a thick rug shifted like grass in a breeze. I gazed suspiciously at the multitude of armchairs positioned around a coffee table in the middle of the room—they appeared comfortable, but who knew what would happen if I sat in one.

There was no sign of their domestics though Melody was shouting for someone called Roger. And with that, the Walstrands scattered, disappearing up narrow stairwells. I gestured to one of the guards to follow me, powering along behind Cuthbert, not letting him out of my sight.

"It's in the top left drawer," said Cuthbert, throwing his top hat on a chair and flopping down on his bed, his head in his hand, watching me. The guard standing in the door-way frowned at him, but I tuned him out, focusing on the treasure trove of information in front of me.

Ernest's generosity and enthusiasm for invention did not extend to his son's room. The edges of the curtains were rotten, tufts showing in the arms of his chair and his desk, with its broken lock, looked like something picked up off the street.

"I'll just make sure we aren't missing anything important," I said, methodically opening every drawer.

He groaned and thumped back onto the bed. The lamps, already burning, highlighted the disturbed dust. That, and the fact that the room smelt of old socks suggested that Roger wasn't that fond of cleaning, or Cuthbert. Or both.

I picked up papers, sometimes adding them to my pile,

other times returning them to the desk but reading every piece.

A personalised jotter with a few poems written on it caught my eye. While not relevant to the investigation I picked up one that had been ripped off.

Oh, to be one of the noble artists
To brush, sculpt or write my interest
But I must have the skills
To pay my bills
Or become one of the harnessed

Life choices

Someone had taken the time to imprint a top hat with dice on it and his name in the bottom corner. As a gift, it was both thoughtful and a bit judgemental. The kind of gift a sister would give. Though considering the quality of the poems, I doubted there was enough pneuma inspiration in the words for him to even qualify for the base stipend. He would be better off getting a job like the rest of us.

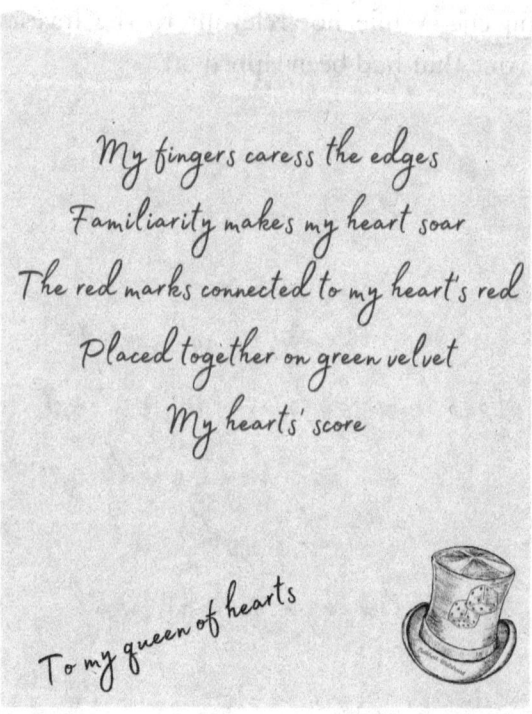

My fingers caress the edges
Familiarity makes my heart soar
The red marks connected to my heart's red
Placed together on green velvet
My hearts' score

To my queen of hearts

Drivel.

Turning my attention back to why I was here I collected every business paper I could find. Ignoring Cuthbert's and the guards' sullen expressions, I gathered my collection together.

"These will do for now." I pulled out my jotter and wrote a receipt. "Once the investigation's completed you can request them to be returned to you."

"Yeah great, thanks." Cuthbert sat up, staring at me, tiredness dominating his expression.

We left and I re-entered the living room, expecting to find Ernest waiting for me. But it was empty, and I wasn't one to waste the opportunity.

I wandered through the room, picking up books and any scrap of paper with writing on it.

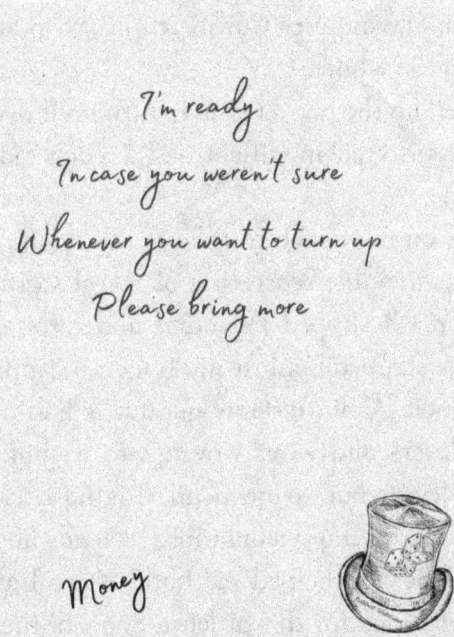

I'm ready

In case you weren't sure

Whenever you want to turn up

Please bring more

Money

I fully believed he was ready. I just wasn't sure any was

going to come his way with this quality of work. While Cuthbert might not be a competent poet, he was prolific. I found more scraps of paper with terrible poetry on them.

Unable to handle any more I left the main living area and moved to a small desk at one end, the majority of it covered in open ledgers, the house accounts. The patent office paid well. Something to consider for a future career move.

A bench ran under a window with a nest of cushions at one end, a scattering of books around it, and a pocket watch sitting on the window ledge. A favourite reading spot of someone's. Having met Cuthbert and Melody it didn't take much to guess whose.

I picked up the pocket watch, turning it over in my hand. Some unregistered modifications? I pocketed it to investigate later.

I knelt on the bench to take in the small garden beyond and its fashionable scattering of metal statues. Something dug into me. I slipped my hand under the cushion and a sharp edge scraped against my fingers. Gripping it, I pulled out the book. A diary. How quaint. It had a complex network of levers and wires woven into its binding. I fiddled with the levers but to no avail. Taking a chance, I fed a small amount of my pneuma into it. I was no artist, but my love of music had helped me build control as a child, and enough remained for this at least. Some of the levers glowed and I pushed in a bit more, my breath sped up and sweat collected under my arms. Click. The diary opened, revealing the first page.

From the desk of Ancilla Walstrand

Dangerous to keep a diary, even a locked one, in a high-traffic place like this. I tried to read the first page but found it further encrypted. A scuff on the rug jolted me and impulsively I ripped out the last entry. A stretch to say the act was covered by my authority to recover documents, but arguable.

The pages separated easily but small wires hung loose, quickly weaving themselves back into the paper leaving the encryption intact. Fascinating. Something to be explored later but if this invention was for sale I was buying. To avoid inopportune questions, the papers, joined the pocket watch in the inside pocket of my waistcoat. The matter might be serious, but it didn't stop puzzles from being fun.

I turned around, Cuthbert's papers still clutched in my hand, the guard on the door, watching me.

"We're done here," I said, waving Cuthbert's papers.

The guard gave a short nod. "Yes, zer."

"Someone has to drive me back to the Way."

The guard sighed. "Yes, zer."

The fact that it turned out to be Hopperton was unfortunate. The guards on the door, nodded at their colleague as we left. Beaumont was probably at home already, happy to leave this all to another day. But I wasn't one to waste time sleeping when there was a mystery to be solved.

On the street, Hopperton paused.

"Is there a problem?"

"Sorry, zer, I left the starter with Dalley."

"Dalley?" I didn't remember seeing her. But then I hadn't been paying much attention to what the guards were doing.

"Yes, she's inside...I'll just..." He indicated back at the house, and I waved him away.

The street lamps, hazy in the early morning mist, created a scene of light, shadows and glistening cobblestones. For a moment Noxrath was almost beautiful.

The following crunch, blinding pain and a close-up of the stones of the street weren't quite as picturesque.

A chemical cocktail, reminding me of the morgue had swirled around me. My stomach rolled and I swallowed.

Alive. Check.

Light knocked on my eyelids and I opened them to find the sun creeping in through a window, highlighting the lines on Beaumont's face and the blonde, and greys, in Beaumont's curls.

"Zer," I said.

"Hoadley..." He gazed in my direction but didn't meet my eyes. "How're you feeling?"

His voice was even more gravelly than usual.

"What happened?" I examined the room. A mistake. Pops of pain travelled through my head. I had blinked rapidly and stilled.

Would my parent's fate be mine as well?

"Someone jumped you for Cuthbert's papers." Beaumont scowled.

I exhaled. Not a steamer then. I wanted to jump up

and shake him. Demand that he tell me everything. "Who?" When? How?"

"We don't know." His lips thinned. "But we will. I've assigned two inspectors to track down...your attacker."

And just like that I was a victim. At the mercy of fate and an indifferent gendarmerie.

But I wasn't. This time I was the inspector, and I could take control. Make sure it was done right.

"Cuthbert's papers? Why?" I risked letting my eyebrows move closer together. "I read them. They weren't anything strange, just the terms of the agreement."

Beaumont tapped the end of the bed frame, making its myriad of joints rattle. I stiffened, waiting for the bed to collapse.

A mirror hung on the wall opposite me. The bed, and its network of metal rods held together by adjustable joints, presumably for the patient's comfort, reflected back at me. With multiple metal legs and feet underneath, it resembled a spider. Hopefully a well-put-together one. I was sceptical that a bed scurrying down a hall would be anything but terrifying.

It had been a long time since I had been in a hospice. After months of watching my parents die a slow and painful death, if you had asked me if I liked anything about them, I would have flatly denied it. But now, I found myself remembering the simple stretchers they used to have with fondness.

"What do you remember?" Beaumont's fingers dug into the skin on the side of his jaw, leaving red marks on areas already rubbed raw.

How much of the trail of our murder investigation had gotten cold?

I blinked. "Er...I can't..."

"It's alright, take your time. When you feel up to it, write down what you can recall for now."

"How long?"

Beaumont shuffled over, placing a large jotter, and a quill with an automatic ink generator attached, on the table next to my bed.

The quill drew my gaze. A self-inking quill. I had heard of them. Even saw one in a shop window once. But I hadn't expected one to just be handed to me. I gripped the metal frame of my bed. Forcing myself to keep still.

It was frustrating that I couldn't turn, that I couldn't reach over and play with it immediately. But if getting hit over the head meant I got to keep the quill, it had almost been worth it.

"Only a few hours. It's the next morning." The lines on his forehead deepened. "The murder is not your main concern right now."

"But, the attack, the murder, surely they are connected?"

He nodded. "Yes, and for both," he said, glancing down at the jotter. "For both, I need the entirety of what you remember."

I narrowly avoided an instinctive nod. "Yes, zer." I would capture everything. One day I might even turn it into a story. My first murder. Written with a self-inking quill. I could imagine it in a gendarmerie museum. Something to be admired by future generations of guards dreaming of being an inspector.

Beaumont shrugged. "They want to keep you under observation for a bit." He rested his hand on my bed again. It creaked alarmingly. "Take all the time you need."

"Yes, zer." I couldn't stop myself from shivering. The stiff sheets of the bed and the thin blanket over it offered little warmth. "How long before I can..."

"No job is worth dying for Hoadley." He peered down at me, his eyes barely open and his mouth resting in its usual morose position.

"Not even to catch a murderer?"

He let out a heavy exhale and gripped the edge of the bed. "How would another death, your death, help that?"

"What next?" I twisted the sheet under my hands.

What would be happening without me?

"We're checking out Overton's residence, see if we can find copies of the documents."

I cleared my throat. "And his workroom in Atwaters Place."

Beaumont wiped his hand across his face, attempting to hide a small smile. "Already checked."

By whom? And how thoroughly?

"Just focus on getting better," said Beaumont.

Soon after he left, a doctor dropped in to tell me I was going to be fine. A couple more hours for observation, something for the pain and I would be free. I asked for my clothes which had somehow disappeared. Why remove them for a smashed head?

A few minutes later an orderly appeared with them, clean and folded, and my ruined hat.

Ragged edges tickled my finger as I traced the dent. My top hat, not a fancy one, solid, reinforced on the sides, had probably protected my skull from a more serious injury.

Putting it aside I picked up my vest. I unsealed the inner pocket to reveal two pieces of paper and a pocket watch.

6

The Diary of Ancilla Walstrand

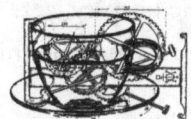

While Hoadley was being attacked, Beaumont had been grateful for the softness of the bed, the warmth of his quilt. His brushed cotton sheets trapped the warmth of his body and reduced the need and cost of the oil heater.

Oil wasn't out of his price range but considering Noxrath was cold most of the year it quickly added up. His parents had been huge fans of blankets.

Instead of staying with her, as soon as Hoadley had left with the Walstrands he had excused himself from the Atwaters and left the guards to keep them safe.

And why not? Marcellus Overton was dead and the world wasn't going to end if they left the investigation to morning, giving the lab, and Dr Morten, time to complete their tests.

He needed to stretch, lie down. Give the muscles in his back some rest.

The pounding on the door had ripped him out of sweet oblivion, his stomach twisting at each step to the door.

"Prime Inspector, Inspector Hoadley's been attacked." The messenger, still young enough to enjoy the night shift, stared up at him with wide eyes, her face flushed with excitement. A murder and a gendarmerie attacked, it was more than Noxrath had seen for years.

Beaumont's heart stopped. "Where is she?"

"They took her to the hospice, zer."

The hair on his skin rose and he shivered. "Tell them I am on my way."

It was only after he closed the door that he realised he was in a cotton nightshirt and that he had forgotten to put on his robe. No doubt the messenger would include that commentary in her message. He just hoped the inevitable tale wasn't embellished to the point he ended up answering the door naked.

He arrived at the hospice to find Hoadley unconscious. He forgot sometimes how short she was. When awake she dominated the space. But with her head wrapped in bandages and only pale white gas lamps and the first light of the day illuminating her, her solid frame appeared small, swamped by the hospice gurney's spider web of metal.

He had sent for the shift supervisor to come and deliver an update and bring supplies. An empty visitor's area, where dirt collected in its corners from years of indifferent cleaners, and any colour in the seats had faded leaving nothing but a pale hint of green, offered sanctuary. Dust softened the hospice's brew of chemicals.

The squeak of rubber against oil-cloth floors, sharp and even in tempo, made him look up. Alfred's bright eyes and gendarmerie signal ablaze on his waistcoat, a welcome sight.

"Alfred."

"Prime Inspector. I have the jotter and quill requested." Alfred's voice echoed, overloud in the empty room.

In his hands was a full-sized jotter and self-inking quill. Beaumont suspected that Hoadley would need to stay in the hospice for a while, but she wouldn't want to stay for long without something to do.

"Thank you," he said taking them. "What do we know?"

There was a drink station that had never been restocked, but it did have a small beaker for heating a cup of water. He fiddled with it trying to get it to light. Alfred joined him and magically managed to get it started.

"Let me, zer."

Beaumont shifted out of the way, watching Alfred. The drink station might be empty, but Alfred still managed to put together two cups of tea. Beaumont would not have been surprised to find that Alfred carried an emergency tea-making set on him at all times.

"Thanks, Alfred."

Alfred nodded and they sat on the two seats that seemed to have the most padding left. There were no arms though and Beaumont shifted trying to get comfortable. It left him sitting overly straight and at right angles to Alfred.

"You alright Prime Inspector?" Alfred's voice was softer, his face creased with concern.

Beaumont glanced sideways at him. "I'm not the one we need to worry about today." He shifted in his seat again, angling more towards Alfred. "Do we know what happened?"

Alfred balanced his cup on the chair next to him. Beaumont stared at it. It would not take much for it to fall and spill.

"Looks like she was left out on the street alone while one of the guards went back inside to get the starter."

Beaumont tore his eyes off the cup, turning his attention back to Alfred.

"How long was she alone for?" he asked.

"That's where it gets a bit hazy, zer. Some say a moment, others say a few minutes." Alfred shrugged. "We are taking statements but so far no one has seen anything useful."

"Any sign of the weapon?"

Alfred shifted, settling back, adjusting his waistcoat. "No, zer. It is a fairly clean street. It looks like they took whatever they used with them."

"Pipe it." Beaumont stared at his tea. It was cooling rapidly so he gulped some of it down, knowing it was probably the last he would have for a while.

Alfred picked up his own but didn't drink any. "Did you want me to explore any other avenues, zer?"

Was it worthwhile canvassing the neighbours?

He finished the tea and rose, throwing the flimsy cup into the small waste device, another Atwater invention. It hummed as it started up, breaking the waste down.

"See if any of the neighbours were awake." It only took a couple of steps to pace the room. "We might get lucky." He shook his head. "I thought we had a whole steamer full of guards with the Walstrands?"

Alfred followed his lead, finishing his own tea and throwing the cup away.

"Three, zer. Two were in the Walstrand's residence getting ready for the night and the third was going to drive Inspector Hoadley back to the Way."

Beaumont rubbed the back of his neck. "I'm going to want to talk to all three." He raised his voice a little, as the device enthusiastically started breaking down the second cup.

"Of course, zer, now—"

Clomp. Clomp.

They both turned. A man, a nurse by the looks of their pale green hospice waistcoat, entered the room.

"Inspector Hoadley's awake."

And now here Beaumont was. Twenty-two hours, five minutes and three seconds after being notified of Hoadley's attack. Sitting in his office reading her notes.

Beaumont had been right. She had not wanted to stay in the hospice at all. He suspected she would have left with him immediately if they hadn't taken her clothes. But he had bought her some rest time.

Now it was twenty-seven hours and forty minutes and twelve seconds since Hoadley was taken to the hospice and he had an overly comprehensive transcript of everything. With nothing in it about who attacked her.

But if someone asked his opinion right now his money was on Cuthbert. And it was his papers that Hoadley had collected.

Mostly.

Unless Ancilla Walstrand realised some of her diary pages were missing?

The authority to remove documents from the Walstrand's residence, might, arguably, include Ancilla Walstrand's diary, but it didn't solve the problem of the pages being encrypted. He flipped through Hoadley's notes hoping that she left some clue on how to get them to show him their secrets.

The one thing she hadn't written down.

He picked up the pages, turning them over in his hands, pushing away the irritation of having to spend any amount of time on this.

Hoadley used pneuma, he didn't know she had it in her, another surprise, to open the diary, and they knew Ancilla had enough control to be Marcellus' assistant. It wasn't a stretch that this device, this paper, needed pneuma to open it. The question was if his was strong enough.

A long time ago his parents, like most parents, had aspirations of him being a painter and encouraged him to train hard. But it had not taken him long to realise he did not have the drive for the hours of practice needed. So instead, he had dismayed his parents and answered a recruiting call for the local guards. Twenty years later he only allowed himself to paint in his judgement-free flat.

He breathed in deeply and tried to picture himself painting. To imagine the stroke of the brush, and the small part of him that was his very own pneuma infusing the paint, making it unique, a part of him. He caressed the pages, visualising his pneuma brushing across it. The wires in the pages hummed. He brushed it again and the paper sighed.

His parents would have been proud, or at least less disappointed in him. After a few deep breaths, he was able to bring the untangled words into focus.

 From the desk of Ancilla Walstrand

She's going to sing tonight I just know it. Why did family have to be included? But then nothing would have kept Ernest away. Everyone would hear about how he supported the illuminier's development and registration, over and over again. Retold until it sounded like he practically built it himself.

Cuthbert is coming too. The pipes know why. He was going to be bored and a bored Cuthbert is dangerous. He will embarrass me somehow. The fun and games will be discovering how.

Seriously if they put as much effort into building their pneuma control as they did in interfering with my life, they would all be able to channel like the greatest artists.

What a terrible day. No stop that. This is it.

If I pull this off, no one will know about it...but still. Plus, there is the prototype Marcellus has promised me if it all runs smoothly. As long as I don't collapse from exhaustion before receiving it.

Stop that. I can do this.

I had tried to skip the family invite. I think Ernest knows. It has been a bit chilly. But Alistair, or Felicia Atwater, must have mentioned it, so now they are coming. The Atwaters are too kind to him.

What will be will be. I can't control them. Would I want to?

Marcellus, the man has gone crazy. That was the only explanation. I get that he was upset. Felicia registering the illuminier, without talking to him or Alistair, and in her own name, was bad form. But in her defence, the changes in the patent laws are barrelling along. She didn't have time to pander to their egos. It wasn't her fault she didn't realise the exact wording of what the bill was going to be. No one did.

And she was right. Look what happened to the patent office as soon as the bill was tabled. If she hadn't registered when she did...who knew if they would have gotten it through in time. She did what she had to do. And it wasn't like it wasn't her right. Every prototype she invested in was registered in her name. Both of them, childish.

At least Alistair had gotten over it, Marcellus, still reeling, unable to let it go, making all sorts of unhelpful decisions. Tonight, being a prime example. Felicia is barely leaving her conservatory these days. Her plants being better company.

Now I'm not saying I can't do it. I might have a greater affinity for metal, like most people, but I had wrangled at least some ability with light. But how he thought he could...future Marcellus and Felicia's problem. Or maybe it is mine. If they split, would I still have a job as Marcellus's assistant? Perhaps not. All the more reason to make sure that tonight goes smoothly. A perfect demonstration, everyone happy and Marcellus realises he is being a fool. One could only dream.

First, get out of bed. But it is so comfy. Soft, but not too soft. My quilt, with my own little device woven in, the perfect fluffy weight without being too hot.

My stomach is growling. Did I eat last night?

With the amount of pneuma I am going to be burning through today, I need to eat and drink. Fainting during the presentation will not be helpful to anyone.

How to get into the kitchen and out again, without waking any of the sleeping beauties? All nightmares if woken before noon. Wish me luck.

Success! Back in bed, with food and coffee. Add some books and I'd be set for the day. A different day. A better day.

I need to focus. I need to be a different person is what I need.

Deep down I know I am meant to be a quiet person who runs a little shop, creating metal sculptures and useful devices and whose biggest problem is getting the cat to not sleep on top of my best-selling inventions. I will smile and say hello to some customers, occasionally, but that is it.

A dream or a possible reality? Perhaps the desire for escape is in our blood. Melody has a plan. I know it. Cuthbert, delusions.

It has taken me over a decade. A decade of living with my family, no small price to pay. I just needed the promised schema.

The dream could be a reality.

First, get out of bed. Survive the day. I could do this. Could I do this?

Did I want to do this? Maybe I should just...what? Stay here? For the rest of my life?

NO.

I've got this. May they all kneel before me and be amazed at my glory.

Possibly.

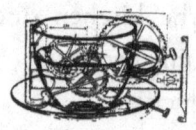

Be amazed at her glory?

Beaumont tossed the pages aside. A lot of effort for nothing. The clock ticked, mocking him.

So, it wasn't Marcellus using the illuminier that night. And Felicia and Alistair didn't know. Or Ancilla thought they didn't. But why? Why wouldn't the greatest illuminator of all time be running this illuminier invention?

All that tea started to make itself known and he rose, stretching out his back, heading to the washroom.

There were more people in the Inspectors' pen now, and someone had caved and propped open a few of the windows.

It was cold, but the air had lost its stale sweaty edge and Beaumont sent them a silent thanks. After a few hellos, and a blessedly empty bladder, he skuttled back to his den.

"Zer."

Beaumont grimaced, but his face returned to its usual pleasant expression by the time he turned around.

Two guards stood there, their heads hanging, shoulders slumped. He almost didn't want to know.

"Guards...Dalley and Hopperton, is that right?" He remembered them from a case he had worked on a few years ago. Dalley had a decent head on her shoulders, but if he remembered correctly Hopperton had trampled on some evidence.

"Yes, zer," said Dalley. When she glanced at Hopperton, he just stared at the ground.

"How can I help you?" asked Beaumont, his mind flicking through the evidence of the case. Which bit had they lost?

"It was us," said Hopperton.

Beaumont blinked. "I'm afraid I'm going to need you to be more specific."

Dalley took a deep breath. "We left Inspector Hoadley on that street alone, the night before, outside the Walstrand's residence."

Beaumont's pleasant expression congealed.

"Why? Did someone pay you—"

"No," Dalley's voice echoed through the pen.

A few of the inspectors turned and stared at them but Beaumont waved them away. They pretended to go back to what they were working on. He probably should have moved the conversation, given this confessional some privacy. But he wasn't going to. If they had something to confess, let them do it here.

"Okay then, why?"

Hopperton and Dalley exchanged glances.

"I forgot the starter for the steamer," said Hopperton. "Genuinely."

Beaumont's forehead furrowed. "Okay..."

"So...I went back to get it off Dalley."

Beaumont waited. Dalley took another deep breath.

"I handed it over to Hopperton, but we..." She glanced at Hopperton, who stared down at the tops of his shoes. "We didn't rush. Didn't think about her out there on her own."

Beaumont dug his fingers into his eye sockets. They had created an opportunity due to their pettiness. Was it the only time? Or had they left her alone last night as well?

"Did you see anyone?" The drumming of his blood increased.

"See anyone?" asked Hopperton, tilting his head.

Beaumont's nostrils flared as he tried to breathe in through them and not have them both arrested immediately.

"Who might have attacked Hoadley. You were standing around, wasting time...did you see anyone leave the house? Or on the street?"

Dalley scuffed the floor with one of her shoes. "Possibly?"

"Possibly?" Beaumont clasped his hands behind his back to stop from grabbing her shoulders and shaking the information out of her.

"There was something." Dalley squared her shoulders and

faced him. "I thought I saw a couple of people walking past on the street."

"A couple." Beaumont stared at her. "On the street, not from in the house?"

"No, they crossed the street. I remember thinking it was an odd hour to be out for a walk."

"And you told the inspector investigating Hoadley's attack this?"

Silence.

Beaumont growled and they both took a step back.

"No, zer." Dalley swallowed.

"You could have shared this information without implicating yourselves." Beaumont shook his head. "Fine, go give a statement, a whole statement." He stared at Hopperton. "Did you see them too?"

Hopperton pinched the back of his neck. "Err...maybe, zer. Out on the street, there was a steamer parked a bit down which had two people in it."

Beaumont went temporarily blind. He forced himself to take a few breaths.

"You left a fellow gendarmerie alone out on the street, on the night of a murder, with two strange people parked in a steamer in the early hours of the morning?"

Muteness.

He stared at them. Too little too late.

"Make your statements to Alfred. The High Protector will be informed."

They blanched but nodded and backed away.

All the pipes.

Suspension was too good for them.

Though right now he was more interested in two people invested enough to risk attacking a gendarmerie inspector. But why?

And who were they watching?

7

Death of the Day

Lavina Hoadley, Inspector
Noxrath Gendarmerie
Great Espya

I was free.

It had taken a few hours, which I had put to good use immortalising the most important case of my career, but finally the doctor released me, admittedly with a bandage around my head. But still, I was free.

Stumbling out of the hospice I stared around blankly. Perhaps I should have told the guard on my door I was leaving. But he was napping so I left him to it.

A guard on my door. An embarrassing reminder that I hadn't been able to protect myself. Time wasted. I sidled along a path around the hospice until I reached the laboratory wing.

Once I ignored the unhelpful signs and asked for directions I located the forensic lab, which turned out to be a large open space with rows of benches in the centre and cabinets full of curiosities. Every surface was covered in beakers, tubes, and a myriad of devices, and unmoving technicians draped over their benches and slumped in their chairs.

A rhythmical whooshing from a giant pendulum hanging against the wall filled the soundscape.

"I'm Inspector Hoadley and I'm here for the test results from last night's death."

I couldn't see what the pendulum was connected to. Perhaps it was art? Sound, like light, was a popular form of artistic expression these days, leaving metal sculptures and paint considered old-fashioned and only valued by the wealthy.

"Oh, are you just?" A technician close to me sat up, pushing his hair back.

"Yes." I stared at him. "Can I have your findings?"

A ripple spread as technicians woke up and snickers fluttered throughout the lab. The laboratory itself was fascinating. One of the cabinets had an open shelf and on it a row of skulls. Each skull was covered in colourful markings and had a large magnifying glass attached.

Grief might have blocked my own connection to music, but if I had gone into forensics, I would have made an excellent career out of it. Instead, I had chosen to be a guard. I'm still not sure I made the right choice.

I frowned at them. "Is there a problem?"

"No, no problem, Inspector." The technician pushed himself to his feet. "We live to serve after all."

I nodded. "Yes indeed."

He said the right words, but I suspected he wasn't going to be that helpful.

He examined me. "What happened to your head?"

"That's not relevant." I stared back at him.

He glared at me. "Pipe it."

Alcohol permeated the room. But not the type you would find at a bar. More like home-distilled alcohol. I could only hope it was a solution, not something they had all been imbibing.

I tilted my head. "Pipe what?"

"You're an inspector?" The technician picked up some paper that had been crumpled under his arms while he took his nap. "Marcellus Overton, right?"

Really what other murder could it have been? Even Noxrath didn't have more than a handful every year. Precious time was being wasted.

"We have confirmed that there was nothing in the decanter or glass but very fine whisky. Not that we could find anyway."

"Nothing?" I frowned. "Are you sure you did all possible checks?"

The technician's cheeks flushed.

"We've some more to do," he gestured at technicians slumped at various long high tables. "But based on the common tests, we couldn't find anything."

"Hmm..." I glanced around the messy laboratory. I wasn't one to judge but it didn't give me much faith in the methodical approach of the team. "No doubt the doctor will be sending some blood for testing as well—"

"Already received it," he motioned towards a couple of lab techs who blinked blearily at us and started playing with glass tubes and a variety of solutions in droppers. "They are analysing it now, but so far nothing."

"Very well." I frowned at the puzzle in front of us, hoping that the doctor at least had found the cause of death. I headed towards the exit.

"That's all then?" asked the technician, his voice loud over in the room.

I blinked, glancing back at him. "There is one thing..."

"Yes?"

He stood there his arms crossed staring at me rather intently.

"What are the markings on the skulls for?" I asked, gesturing towards the open shelf on the cabinet.

He took a deep breath. "They highlight the different types of wounds on a skull."

"Right," I said, examining them. "Interesting."

As I hurried from the lab, he said something, but I didn't have time to engage in more chit-chat.

The sun was out.

It was worth noting as it hadn't been out much in the last week. It is also worth noting that it was the only bright part of the day.

After the lab I went back to my room and woke up the guard who was napping outside it and requested a lift back to the Way. He briefly tried to tell me that I had been ordered to stay at the hospice, but I had pointed out that if that was the case then he had been ordered to guard me. We had then mutually agreed that the orders weren't clear, and we had best get back to the Way.

I was glad I did.

Beaumont shuffled—I wish I could say strode, but I want these notes to be accurate—out of the front entrance of the Way just as I was exiting the steamer.

"What're you doing up?" he asked.

"They released me." Technically this was true. As long as the interpretation of they included myself and a doctor who was happy for me to go as long as I signed a document saying the hospice was no longer liable.

Beaumont squinted at me. "Are you sure? You've got a bandage on your head."

"Right." I blinked. "Doctor said I was fine, let me just..." I ducked inside the Way and found my spare bowler. I half thought he would leave without me, but I made it outside to find him standing in the sun, his face tilted up, eyes closed.

"Ready, zer."

He blinked, glancing over at me, pausing on the bowler, and shrugged. "I'm heading to the morgue."

I nodded and swung around, matching my step to his. In most cities, the morgue was located under the hospice or, in the smaller towns, attached to a medic facility. Here it was several blocks away from the hospice, crammed between the Way and Noxrath's administration headquarters. One thing

I hadn't worked out though was why the morgue always had a crowd of people coming and going at all hours of the day.

"Why is the morgue so busy?" I asked. "I wouldn't have thought Noxrath's death rate that high?"

The street was paved with an older style of cobblestone, which combined with the cul-de-sac meant most steamer drivers avoided it, making it a largely pedestrian area. Except for gendarmerie steamers which had a bad habit of tearing along and giving everyone a fright.

"Tours."

My feet fused with the stones beneath them. "What?"

A cold gust of wind wrapped around me. I fumbled with the buttons on my coat, closing them all the way up to my cravat. The air was fresh and clear. A relief to my olfactory senses after the chemical-laden hospice and laboratory, but it didn't stop the shiver.

Beaumont paused, glancing back at me.

"Tours. They run tours of the morgue."

"Even...at night?"

"The most popular. Everyone likes to see a dead body, when it isn't their own."

"Surely the families of the deceased object?"

"Not really, you can choose to opt out, but most people have it in their will that they want to be displayed."

"But why?"

Beaumont shrugged. "Maybe they're afraid their family won't remember them; strangers are better than no one." He moved forward, sidestepping the group exiting the building and headed inside.

The guards, at least they had those, nodded us through. Inside was everything a morgue should be. Sealed windows, and long dim corridors weaving between rooms where metal frames held the large glass doors, allowing visitors to see the pathologists playing with the side products of death. The frames themselves were overly ornate for their purpose with wires twisted and gathered in patterns. Not that I begrudge the morgue for having art. If anything the people who worked here deserved it more than most. But still.

Beaumont headed off down the corridor and I followed. As I passed a door, I ran my fingers over the metal. Little hinges in the wires suggested that they were for more than just appearance.

We found Morten hunched over the body of Marcellus Overton, and a blast of cold air carrying a combination of formalin and the slickly sweet smell of death hit us. I blinked clearing my eyes.

I jerked myself to a halt. "The tours..."

"The tours won't see him until the investigation is finished," said Beaumont, scratching his chin. "Not that I am sure why...I doubt it would make any difference."

Breathe in, breathe out. I coughed as the chemicals in the air entered my lungs.

"Bloody tours," said Doctor Morten. She had finished the autopsy, but the corpse was still partly open. The doctor was sewing the dead skin back together with dark thick thread. "A foolish idea."

"I thought it was yours?" Beaumont moved further into the room.

"It was a joke," Morten snorted. "I didn't think the fools would run with it." She glared at the glass door. "The next one is due to start soon." She glanced at her gloved hands and her work. "Beaumont, can you get the door?"

"But you don't mind enjoying the fruits of the folly?" Beaumont strolled back towards the door and flicked something.

I couldn't see what he did but on the other side of the glass, slithering. Hisses slid across the glass like snakes, weaving together until the corridor beyond was obscured, trapping us in here with the dead body.

Beaumont, apparently unphased, moved over to an impressive machine with lots of compartments and levers. I wasn't sure what it did, but there was a gurgle of liquid and a strangely comforting ping every ten seconds or so.

"I'm assuming..." The doctor pulled together the last bits of dead skin. "You've made your way down here as you don't trust me to send the results?"

I forced myself to look away from the now obscured exit and refocused on Dr Morten and the comforting ping.

"Time is of the essence," said Beaumont, finding a set of shelves, overflowing with containers full of things floating in greenish liquid, I was pretty sure one was someone's hand, to lean against.

"Doesn't matter how much pneuma you can channel, you can't make more." She tied a knot in the last stitch and reached for her scissors to cut the thread.

"Of what?" I asked.

"Of time." Doctor Morten frowned at me, straightening. She turned to Beaumont. "Where do you find these people?"

"Hoadley's alright," he flicked me a half smile.

A rousing endorsement. I struggled between feeling the warmth of Beaumont's approval and the indignation of a suspected slight.

Doctor Morten hmphed and focused on her notes.

"Speaking of time..." His lips attempted to curve into a smile but didn't quite make it.

I wasn't sure it was normal, or appropriate, for an inspector, especially a prime inspector to smile that much. Though the whole gendarmerie at Noxrath smirked too quickly, in my opinion.

The doctor snorted. "You do realise that it's been less than eight hours?"

I had the displeasure of running into Inspector Gordon, or perhaps I should say prime inspector now, the other day. It was barely light, and she was running around smiling and laughing like she was organising a trip to the park, not attempting to deliver justice.

"Cause of death would be nice," said Beaumont, once more flashing his teeth.

"Yes, I'm sure it would, but unless there's a knife sticking out of the chest...these things take time." The doctor lifted the lid of a large flat container next to her, putting her instruments in a bath of liquid that made my eyes water from across the room.

Beaumont rubbed at his eyes. I wasn't sure if it was exasperation or the chemical haze.

"I'm not here to ask for your formal report..." said Beaumont. "I just need to know if it is poison."

Doctor Morten shook her head, her eyes never leaving her task. "Is that all? A definitive cause of death, thank you nicely?" She stomped around the room slamming drawers closed, some she even had to open first.

"Tabitha..." Beaumont shifted his weight and gazed at her, a small frown on his face.

If he had asked I would have told him exactly what was going on. I knew delaying tactics when I saw them.

"Fine," Morten swung away from Beaumont. "But don't you think you can charm me."

Beaumont flashed her, yet another, small glimpse of his teeth. No doubt distracted by the implied compliment.

"Poison?" I asked, trying to end the ducking and weaving.

"No." Dr Morten's eyes dropped down to the drawer she was holding. She closed it and moved back to the central slab, and the body.

"Ah, a natural death then."

He didn't glance at me, but I knew he wanted to. "Smothered." Dr Morten found more equipment to put away. Though she had to rearrange a few pieces she had just moved to do it.

"What?" Beaumont's voice rose sharply at the end. "But..." Beaumont tapped the hat he hadn't bothered to let go of against his thigh.

"Do you want to hear my results or not?" This time she turned back and faced him squarely.

Finally, some answers.

"Any sign of a struggle?" Beaumont straightened.

"No." Dr Morten rested her hand on the edge of the slab, Overton's body spread out on display between us.

I examined it, looking for bruises, marks on the body or anything that suggested asphyxiation.

"Are you sure?" I asked.

Beaumont cleared his throat and Dr Morten shot me a sharp glare.

"Do we have an estimated time of death?" asked Beaumont, his shoulders slumped.

"I would imagine," Dr Morten said, gaze dropping to the body, "it was between when he was last seen and when his body was discovered."

She was probably right, in that it gave a more accurate time of death than any she could. But it was the way she said delivered it—the hairs on the back of my neck stood up. Or they would have if I hadn't tied the cravat a little too tight.

Beaumont snorted. 'Thanks, Tabitha."

I tore my eyes away from the body towards something that moved in a container.

Morten stood there, arms crossed.

"We'll just leave you to it then..." Beaumont cleared his throat, "shall we?"

If something had moved in the canister it had stopped again, but either way, I was more than ready to leave, relieved when the door opened without any resistance.

The wires, which had been gathered in the frame, were stretched out across the glass in a lattice that obscured the room beyond. At least it was static and not a continuing writhing mess of wires twisting. Though I wouldn't be sur-prised to find that someone was working on that.

Back on the street, Beaumont stood there, shoulders hunched, reinforcing the groves etched into his forehead.

A spilled glass, an assumption, and everything wrong.

8

Pick Me, Pick Me

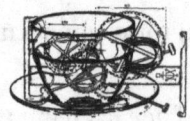

The morning's wind had swept away the fog, leaving the city crisp and clear, Beaumont wished he could say the same for his brain.

After the morgue, Hoadley hadn't been happy when he insisted on walking to the Atwaters. It was a windy day and unlike the morgue, which was right next door, Atwater Place was several blocks away. But whatever loss of dignity they suffered in walking was a small price to pay for a clearer head.

"It's important to stretch the legs," said Beaumont. "Gets the brain thinking." And gave his back some welcome relief. It could have been natural causes, or even one of those rare overuses of pneuma cases. But it wasn't.

Pipe it.

Mistakes had been made and he had been right that Hoadley was writing them all down.

A chilly gust whipped around them chasing any lingering traces of the morgue away. He exhaled and a few muscles unclenched.

"Yes, zer." Hoadley pulled her coat tightly around her with one arm, keeping a hold of her bowler hat with the other.

He was a little surprised she didn't have another top hat. But he had asked Alfred to lodge the necessary forms, the gendarmerie would pay for a replacement, hers being lost in the line of duty.

But the bowler suited her, even if it wasn't quite regulation.

The street leading from the Way to the Atwaters was wide and clean. Large tree sculptures framed it on each side, leaves retracted, they let the winter sun through, their elegant bones reaching up into the sky. Beaumont tilted his head, capturing as much of the weak sun as he could before it disappeared behind a cloud.

"Do you think it'll rain?" asked Beaumont. His stride lengthening. A lot of ground needed to be recovered.

The street was busy with people getting on with their day and a few smiled, nodding hello at him. He smiled back, pleased to be welcomed into their day. He really needed to get out more.

"No."

The only dark rain cloud plodded along next to him. Beaumont stopped and stared at her.

"No? That is a very definitive answer."

Hoadley and her absolute answers. The hard part was identifying when the confidence was justified.

"The clouds aren't the right type for rain."

"The clouds..." he peered at her quizzically. "Hidden depths Hoadley, hidden depths."

"Yes, zer."

Right, no small talk.

They turned the corner off the Way onto Trecarres Passage. Beaumont stepped closer to Hoadley as people pushed passed him. Heading towards the clatter of placards ahead.

It was starting.

The first block was full of official buildings, the patent office being the largest.

Beaumont, whose main goal had been to get past the crowd, glanced over his shoulder.

Hoadley stood there examining the tall, elegant building with a sweeping curved half-pipe wrapping around its three storeys of offices.

He headed back towards her, dodging around a couple arguing, both holding placards, but each with a different slogan on it. He wouldn't want to be joining them for dinner over the next day or so.

"Hard to imagine, isn't it?" he asked. The crowd wasn't too loud, not yet, but he still had to raise his voice to be heard.

She tilted her head and peered at him. "Zer?"

"That this building's where fortunes are made, and destroyed," he said.

"Yes, I suppose so." Her gaze traced the curve.

He had studied her. Her interest in everything around her was also so intense.

"It's a moving stairwell," he said.

"What?"

"The curve on the outside of the building," he pointed in the direction of the building, "it's a large moving stairwell, powered by massive pistons in the basement. It wraps around the whole building, linking the floors."

"I take it you've been inside?"

"Yes, a few times. Amazing architecture, and a bunch of people sitting in rooms pushing paper. Except for the prototype room of course."

"Do you think it will pass?"

"The abolishment of perpetual patent inheritance bill?" He adjusted his outer coat, glancing around, even in the few minutes they had been there the mob had expanded. It was perfect weather for protesting. They needed to get moving. "Yes, yes I think it will."

He resumed his march to the Atwaters, though it took Hoadley a while to catch up with him.

"And what will that mean for people like the Atwaters?" asked Hoadley.

The clamour of people protesting faded and he slackened his pace.

An interesting question. So far the Atwaters hadn't talked about it much. Perhaps that itself was strange.

"It will depend, on how long their old inventions meet the new threshold for patent protection, the registered owner's lifetime for any new ones..." Beaumont grimaced. "It's both a blow to the safety of their income streams and an opportunity for new profit pathways." His eyebrows drew together, and an invisible weight dragged the edges of his lips down. "I suspect if it passes, we'll be in for a busy time of it."

"I would've thought most people would be in favour of it." She glanced back, frowning.

"Yes, you would think so wouldn't you. But people don't like change, and some see the families' wealth as the origin of their own income, they'll be afraid for themselves and their families."

"But surely they realise it will mean more innovation—"

"Never assume anything, Hoadley. Some people...ah here we are." Beaumont turned into the Atwater's street. "Today that's someone else's problem. Ours is trying to work out which lies are important."

They had arrived. Time to get this murder investigation started. He put his foot on the first step and peered up at Atwater Place.

"Don't you mean who's telling the truth?" asked Hoadley.

"No one tells the truth in an investigation Hoadley." He glanced at her with a small smile. "You can make a note of that."

They climbed the front stairs of the Atwater's residence.

"The Atwaters first—"

Beaumont's brow furrowed. "The Atwaters wouldn't be up yet."

"Wouldn't—"

"If we have to do this, we take it calmly and carefully, teasing out the information."

Murder investigations, especially complex ones like these, always took so much longer than expected.

She gave a short nod. He wasn't sure if she agreed, but he took it that she would at least follow his direction.

The metal of the doorbell was still cold despite the sun.

He couldn't hear anything. But he trusted something had happened.

"Where are the guards?" asked Hoadley, her face pinched.

Beaumont's stomach tightened; she wasn't going to like this answer.

"Forensics are finished, and they were needed for crowd control."

Hiding what she was feeling was not one of Hoadley's strengths.

The door was opened by a tall woman of indeterminable age with pale blue eyes and white hair who examined them, critically.

"Prime Inspector Beaumont and Inspector Hoadley," said Hoadley, flashing the insignia set in her vest.

Unless he missed his guess, this was Necket the butler. One of the guards had taken her statement. She had spent the whole night watching the guests in the ballroom and witnessed Overton walk down the middle of the room through the gallery.

"Zer Necket?" asked Beaumont, sweeping his own hat from his head. His hair tumbled loose. He had forgotten to find a tie for it, again. It didn't seem to matter how many of them he bought, somehow, he could never find one when he needed it.

"Indeed." A small crease in her forehead, but she stepped back, allowing them inside.

With their hats in their hands, they stepped through. The painting captured his attention again. Taking up most of the wall it depicted Felicia Atwater, before her hair turned silver, at almost twice her normal size singing. What made it special though was the sense of motion. You could almost hear the powerful note arching through the air, resonating in the room.

"Your hats." Necket's voice was crisp.

He blinked and handed his over. Hoadley slowly took hers off and held it out.

Click.

At a signal, he didn't see the wall as it unfolded. Well-oiled metal joints muffled the clanking of the descending mechanical arm. Necket placed both their hats on the tray attached to the arm and it lifted back up, carrying the hats to a recessed cabinet in the wall. Perfectly sized for top hats. Hoadley's bowler disappeared into its depths.

"We have..." His words trailed off at his hat's departure, the cabinet's door sliding closed. "...some more questions."

He had once been told he had a reputation for eloquence, if he did, it was absent at the moment.

"What were Marcellus Overton's movements last night?" Hoadley asked, her tone clipped.

Necket's smooth face was unchanged. "My attention was otherwise engaged."

Hoadley's lips thinned. "Do you know when Overton left the ballroom?"

Necket stilled, and for a moment he wasn't sure if she would respond.

"Just what I said in my statement." Her expression, disinterested at best. "He wasn't my problem that evening."

Beaumont doubted that she hadn't been very aware of every breath Overton took. Her jaw was tight and her face, marble. She was not in a sharing mood. Her bright intelligent eyes stared at him.

"Whose problem was he?" Hoadley asked.

He should have been taking the lead on the questions, but one advantage of Hoadley was she wasn't afraid of jumping in. Regardless, he was interested to see where Necket wanted their attention directed.

Necket's mouth curved. "Come with me."

Franklin Reginald Vyner didn't make a great first impression.

Beaumont examined the pleasant enough shaped head crowded with oversized features and an undersized nose.

"Vyner," Necket stood in the doorway, her toes just outside the threshold. "The Prime Inspector would like to talk to you about your statement last night and Marcellus Overton's movements."

"Yes of course," He rose, rubbing at his chest, causing the pattern in his waistcoat to whirl faster. "A terrible tragedy." His lips trembled slightly until he pressed them together.

A rare display of grief. Even the Atwaters had come across as more concerned about the device and the investigation than Overton's death.

Necket mumbled something and disappeared. Probably for the best, though he had more questions for her.

"Yes..." said Beaumont, stepping into the room. "I'm sorry for your loss."

A couple of years ago they had a festival of light and all the illuminators from around the world had gathered at Noxrath. Some of the light installations had been spectacular. But as much as it pained him to admit it, he agreed with the overly pompous Ernest. He preferred more tangible art like paint, poetry, and prose. Something he could take the time to enjoy more than once.

"Everyone will feel his loss." His shoulders slumped and he folded back down into his chair.

Vyner's office lacked the sophistication of the rest of the house and Hoadley had to drag two chairs across the room, allowing them to sit opposite Vyner.

"Zer Vyner." Beaumont leaned forward. "It's important that we build an understanding of Overton's and the guests' movements."

"Tricky," said Vyner, examining them. He rubbed at his eyes and then mirrored Beaumont leaning forward, his elbows on his desk and his fingers steepled in front of him.

Beaumont suspected that Vyner had invested in the desk himself. It was overly large for the space and designed to reinforce Vyner's presence in the room.

"What are the duties of a..." Beaumont blinked, his brain empty, what was he called? "...house person, on a night like last night?"

"Manager, house manager. I'm responsible for ensuring

the evening runs smoothly. Food, drinks, rosters, and everyone knowing what they need to do."

"Forgive my ignorance..." Beaumont ran fingers through his hair. "But isn't that what a butler does?"

Vyner sniffed. "Butler Necket considers those things beneath her." His eyes were unfocused. "To host an event like last night...We were all a bit rusty, so everything took time." He brought his attention back to Beaumont. "We pulled it off in the end though. It was a great night."

"Except for Overton dying," said Beaumont, his eyebrows slightly raised.

"Yes." Vyner sighed. "It's a great loss." His mouth twisted. "A great loss."

"Were you close to Overton?" Hoadley asked, going straight to the point, as always.

Risky.

If the suspect or witness got their back up and shut down it didn't leave many options. Better to lead them to admissions.

Vyner shifted in his seat. "Yes, in a way. He didn't live here, as you probably know, but he was here at least a few days a week. Our paths crossed regularly."

"And you were fond of him?" asked Beaumont.

"He was a very generous man." Vyner shifted in his seat.

"Generous...?" Beaumont peered at him expectantly, his jotter limp in his hand.

"Not that he was expected to tip the household staff, but he would often...offer a thank you to anyone who helped him out." Vyner glanced at Hoadley's scribbling hand.

"What kind of things did he need helping out with?" Hoadley asked.

Beaumont tried to hide his grimace. Every time she pushed they risked him shutting down.

"Oh you know—"

Hoadley's hand was paused over her jotter, waiting. "Exactly." Her voice was strong, flicking out at him.

Vyner's body winched.

"Er..." He shifted a piece of paper on his desk from one pile to another. "People like to have things a certain way. Marcellus was in the difficult situation where he was both a guest and not a guest in the house. I helped him feel more comfortable."

"And how, specifically, did you do that?" Hoadley's lips thinned.

Beaumont needed to step in, and without making Hoadley feel undermined.

Vyner leant back, his eyes narrowing. "Drawing materials, metals for his inventions, food for when he was in the throes of creation."

"What about drinks?" snapped Hoadley.

Was it time for a nap yet? A cup of tea was in order.

"Zer Felicia Atwater believes a great deal in the mastery of the physical. She prefers the consumption of water infusions, tea or, if you must, coffee."

"Zer Vyner..." Beaumont drew Vyner's attention back to him. "You understand he was found with whisky in the library?"

Hoadley huffed, sitting back in her seat.

Vyner shrugged. "If Overton chose to keep his whisky here then it wasn't my place to stop him."

"Did you inform your employer?" Beaumont asked. He kept his voice soft, inquisitive.

"No." Vyner frowned at him.

Beaumont tapped his quill against his lips. "And was Overton, "generous" for this silence?"

No point trying to be subtle now.

Vyner flushed, his mouth twisting. "If Marcellus chose to be grateful for services rendered, whatever they may be, I was not going to be rude."

"But was it a choice, Zer Vyner?"

Vyner stood up.

"I won't—"

"Sit down, Zer Vyner." Beaumont's low voice sharpened.

He would have preferred not to risk playing the authority card but if that was the hand he was dealt then he could bluff with the best of them.

Vyner sat. "I don't appreciate what you are insinuating."

"I wasn't trying to insinuate anything." Beaumont straightened. "I was trying to establish whether you charged a price for the supply of alcohol to Overton while he was here, and for your silence."

"Marcellus and I..." Vyner's lips barely moved, "had a mutually beneficial arrangement in regard to that particular vice of his."

"Any other, arrangements?" asked Beaumont.

"No." Vyner sat back in his chair. His body was straight but centred and his arms were relaxed. Calm and stubborn.

Beaumont kept his expression blank. He had made a mistake following Hoadley's lead.

Time to move on.

"Let's talk about Overton's movements last night," said Beaumont.

Vyner settled back, his shoulders relaxing while Hoadley's shoulders were hunched, and she stared down at her jotter.

At least one person was happy.

"Yes of course." He picked up a cup on his desk, taking a sip. "He was the man of the hour. My recollection is: he was in the ballroom from the moment the guests started to arrive until that unfortunate performance of the Walstrand sister."

"The whole time?" Beaumont leaned forward slightly. "Does that mean you were also there?"

"Yes, I was near the door to the hallway, a point of contact for those on duty. I'd a direct view of Marcellus and his assistant."

"And after Melody Walstrand's performance?"

"I remember there was an issue with one of the dishes, one of the kitchen domestics had come to ask me a question and by the time I turned back to the room the assistant was on her own."

"Which door did he leave by?" Hoadley asked.

"I don't know." Vyner scanned us, his eyes narrowed.

Hoadley's gaze flicked him.

Beaumont hummed, his body shifting forward slightly. "Would you've noticed, if he went past you?"

Hoadley returned her gaze to her jotter.

"Definitely. The kitchen domestic was standing in the doorway, she had to move to let someone past."

Hoadley flicked a glance up. "A man?"

"No, a woman, I think. It wasn't Marcellus, I would've noticed that."

"Thank you." Beaumont tapped his quill on his largely unused jotter. With Hoadley furiously writing it seemed a waste taking notes.

He preferred to pay attention to what was going on in front of him anyway. "Did you notice anyone else leaving or entering the ballroom?"

"Alistair came in off the balcony after that terrible performance by the assistant's sister. I saw the brother come in as well, mooching near his father."

"Was there anything else that struck you as unusual..." asked Beaumont.

"No, it was, until Marcellus' death, a very successful evening." Vyner frowned. "It's going to be a real blow for morale. I'd promised them a massive celebration if we pulled it off but now...it seems lacking in taste." Vyner ran his hand over his face, his shoulders slumping.

It crossed Beaumont's mind that his grief for Overton might be more about one of his income streams being cut off, than anything else. One of. He studied him.

What other silences had been bought?

9

Ancilla Illuminates

The house's metal frame hummed, reminding Ancilla of the cage she was in, for all it was dressed up, trapping her here, forever.

Nothing like a death to make the walls close in. Only six hours ago she had been congratulating herself for carrying it all off. But then her brother Cuthbert stumbled back into the ballroom, all a tremor and screeching that Marcellus was dead. She hadn't believed him of course.

Since she was going to be stuck here for the foreseeable future, at least she liked her room. And not just because of the lock on the door.

The metal frame of her bed, softened by velvets draped on its high corner posts and a perfectly stuffed cotton mattress, cocooned her in warmth. Protection from the cool air of the early morning.

She had created a thick ribbon which, when she tied it around her head and across her eyes, allowed her to sleep longer. To ignore the light of the day. But in her exhaustion last night she had forgotten to tie it on and for the first time in weeks, the sun was up. She lay there, in her warm dark nest. A few minutes later she flung her sheets back and rolled herself up into a sitting position. The time had come. She swung her legs over the side of the bed, groaning as her abused body protested.

Despite joining Marcellus every day in his training, her physical recovery after manipulating light was her greatest weakness. Her lips thinned. The reality was she did not have an affinity for light. Like most people, her pneuma flowed the most easily with metal or base materials. And after a week of using that stupid illuminier, she was paying the price.

She would also swear that Marcellus had deliberately designed the illuminier to make it so that only the most skilled illuminators could use it.

She needed to dress, consume some food for her poor depleted body and capture the events of last night.

Shuffling towards her desk, she collapsed onto the chair, leaning forward on her elbows, her head in her hands. Everything hurt. Her stomach grumbled, reminding her that giving up was not an option.

What a steaming pipe of a day.

Despite the haze of stress and fatigue and a few internal freakouts, she had kept her side of the bargain. Now she just hoped that Marcellus kept his. If he wasn't dead.

What if he was dead? What was she going to do now?

She shifted things around on her desk but couldn't find her diary.

When did she have it last?

She glowered at the image of herself carrying it out of the room and threw her head back, stared at the ceiling and groaned. Downstairs, pipe it.

Another stretch, and groan, and she shuffled over to lay her palm against one of the drawers of her floor-to-ceiling cabinetry, the metal and wood soothing as her pneuma naturally flowed.

Metal unfolded, creating temporary walls around her, until she was surrounded by the workspace she had built. It was a sad fact that metal inventions only received the most basic of dividends these days, and hers weren't selling.

With a grunt, she manually cranked up her workbench. She had been meaning to create an automatic lift for it but never had the time. Hopefully, she would remember how much this hurt and find time soon. One small section of her workspace also functioned as her wardrobe. She prided herself in only having four outfits, two work ones, one evening and one morning. All customisable as needed.

Contemplating the day ahead, she pulled out her soft grey morning outfit. It had a light pattern that shifted so subtly that it would take several minutes of observation to notice. Laying its pieces out on the bench she pulled her tool kit towards her. The diary, food and water, were all critical, but she wasn't going to get any of them without her clothes on.

She had no wish to be a modist and hadn't resented having to pay someone to design the hats, waistcoats, waterfalls and britches. But the fabric. She ran her hand over its rough texture. Close to indestructible, yet too uncomfortable to be a commercial success. But still hers, registered in her name. Her lungs expanded, the edges of her lips turning up.

Her name.

It had taken some doing without Ernest finding out, but the fact she had done it without him knowing, made it all the sweeter. The cash she made from selling the fabric to clothesmakers whose clientele valued longevity over comfort helped too. One step closer to freedom.

She forced herself to focus, placing all four parts of the outfit next to each other and opening seams to access the patterns' mechanism. It was important that she did all four at once to ensure the continuity of the adjustments. She hated it when the patterns got out of sync.

The adjustment would require some pneuma usage, so she took a breath and centred herself, picking up her favourite micro wrench that was so familiar to her hand as to feel a part of it, letting as little pneuma as possible dribble through.

The miniature mechanism embedded in the fabric allowed her to push the colour orange into it and flow through the pattern. She was careful not to change the timing and soon a grey outfit appropriately touched with the burnt orange of death was in front of her.

It took a bit of moaning and groaning, but she was finally dressed. The workshop packed away as she unlocked the door, pausing in its frame way. Time to sneak downstairs. The last thing she wanted to do was wake anyone. One because of the whining and two, oversharing of whatever inane thought was in their head. She needed time to think.

Despite an urgency to find her diary, she listened to her body and went to the kitchen first. Roger might not be an early riser, and as a heavy socialiser, he appreciated a household where the master got up late, but he did leave the kitchen stocked with snacks.

Ignoring the plates she grabbed a tray, piling it high with cheeses, ham, breads, butter, marmalade, and fruit. Not to mention a large pot of tea. It was too heavy to carry so she loaded it up on Roger's trolley and pushed it into the living room at the centre of the house, after turning off the ridiculous moving floor at the entrance, she manoeuvred the trolley to her favourite spot.

Foolish to bring her diary down here. Whatever small comfort it gave wasn't worth the risk of reminding them that it existed. Not that anyone here had enough pneuma control in them to break the encryption. She shoved her hand under the cushions, exhaling heavily at the scrape of its hard metal edge against her fingers. She settled down in her spot, placing the tray of food across her lap.

Pipe it. She'd forgotten a quill. Clambering back up, she found a quill amongst Melody's ledgers and resettled back down again, pouring herself a cup of tea, and shoving cheese and bread into her mouth. She opened the diary, and a spray of broken food and tea decorated the tray.

Bloody beetle-crushers.

If she had to guess, Inspector Hoadley. The Prime Inspector was half asleep most of the time. She wasn't sure whether to be pissed off that Hoadley ripped pages out of her diary or impressed she had the level of pneuma control needed to open it in the first place.

Pissed, definitely pissed. She wanted to throw the tray across the room. Except she didn't want to lose any more tea or food, and the tray was heavy.

Tossing the diary down next to her, hiding its ripped insides, she cleaned up what she could and channelled her anger into the food her body needed.

Her attention was captured by the meld of the marmalade and the soft cheese together, the pleasure of the flavour distracting her. A few bites and she calmed down to savour it, and to avoid choking.

Once half the tray was gone, she liked to think of it as making room for writing, Ancilla picked up the diary again. The jagged edges stared back at her. Remnants of her last entry. What had she written? She had talked about how she was the one using the device that night, but that was it, right?

Bloody foozler.

What if they suspected she was involved somehow? Should she just tell them what happened? She needed to write it all down, but her diary had been violated.

May they all get stuck in a pipe.

She could fix this. She just needed to adjust the diary so it took a massive amount of pneuma to open, much more than any pigeon-livered inspectors could ever have. She breathed in and then exhaled, letting the tension flow out of her. It was possible for it to be safe again.

Despite the desecration of her diary, she liked Hoadley. She took things way too seriously, but she was intelligent, and regardless of what she said, was clearly loving the murder investigation. Hoadley's body hummed with excitement, though she probably thought she was being all cool calm and collected.

It was a smidge concerning that Hoadley saw her as a suspect. But that was probably just her intuition telling her that Ancilla wasn't sharing the whole story. This meant that Ancilla couldn't just sit on the sidelines and watch the gendarmerie fumble, or in the case of Hoadley, storm, their way through this.

She needed to find Marcellus.

"It's a nightmare."

Ancilla glanced up from her empty tray. Her sister flounced into the room in full orange regalia, collapsing into one of the enormous armchairs.

Ancilla often mocked Ernest, internally, for buying the most useless devices, but she agreed with him on the chairs. Even after removing the upholstery and examining the mechanism underneath, she had not been able to work out how they functioned, but she admired how it adjusted to support Melody's head, stretching its frame and fabric for optimal comfort. Considering Melody had collapsed onto it lengthwise, it now more closely resembled a daybed than an armchair.

"Good morning, Melody," said Ancilla. "You're up early."

"Who can sleep?" Melody lay there, stretched out, staring

at the ceiling with her arm across her forehead. Really, she should give lessons. "Aren't you devastated? I mean, you're unemployed now, aren't you? And I don't have a sponsor..." she exhaled heavily. "It's all a disaster."

Ancilla tried not to let a frown gather. Not that her sister was wrong. But it wasn't necessarily helpful for her to point it out.

"Am I? Technically I'm employed by the Atwaters..."

She scanned her sister's outfit. Not only was it a bright orange, but the pattern also had small sunsets happening all over it, on a continuous loop. It was quite tricky to have a distinct image repeat itself. A lot easier if it was a general pattern with subtle shifts. Melody must have had it prepared.

And why was it a disaster for Melody?

"I thought he rejected—"

"He would've come around." Melody's eyes sprung open, and she glared at Ancilla. "He just needed time to realise how art has evolved." She held her hand to her mouth and closed her eyes again. "But time is something he'll never have."

Ancilla dropped her gaze.

A soft ping echoed throughout the room advising them someone was at the gate. Ancilla doubted Roger was up yet.

"I'll get it," she said, unnecessarily as Melody showed no indication of rising.

As she left the living room, she flicked the lever that stopped the ridiculous floor from moving and opened the front door, to find a messenger waiting down at the fence.

Ernest had retracted the stairs, so they had to awkwardly

stare at each other as they waited for them to unfold and then for Ancilla to get to the front gate.

"Sorry about that," she said.

"Sure." The messenger pulled out a scroll, the string tying it was sealed with wax, with the Atwater's emblem pressed into it, a collection of cogs on fire, presumably to symbolise their ongoing creativity and power of their inventions. It had however always given Ancilla a sense of foreboding.

She gave the messenger an extra coin, an apology for having to wait, and unrolled the message.

Dear Ancilla,

As I am sure you appreciate today is a day where we all come to terms with the loss of our beloved Marcellus.

Please take this day as a day of mourning.

I will of course have to meet with you to discuss the next steps regarding the illuminier and your employment, however let that be tomorrow's worry, at ten o'clock at Atwater Place.

Thank you for all the support you have provided Marcellus these last few years.

Kind Regards,

Felicia

Maybe Melody was right.

Pipe it.

She dragged herself inside, leaving the stairs down, but

locking the front door, the weight of it only reinforced when she found her father Ernest and brother Cuthbert in the living room as well.

"Who was that?" asked Ernest.

"A message giving me the day off," said Ancilla.

"See?" said Melody, not opening her eyes.

Ernest sniffed. "Quite right. I think we all need a day to recover from the tragic events of last night."

Great, a day home with the family. Life just got better and better.

"Seriously?" Cuthbert vibrated in another armchair. "I cannot be stuck here all day."

Ancilla shook her head at his chosen outfit of robin blue and dark green, a beacon of his absence of mourning. She glanced at Ernest. An orange cravat and cuff links. Respectful, not too over the top. Her eyes tuned out Melody's outfit in silent protest.

Ernest pulled the cord until a bleary-eyed Roger stumbled into the room. Somewhat put together at first glance, except for the half-opened eyes, and the two different shoes.

"Zer?" asked Roger, the word slightly garbled.

"Breakfast, coffee, tea and best be prepared for visitors today." Ernest moved to one of the spare armchairs, which, despite its attempt to make him comfortable, he managed to sit awkwardly straight in.

"Visitors?" Ancilla asked. "Surely it's too early—"

"Intrigue always brings interest." He stared down his nose at her from across the room, glancing down at the empty tray in front of her. His features pinched together. "I see you've helped yourself to a repast already."

"Replenishing the reserves," she said. Her eyes dropped down to the grass-like rug, making her wish she was outside, far away from Noxrath, amongst real grass instead. She could imagine stretching out, allowing dreams of light and steam to chase away the shadows of death and unemployment dancing through her head.

"Tired from standing around telling Marcellus how great he was?" Melody snorted as she laughed.

"Melody Walstrand." Ernest's voice snapped out. "Have some respect."

Melody rolled her head towards him, gesturing to her overly orange outfit. "I'm being respectful. If you want to talk about respect..." She gestured at Cuthbert. "Talk to your popinjay over here."

Ernest scowled, paying attention to Cuthbert's attire. "What's the meaning of this?"

"I don't see why—"

"Go get changed into something decent."

"I—"

"Now"

Cuthbert and Ernest stared off but, in the end, Cuthbert threw himself out of his chair and stormed off up to his room.

Ernest exhaled heavily.

"What did I do to deserve being surrounded by fools?"

Ancilla and Melody shared a quick glance before going back to avoiding each other's gaze.

Ancilla settled more deeply into her cushions, staring out

of the window, leaving Ernest to the contemplation of how hard done by he was.

Roger eventually returned with a breakfast tray for the others and unexpectedly came over with a fresh pot of tea for Ancilla. He didn't usually see serving her as part of his duties, so she was grateful for this moment of kindness.

"Thank you, Roger." She smiled warmly at him. He gave a brisque nod back. Ah well, at least she had the tea. The steam had hints of lemongrass, one of her favourites.

He was shuffling back to his duties, or more likely his bed, when a peel rang throughout the house.

Roger's shoulders slumped but he headed towards the front door and Cuthbert appeared, dressed in a purple suit, but at least with an orange pattern in it.

"This is the best I can do," he stated to the room, flopping back down into his chair.

The only response he got was a quick scan and humph from Ernest.

"Zer Alistair Atwater," declared Roger.

They all turned towards him, and Ancilla was pretty sure they all had equally surprised expressions. Certainly, there was one on hers.

"Ernest, Melody, Cuthbert, Ancilla." Alistair nodded to each of them in turn. "Sorry for the unconscionable early hour, but I see I was correct in my estimate that you would all be up. Hard to sleep after the events of last night."

"Alistair. What are..." Ancilla rose to her feet. "What brings you..." She gazed around the room, at her family. "Err..."

Ernest stood. "Alistair, welcome." He gestured to an arm-chair near him. "Please take a seat. Have you had a chance for breakfast? Roger, bring more food for our guest."

Ernest smiled, as warmly as he was able, and Alistair gave a strained smile back but sat, his body settling into the chair.

"Thank you, Zer Walstrand—"

"Ernest please." Ernest sat, turning his body, tilting towards him.

"Ernest," Alistair inclined his head. "I was just coming to check on Ancilla," he smiled at everyone in the room, "and her family, after the unfortunate events last night."

"A tragedy." Melody remained reclining. "The world has lost a great artist."

Ancilla had to stop herself from rolling her eyes when Melody rested the back of her hand against her forehead. She really needed to cut down on those tawdry melodramatic plays she was so fond of. Of course, the advantage of the hand's placement was that it left an unobstructed view of the audience. Alistair gazed at Melody, but Ancilla was unable to determine if there was any of the affection that Ernest so often claimed was there.

"Indeed," Alistair blinked. "A great loss."

"I thought you said he was past it?" asked Cuthbert.

Ancilla tuned out Ernest's attempt to restore order in front of their guest. What part did Cuthbert play in this? He was the first to identify the body as Marcellus. How much of a fool was he?

She blinked her family back in focus to find that Ernest

had taken control of the room, Cuthbert gone and Melody trying to force Alistair to comfort her.

Alistair, however, was staring at Ancilla.

"Are you well?" he asked.

Melody and Ernest both glared at her. She had been well until his overly solicitous concern made her a target.

"Yes." She wanted to lower her head, to close her eyes for a brief moment of respite from their gazes. But she didn't dare lose sight of them. Tricky waters ahead. "It doesn't quite seem real."

"Thank you for your kind words, Alistair," said Ernest. "As you can see, we are all suffering from heightened emotions today." He handed Alistair a cup of coffee.

Presumably to trap him here, at least for the time it took to drink it.

"It's just too horrific for words," bewailed Melody.

If she was aiming to show off the power of her voice she succeeded or she just hit it a bit harder than expected. From the expression on her face, Ancilla suspected the latter.

"Indeed Melody." Alistair sipped his coffee, his eyes warm with concern. "The fact that such a thing happened, in our house, to Marcellus." He lowered his cup. "Quite horrific." He leaned forward placing the cup and its saucer on the table in front of him. "I'm sorry for your family's shock." He rose, gliding over to take a seat next to Ancilla. "I particularly wanted to talk to you Ancilla."

His personal scent, which his partner Vivian, had crafted for him, wafted over her. It wasn't unpleasant but it permeated everything he wore. Had he ever wanted to wear a different one? Or perhaps he couldn't sense it anymore, that was just how he smelt.

Melody snorted.

"Me?"

"Yes." He leaned forward, his elbows on his knees, frowning at the floor. "I know that Marcellus' death brings both grief and uncertainty for you."

Ancilla stared at the side of his head, trying not to get distracted by the lushness of his hair. She guessed he and Felicia hadn't talked this morning. Interesting.

"Yes," she said.

He tilted his head, gazing up at her. "I want you to know that your employment by the Atwater Family is secure. There's plenty of different types of work to do and you've shown your capability repeatedly." He smiled warmly at her. "We won't forget that."

She gazed back at him. He seemed sincere. But in the end it wasn't his decision to make.

"Thank you for your kind words and assurances Alistair, they're a great comfort." Ancilla had had enough of having someone else sitting in her spot and wobbled to her feet.

"Are you hurt?" He jumped up, reaching out to help her stand.

"No," she shook her head. "That illuminier..." She straightened slowly. "Even testing it seems to leave me drained."

Ernest flicked a sharp glance at her.

"Yes." Once Alistair had assured himself she was fine he took a step back. "A testament to the loss the world has suffered with Marcellus' death. He is not someone easily replaced." He bowed towards Ernest. "Zer Walstrand, Ernest, I'm afraid I must return to my mother's side, but thank you for allowing me to visit at this early hour."

"Not at all not at all, let me show you out."

Melody was not one to be left out and insisted Alistair stop and bid her goodbye. After they left, she could still hear Ernest's voice, flooding the space.

"You should go for a walk," said Melody. The chair under her adjusted as she shifted until she was draped elegantly but facing somewhat in Ancilla's direction.

"A walk?" Ancilla blinked at her.

"When I channel pneuma a walk helps." She shrugged and shifted away. "Something about nature and new sights along with warmed-up muscles. Or at least that is what one teacher told me."

Ancilla patted her hair. It was a simple pulled-back style, but sufficient for a morning walk. Especially when hidden under a hat.

A wall of sound, which was Ernest's, and now Cuthbert's, voices sharing their views of the world with Alistair, assailed her. It would also have the bonus of getting her away from her family.

Melody reached out signalling for Roger, who was surprisingly prompt.

"Ancilla's hat and coat," said Melody gesturing from where she lay, her eyes closed.

Ancilla suspected that she was imagining herself singing, delivering a rousing performance at Marcellus Overton's funeral. The very launch she had been wishing for.

"Yes, zer Melody." Roger was being very felicitous as well. Perhaps intuiting that today was not a day to push the boundaries.

He soon reappeared with her hat and even a few pins to help her secure it. She went to smile gratefully at him, but he was already gone.

"Thank you, Melody. That was...kind."

Melody gestured her away without opening her eyes. Ancilla snuck out the back, weaving between the metal sculptures that Ernest had littered the garden with, and out through a simple gate that had escaped his innovation fever.

The Walstrand house might just be waking up, but the city was in full swing. Dirigibles flew so low she wanted to wave at the passengers inside. Steamers grumbled on by, honking at each other as they attempted to get to their destinations a few seconds earlier. A food cart set up on the street, its chimney puffing out sweet-smelling smoke, forced her to remind herself she had already eaten.

And the people. The streets teamed with them, many holding placards. News of Marcellus' death perhaps? But there was no orange.

A glimpse of a sign made her groan. The protests. Everyone was dressed in their smart clothes, greeting friends cheerfully and sharing stories of dinners the night before. That would change once they reached their destination.

Ancilla turned and scurried in the opposite direction, taking the thoughts of how her siblings' lives would be improved if Marcellus was dead, with her.

10

A Cake of Lies

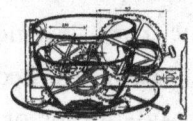

At precisely twelve hours, three minutes and ten seconds after the knock on Beaumont's door had advised him of a man's death, Beaumont had been standing outside Atwater Place. A sharp wind, infused with traces of metal and stone slapped at him and Hoadley, while he attempted to hail a steamer.

After they finished their interview with Vyner, Necket had taken great pleasure in telling him that both Atwaters had already left for the day before ending up on the street.

Hoadley had kicked at the bottom step. "I'm not sure why you want to visit the Walstrands." Her bowler hid her expression. "Wouldn't we be better off—"

"There's a piece missing." Beaumont frowned at the street. It was stereotypically broad, well-maintained, and food cart-free.

"I was thorough," she said, her lips stiff, "and it wasn't like I lost the papers, I was attacked."

Beaumont jolted around, staring at her. "I know." He adjusted his hat, pressing it down into his hair to keep it back from his face. "It's not about Cuthbert's papers. I want to know how this illuminier works."

She lifted her head, gazing at him intently. "You think it was used to hide the crime?"

"I don't know. That's what we're going to find out."

Hoadley scanned the street. "We need to—"

"Here we are." Beaumont grunted in satisfaction as a very smart steamer, the advantage of being in a prosperous neighbourhood, pulled up beside them. Engine chugging, ready to go.

"Are you taking rides, zer?" Beaumont touched his hat in greeting. "We need a lift to Viliside."

"Hop in zer," said the driver, touching her own hat in response.

"Thank you." Beaumont jumped into the back, settling in. Hoadley hesitated near the front seat but exhaled heavily then stomped around the side and clambered in next to him.

"Where in Viliside are you heading?" The driver shouted over her shoulder. She was rugged up in a thick windproof coat and Beaumont was a little envious, though he was grateful for the steamer's drawn cloth and the small amount of protection it provided from the breeze, sharpened by the steamer's movement.

"South Street," Beaumont projected his voice over the clank of engine pistons speeding up.

"Rightio."

The steamer jerked forward, and Beaumont winced, grabbing onto the side, and finding it slightly sticky. He lifted his hand, sniffing it. Whatever it had been it had been something sweet.

A piece of fabric appeared in his peripheral vision.

"Here," said Hoadley. Her arm extended. She held out a quill wiper. "It's one of those with a built-in oil scraper, to help get ink stains out."

He nodded his thanks and took it, scraping it across the glaze on his hand.

"Thanks, it's working." And it was.

He contemplated her. One moment she was looking at him like he was the most useless person in the world and then next, she was interacting as if they were friendly colleagues.

Hoadley turned her head away, observing the road outside. The conversation between them over.

With the grand houses left behind, narrower roads lined with tenements huddled together. Even the air thickened with the Noxrath mix of stone and metal infused with wafts of frying oils from the occasional street cart.

"This is it," said Beaumont. The steamer pulled over, its engine clunking into idle, and he handed over some coins and carefully stepped onto the footpath.

"Is it possible to have a receipt?" Hoadley asked, her voice easy to hear over the engine's whirl.

Beaumont huffed. As if he would waste his time with the paperwork required to make the claim.

"Not a problem, zer." The driver scribbled illegibly on a piece of paper and handed it over to Beaumont.

He could make out the amount but doubted it would hold up to the accounts department's scrutiny. "Thank you."

He aimed the thanks at both of them, tucking away the useless paper and turning his attention to the tall slender house with three levels of windows in front of them.

"Do you think they're expecting us?" asked Hoadley, pointing at the stairs.

Beaumont wasn't sure why having stairs at the front of the house was an indicator of expecting visitors, but he shrugged. He wasn't really looking forward to this. More conversations, more half-truths and lies. But he needed to know what part the illuminier played. Why did the death occur on this night of nights? It had to be connected. And if the Atwaters were avoiding him, he would start with the assistant.

"I do hope they haven't had morning tea yet," he said.

Hoadley glanced at him, rolling her eyes as she turned and pressed at the gate. It swung open. Hoadley tilted her head staring at it for a moment but stepped out of the way to let Beaumont past. He navigated the front stairs only to find that Ernest Walstrand had replaced his front entrance with a vault door. A sign of wealth, or paranoia?

Hoadley reached out to a small dial to the right of it and spun it. A hiss of gas set wheels in motion, hopefully setting off a bell in the house.

The vault door creaked, swinging inward, revealing a young man dressed in dark unmoving colours, a shockingly bright orange cravat and mismatched shoes.

"Walstrand Residence."

"I'm Inspector Hoadley and this is Prime Inspector Beaumont, we'd like to speak to the Walstrands please." Hoadley touched her waistcoat, flashing the hidden pattern of the gendarmerie.

"Only Melody Walstrand is receiving visitors."

He continued to stand in the doorway. Beaumont wouldn't describe it as blocking, but he certainly wasn't getting out of the way.

Beaumont tried for one of his most harmless smiles. "Then that's who we'll speak to."

The domestic, who if Beaumont remembered correctly was listed as a Roger something or other, grunted and stepped back, opening the door, gesturing for them to enter.

Hoadley stood at the entrance and poked at the floor with the tip of her shoe. He remembered gazing at her quizzically. Eventually, she stepped forward and he followed her, taking the necessary steps to enter the living room.

They found Melody, seated at the desk, ledgers and counting devices next to her, decked out in the most lavish display of orange Beaumont had ever seen in real life. She finished writing down her calculations before gazing up at them.

"Inspectors," she drawled, rising. "Couldn't stay away?"

The curtains were drawn back, displaying a garden full of sculptures. The closed windows trapped the must and metal that permeated the room.

"When will Zer Ancilla Walstrand be back?" asked Hoadley. Her voice shattered Melody's welcoming expression.

"Ancilla?" Melody sneered.

"Perhaps you can help us?" Beaumont smiled at her. They were here after all. Might as well use the time to get more information about her visit to the library. "You strike me as an observant person with an excellent memory."

Melody blinked, her smile returning.

"I am. Would you like some tea?"

Beaumont nodded, even he would admit, a little too enthusiastically.

"Yes, thank you, and perhaps something small..."

She smirked. "Roger, tea and cake for three." Her voice rang out, crossing dimensions.

Beaumont used the opportunity to make his way to her desk and examine her work.

He put down the ledger she had been working, smiling at her, again. "A woman of many hidden talents it seems."

Hoadley cleared her throat. It wasn't just a normal clearing, like you would expect to get someone's attention. It reminded Beaumont more of a train passing.

"Marcellus Overton's movements before his death." Hoadley's voice was the whistle of the train leaving the station.

"The party was a crush," Melody flopped down into one of the armchairs arranged around a coffee table in the centre of the room.

"After your..." Beaumont began as he joined her, taking an armchair near her, "...altercation with Overton, you said you walked through the gallery searching for Felicia but ended up with your father instead?"

"That's right."

"Do you remember when you next saw Felicia Atwater?"

"Do you think she did it?"

Hoadley shifted out of the doorway to allow Roger past. He was pushing a trolley loaded up with a large teapot, teacups and an impressive amount of cake.

Beaumont discretely swallowed the saliva that pooled in his mouth.

Roger transferred the tea and cake to the table between them. "Anything else?" he asked.

Melody waved her hand dismissing him.

Roger left, his air of disinterest appearing genuine.

Hoadley inched onto the rug, peering at the armchairs. She lowered herself down and then sat still, holding onto the arms. Beaumont leant back enjoying the chair's adjustments as it rearranged itself to support his back. He had been wrong to delay coming here.

What was of more interest however was the repast in front of him. He leaned forward to see if he could make out what kind of cake it was.

"Tea and cake, Prime Inspector?" asked Melody, giving Beaumont an overly warm smile.

"Don't mind if I do," Beaumont smiled back at her.

The teacup was a fragile affair even tinier in his large hands, unlike the tea bowl he had back in the station. Melody also gave him a plate with two pieces of cake, thankfully realising that he was going to need more than one.

"Felicia Atwater?" asked Hoadley. The wave of her hand

dismissed the offer of tea, almost sending the quill in her hand flying. She fumbled, getting it back into position.

Melody glared at her. "I'd joined Father and was sharing how...what had happened. I remember searching for her, I still had plans to let her know about the whisky but when I eventually did see her, she was surrounded by people and—" Melody took a sip of her tea "—my nerve failed me I suppose. I also doubted that she wasn't perfectly aware of what was going on in her house."

"How long after you came back from the library was this?" asked Hoadley.

He probably should be leading the conversation. But he doubted that Melody had anything of interest to add. The tea was nice too. He wasn't familiar with the blend, but the aromatics were clean and pleasant.

"Five minutes? Certainly not more than ten." Melody tapped her finger against her lip. "Is this terrible business going to be over soon? We need to start thinking about an appropriate memorial." She folded her hands in her lap and peered at Beaumont.

"We'll move as quickly as we can." Beaumont hummed as he finished his first bit of cake. "What's in this? Are these actual raspberries?"

"Freeze-dried."

Freeze-dried raspberries. Now that was worth making a note about.

"Delicious." He took a sip of tea. "Zer Walstrand, we have had some witnesses talk about seeing you with a person in the atrium. Now you mentioned following Overton through it, but did you speak to him in the atrium itself?"

Hoadley narrowed her eyes at him. What had he done wrong this time?

Melody flushed, "I..." she put down her cup, "attempted to talk to him in the atrium as well."

"And what did he say?"

Her gaze flicked between them and she buried her face in her teacup. Or attempted to. The size of the tiny porcelain cup made her attempt futile.

"Zer Walstrand," said Beaumont, after he swallowed his mouthful of cake. After all priorities.

"He ignored me." She patted at her elaborately made-up hair.

Overdone, like her outfit. Where exactly was she planning to go?

"Ignored you?" Beaumont's forehead furrowed.

"Yes, I attempted to talk to him a number of times, but he kept walking."

"Did you touch him?" Beaumont tried to sit forward but the armchair kept adjusting so he was forced to lean back. "To get his attention?"

"Yes," said Melody, waving her free arm through the air. "Yes, a caress of the arm, I suppose you might say. Not that it made a difference."

"And then you followed him into the library?" he asked, ignoring the look Hoadley sent him. It was getting to the point where they needed to have a bit of a conversation on how they were going to work together. Especially in front of witnesses.

Melody frowned. "Not right away. I stood outside the door, I was upset. I wasn't sure if I should continue the conversation or leave it. After a couple of seconds, I decided to try one more time which is when I entered the library."

The door clicked, opening to reveal Ancilla Walstrand. She was a perfect picture of mourning. Dressed simply, her hair pulled back in a low bun and her outfit a coordinated soft grey with a subtle orange pattern.

Did the whole family have their mourning clothes just ready to go?

Lavina Hoadley, Inspector
Noxrath Gendarmerie
Great Espya

I do think that it would have helped if he brushed the crumbs off before he greeted the suspects.

"Zer Ancilla Walstrand..." said Beaumont, standing.

"Prime Inspector Beaumont, Inspector Hoadley." Ancilla moved towards us, sitting, fearlessly, in another armchair.

"We need to...speak with you." He was now in an awkward half-standing, half-seated position.

"Very well." Ancilla reached out and poured herself a cup of tea. Her eyes flicked to my head. "Inspector Hoadley, are you okay?"

I nodded. "Yes." I touched the cloth wrapped around my

head, its fabric rough against my fingers. The indignity of having to wear it was only trumped by the fact I had an unpleasant gash on the back of my head. Not to mention the doctor had gone on, at some length, about the importance of keeping the wound clean. At least he had let me cover it in a black cloth. Maybe I would start a new fashion.

She blinked and gave a small smile. "Glad to hear it."

I examined her. Less stiff. More centred. What exactly had she been up to this morning?

"We'd like to understand...how the illuminier works," he asked, finally making the decision to sit back down again.

"The illuminier?" Ancilla leaned back in her chair, sipping her tea. "That's Felicia Atwater's..."

"Yes of course," Beaumont inclined his head. "But I would like to understand...what it can do."

"I can try," said Ancilla, and in a rare moment of verbosity, Ancilla Walstrand, accompanied by Melody's yawns proceeded to expound on a whole bunch of peculiar.

What I think I got out of it was: the illuminier focused light—it reflected off small bits— Overton, or any artist with enough pneuma, can use the light to shape images—these images were realistic—appearing in the centre of the room—not just an image projected on a flat surface.

"Can you touch them?" I asked. All much ado about nothing really. What difference did it make if the light was on the wall or in the middle of the room?

Ancilla frowned. "Not really. It's light...there's no...resistance."

So not useful at all then. I made some notes in my jotter.

More to appear like I was writing something than capturing my understanding of what she just said.

"What kind of images can you create?" asked Beaumont.

I am ashamed to admit, that it was only at that moment I realised why we were here and what Beaumont was trying to establish. If I blushed, I could only hope he didn't see it.

Ancilla tilted her head, examining him. "Last night's demonstration was of a chair and an ornate desk."

"What about...a person?" asked Beaumont. He did a bit of a twist and managed to lean forward.

I was impressed. My chair still held me captive in a more, reclining position.

"You mean sitting at the table?"

"Could Overton..." Beaumont cleared his throat, "create an image of a person walking and moving around?"

That surprised a laugh out of her, and Melody snorted.

"I'm afraid we aren't—"

"If you saw the table and chairs—"

Ancilla and Melody glanced at each other, smiling. Ancilla touched her throat and turned away.

"In short, no," she said.

"I mean there were definitely tables and chairs," said Melody, "but besides from being terribly old fashioned, like their creator, you could practically see through them."

"See through them?" asked Beaumont.

"It's a step," Ancilla shrugged, "an important one, but it's the beginning of the journey."

"And will you be leading that journey?" I asked.

"I..." Ancilla shook her head. "It is up to Felicia Atwater."

She rolled her shoulders, hunching them forward. "Only the most skilled of artists can manipulate it."

"But you can use it," I said.

Ancilla stared at me. "I can do what is needed, but I am not..."

"Not an artist?" I asked. "How many artists could do what is needed?"

She shrugged. "I'm sure Felicia will begin the search for one soon."

"Indeed," said Beaumont.

He sat back in his chair and ate the rest of his cake in a couple of bites while we all watched him. A crumb dropped off the edge of his plate, but it never hit the rug. The coffee table moved just enough to catch it.

Of course, it did. The only question was how far it was willing to go to protect its friend the rug.

"Is there anything else we can help you with today, Prime Inspector?" asked Ancilla with a slight twitch in the corner of her lip.

If I ate that much cake, I would be wobbling down the streets. It was unjust that he could eat with such abandon and still appear healthy.

"Zer Overton's movements last night, is there anything else you remember, after the demonstration?" I asked.

Ancilla's nose scrunched and she shook her head, glancing at Melody who also shook hers.

"Sorry, no. It was all rather exhausting." She shrugged. "I was smiling and nodding at people, wishing for it to be over."

"I will say no one was having a great night though," said Melody.

"How's that?" asked Beaumont, washing down the cake and any other peripheral thoughts with some more tea.

Muddling your insides with that much tea couldn't be healthy for you.

"What? It's true," Melody said, giving a little smirk when Ancilla frowned at her.

"It all went down before the demonstration."

"What went...down?" asked Beaumont, settling back in his chair. Like a man preparing to hear an enjoyable tale.

And why did she not tell us this yesterday?

"Oh everyone was very grumpy with each other." Melody stretched out, almost horizontal, the chair following her movements and allowing her to drape herself over it. "The only civilised person was Necket."

Ancilla gave a soft chuckle. "That's true."

"This is a murder inquiry, not a tea party." I reminded them.

They simultaneously blinked, staring at me. I was not going to apologise for reminding them why we were here. A man was dead.

Ancilla raised her hand. "We know that." She glanced at Melody, who was now glaring at me. "Everyone was stressed that's all. Alistair was constantly checking to make sure the device was working, Felicia was still riled up about the wording of the patent bill, and Marcellus...he was..."

"He was bouncing off the walls was what he was," snorted Melody.

Ancilla frowned. "He was not himself."

Melody gave a dry laugh. "That's one way to put it." She patted her overly elaborate hair. "I had never seen him that skittish."

"Sounds like a stressful evening," said Beaumont. His gaze pinging between the two sisters.

I stared somewhere in between them, not wanting to miss a single beat. Ancilla's expression was rueful and Melody's excited.

"Alistair snapped at both of them," she crowed. "I've never seen him lose his temper before."

"He...snapped...at both Zer Atwater and Zer Overton?" asked Beaumont.

Melody swung herself upright and leant forward.

"Well Marcellus didn't stay around for it, but Felicia was not okay with her son telling her what to do." Melody's eyes were bright. "She went into a full-on rant about how everyone was ungrateful, how much she had done for them." She sat back, letting her clasped hands rest in her lap and smirked at the room.

"And where were you when this fight occurred?" asked Beaumont.

"I'd been talking to Alistair—"

"All afternoon while we were trying to work—" murmured Ancilla.

Melody waved her sister's words away.

Beaumont's eyebrows rose. "And how did the argument end?"

"Felicia stormed off, saying she had to get ready," said Melody, gesturing upwards.

"And what did you do during all of this, Zer Ancilla?" asked Beaumont.

Tea and cake had a positive effect on him.

"It wasn't quite the argument that Melody makes out. A short, albeit heated, discussion. Once it was over, I got myself, and Alistair, a cup of tea and we went back to work."

"And did you have any problems using the device?" I asked.

Ancilla blinked. "No. However, I was only...testing."

Beaumont nodded and made some notes.

"Thank you and thank you, Zer Melody." Beaumont rose.

Probably because he had run out of cake. The coffee table shifted, catching crumbs and getting dangerously close to his kneecap.

I closed my jotter and followed suit, muffling my sigh. Everyone stared at me.

Beaumont bowed in Melody's direction. "I won't take any more of your time—"

"And how much time have you been taking Prime Inspector?" Ernest Walstrand had stood in the doorway, bristling.

"Zer Ernest Walstrand." He tilted his head, giving a small bow and nodded a welcome to Cuthbert. Exactly the kind of courtesy that had everyone thinking he was something delightful.

"You're in my home without my consent Prime Inspector," said Ernest, frowning.

"It's alright father," said Melody, "I let him in. We have been having a very nice time with tea and cake."

"Have you?" Ernest pulled at the gloves on his hands, ripping them off and slapping them into Cuthbert. "And what exactly has been the topic of conversation?"

"Just the demonstration last night, and the argument between Alistair and Felicia." Melody reached out, pouring herself another cup of tea.

Ernest took a deep breath. "What argument between Alistair and Felicia?"

"The one before the party." Melody opened her eyes wide at her father.

Ernest's jaw twitched. He stared at Beaumont. "Indeed."

"Indeed." Beaumont smiled back.

What a fun morning. We really didn't have time for this.

"Since you are here," I stared at Cuthbert. "We've questions." Such as did he swing something resembling a large metal pipe at my head and steal his papers back?

Beaumont had promised me that he was having one of the other inspectors investigate it, but I doubted they would return anything useful.

Cuthbert, still standing there with his father's gloves hanging loose in his hands, jumped a little. "Er...do I get a choice?"

"Yes, here or back at the Way." I followed Beaumont's lead and tried a smile.

Cuthbert gave a rather ragged laugh. "Sure whatever. Father," he said, giving him the gloves back. "Let's go—"

Ernest took his gloves but didn't move out of the doorway. "Sit down Cuthbert, whatever the gendarmerie needs to know you can share here. There is no objection is there, Prime Inspector?"

There should be every objection. This was an investigation, not a family tea party.

"As long as Zer Cuthbert's comfortable?" asked Beaumont.

Right, because the comfort of the suspect, who potentially had assaulted an inspector, was our priority.

Cuthbert sat in an armchair, putting his feet on the table and hands behind his head.

Beaumont's smile continued, and he sat back down, leaning back in his chair with his long legs stretched out in front of him, mirroring him. "Thank you for making the time."

I struggled to suppress my frown, resuming my own seat but refusing to give into the chair's desire for me to relax. This was highly irregular and was most certainly not following the gendarmerie guidelines.

Another slice of cake was offered, which he, of course, accepted.

Ernest glided to another armchair. I counted at least six of the oversized, overly enthusiastic, armchairs and a collection of other seats scattered around the space. It was practically a chairitorium.

"We understand that Overton was...unhappy...with his business arrangement with you." Beaumont gave an almost apologetic smile. Though what he had to be apologetic about I didn't know.

I remembered enough from my flick-through to know Cuthbert's approach was completely unethical. Overton was either completely incompetent in managing his own affairs, or extremely drunk at the time. Or both.

"These things take time, and always cost more than you think they will." Cuthbert crossed his ankles.

From what I could remember, the long and short of it was that Overton had given Cuthbert a huge amount of money to invest in an invention.

"These things..." Beaumont raised his eyebrows.

"The invention." Cuthbert rolled his eyes. The picture of disinterest, except for the tapping of his hand on the armchair.

"What did this invention do?" I asked. Nothing in his paperwork had mentioned anything by name. Presumably to protect the invention from being copied before it was registered, if that was the plan.

"It," Cuthbert pulled at his cuffs, "well it used light to create replicas of things." He adjusted his cravat.

"What? How?" asked Ancilla, jerking upright.

I glanced at her. "Have you heard of this?"

She shook her head. "No, no I wasn't aware of any-thing that could do something like that." Ancilla frowned at Cuthbert. "Was it real? Or was it all just a scam?"

Cuthbert straightened. "It was in development."

I narrowed my eyes at him. "With the bill before

parliament I would have thought registering this...duplicator...would've been a priority."

"Yes, it would have been better if we could have, which was why it needed the injection of funds, but the people working on it hit a few snags."

"What, that the money didn't get to them?" I asked, my voice dry.

Cuthbert flushed, his eyes narrowing. "I completed my part of the contract."

Beaumont put his plate down. "It's interesting that you say that." He pulled out a small folder from a hidden front pocket in his waistcoat.

"Why?" asked Cuthbert his eyes darting to the folder in Beaumont's hand.

"I've a report from some of my colleagues of an altercation at a bar called SteamMasters where a group of device crafters beat up their investor for not turning up with the promised funds. And from what I can see," Beaumont glanced up from the report to Cuthbert, "that person appears to be you."

Great, thanks for keeping me in the loop Beaumont. In all the walking he could not find time to brief me?

"I'm not a device crafter."

"No." Beaumont peered at him over the top of his glasses. "I didn't think you were."

"When was this?" asked Ernest.

"Three nights ago, zer," said Beaumont.

Ernest twitched. He glared at Cuthbert, irises pinpricking. "Is this true?"

Cuthbert grunted and rose, heading over to a spare space

in the room. He pressed his foot down on a patch on the floor, causing it to squeal.

I jumped to my feet. The floor folded back and something lifted up. Like everything else in the house, it was overdone but certainly eye-catching. Metal wings, filled in with glass half opened up and curved metal wove around the structure. A piano.

Cuthbert wandered over, letting his fingers rest against its metal keys.

"I remember that night," said Melody, "Remember Cuthbert, that was the night you tore your favourite waistcoat. You were quite upset about it."

He shot her a sharp glare but returned his attention to the instrument, settling into the small bench.

I glanced around the room. Everyone was watching Cuthbert with various layers of disapproval, only Ancilla tried to hide it.

His fingers moved on the keys and a soft wistful sound filled the air. My eyelids twitched. I hadn't heard live music since before my parent's death.

The piano was integrated with the room, so the sound flowed through the walls, wrapping me up in each note. I am ashamed to say my hands trembled.

"I can't remember. All the nights blur together you know." His fingers danced and the soft melody continued.

Why identify as a poet if he had a talent for music? I could not feel any pneuma infusing the sounds, as I would expect from an artist, but it was a lot closer to it than his poetry.

"You don't remember being beaten up?" I centred myself, tuning out the music. There was work to be done. "I would remember."

Cuthbert shrugged and kept playing. I assessed it would be unprofessional to stride over to him and slam the lid on his fingers.

"Even if it was Cuthbert, what does that have to do with Marcellus' death?" asked Ernest.

"You see..." Beaumont cleared his throat. "Overton's money somehow got lost in the two hours between when he gave it to Cuthbert and when it was due to be delivered to the crafters," said Beaumont, with a tsk. Though he always took his time to say things, right now each word was almost glacial in speed.

"How much money are we talking?" Ernest scowled.

Beaumont named a sum which still made my heart jump, but it did help me get back in the game.

Ernest stopped breathing, his face going a strange mix of colours. I contemplated calling a medic, but Ernest managed to start breathing again.

"Cuthbert..." he glared at him. "Is this true?"

Cuthbert shrugged. "Numbers are more Melody's thing than mine." He moved on to another song.

"Where is it?" Ernest slumped in his chair.

Cuthbert's gaze was down, focused on his fingers. He shifted into a tune I hadn't heard before and sang:

A shot

A shot

Liquid makes smug

> *A shot*
> *A shot*
> *Luck is dug*
> *A shot*
> *A shot*
> *The glint is a drug*
> *A shot*
> *A shot*
> *I am a mug*

Ernest threw himself across the room, slamming the key cover down. Cuthbert moved fast, flinching back, and curling his hands against his chest.

"You fool," Ernest hissed, swallowing as he tried to regain his composure. His eyes flicked to Beaumont.

"To give your son credit," I shifted my weight forward. I did not have much space or time for Cuthbert, but despite his bravado, there was pain in his eyes. "He knows how to write a contract to protect himself."

Ernest breathed deeply. "More a motive for Overton to kill Cuthbert, not the other way around." He stood with his arms crossed glaring at everyone. "A motive I fully understand."

Melody joined him in glaring at Cuthbert while Ancilla poured herself another cup of tea.

"Perhaps..." Beaumont inclined his head. "You understand we need to follow this?"

Ernest's lips thinned and he glared at the back of Cuthbert's hunched form. He jerked his head in Beaumont's direction and strode from the room.

Something crashed against a wall.

"You're a fool," said Melody. She dusted the crumbs off her orange monstrosity, setting the coffee table scampering.

Ancilla sipped her tea, watching.

"Don't pretend you're so perfect, either of you." He pushed back from the piano, throwing himself out of the room.

Melody groaned. "I suppose I better check on him in case he does something stupid." She moved to a doorway. "Prime Inspector it's been a pleasure." Her over-the-top waterfall flowed behind her, adding gravitas to her exit.

Ancilla put the last remaining slice of cake on a plate and took a bite. Beaumont watched, his shoulders and the edges of his lips drooping.

"You aren't going to check in on him too?" I asked.

She shook her head, her eyes down. "I doubt my presence would be helpful."

Ernest appeared back at the entrance to the room. "Prime Inspector, a word."

Beaumont stood, though he would have been in his rights to send Ernest Walstrand packing.

"Of course, Zer Walstrand." Beaumont bowed slightly in Ancilla's direction. "If you will excuse me.

Ancilla's gaze followed his exit while she finished chewing. Once they left she turned her attention back to me and flicked me a grin.

"Having fun yet?" She settled back in her chair and took a sip of tea.

"With the investigation?" I asked.

Ancilla rolled her eyes. "No, with the other major thing going on."

I reached into my waistcoat pocket and pulled out her pocket watch. Her eyes widened.

"Yours?" I asked, rolling it around on my palm.

"I wondered where that went." She laughed. "You know of all the things I thought had happened to it, being stolen by the gendarmerie was not one of them."

"Impounded."

She waved my word away and leant forward with her hand outstretched. "Any chance of having it back?"

"How many unregistered modifications have you made to it?" I asked, my eyes narrowing.

Her fingers curled closed and she sat back. "Nothing worth the gendarmerie's attention."

"All illegal activity is worthy of the gendarmerie's attention."

She held her hand out palms up. "If you want to spend your time doing that rather than chasing a murderer..."

I turned the watch over. So far I hadn't been able to work out what it did. "The modifications."

She huffed. "It records."

"What?"

"Sound."

I blinked. That sounded like a significant modification to me. "I am assuming you aren't paying the relevant royalties to the Hawkes Family?"

"Personal use." She grinned at me and held her hand out again.

I dropped the offending watch in it.

"How does it work?" More importantly, where did I buy one?

"You want one?" She tilted her head, her smile broadening. "Press on this side to record"—she pointed to the left of the watch—"and this side to play back"—pointing at the other side. "It can only record short messages, but useful when you need to leave a note to yourself."

I nodded, wishing I hadn't given it back.

"If we survive this, I'll make you one."

I stared at her. "Has someone threatened you?"

"No." Her gaze lifted up to the bandage on my head. "How's the head"

My hand touched the bandage, but I forced it down and successfully freed myself enough from the chair to lean forward.

"I am more interested in Marcellus Overton's movements on the night he died."

She gazed down at her watch, leaning back in her chair. "Why Marcellus' movements? Shouldn't you be worried about everyone else's movements?"

"I'm trying to confirm how he entered the library as that may make a difference to who was the last to see him alive."

"I would imagine it was the killer."

"Call us crazy." My lips twisted. "But we like to know where everyone, including the victim, was. It's still not clear how he moved from next to you to—"

"Out the back behind the stage." She shrugged like it should be obvious.

"What?" I snapped. She could not have mentioned this last night?

She blinked. "What?"

"He left the ballroom behind the stage?"

"Yes, there's a service door."

Ancilla examined me in a way that made me think there was a lot more going on behind her eyes than the casual stance of her body indicated. What was she hiding?

"Would others have seen him leave that way?" I asked.

"Yes, the two guests directly in front of me."

Her gaze scanned me, for what? To see if I believed her?

"Hoadley."

I glanced up to find Beaumont standing in the entry, listening. He jerked his head towards the front door and left. I rose.

"Thank you for your help Ancilla," I said.

She gave a small smile. "So it is back to Ancilla again is it?"

"If that's what it takes for you to share what you know."

Her lips thinned.

I gave her a small bow and joined Beaumont out on the street.

"How many Overtons do we have now?" Beaumont asked.

I placed my hat on and pulled at my coat to keep it tight. "Four, zer."

"Four." He peered up at the sky. "Send a note, let's ask the guards to check the statements from those two witnesses and see if they corroborate Zer Ancilla's comments, if they don't tell them to go and interview them again. We still need to follow up on Cuthbert, and who he had this gambling debt with, but later tonight."

"Couldn't we track them down in their homes?"

He gazed at the sky, for what? Inspiration? A closer inspection of the world in front of us was bound to be much more fruitful.

"Do you know their names?"

"No, zer," I said with, I admit, a bit of a flush to my cheeks.

"Let's use this afternoon to go through all the witness statements. I don't know what is going on, but I don't like it."

I nodded and searched for a messenger. Noxrath didn't keep its own messenger service like we did back in Solverde. Too substantial a city to make it worthwhile, perhaps. Instead, I had to trust that the higher rates of pay that the Way offered to them would keep my message safe. Worth exploring the costings of a dedicated service for one of my future recommendations.

"Done, zer."

Beaumont nodded but didn't take his eyes off the weak sun struggling to reach its halfway point in the sky. "Excellent. First things first though. Lunch."

11

One Tentacle at a Time

Ancilla paced.

Her bedroom rug, old-fashioned and unmoving, cushioned her feet and protected them from the cold floor beneath.

Not that she noticed.

What was the right thing to do?

She forced herself to stop, to lean on her window frame, the promise of the morning sun had muted to silver as the day matured. Her fingertips tapped the glass, and she shivered as the cold of the outside pressed against it and ran up her arm.

Sculptures, scattered throughout their garden, caught her gaze. Ernest was a collector. Of inventions and art, and of course, the ones that combined both were the most highly prized.

She liked them, sort of. Her favourite was the cage with

an octopus escaping. A gift from their mother, though no one ever told Ernest that, otherwise it would have been destroyed alongside everything else.

Hours had been lost gazing at it, inspiring her with its slow and steady escape. The octopus had started with merely the tip of one tentacle reaching through a small opening. Across the years she had been watching, the bars pushed back enough to allow two tentacles a taste of freedom.

How long would it take for the octopus to be free? She would be very disappointed in herself if she was here to see it. The sketch in her diary was the only memory she needed.

But she had more immediate problems. The inspector's questions about the device meant they were on to Marcellus' ruse. Or at least aware that something wasn't adding up. She needed to talk to him. But would he be fool enough to go to his flat? The only other place was the Purple Door. But they didn't know her and there was no way she was getting in before it opened tonight.

And Cuthbert. What was he thinking? Was he really so stupid?

Cuthbert didn't seem to realise that those 'overnight' successes he was so envious of came after slogging away for years.

Ernest had once found him a rare opportunity to work with Noxrath's oldest living poet, the head of the Hawkes Family. The interview was set. Instead, Cuthbert decided it was all a waste of time. That if he wasn't already famous there was no point putting in the effort. He really was a gasser. Ernest, furious and embarrassed, had sent an apology and the household had been very chilly for a long time afterward. But she didn't mind the cold. For her, it had probably been the calmest time she could remember.

She lost her own money a few times trying to be supportive but even Cuthbert knew not to bother Melody for a loan.

Ancilla winced as she remembered the orange dress. What had Melody been thinking? Her over-the-top colours were extreme even with the current bright trends. It was strange that such a frugal woman would be willing to spend that much money on clothes.

Unless her clothing choices were dictated more by the sale price of the fabric than a sense of style?

She startled herself with an overloud laugh in the cold quiet room.

Poor Melody, forced to a life of art and music when really, all she wanted to do was play with her coins. She certainly didn't do the bookkeeping for free, much to Ernest's disgust.

The bed groaned, Ancilla's weight ramming it with some speed. The mattress absorbed the hit and Ancilla sprawled across the bed on her back. Her fingers twisted at the quilt, grabbing a section and dragging it across. Her body shivered, beginning to warm up.

The Atwaters didn't seem to be in any doubt that Marcellus was dead. Surely Felicia would know? Ancilla just wished she had seen the body.

After Alistair's visit this morning, she had escaped the house, her feet leading her to a small park, with a picturesque brook and a lover's bridge. Her mind blank she stood there, gazing at the water contemplating the events of the last few hours.

The morning sky had misunderstood the solemnity of the moment and had been bright and cheery, throwing the world into colour and the birds into song. She had brought the grey to the scene, standing there, like some sort of dramatic hero, until the scent of a food cart with deep-fried dough and sugar seduced her.

She couldn't hide forever.

One of the nicer steamers idled next to the park, waiting for fares. With a sudden sense of urgency, she had hailed it, hiding her freshly fried treat from the driver's gaze in her pocket. She had intended to wait, but couldn't resist sneaking a bite in. The warm sugar exploded in her mouth, and she groaned.

"Everything alright?" asked the driver. The driver was too layered up against the cold to fully turn around, but she managed to shout over her shoulder.

"Yes, thank you," said Ancilla, carefully angling herself so the driver couldn't see her take a second bite, the adrenaline only adding to the pleasure.

She had regretted rushing home as soon as she stepped inside and found the gendarmerie waiting for her, with Melody, in her garish orange dress, entertaining them like they were fine guests.

She wasn't sure about the Prime Inspector, but she liked Hoadley and at least their brains worked. Well hopefully. The bandage around Inspector Hoadley's head had been concerning but didn't seem to have inhibited the Inspector's sharp insight.

If she was going to tell anyone it would be Hoadley. After she spoke to Marcellus.

And then there was Cuthbert. What was going on between him and Ernest? Ernest oscillated between supporting him and leaving him to sink. With them raging, Ancilla and Melody both made the strategic decision to retire to their respective rooms.

And here she was.

Trapped, again.

Ancilla rolled out of bed and paced back towards her bedroom door, using it as an excuse to double check the lock. The latch was engaged.

She ran her fingers over the hinge feeling for the stick of metal she had jammed in there. Its edge dug into her skin and she exhaled. The next step was to install some extra material to muffle the noise of her family.

Shoulders hunching, she kicked at the rug, flinching when her bare toes missed.

Pipes.

She should have been thinking about finding her own place by now, not bunkering down here. And she certainly wasn't going to spend the whole day hiding in her bedroom.

She pressed her ear up to the door. No yelling, no footsteps. Everyone retired to their corners. She dressed and with her hat in her hand, she unlocked her bedroom door, tiptoed down the stairs and shuffled quickly out the back door.

She tapped hello to the octopus as she hurried past,

imagining its tentacles gave her a little wave back. Would Ernest let her take it when she left? And tulips would start growing out of metal.

Once on the street, she took a breath, inhaling the smoke from a nearby food cart. Her stomach grumbled. It was almost lunchtime, and she needed something substantial after a morning of sweet treats.

The residential area they lived in didn't really lend itself to restaurants, but the Treadways, near the dirigible yards, and Marcellus' flat, did.

The only problem was getting a steamer.

The street was quieter, the crowds flowing along to protest having died down, most of them were now likely set up outside the patent office, and the only steamer on the street already had two people in it.

In the end, she had to walk a block before she could find a free one, but she didn't blame everyone for being out and about enjoying the sun filled day.

"Where to?" asked the driver, barely glancing in Ancilla's direction. Ancilla was relieved that he wasn't a chatty one. She wasn't sure she had more small talk in her today.

"Sixsmith Road, up at the Treadways end, thank you kindly."

She had the steamer drop her outside Marcellus' flat on Sixsmith Road. Her stomach rumbled in disagreement with her choice of priorities. But if Marcellus was here that was more important than food. She patted her stomach in apology and scanned the facades of tenements until she came to the blue door covered by a complicated grid of metal.

Keys were not something Marcellus was capable of keeping track of. He had instead installed a complicated lock system that required just the right configuration of dials and levers.

She strode up to the metal grid and followed the pattern he had drilled into her. She would have been touched by his trust if it hadn't been clear that she was only being shown to help when he was too inebriated to navigate them himself.

A click and a grinding sound heralded the metal grid swinging out, forcing her to take a step back.

The days before the launch had been hectic, but Ancilla remembered the conversation with Marcellus that had rolled the dice on their fates.

He had been hunched over the illuminier, digging around in it, while she bit her nails. Marcellus was a genius but not all experiments, by their very nature, led to success.

"I don't know what's wrong with this dastardly device," grumbled Marcellus. He squinted at a part and shoved his tweezers inside the illuminier.

The workroom smelled of dust and metal. He didn't like the domestics, or her, disturbing his stuff. But he didn't like cleaning either. Traditionally this impasse continued until Felicia stepped in.

"There's nothing wrong, your test worked," said Ancilla. The truth was they had had this conversation a thousand times but if they needed to have it again, so be it.

"The image might form but..." He paused, pulling back,

scowling down at it. "It shouldn't drain me...quite so thoroughly."

The illuminier would make the history books, and they might too—or at least Marcellus would.

"It's exciting times."

"Every time I use it, the amount of pneuma required seems to increase." He rested his hand on it, his expression a mixture of exasperation and affection. Like a parent might show a troublesome child.

"We just have to practice more," she said. Practice being her answer to everything.

Marcellus stared at her, his gaze distant. "It could be, but..." He peered at the illuminier. "I've spent my life spinning light...this is different."

At the time she had dismissed it as nerves.

"Do you want a drink? I could get some tea?"

"Fine." His lips tilted up, but his eyes stayed empty.

Felicia had given Ancilla strict instructions that Marcellus was to practice with the device at least three times today. Only days out from the demonstration, she wanted to make sure everything was working. No blocked pipes were going to ruin her night of triumph.

"Do you want me to do the next practice run?" she asked. She did not want to. If it was exhausting for Marcellus, it was triple for her.

Yes." Stepping back, he flopped down on his daybed, closing his eyes.

Pipe it.

Ancilla could almost feel his mind leaving the room, like a caress of a breeze that wouldn't be back.

She checked the gas levels of the illuminier, shifting the lever to the on position. Cogs started to turn. Her hand rested against the artist's controls, and she let her pneuma flow through her skin, into the metal, the pipes. By shifting the lever, she allowed more and more light into the illuminier and when her pneuma tangled with it, the light started to dance.

Marcellus had already set it up so all she had to do was feed more and more light and pneuma in.

Slowly, much more slowly than Marcellus, a table and chair took form. It wasn't sharp, but it was visible.

"You'll need to do better than that," Marcellus grunted.

Ancilla blinked in surprise, and the table and chair dissolved back into amorphous light. Her mouth was dry, and she hobbled over to get a glass of water. She was also suddenly starving.

"I completed the test."

Which was no small feat. She was an assistant, not even an artist by most standards. The fact that anything appeared at all was a miracle.

He swung himself back up to his feet.

"You'll practice five times a day until the presentation." He stared at her intently.

Ancilla blinked. This was something different from Marcellus' usual mercurial moods. "Why?"

"I've an appointment that clashes with the demonstration at the party."

What the pipes?

She glanced around the workroom. They had just spent the last two weeks here preparing for the demonstration and now he had an alternative engagement.

"Does Felicia know about this?"

He stared down at his hands which had closed into fists.

"No, she doesn't need to know. I've hired an actor to be me."

Water sprayed out in front of her. The lack of food today was affecting her hearing.

"To be you? At your appointment?" she asked, her voice rising.

"No at the demonstration." He stood facing her, his arms crossed across his chest. His eyes, flat.

She gulped some more water, trying to get the suddenly sour taste out of her mouth.

"Felicia's going to notice..."

"Not if he keeps moving."

At least the actor was a male. She mentally slapped herself, as if that was going to make a difference.

"People will want to talk to you." She dragged her fingers through her hair, destroying her neatly tied back mop and sending it flying.

"I never talk to people at parties."

While this was true, they still wanted to speak to him.

"They'll know it isn't you."

"People see what they expect to see." He came over to the illuminier, glaring down at it.

Yes, and what they will expect to see is a completely

different person. Had he taken something before he lay down on the couch? She tried to remember if he had drunk or eaten anything that day.

"Felicia..." She shook her head. "There's no way—"

"The only thing she will be watching is the demonstration."

"Which will obviously not be you." She gestured at him, and then back at where the light danced, unformed and weak.

"You'll need to practice."

"There's no way..."

"Do this..." He stood there, his hands on hips, staring at her. A smirk crossed his face. "Do this and I'll give you everything you need to escape your father's house."

She had gaped at him, puffing, unable to catch her breath.

Marcellus never really had a home. Or at least if he did she had never seen it. His room at Atwater Place was more workshop than a place of rest and his flat was no different.

The only word to describe it was chaos.

Scraps of metal, broken cogs, springs and half-finished devices covered every surface, then the floor, and then each other.

Ancilla kicked a broken device out of her way and stepped in, closing the door behind her.

The flat hadn't changed. A myriad of benches and stools were scattered throughout the main living room. It crossed her mind that she had kept her side of the bargain and Marcellus would most likely have kept her payment here. She could search for it, but the sheer volume of bits and pieces she would have to test to find it meant she would be here a couple of days. Her gaze bounced towards the bedroom door at the back of the apartment.

The closed door.

Marcellus' pneuma flow was so strong that sometimes she could feel the force of him across the Atwater house. But lately, it hadn't been.

She dodged and weaved through the tangle of scraps, heading towards the closed bedroom door.

Knock. Knock.

Her hand dropped down to the doorknob as the sound echoed back. She twisted it and pushed it open.

Crumpled sheets and discarded pillows on an empty bed greeted her. His clothes, scattered around the room, evidence of Marcellus' presence.

Familiar with the way he lived, there was nothing to indicate whether he had been here recently. The washroom had been used, but again it was hard to tell if it was today or yesterday.

Closing the bedroom door behind her, she waded through the mess until she made it to a small kitchen in the corner, the muscles in her neck relaxing at the sight of coffee and a plate covered in crumbs in its sink.

She picked it up and gave it a sniff. It wasn't old. From this morning would be her guess. Which meant he slept here last night. But why hadn't he let her know? And if it wasn't him who was dead in the library then there was only one other person it could be and to be honest, she wasn't sure if that wasn't worse.

Ancilla's stomach rumbled. She needed to find Marcellus, but she wasn't going to be making effective decisions on an empty stomach.

What a piping mess.

She double checked to make sure she hadn't left any evidence of her visit and sealed the flat behind her.

Back on the street, the scents of spices and oils made her stomach dance and she headed to one of her favourite pneuma-inspired restaurants. How many times had she been grateful for the patented device that could identify your nutritional needs in the moment?

The restaurant itself didn't have a name. One of the latest trends she was not a fan of. As she arrived a group of six were leaving and she managed to squeeze in behind two couples. She handed over her coins, there was a standard upfront payment, a gamble on both sides, and grabbed a spare seat.

She placed her hand on the melted glass embedded in the wooden table, watching as the small gas lines started humming, the cogs turning. What she would give to be able to take it apart and look at it. Her work might have forced her down the manipulation of light path, but all devices were fascinating. In particular, the ones that interacted with pneuma itself. Perhaps after the illuminier tour she could ask to be transferred and join the Atwater's inventors in that space.

She placed her top hat on the hook on the back of the chair and her watch on the table. She was grateful Hoadley had returned it. While only a small brass pocket watch, it was designed to be able to sit up and assist her in keeping an eye on the time, along with the few other minor modifications of course. All it told her right now was that it was past midday and her stomach was very clear it had not enjoyed the delay.

A plate of mixed seafood, steamed greens and a small bowl of soup were placed in front of her. Ancilla huffed. No potatoes or bread. Stupid pneuma reader. Despite being packed the restaurant was only warmed by the slight hum of conversation. Most of the diners were too busy with their food to waste time with idle chit-chat.

She sipped her soup first, reminding herself that was why she was here, not outside having something yeasty deep-fried in cheese.

Purple Door tonight. Not that she wanted to. Gambling halls on the southside didn't hold any appeal, but Marcellus had become a regular in recent months. And now Cuthbert was also involved.

Who would use Cuthbert? Surely no one would be that foolish?

The evidence was to the contrary.

She finished the soup and speared some greens and fish. The pleasant light flavours of the warm crunchy vegetables with the fish flooded her body with welcomed power.

She wished Hoadley was across from her. They could brainstorm possible scenarios, solutions. But if Hoadley was sitting there she would take Ancilla's information and run with it, and Ancilla would have nothing, except a potentially annoyed Marcellus who saw it as a breach of their agreement.

No, she needed to find Marcellus. Work out what his next steps were and then, and only then, would she know what to tell Hoadley.

It would be hours until the Purple Door opened. In the meantime, best to stay home in case the inspectors dropped by again.

12

Pinning It Down

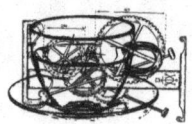

The Walstrands' tea and cake bubbled through Beaumont. His body buzzing and his mind a maelstrom. He had needed something to ground himself.

"Lunch?" asked Hoadley.

"We need food if we are going to spend the afternoon reading a bunch of statements. Brains need fuel, Hoadley."

"But you...half a cake, zer."

"Cake's important, but we need something a bit more nutritious if we're going to be using our brains. Come on." He flagged down another steamer.

Hoadley stared in the direction of their headquarters.

"Wouldn't somewhere near The Way..."

He shook his head. "Best place is the Treadways, near the dirigible yards."

The restaurant would also take them away from the

Patent Office and the crowds. They were getting bigger every day as the day of the vote came closer. It would be a nightmare trying to find anything near the Patent Office at this hour.

He climbed into the back of a steamer and tried not to take it personally that Hoadley got up front with the driver. It made sense. Meant she did not have to walk around into the traffic.

They left the formal part of the city behind and soon, narrower streets crammed with narrow buildings. There was also a myriad of stores and restaurants smashed between them. But they continued on and soon came to a large plaza filled with a myriad of street carts that had ingeniously stacked themselves so people could order from the higher-up carts through a sound funnel and then the food would be delivered down to them by triple-joined, spider-like metal arms. The result: a wall of spices, frying meat and baking weaving with smoke and ash, and chaos.

Beaumont inhaled deeply as he exited the steamer. He glanced over at Hoadley as she joined him. She hadn't had any cake and was practically drooling. She swallowed and straightened her shoulders.

"Should we grab something to take back—"

"No no no, we need to stop, take a moment, eat fine food." He gazed at the scene in front of him with a smile. "Trust me."

Hoadley's shoulders slumped but she shuffled along behind him.

He went up to a narrow, unmarked door, stepping aside

to let two people pass, entering a small room with bench seats and long tables. It was packed with only the two spaces, recently vacated, free. A woman standing near the entrance smiled at seeing them. Beaumont greeted her, handing over some coins. Seated without a word being exchanged, Beaumont placed his hats on the small hook on the back of his seat.

Hoadley followed suit.

The seat was hard, Beaumont shifted trying to get comfortable.

"Where do we order?" asked Hoadley. Her hand reached out around her to touch her hat. To check it was still there.

"There isn't a menu. Put your hand there." He pointed at the table, the glass melted into the wood. There was one on his side too and he had placed his hand on it. A liquid or gas moved, and a thousand small cogs were set in motion. Hoadley followed. The glass was cool at first but then it hummed.

"What is it..."

"It's checking what you need to eat." He grinned at her.

"What?" Hoadley recoiled and scowled at him.

Beaumont winced.

"What's wrong?" He peered at her, rubbing his lips. "It checks how your body's going and then prepares a meal that is perfect for it."

A sign hung up on the wall above their table declaring all who sat gave permission for pneuma testing.

"Two things, you don't touch someone's pneuma without asking permission," Hoadley breathed through her nose. Her face tightened further. "And secondly what if I don't like it? I'll have paid for something I don't want to eat."

Beaumont cleared his throat. "My treat, a belated welcome to Noxrath and if you hate the food you don't have to eat it."

His chest tightened. What had he done to make her feel welcome? He had been so caught up in his own existential crisis that hadn't done more than say hello and give her some easy cases to get her started. Had anyone else made an effort?

Hoadley gave a short nod and sat there without talking.

The distraction, of a decent platter of seafood, steak, roasted vegetables, and pasta was placed in front of him.

He winced seeing the two small bowls in front of Hoadley. A single portion of rice, greens, some sort of fried protein, and seeds, and a second smaller bowl full of broth. Very healthy. She stared at it and then at his decent-sized platter.

Another heavy exhale and she picked up a fork. Taking a bite she paused, seeming to savour it.

At least she was eating. He was surprised she needed so little. But the reader was never wrong. Look at him, he had a full range of proteins and vegetables. This would at least get him through to afternoon tea, potentially even dinner.

By the time he glanced up again, she had finished her bowl and was sipping from the smaller bowl of broth, watching him.

She would be less stressed if he made this a working lunch.

"What do you think is happening?" asked Beaumont between bites.

"I think your stomach is becoming distended with the amount of food—"

He laughed. "No about the case."

At least she could make a joke.

Hoadley sniffed. "I don't see how it could have happened the way everyone said. If he couldn't have used the illuminier—"

"Another device?"

"I'm dubious about the technology existing. I mean we are talking about a device that not only creates an illusion that you can walk around but that you can touch.

"Okay then if it wasn't a device what do you think it was?" Beaumont used his fork to spear a well-roasted glossy potato.

Her eyes tracked it.

"What?" she asked, blinking and returning her gaze to his face.

"If it wasn't a device then what do you think's happening?"

"If it isn't the device..."

Beaumont ate another potato. Hoadley finished her broth and put the bowl to the side.

"Yes?" he prompted when she didn't resume her sentence.

"I don't know. I don't see how it could have happened the way they say it did."

"Exactly." Beaumont had finished all the protein on the plate and was now working through the vegetables.

"You think they're lying?"

"In short yes. Or at least someone is. We need to check the

statements and map out Overton's movements from them, not the say-so of our prime suspects."

"Is it time yet to go back to The Way and start doing that?"

Beaumont pierced the last vegetable on his platter.

"Yes, let's go." He wiped his mouth and stood.

Something pressed up under his shoe, so he glanced down. He had stepped on someone's pocket watch. He navigated the other diners and reached down to pick it up. A simple brass device. His eyebrows drew together. It wasn't anything particular, but he was sure he had seen it before.

"What's that?" asked Hoadley, peering at it, a scowl on her face.

"Excuse me."

They turned to find one of the servers standing next to them.

"If you're finished..." the server gestured to the line of people waiting for a seat.

Beaumont flushed and nodded.

"Quite right." He turned to Hoadley. "Time to get to it don't you think?"

As they left the restaurant Beaumont could tell Hoadley's energy lifted. The marvels of nutritional food and brisk air.

Beaumont loved this part of town. When he wasn't on duty he often just wandered around, stopping for conversations and the occasional tasty treat. Noxrath wasn't an awful place to be.

He had always been proud of Noxrath and the fact it was a hub of invention and art, but once it had moved one of the larger patent offices here it had really become a place to be. And the increasing number of excellent restaurants was certainly evidence of that.

He just wanted to be free to spend the afternoon here, while away the afternoon with tea and pastries.

But death beckoned.

Beaumont peered over the bobbing top hats of others in search of lunch.

"What are you holding?" she asked.

He blinked, looking down at the pocket watch in his hand.

"Oh, I stepped on it, I probably should have left it with the restaurant." Beaumont's brows gathered together.

Hoadley held out her hand and he dropped it into it. She examined it.

"I've seen this before. When I got Cuthbert's papers, there was a pocket watch, I took it to examine later."

"Are you sure?"

"It was Ancilla's." Hoadley scanned the people pressing around them.

Beaumont frowned. "So how did it end up in the restaurant?"

"She must be here?" said Hoadley, adjusting her bowler so it hid more of her bandage.

Beaumont joined Hoadley in scanning the crowd.

No Ancilla magically appeared.

"Well, I don't know if it matters," said Beaumont.

Hoadley grunted.

A steamer for hire, its available flag fluttering, rolled down the street.

"Come on, we have statements to get through."

He flagged down the steamer and turned to Hoadley, his eyebrows raised.

She gave a short nod but never took her eyes off the crowd as she awkwardly got in.

It took a while to get clear of The Treadway, but eventually the steamer entered Clearwater Way, a long meandering street that hugged one of the wider creeks that fed into the Cimmerian River, which ran like a black blood artery through the city. His neck muscles tightened as they progressed along. He would not miss this drive when he joined Wilhelmina on the mainland.

"Why is it called The Way?" she asked. "The gendarmerie headquarters?"

Beaumont shifted, opening his eyes. "It is the end."

"The end?"

"The end of the Way. People would say, go to the end of the way, and over time it got shortened to The Way."

"That's it."

"Yep," said Beaumont, his hat askew and his blond curls flopped forward. "Sorry, were you expecting something a bit more profound?" He tried to sit up straighter, bring himself in order, but really, he just wanted a nap.

Hoadley gave a bitter smile.

Perhaps she hoped for the way of justice or something more profound. If she was, she wasn't going to find it in Noxrath.

At the end of The Way the gendarmerie headquarters loomed. A huge building, with turrets and ancient archer slits in the walls. Beaumont suspected it had started out life as a base for soldiers. Most likely protecting the inhabitants from threats coming up the Cimmerian River. Now it was a hive of activity of smartly dressed inspectors and guards working hard to protect the people's intellectual property.

Every space inside had a desk, regardless of whether it fit or not, so they had to weave through the rabbit warren to get to the small set of rooms reserved for inspectors investigating the more complex cases, more commonly known as the pen. Death was rare so they usually worked on the sale of counterfeit and unregistered prototypes. A prime inspector could go their whole career without a death case. But not Beaumont. This would be his fifth.

Lucky him.

He suspected that was why Hoadley had asked to work with him. And that he was not living up to her expectations.

"Right," said Beaumont, peering around the room. Empty, most likely everyone was out getting lunch. "Who knows when they'll be back, best not to do it out here. You can work in my office for this one. Grab what you need, and we'll start going through these statements."

Hoadley moved to her desk, opening a drawer and pulling out a small satchel. She filled it with the jotter Beaumont had given her, quills, a quill wiper and some bright inks, though Beaumont was not sure what they were for.

"Hmmm..." She scanned her desk.

"You can come back and get something if you need it," said Beaumont, his eyes wide.

"Yes, of course." She folded the satchel shut but didn't buckle it up.

Standing in Beaumont's doorway she scanned his office.

Beaumont walked past his desk to the other end of the office where cork had been glued to the wall, floor to ceiling and from edge to edge, with millions of tiny little holes peppered in it. A testament to its previous use.

"We'll be using this today." He stroked it. They probably didn't need the desk but he wanted her to feel she was welcome in his space. A small wheel on its side released another partition, the mechanism and brace clicking into place.

"Pop the legs down would you?" Beaumont grabbed a chair tucked in the corner while Hoadley prodded under the desk, releasing two metal poles that clicked into place.

Hoadley stepped back and peered under, pulling the legs down.

Beaumont was rather proud of his desk. It wasn't a patented invention or anything, but he had a friend who liked to tinker and when Beaumont explained what he had in mind had worked hard to make it a reality. Technically he probably shouldn't have altered gendarmerie property, but after so many years sometimes he forgot that the chair and desk didn't belong to him. Even if the gendarmerie would let him take them when he left, his flat wouldn't fit them anyway. Besides, he was going to be travelling, studying painting, not sitting behind a desk pushing papers.

Hoadley carefully placed her satchel on the extension of the desk.

"I..." her gaze took in the desk's position and the corkboard.

Seated, they would both be able to view it. "I don't know what I was expecting but it wasn't that."

Beaumont laughed. "No one does. Shut the door, will you?"

Hoadley took her seat at right angles to him.

He was grateful that the desk was long and wide enough that it didn't feel crowded, but clicked on the fan to at least give them some air movement.

"The statements..." Hoadley pushed back her chair to stand.

Beaumont waved her words away. "I have them." He pulled out a massive pile of folders off the floor and plonked them between them.

"How do we approach this?" she asked.

Beaumont prepared himself for the examination he was going to fail.

"We read them and any sightings of Overton we put up on the board."

"Oh." Her voice dropped low.

Beaumont snorted. "It might not be the glamourous detecting you had envisaged but it's an important part. First, let's map out the space."

Beaumont had enjoyed that afternoon, not that he would admit it if asked. He had loved the board since he first bought it, using it on every case, sometimes even when not needed. To the point, Gordon refused to come into his office.

"For every guest..." Beaumont searched for his bags of tacks in his desk drawer. The last time he had used them they had helped solve one of the darkest cases of his career.

Too late. Small, still bodies hovered at the back of his mind, reminding him that he was no longer of any use, to them or anyone.

The rough fabric of the pin bags scraped against his skin. He focused on his fingers, watching them close carefully over the top of the bag and noting the colours in the drawstring ties. He took his time. Deliberate in his movements until the tremors ceased.

He handed over some of the bags to Hoadley. "Put a tack where they said they were."

Hoadley stood there with her arms crossed. "And if they didn't say anything?"

He massaged his jaw, trying to get it to relax. He admired her intellect but interacting with her was hard work.

"Put them in a follow-up pile. We may need to interview them again." Which should have been obvious. Did she think this was a waste of time? "Do we know if we have the statements of the two guests near Ancilla?"

"I haven't checked."

She had at least taken the bag of tacks.

"Let's keep an eye out for them while we do this." He smiled encouragingly at her, but she just sighed, picking up the first statement.

But regardless of her attitude, she was a decent investigator, and it wasn't long before she had pulled out a jotter and started making notes.

Beaumont picked up some statements as well and started trying to tack them out, when a large exhale distracted him. He turned to find her frowning at the pile of paper in front of her.

"Tea," he said, stretching his arms over his head.

She glanced up. "Tea?"

"Yes, I'm getting some, do you want one?"

As a first, she nodded.

Beaumont tried to stride but it deteriorated to a waddle as his stiff legs and tight back refused to respond.

He was glad he had made them stop for lunch. Her head was probably still throbbing from the hit last night.

The fact she was not asking more questions about her own attack was a surprise. However, the intensity she was putting on the murder investigation did suggest some transference.

His brain was tired from the mill of meaningless words in it, but he delayed his quest for tea to check in with the inspector he had allocated to Hoadley's attack. A mistake. It had just made him thirstier. And annoyed.

From what he had seen the inspector had done very little. No questioning of the guards who had left her alone on the street, no questioning of the Walstrand residence to see if anyone had seen anything. The excuse given was that they didn't want to get in the way of his investigation. His jaw tightened. One of their own had been attacked. They didn't have to like her, but this was not right. He could only hope that his terse, and explicit, instructions got them moving.

Perhaps it was guilt, but he piled all the sweet muffins in the breakroom onto a plate, adding it to the tray along with his refilled perpetual teacup, and a large pot and cup for Hoadley.

He got a few sharp glances as he manoeuvred through the pen with it. He tuned them out. They only had themselves to blame.

"Brains need sugar." He said, putting the plate down between them.

She glanced at them, not moving at first but eventually reaching out, picking up the largest. He smiled.

Beaumont picked one. The first bite flooded his mouth with blackberry and peanut flavours. If he hadn't been at work he would have moaned. He tried to slow himself down, but couldn't take his attention off the muffin and too soon it was finished. He sipped some tea and forced himself to glance away from the remaining ones on the plate.

He peeked at Hoadley expecting her to be watching him, but she was lost in her own thoughts.

"I think..." When she didn't immediately glance up, he cleared his throat to get her attention. "We need to take a systematic approach."

She blinked, examining him. "What were we doing before?"

"Reading them, noting what they said, marking where they were...but we need to consider it from a different angle." He moved the tray, and the muffins, out of the way. "We have four possible sightings of Overton. We need to organise the statements into piles for each of those sightings and then read them together to see what they have in common."

"What kind of things?"

"There is another dimension to this." He started sorting his own statements. "Position?" He glanced at the board.

"Why would that matter?" Hoadley bit into her muffin.

"No one mentioned seeing four versions of Overton at once, did they?" He lent his hand against the cork.

"No," She slumped in her chair, frowning. "He was the man of the hour, if there were multiple versions of him running around, they would have noted that."

"Exactly, so let's see where everyone was when they noticed Zer Overton making his exits."

He handed Hoadley some cards he had in his desk and she carefully labelled them the four Overtons, Veranda, Backstage, Atrium and Gallery. The specific search sped things up and soon, four neat piles were on the desk.

"Now we put it up on the board." Hoadley helped him tack out where everyone was, compared to where they had seen Overton.

They sat back down. Beaumont topped up Hoadley's cup from the teapot, and he reset his own cup, flooding it with hot water.

They gazed at the tacks and names scattered across the surface.

"What are we missing?" he asked.

"Time." Her voice, soft.

He turned and stared at her. She was right. If they accepted that one person couldn't be in the same place at once, then it naturally followed that there was going to be a time difference.

They did have to reread the statements in full. It was difficult. They had to use key events to map out the timeline.

"Not at the same time then," he mumbled, examining the board.

"Tight," said Hoadley.

He poked at the muscles on the side of his neck. She was right. The timing was tight, but possible.

"It would be helpful to know how long Melody sang for," he said.

"One of the guests described it as indeterminable."

A chuckle escaped, surprising him. He suspected Melody would be pleased to know that her performance was so memorable that it became the thing that all others related to.

He wasn't sure how it helped them though.

"We've sightings ranging from right after Melody's performance, to later in the song and some," he exhaled heavily," the one down the centre of the room, happened when the band started playing again, after Melody's performance..."

A fog encompassed his mind. At the end of the day, it was a bunch of words and facts that didn't mean anything. He was just grateful that no one's life was on the line, waiting for him to have a moment of brilliance that was never going to come.

"After this, we'll have to go back to the Atwaters." Hoadley straightened. "I know that they're hiding something behind those walls, I found—"

The door to the office received a sharp tap and opened.

"Lab report, zers." The guard handed over a message.

Beaumont thanked him with a smile. The guard, giving him a small smile in return, closed the door behind him.

"What is it?" asked Hoadley.

Beaumont opened the envelope. He unfolded the report and glanced at it.

He snorted. "An update about nothing."

"Nothing?" Hoadley glared at the paper. "Why would they send a report about nothing?" She transferred the scowl to his direction, like somehow it was his fault.

"Perhaps to remind us they are working on it?"

"Why wouldn't they be working on it?" her scowl deepened.

Beaumont manipulated the muscles in his jaw. He was doing a lot of that lately.

"They're, they just want to..." air hissed out between his teeth. "Never mind, let's just focus on this."

"Shouldn't we follow up on the lab?"

"Of course, we'll visit them next, but first..." he gestured to the board.

She grunted. They did, however, get back to work.

A plate of crumbs was all that remained of the muffins and there had been at least two trips to the bathroom. He might love tea, but his bladder wasn't as much of a fan. He couldn't remember Hoadley going through which was slightly concerning. Admittedly she hadn't had as much tea as he had, but still.

"That's it." Hoadley stretched her arms, with crackles and pops, towards the ceiling,

"No more statements?" he gazed down at the desk, but she was right, all statements had been sorted and cards created for them. Only a handful didn't have anything useful in them.

Hoadley shook her head, leaning against the desk, her arms crossed. "Backstage first."

"Yes..." Beaumont scanned the board. "The outside,

argument with Cuthbert..." He pushed off the desk and stood, his hands on his hips. "Then back into the ballroom..." He glanced back at Hoadley who stayed where she was.

It was interesting. He didn't know if she was doing it deliberately or if it was just who she was. It actually took a lot of effort not to follow the physical cues of others.

"Atrium, an argument with Melody."

He turned back to the board.

"Then back to the ballroom, and down the middle," he shuffled up to the board and ran his hand across the majority of the cards, "to be seen by almost everyone, through the gallery back to the library."

"It's not possible," she said.

"But it happened." Beaumont shrugged, frowning.

"How?"

"There are a few options. One, there's a device we aren't aware of, Two, everyone is lying. Or three, they were all hallucinating." He tilted his head, examining the board. "Of course, there might be a fourth, but I can't think of it right now."

"I'd start with everyone's lying...but the statements..."

"Hmm, yes." Beaumont examined the board. "If they are lying, they are all doing it very convincingly. No two stories the same, everyone noticing different things."

"What about the hallucination? I mean what if the device that does the chair and table etc, what if it doesn't work and the whole thing is a hallucination?"

"What for?"

"The bill, they are running out of time to have it registered before the inheritance laws for patents change so everyone is in a mad scramble to have theirs registered. Maybe they wanted to register it before it was actually finished?"

Beaumont flashed Hoadley a grin. "Now that's fine thinking." He stared at the corkboard. "We have to assume, for now, that the patent office would have checked the prototype as well...but don't discard that thought." He contemplated the board. "We also need to know if he was drugged."

Hoadley blinked at him. "What does it matter?"

Beaumont's head tilted in her direction. "What do you mean?"

"What does it matter if he was drugged or not? We know someone smothered him."

"True, but if he was unconscious, it changes who could do it. He didn't struggle, we need to know why."

"He wasn't a small man," she drummed her fingers on the desk edge. "An artist, very fit."

"Exactly. So, he what? Lay there waiting to be suffocated?"

"He did spill his drink."

"I would expect a lot more than that, a scratch, a whack...something."

They both stood there staring at the impossible wall.

"Okay..." Beaumont turned towards her. "We're pretty sure there weren't two versions of him in the room at the same time."

Hoadley gave a short nod. "And we know that he died by being smothered with no defensive wounds."

Pipe it. This case would never end.

They both turned and stared at the board for a while longer.

Lavina Hoadley, Inspector

Noxrath Gendarmerie

Great Espya

We stopped at the lab first. The technicians once more draped over their benches, napping.

"It was like that this morning," I scanned the room, my lips tightening.

"They did an all-nighter." He smiled at me and turned back to the room. "Hello, lab people." Beaumont stepped forward, projecting his voice to the very ends of the room, throwing his arms wide like he was giving a massive group hug.

Several people jumped, and those asleep jolted awake, blinking at him in confusion.

"What's happening?" one of them asked.

The same lab tech I had spoken to that morning came over to us.

"She's back...and she's brought a friend."

Beaumont grinned. "Timothy, my dear fellow it's always a delight to see you."

"Wish I could say the same Beaumont. Why is it that whenever you're involved, I don't get any sleep?"

"How can I help it if you're tossing and turning with dreams of me?"

Timothy snorted. "In *your* dreams." His eyes flicked to me. "She works with you uh?"

"Yes, this is our new Inspector Hoadley who has the rare privilege of being assigned to me."

Timothy glanced at me with what appeared to be sympathy. "Sorry for your pain."

Considering I had asked to be assigned to work with Beaumont, it seemed churlish to acknowledge the comment.

"Timothy..." Beaumont said, smiling again. "What do you have for us?"

Timothy scowled at Beaumont.

"As I told Hoadley here this morning, some tests take time, and it doesn't change how long that time takes with people like you coming around asking—"

"Now now, no need to get upset," Beaumont made soothing noises, but Timothy didn't appear to be mollified.

"Timothy..." another lab tech came up besides us.

"Not now Joan," he said. "Now look here Beaumont. This might be amusing to you and your inspector, but you aren't the only inspectors we're doing tests for, and we've wasted more time—"

"Timothy..." The tech tapped his elbow.

"Answering your questions about how long it will take, rather than actually doing the tests—"

"We need to know if Overton was drugged," said Beaumont, his voice soft and low.

"And that test takes time, I told you—"

"Timothy..." Joan pulled at the back of his sleeve.

"What?" Timothy glared at her.

"The test results are in." She handed him a report, wandering away, until she found a stool where she sat, leaning against the wall behind it and closing her eyes.

Exactly what did these tests entail?

"Is she okay?" I asked.

Timothy glanced up from the results in his hands and followed my gaze. "Yes, she's fine...tired. As we all are." He flipped through the notes in his hands. "Huh."

I wanted to reach over and rip them out of his hands. The only thing that stopped me was I wasn't sure if I would understand them.

"Huh?" asked Beaumont, perching on a stool, his eyes bright, watching Timothy's fingers stroke the pages of the report.

"Hmmm...," said Timothy. He reread the first page.

Beaumont's leg started to swing, the only sign that he wasn't perfectly willing to sit there all day watching Timothy read.

"Any thoughts you would like to share?" I couldn't help myself. Beaumont flicked an amused glance my way.

"Yeah..." Timothy continued to reread the entire report.

I took a seat, making sure to put Beaumont between me and the annoying Timothy.

"Tim." Beaumont's voice was soft.

Timothy blinked at him. "Sorry, it's..." he stared at the report, shaking himself. "It doesn't make sense."

Beaumont held out his hand and Timothy passed the report over to him. Beaumont flipped through it and then shrugged, handing it to me.

Some of the substances had names next to them.

"What are the unlabelled ones?" I asked.

Timothy rolled his eyes. "We don't know, they are quantities of something, we just aren't sure what." He flicked a glance at Beaumont, but Beaumont didn't engage. "Which is why they are unlabelled."

Beaumont sat there frowning at the report in my hands.

"Even if you don't know what the substances are, what type or what are they related to or similar to?" I asked.

Timothy slumped into a seat. "Fair questions." He rubbed the side of his face. "Okay, there are two main things that report shows." He stretched his neck side to side, and I was pretty sure I heard a crack. "One that he has been dead for about three days, and two that an unknown or unregistered substance was in his system."

I don't remember Beaumont, or I, saying anything for a while.

"Three days," said Beaumont.

"How can you be sure?" I asked.

"The chemical makeup in the blood contains certain structures that take time to break down."

"Could the unknown chemicals cause that change?" asked Beaumont.

Timothy frowned. "No. While we don't know exactly what they are we can tell that they most likely belong to a sedative family."

"What about the state of the body?" I leant forward. "How could Dr Morten miss that she had a three-day-old body rather than a body of only a few hours?"

"The body could have been preserved in stasis. All designed to confuse." He straightened. "But blood will tell all, and you can't hide the degeneration of key structures once the heart stops pumping." He shrugged. "To be honest if this hadn't been such a strange death, we might not have done the in-depth tests and never would have known."

"Too clever."

I glanced at Beaumont, "What do you mean?"

"They're trying to be too clever, to confuse the issue, but instead giving us more information." Beaumont made a few notes in his jotter. "Timothy, I need to know what those substances are, or at least what the effects of them are. I need to know if Overton was conscious when he died. Also, I'll need to contact Dr Morten and discuss this with her. No disrespect, but I want her to verify your findings."

"Fair enough," said Timothy.

I handed the report back to him.

"What now?" I asked Beaumont, lost amongst all the inconsistencies and information we had on the case.

"What happened three nights before?" asked Beaumont.

My eyes widened. "Cuthbert stole Overton's money."

"Yes, he did," said Beaumont, straightening, his feet planted shoulder's width apart. Apparently, he had joined the investigation.

13

Family Closes In

Ancilla came to the conclusion that Ernest must hate fresh air. The warm bodies in the living room amplified the stale air's mustiness.

Curled up in her usual spot next to the window, Ancilla cracked it open to let a slither of fresh air through. She adjusted her shawl to protect her skin against the icy afternoon air while breathing it in deeply.

"I can feel a draft," said Melody.

Of course, she could. Melody, like their father, could feel a draft at the other end of the house if even a slither of a window was open.

"Can you?" asked Ancilla, glancing around the room, ostensibly in search of one.

"Yes," Melody didn't look up from her own favourite seat

at the desk, surrounded by the household ledgers. "Check that window near you will you?"

Ancilla exhaled. It wasn't worth the drama. She pretended to check all the windows near her, disguising the closing of her small rebellion.

Ernest was at the piano practising. He didn't have enough pneuma control to ever be a real artist but his thirty minutes a day routine had resulted in some skills. Which was more than Ancilla could say about Melody's singing.

"Best have Roger check all the windows," said Ernest, raising his voice over his playing. He had chosen a rather robust piece tonight with lots of crescendo and Ancilla had found her heart rate increasing and her shoulders tensing at certain passages. She wished he took requests and would play something a bit more soothing.

Ancilla hummed an acknowledgement and went back to the book in her hand. Not that she could concentrate with the death and deception of her real life being so much more dramatic than anything an author could think of in a book.

But she needed to let her brain rest. She had a long night ahead and if she could have forced herself to sleep she would have. Instead, a book would have to do.

Thud. Thud. Bang. Thud. Thud.

The door to the living room crashed back into the wall. The piano music stopped, and they all turned.

Cuthbert stood in the doorway, his hair jutting out all over the place, the victim of rough hands, his cravat askew and a newspaper held high, being shaken at them.

"Did you know about this?" he asked, his voice ricocheted

around the room. Ancilla's muscles clenched and she forced herself to stay still.

The newspaper fluttered and small tears appeared where his fingers tightened.

"Today's newspaper is filled with many things Cuthbert." Ernest dropped his hands into his lap but didn't get up from in front of the piano. "What specifically are you seeking to know?"

Cuthbert unfolded it. His hands shaking, it took him a couple of goes to get it open.

"Noxrath is delighted to find that one of the top ten up-and-coming poets of Great Espya is a Noxrath local. Poetry, an art form that hasn't had much attention lately, is having a resurgence, all due to these amazing new artists who are bringing a fresh influence into today's poetry. And none more than our very own Roger Latimer, twenty-eight years old, and a resident in domestic service, for now, in Villiside and being mentored by Noxrath's oldest living poet, Hepzibah Hawkes."

The paper crumbled in Cuthbert's fists and more small tears appeared.

Go Roger.

Ancilla blinked and tried to keep her face as empty as possible. Not that it mattered as Cuthbert was glaring at Ernest. Perhaps if she was quiet she could exit without anyone noticing? Melody glanced at the doorway closest to her, probably thinking the same thing.

"Well..." Ernest frowned. "No I didn't know, but I'm impress—"

"It gives an example of one of his poems." Cuthbert shook the now bedraggled newspaper above his head. "It's absolute...twaddle. The most banal kind of poetry ever. How did he..." Cuthbert started pacing, throwing down the newspaper and burying both his hands in his hair.

Ernest rose. "Let's ask shall we?" He walked over to the cord that connected to a bell in the kitchen.

Roger had finally fixed his shoes and found a comb for his hair. But his eyes were still bloodshot, evidence of a party last night perhaps.

"Yes, zer?" asked Roger as he shuffled into the room. His gaze was disinterested as he took them all in but settled on Ernest with at least the resemblance of curiosity in his expression.

"I understand congratulations are in order Roger?" asked Ernest.

Roger blinked and peered around the room, his gaze dropping to the poorly treated newspaper. His jaw tightened and he raised his gaze to Ernest's.

"Thank you," he said.

Ancilla thought he might have been about to say more but his lips firmed, fusing together.

"You'll have to let me sponsor you," said Ernest, taking a step forward. "It would look pretty damaging for me not to take an interest in a poet working in my own household."

Cuthbert and Roger paled.

"No need zer," said Roger.

"What I want to know," Cuthbert's voice trembled, "is exactly how *Roger* came to be mentored by Hepzibah Hawkes?"

Ernest's forehead creased and he examined Roger. "If my memory serves me correctly, I sent you to deliver Cuthbert's regrets."

"Yes, zer." Roger examined them all and shrugged. "We got to talking and she was of a mind to share."

Well, that explained all the late nights.

Cuthbert's neck had gone a dark red and the muscles on the side flexed.

"Enterprising." Ernest nodded, his expression pleased. "I admire your—"

"Are you kidding me?" Cuthbert grabbed the back of an armchair, shaking it sending it clattering in confusion.

Ernest flicked him a glance. "You only have yourself to blame for this."

"I'm the poet in this household." Cuthbert's hand tightened and metal groaned. "I—"

Ernest held up his hand. "You have wasted every opportunity. Meanwhile Roger," Ernest bestowed a warm smile on him. "Here has worked hard and taken opportunities when they came. You could learn something from him."

Roger huffed out a short breath. "Thank you, zer."

"Father..." Melody glared at him.

Ancilla was surprised that Melody bothered but a glance at Cuthbert showed that he didn't appear to be breathing, going an unpleasant mix of red and blue. Perhaps she was right to intervene.

"Finally," Ernest rubbed his hands together. "Finally an artist in the household." He strode over to Roger and dropped his hand on his shoulder. "I won't lie, I thought it would be one of my children but that doesn't mean we can't make something of this."

Roger shuffled back a few steps, his eyes wide. "That's not necessary, zer."

"Nonsense, I need an artist to gain access...to be a part of certain gatherings, and you need money." Ernest smiled at Roger.

It was the most excited that Ancilla had seen him in a long time. Roger's face however did not express anywhere near the level of excitement.

"Not really, zer—"

Ernest frowned. "I'll have you remember the latitude I've allowed you in the deliverance of your duties, not to mention the introduction to your mentor."

Ancilla was always impressed with Ernest's ability to re-write a situation so quickly and so thoroughly, but this was another level.

The armchair screeched as Cuthbert flung it away from him.

"I'm not staying and listening to this *steamless pipe*." Cuthbert stormed over to the doorway to the living room. "I expect dinner to be served in one hour, I'll take a tray in my room." Cuthbert's mouth opened and closed before he spun away. The thud of his footsteps running up the stairs to his room shook the house.

Ancilla wished, for his sake, that he had been able to think of something witty to say.

Ernest scowled at the empty doorway. "Never mind that," he turned to Roger, "I want you to know that I consider you practically part of the family and I think that what we should do—"

"No, zer." Roger straightened, his shoulders back.

Melody chuckled. Ancilla glanced to find her sitting back her fingers clasped in front of her, her eyes bright. Now Cuthbert was gone she appeared happy to enjoy the drama.

Ancilla was glad it was all so amusing for her. Personally, she suspected that the end result was no dinner tonight.

"What do you mean no?" Ernest glared at Roger. "I made you—"

"No, you didn't." Roger's feet widened to just under his shoulders, his weight forward. "You, none of you," his glance took in Ancilla and Melody, "did anything for me."

"We gave you employment," snarled Ernest, "a roof over your head—"

"You didn't give me anything. We had a contract for an exchange of services." Roger's lips thinned. "A contract that is at the end."

Ernest's eyes narrowed to slits. "You can't just quit, what will that look like?"

Roger glared at him. "Honestly? I don't care."

"Don't expect a reference from me." Ernest's face hardened. "And don't expect to sleep here tonight, or ever again."

Roger jerked his head and strode towards the door. He swung back to them when he reached the doorway, focusing on Ancilla and Melody.

"It started well, Kindness meant, But time palls, Ruining intent, Now it is a cage, Trapped and discontent, Fare thee well, And freedom from what is bent."

His pneuma-infused tones were powerful and in that moment Ancilla had no doubt that he would make it. She also suspected that Ernest, and Cuthbert, would appear, most likely as villains, in a lot of future work. Don't annoy the writers.

And what exactly did he mean by what is bent?

Time to find Marcellus. Even without dinner.

She sealed her room behind her and fitted a small selection of wires that reinforced the lock. It wasn't as effective as sealing it from the inside, but no one would be able to enter without breaking the lock.

The house was in mourning. They must have all adapted as Roger's pneuma control grew, his core, like Marcellus', had become stronger. Infusing the house, like a faint comforting background hum. And now it was gone.

Without turning the lights on, the glow of the moon and streetlamps allowed her to navigate the stairs. The moon was waxing and drenched the sculptures in the garden in silver. Ancilla let her feet roll, reducing the crunch of the gravel under them as she navigated the sculptures.

The octopus' tentacles beckoned her. Detouring she took the time to tap the two that had broken free a hello. She liked to think it knew she was cheering it on.

She lifted the gate as she swung it open, reducing its squeak and stepped out onto a strangely quiet street. After the bustle of the day, she would have expected to find people roaming but perhaps everyone had gone home for dinner.

The only steamer she could see was already taken. The

occupants stared at her, but she wasn't going to pinch their ride. She strode down the street until she was at the corner, just as a steamer for hire drove past.

A sign that her luck was with her tonight.

The driver pulled over.

"Evening, zer." He touched the rim of his hat and she touched hers in return.

"Evening, heading to the Purple Door, Southside."

He peered at her. "The Purple Door?"

"Yes." She gave a short nod, her face still. She shoved her fingers in her pockets to hide their tremble.

"Rightio."

She scrambled onto the steamer and settled in, her muscles relaxing.

The steamer itself was clean, but the top was down. Which was fine while they were in the northside of Noxrath but as soon as they crossed the bridge, they lost the protection of Mount Nox, exposing her to the southerly gale. She almost lost her hat.

Everyone she had ever met from Southside was fiercely proud of this section of town. She was aware that some great physical art had come out of there in recent years and the wind walls, an attempt to buffer the winds sweeping across the plains while they worked on regrowing the forest, were a marvel. But other than that, as far as she could ascertain, it was just an extremely windswept part of the city. The same as any other, though perhaps less comfortable, and hard on hats.

The steamer pulled up in front of a dark alley. The

streetlamps lacked the well-cared-for glow she was used to, lengthening the shadows that reached towards her.

"The Purple Door," he stated.

The other side of the street was busy with people flowing in and out of buildings. Her stomach rumbled, reminding her that she had missed dinner.

Later.

She handed over a few coins and scrambled out, glancing around. No purple doors or entrances magically appeared, and she turned back to the driver.

"Where—"

He screeched a sharp U-turn, and she was addressing her question to the back of him.

Pipe it. She would find it herself then.

The sharp odour of urine from the alleyway suggested what it was usually used for. That was something that would never happen on the northside.

She shivered, glancing around. For a moment it seemed like she was on her own.

A scrape in the alley caused her to turn and peer down it. She imagined she could make out two tall shapes. The southside had a reputation for some unsavoury types, but she hadn't expected the actual streets to be unsafe, just her money at the gambling tables.

The shapes moved, the scraping sound louder.

The clatter of a steamer pulling up next to her started her breathing again. A couple alighted and she smiled and nodded a friendly greeting at them. They gave awkward smiles back and turned away.

Breathing in the shadows of the alley propelled her forward and she followed her new best friends across the road into the streetlamp's circle of light.

She saw purple.

14

Beaumont Gambles

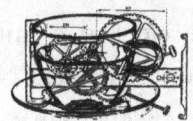

Beaumont's stomach had rumbled. Time had been ticking away and he had calculated that it had been now almost five hours, forty minutes and three seconds since his last meal. He remembered it particularly because he had contemplated whether the muffins counted, but in the end decided they didn't.

"Dinner first," he had said.

"What?" Hoadley stared at him, her eyes wide. "But we need to..."

Her bandage had mocked him from under her bowler. He had known that even if he could have gone without food, she needed a rest. Not that she would admit it.

"We need food. We're already working on limited sleep, if you take away food as well...what's left?"

"People focused on finding a killer?"

Beaumont shook his head. "You'd think that. But what you actually have is a couple of useless people wandering around staring at things blankly, missing clues and saying things like, *this is impossible, no one could solve this*, when what they really mean is they are too tired, and their brain isn't working."

He hailed a steamer. It didn't slow down.

"Now's the time to use the—"

"The last thing we want to do is use a gendarmerie steamer. We would be clocked a mile away. No, let's not frighten people." He glanced at her, "Not yet."

It had taken him a few goes but eventually one stopped, and they were off, leaving the more comfortable parts of Noxrath behind.

"How much of Noxrath have you explored?" he asked.

"Not much," she said.

He waited for her to offer more detail, but none came.

"Did you know that Noxrath was originally two cities? Nox on the north of Mount Nox and Wildia on the south of the mountain?"

"Yes."

Something was up, but the truth was he didn't have it in him to unpack what was going on in her head.

"Wildia originally had a large forest next to it but over the years the land had been cleared, leaving it exposed to the strong winds that wrapped around the mountain. It became referred to as Nox's wrath and when the two towns expanded and combined the name was shortened to Noxrath and stuck."

He peered at her, waiting to see if she would add anything.

"My hometown was called Solverde, it was green."

He blinked. Well, it was something.

She pulled her coat closer around her and grabbed a hold of her bowler as the protection of Mount Nox disappeared.

"Where first?" she asked.

"The southside might be considered a bit on the uncouth side but there is some amazing food down here. Plus, if we are seen dining and then wandering into a club later it will look like we are enjoying a night out."

She gave a jerky nod.

The steamer pulled over next to their restaurant and he climbed out, careful not to do any sharp movements. Hoadley followed, her glare drilling into his back.

Food would help.

This time the unmarked door led to a large room full of curved booths, comfortable for two people but could sit four at a pinch. Beaumont spotted a free one at the back and made his way to it.

"Is this another one where they read what you need?" She asked, scanning the table for the pneuma reader.

"No," Beaumont smiled as a server came up to the table and handed us two large menus.

"Any drinks?""

"Water for me," she said.

"And two of your special teas please," said Beaumont.

The server smiled and nodded and disappeared.

"Special tea?" Her arms clamped tight against her body.

"Don't worry, it is a herbal blend, nothing dangerous it in but they only make it here. Very tasty."

"You don't know what is in it?" Her scowl deepened.

Beaumont shrugged. "Not specifically but I know it is nothing illegal. I do ask a few questions before I taste things marked "special"." He laughed.

Hoadley did not appear to be convinced.

The server returned with a pot of tea and two cups.

"Ready to order?"

Beaumont flicked a glance at her, and she nodded.

"Yes, we are..." Beaumont hadn't even opened the menu. "I'll have the chef's soup and..." He glanced at Hoadley.

"The fish and greens please."

The server nodded but didn't write anything down. Hoadley frowned.

"He'll remember," said Beaumont.

She glanced at him and tried to smooth the frown off her face. "Yes of course."

He suppressed a smile. The butter sauce on the fish she ordered was tasty enough to make anyone's day.

His own day was made when a bowl filled to the brim with chunks of meat and vegetables with bread on the side was placed in front of him.

"That...that's impressive." Hoadley's eye widened as she stared at his soup.

Beaumont beamed.

"The soup itself is different every time but I have never had a bad one yet." He took a mouthful. "Hmm...another amazing one."

"Will you be able to walk after that gallon of soup and loaf of bread?" she drawled.

He grinned back at her. "I'll waddle through." His eyes dropped to the plate being placed in front of her. It smelt amazing.

Her eyes closed as she tasted a small piece of fish, covered in its silky-smooth butter sauce.

He forced himself to eat slowly as he worked his way through the meal. Savouring each bite. When he finished it was to find her sipping her tea, watching him.

"Are you ready to go?" She glanced down at her empty plate. "We do have an investigation to finish."

"Right you are." He folded his napkin placing it to the side and her scowl lightened, until she glanced down at the plate again, going pale.

"What's wrong?" he asked.

"Nothing," She tried to smile at him. "Can we go?"

He nodded and stood. Immediately the server appeared.

"Leaving, zer?"

"Yes, we need to pay."

Hoadley shifted next to him, tension radiating off her.

"Yes, this way."

They stepped out of the booth and Beaumont leaned over towards her.

"I think we can call this a working dinner, so I'll settle here and claim it back."

She nodded, and let out a breath, her shoulders relaxing.

"Where's this club?" she asked.

"Only a couple of blocks from here. Keep close to the

side of the buildings and we should be able to make it there easily."

She did better than that, she kept close to the buildings, and his larger frame was between her and the winds. He supposed that there had to be some advantages to being smaller.

The wind made his eyes water, and the pale, ill-maintained streetlamps made navigating difficult. He stopped, scaping his hand against the wall.

A scuffle of footsteps made him glance over his shoulder at Hoadley, who was gripping the wall to avoid crashing into him.

"We're here." He stepped up into the sheltered entrance of an extremely elegant home. Its dark stone exterior and amaranthine door with vintage gold edging, a beacon.

The guard on the door nodded at Beaumont but scanned Hoadley suspiciously as she walked past.

"Hurry up, I don't want to miss my luck," said Beaumont. She lengthened her stride, and the guard went back to staring into the street.

Beaumont frowned at her. "You need to loosen up a bit."

"I am loose."

"No, I mean your body language, it comes across as...disapproving."

"This is me, relaxed." She crossed her arms in front of her.

He examined her. "Pretend you are having another amazing meal."

She rolled her eyes.

"Okay okay, but just so you know I am going to introduce

you as my disapproving sister who is here to make sure I don't gamble away the family fortune."

"Fine," said Hoadley, her smile bemused.

His heart lifted. If he was going to investigate the case, he might as well have tasty food and a bit of fun while he did it. With a little hop in his step, Beaumont explored the room, with Hoadley following, disapprovingly.

Lavina Hoadley, Inspector,
Noxrath Gendarmerie
Great Espya

What was once the ballroom of a grand house was now a gambler's paradise. The long room's walls were decorated with large murals of food and wine framed in gold and a series of tables, covered in green velvet and scattered through the hall, surrounded by people, leaning forward in their chairs, their attention captured by the games in front of them. In the middle of all this was a long table with an enormous wheel spinning. There were no chairs at this table, and people crowded forward watching every move of a small golden ball as it danced across the wheel.

"Now what is she doing here?" Beaumont was standing off to the side gazing at one of the players.

I followed his gaze to see Ancilla Walstrand.

Beaumont headed in her direction. Considering his concern about keeping a low profile I wasn't sure that was the best option for us, but I followed. He squeezed in next to her.

"All on the orange huh?" Reaching out he put a pile of coins, I wasn't sure where they came from, on the purple. "Bold considering purple is the best."

Ancilla, in a display of good sense, ignored him except to put another coin on orange. She might've been sticking her nose where it didn't belong, but you had to give her points for style.

"Are you going to play?" I blinked, peering at the man next to me. His waistcoat was a beautiful golden satin but without any of the usual patterns or clockwork inlays.

"Play?"

The man gestured to the table. "If you are going to stand here you need to play or let someone else join." I glanced behind me, at the row of people waiting for their turn to lose money.

I sighed and reached into my pocket pulling out one of my hard-earned coins, putting it down on orange thirteen. Orange because there was no way I was going purple, and thirteen...well, if I did believe in luck then thirteen would be my lucky number.

"Happy?"

The man snorted and went back to minding his own business. The croupier called for final bets.

Beaumont was leaning close to Ancilla, his voice too soft for me to make out what he was saying.

The wheel spun and I paid attention to it for the first time. I feel strange for saying this about a gambling device, but it was a thing of beauty. It took up a whole third of the table. The wheel was flat but protected from grubby hands by a wall of fine pipes. The people standing near them could easily see through to what was happening, but the little bursts of flame that popped along them made it clear that getting too close was not going to be pleasant.

The wheel itself was made out of a dark black stone and the alternating orange and purple was framed in brass. A woman's hand gripped the wheel's edge, sending it into a spin.

"Bets are now closed," said the croupier, her voice ringing around the table. Synchronised, everyone leaned towards her, their eyes tracking the small ball dropping from her hand like a shooting star and whipping through the dimensions of chance.

The ball rattled in its final bed, mocking me. I blinked not sure what I was meant to do. The man next to me thumped my back and Beaumont smiled at me.

"I'm pretty sure that means you buy the drinks," said Beaumont.

With only one coin on, I wasn't instantly wealthy, but the long odds meant I was able to pocket enough to cover three people's drinks and tomorrow's meals. Ancilla had a modest increase in her coins as well, with only Beaumont losing his bet. Which I am ashamed to say for some reason added to my win.

"Congratulations," said Ancilla smiling directly at me for the first time. I did not return it but collected my winnings and gestured for her to follow Beaumont. He led the way up onto a balcony with a small bar and a few high tables and stools to sit on. It was also an excellent spot for keeping an eye on the people below.

I left them to find a table and moved to the bar.

"What do you want?" the man behind the bar didn't glance up from the glasses he was arranging. He was dressed in the house uniform same as the security on the door. There didn't appear to be any menu.

"Three whiskies."

I figured if I was buying, I didn't have to waste time asking people questions and if they didn't want it, that wasn't my problem.

Note that I was not at any point planning on drinking all three whiskies while I was on duty.

The server grunted and moved to a series of shelves of liquor at the back of the small space.

Three generous glasses of amber liquid were plunked down in front of me, and I paid, barely getting out a thank you before the server moved on to a couple who had just arrived.

I joined Ancilla and Beaumont, putting the three drinks on the table.

"Whisky?" asked Beaumont smiling. "I wouldn't have guessed. An excellent choice." He picked up his glass and held it aloft. I'll admit that I did have a momentary impulse to leave him there, holding his arm up, waiting for others to join. Instead, I gave into the social pressure and picked up my glass and clinked his, and Ancilla's, whose was already there.

I took a sip, examining her.

"You're a fool to come here alone," I said.

Her eyes widened and she took a gulp of the whisky without flinching. "No bigger fool than sitting around the house waiting for someone else to solve this."

My eyes narrowed.

"Hoadley..." said Beaumont, drawing out my name.

"Yes, zer?"

He shook his head and turned his attention back to Ancilla.

"While Inspector Hoadley could perhaps deliver her observations with more tact. The realities are, Zer Walstrand, that she's correct. But perhaps we are being presumptuous, are you here on your own?" He smiled warmly at her, inviting her to share all her thoughts and confidences.

A rush of colour ran across Ancilla's cheeks and disappeared again.

"Technically?"

Beaumont blinked. "Yes...technically."

"Then yes." She turned her attention back to me. "I can take care of myself."

"I'm sure." I would like to think my expression was neutral, but even I could hear the doubt in my tone.

"Of course," said Beaumont. "But even the most capable of people can still be hit on the back of the head. That's why we," he gave an unnecessary gesture towards me, "travel in teams of two. You need someone at your back."

I took a deep sip of my whisky. *Great.* Thanks, Beaumont, for reminding me of my own incompetence.

Beaumont tilted his head "And to hold the table while you get the whisky."

I peered at his glass. He had emptied it, as had Ancilla. I gazed down at my own half-finished glass.

"I'll get the next round," said Beaumont, slipping away to join a queue at the bar.

Still smarting over the back of the head blow comment I stared down at my drink.

"Do you think Cuthbert is capable of killing someone?" she asked.

"I cannot comment on—"

She raised her hand. "Sorry, it was a silly question."

Yes, it had been.

Apparently, Beaumont's charm extended to bartenders as he returned with another round despite the queue not moving. Either that or he didn't want to leave me alone too long.

"Here you go."

I took my drink and gazed down at my two glasses. I wasn't going to knock back what was left in my first glass, so I set the second to the side for now.

"Ancilla was asking if we thought Cuthbert could have killed Overton," I said.

Ancilla choked on her drink, and Beaumont's eyebrows headed skyward.

"Did she now?" he peered at her. "I hope you told her that we can't give that kind of information out during an active investigation?"

Ancilla coughed, her eyes, red and watery.

"I think the question for Zer Walstrand, is what she hopes to gain by being here tonight?" I frowned at her.

Beaumont blinked but kept a close eye on Ancilla.

"I want to know." Ancilla swallowed some more whisky. This time without choking. "I want this resolved so I can get on with my life and not have to spend every minute of every day wondering if one of my family killed a great man."

"Was he though? Great I mean?" asked Beaumont.

I shot him a glare. "He was the greatest illuminator of our time," I said.

People flowed from table to table. All placing small bets, entertainment, nothing serious. I was contemplating how Cuthbert could have lost so much money he needed to kill for it when a door to the right of the roulette table opened and for a moment, the corner of a large room with a card table and people around it was visible.

"He was...intense...confident...believed he could do any-thing."

I snorted. "He could, he had enough money and status to—"

An older gentleman appeared, decked out in a waistcoat made of ribbons shifting to form, and un-form, a suit of cards, changing colour to match. It was a work of art. He scanned the room and kept moving. I lost sight of him.

"No, no I mean he...believed everything was just a matter of time and effort." She laughed. "Sorry, I'm explaining this poorly."

Beaumont stared at her. "We have witnesses who heard him arguing with Cuthbert, and he was bribing the house manager to hide his drinking." He shook his head. "Is this the same man you have described?"

"Oh, he was no saint." Ancilla's lips thinned. She finished her second drink. "Are you even here investigating anything? Or is this where the two of you come to escape?"

"I'm fully aware that he wasn't a saint..." Beaumont finished off his own whisky. "What I'm trying to—"

"Excuse me?"

We all turned to find that an elderly gentleman had taken a seat at the table behind us.

"Yes?" I asked.

"Your friends seem to be about to have a bit of a lover's quarrel and I was wondering if you would like to have a drink with me? While they finish?" He smiled at me.

I blinked. The ribbon waistcoat. How had he gotten up here? I froze. I will admit I did not, at that moment, know what the best course of action was.

Beaumont frowned. "That won't be—"

I had just seen him come out of that room. Maybe that was where Cuthbert built his debt.

"Thank you. It is always boring to not be part of the discussion." I turned towards him. "Call me Lavina."

The gentleman's smile broadened, "Lavina, it's a pleasure to meet you. I'm Perry." He held his hand out to me, and I reached out and shook it. I was careful to ensure that my pneuma was closed to all but my own vibration. Not that I thought he was an immediate threat, but it is always better safe than sorry.

I stared at him. "Thank you."

"Whisky, hey. Would you care of another?"

I held up my still half-full glass but shifted, joining him at his table. Beaumont grumbled, but I tuned him out. Perry smiled, ordering his own. I noted that he didn't need to go to the bar. He gestured, and the drink was delivered. Well known, then.

"What do you think of our small little patch of paradise?" Perry asked, sweeping out his hand to take in the floor below us.

I took my time, scanning each table before turning back to him and shrugging. "It's nice. I had a bit of a win before which always makes you feel a lot warmer towards a place."

It was his turn to laugh. "Yes indeed." His smile dimmed a little and he scanned the bustling floor. "But you aren't loving it?"

I tilted my head. "It is...very wholesome."

He faked a strike at the heart. "Wholesome? You cut me to the core. We are more than that I promise." He leaned forward and dropped his voice. "We are dark and dangerous as well."

I shrugged. "If you say so."

His smile slipped a little more.

"To be honest I didn't want to come here tonight. I'm..." I jerked a thumb over to Beaumont and Ancilla, who would not be earning actor awards, eavesdropping.

He grinned, glancing over at them.

"It seems we have distracted them. Perhaps we should leave them to it. Would you like to join me at one of the...less wholesome tables?"

I scanned him up and down and tilted my head. "Why not?" I knocked back my drink. Perhaps this whole evening wasn't going to be a complete waste after all.

Beaumont's glare pierced my back, and by the look on Perry's face, he found it amusing.

If Beaumont was any kind of Prime Inspector, he would have read my file when I was assigned to him and known that I could handle myself.

Perry waited for me, offering his arm. "I don't think your friend is very happy about you leaving with me."

"I can look after myself."

Perry grinned. "Maybe he is worried for me?"

"Possibly." The smile I gave was sharp. He squirmed with excitement. Gamblers. I tried not to let my disgust show.

The door opened as he approached which meant either it was automatic and set to recognise certain clientele, or someone was watching, which was my bet. My guess was rewarded when a large woman in a gold outfit, which she managed to make severe, greeted us. Perry received a nod, but she examined me thoroughly. I returned the favour.

"Perry, no guests."

"Now now, she won't be staying long I want to show her where the real stuff happens. She was finding our normal play a bit wholesome."

"Humprhf."

"She can be my lucky charm." He grinned at the watcher.

"Fine."

"Lucky charm?" I raised one of my eyebrows at him.

"Everyone is allowed to bring their lucky charms."

"Even if they are living beings?"

"Oh yes. It caused quite a confuffle when George decided that his snake was his. A very uncomfortable few days. Fortunately, he had a losing streak so that put an end to that."

"He didn't believe the snake was his luck anymore?"

A large man and woman, dressed casually but holding themselves like security, entered the room. For the first time, Perry's attention shifted from me and he glanced at them. The woman shook her head and Perry frowned.

He turned to me with a smile. "Can't claim it as a lucky charm if you aren't lucky, can you?"

His eyes flicked back to the couple and he waved them away. They slinked out of the room like guilty dogs.

Perry promised dark and dangerous, but the only thing I can confirm is that the floor needed a thorough mop. The room with a table in the middle, covered in a light blue velvet, was surrounded by eight chairs and seven people, of different ages and ilk.

One wasn't old enough to be here, but the majority of them were in their middle to later years. The one thing they all had in common was a very expensive taste in fashion. While I had no aspirations of being a fashionista myself, beyond my price range, I could appreciate the finery and intricate work of their outfits especially having moving detail that synchronised beautifully. I examined Perry again, only his ribbon waistcoat was interesting, but wasn't to the same standard as the other players.

"Don't you feel a bit underdressed?" I asked.

He grinned. "I prefer to invest my money in other things."

He patted his waistcoat lovingly. I filed it, and any hidden features, under the potential threat category and made a commitment never to let it touch me.

"Ready to play?" he asked.

15

Ancilla Investigates

Ancilla gazed at the whisky in her hand. She probably shouldn't have sculled the previous one. She swallowed some more. Skipping dinner had been a mistake too.

"It always is," said Beaumont.

She glanced at him sharply but chuckled. "Sorry, I didn't realise that I'd said that out loud."

He was slumped on his stool, but his gaze danced, between the door Inspector Hoadley had disappeared through, the crowd below, and her.

He examined her, his eyes serious. "They do have decent fish half wraps. I could order some."

She blinked. Food would be good. "Err...thank you."

Beaumont stretched out his long form and loped to the bar. He was not what she had expected of a Prime Inspector. If she had been asked before Overton's death to describe a typical prime Inspector she would have used words like stern, abrupt and piercing. Not sleepy, with long floppy blonde curls and an easy smile.

Her lips involuntary shifted into a smile at the sight of him heading back with two glasses of water in his hands.

"Thank you, that's very kind."

"We've a long night ahead of us, we don't want to faint from hunger." He reached into his pocket and pulled out a watch.

"You haven't had dinner either?" She glanced at the familiar piece of clockwork.

"Only a bowl of soup." He gazed at her, mournfully.

She examined him, as he, examined her. His blond hair had a habit of flopping forward. It wasn't as long as most, just long enough to be on trend, but not too long to get in the way. She imagined it was soft.

She glanced down at the watch again. "I can imagine it's hard to stop for food in the middle of an investigation."

Beaumont nodded. "Yes, it's a constant battle." He straightened, pushing his hair back. "I am assuming this is your watch?"

She nodded, "Yes, I just assumed I'd left it somewhere."

"You did, at the Treadways."

Ancilla gulped some more whisky.

"You're having a busy day of it aren't you?" He held out her watch to her. "So why don't you tell me what you're really up to?"

Ancilla took the watch and tucked it into her pocket. "I told you, to find out what Cuthbert—"

Beaumont shook his head.

"Forgive me, I don't mean to be rude. But I sincerely doubt that concern for your brother Cuthbert would bring you here...or at least not *only* concern for your brother."

This being-more-awake thing was not turning out to be a good look on him. And she wasn't sure if she trusted him yet.

"It's not only his honour at stake."

His eyebrows rose. "Even if he was found guilty, how would it affect you?"

"You don't think having a family member a murderer will impact our futures?"

"Oh," he waved his hand dismissively, "only the most conservative will care. The rest...a notorious murder like this? The world will throw their doors open to the poor sisters of the man who killed Overton."

He wasn't wrong. But she didn't need that kind of fame to make her fortune.

"He could be innocent."

"Innocent?" Beaumont snorted. "I doubt it." He tilted his head. "But of killing Overton? Maybe."

She smothered a snort of laughter, and he flashed a grin before turning serious again. Ancilla's cheeks heated.

A large plate covered in small half-wraps filled with crunchy fresh vegetables and deep-fried fish was served, giving her a much-needed distraction. She pulled one off the tray before it even hit the table, shoving it into her mouth. Hard to talk when eating.

Beaumont gave a small smile and picked one up himself.

Their alternating crunches were the only exchange for a

while. After her third half-wrap, Ancilla slowed down, forcing herself to take her time and savour it.

"Would you like another?" asked Beaumont pointing at the two on the plate.

"No, they're all yours."

He grinned happily and proceeded to inhale them. "Right, we can't sit around here all night. Not with Hoadley in that room potentially solving the whole case without me."

"Or being in danger."

Beaumont rubbed his chin. "Hoadley can look after herself. Don't you worry."

She suspected he was right, but her gaze was drawn to the door again.

"If you're sure."

It was his turn to glance at the door and frown.

"We won't get past whoever's watching that door without flashing my badge. And that might make things worse. Not to mention closing up any chance of us getting information tonight." He slipped a glance my way. "Which is why *we're* here."

"Most rooms have more than one door." She peered at him over her glass with a slight smile.

He examined her, his eyes narrowing. "Yes, they do." He threw back what was left in his glass. "Shall we?"

Ancilla's eyes widened. "You want me to come with you?"

"No." he rolled his eyes. "But I'm not letting you out of my sight either."

She swore it was the whisky that made her giggle.

They exited by the front door. She tipped her hat to the watcher, and they wandered off, pretending to stagger around the corner.

"I feel I'm not making helpful decisions," said Beaumont his breath hitting the side of her neck. She blinked.

"We're checking on your colleague. What's wrong with that?"

He managed to smile and frown at the same time.

"True." But he continued to appear confused. She grabbed his arm and dragged him around to the back of the building. A series of windows and doors, spread evenly across the back.

"Strange," he said.

"Why?"

"That's a lot of doors. Do they have one for every room? And why so many rooms?"

"Let's find out." She stumbled up to a door, fumbling for the handle when Beaumont wrapped an arm around her waist, pulling her back into the shadows of a neighbouring wall.

Her body was relaxed. Beaumont's hands turned her so she was propped up against the wall, before dropping away.

"Something's wrong, with both of us." Beaumont swore and he let his weight thud against the wall next to her, "and probably Hoadley as well, if it was the whisky."

"Whisky is tasty."

"I feel..." he held his hands in front of him, examining them. "I feel uncoordinated but invincible." He rolled his head to stare at her. "Do you normally run around the backstreets of southside with someone you don't know, trying to break into criminal dens?"

"No..." She swallowed the giggle, but her body was humming with excitement. "But if I was ever going to do it, tonight is the night."

He groaned. "Hoadley."

She leaned over, hissing, loudly, in his ear. "Can we call for backup?"

He pulled at his ear, frowning at her. "Yes, but it would mean..." he blinked at her. "Yes, of course it's the right thing to do." He reached into his waistcoat, and something flashed.

"What was that?"

"It's a beacon. I have let them know I need assistance."

"What did you say?"

"I can't say anything, I let them know help is needed."

"When will they get here?"

"At night, in southside? Not soon enough. Darn it." He poked at his eyes. "The worst thing is I don't know if it's my own mind screaming at me to get in there."

"I say let's do it."

He rolled his head back towards her. "Of course, you do." Beaumont straightened against the wall. "It's too confusing to work out what is real and what isn't. But Hoadley might be compromised. I'm going in."

He didn't move.

"I thought you were going in?"

"I will...I'm trying to work out which door."

"To the room that Hoadley went in?"

He rolled his eyes. "Yes."

"That's easy, it's the third one along."

He shot a glance at her. "How do you know?"

She shrugged. "From the dimensions of the building, I don't see how it could be anything else."

"Better guess as any I suppose?" He rocked forward.

Ancilla pushed off the wall, swaying slightly. "Do we get to break the door down now?"

"This doesn't make sense," she said, shaking her head. In the dark, a kitchen stretched out in front of her. Its long clean benches a clear statement that this kitchen at least wasn't in use for the night. She glanced back at Beaumont, but he was still blinking trying to bring the room into focus.

"Do you see that?" he asked. She followed his pointed finger and saw a bowl of fruit.

"Yes, but what does—"

"Do you see it? What a glorious bowl of plums." He cantered over, wrapping his arms around the bowl, and snuggling against it.

"How's it going to help Hoadley?" Ancilla shuffled forward trying to make out an inner door that would lead them into the main building.

He cradled the bowl, picking out a plum and taking a bite. His moan filled the room. She glanced around to see if anyone else was there and briefly contemplated leaving him alone. But they needed to stay focused.

Beaumont took another bite of the plum, its red juices dripping down like blood from the corner of his mouth. His wide eyes stared at her.

"I remember, I remember these, I haven't had them in, I can't remember." His mouth was full of bloody pulp, and she tried not to gag.

"Beaumont, we need to keep moving." Noises filtered through the walls. Ancilla wasn't sure what they meant but they seemed to be getting louder.

Beaumont was eating a large amount of the fruit quickly. Like a switch in his brain had been turned off.

"Prime Inspector Beaumont, we need to—"

"This is the best fruit I have ever had in my whole life. It is even better than I remember."

"What about Hoadley?"

"Right, Hoadley," he frowned at the bowl in his arms. "Let's go."

He headed off towards a door with the bowl still clutched in his hands, eating plums as he went. The door he had chosen was at the far end of the kitchen and by her calculations would take them further away from Hoadley. But then her calculations had taken them to the kitchen in the first place. She wasn't sure what that meant about the dimensions of the building.

"You don't want to leave the bowl behind?"

He swung, glowering at her, red smeared across his face. "Stop dawdling."

She wasn't sure if he was like a child in trouble, a blood-sucking fiend, or both.

At least with the rate he was eating he wouldn't need the bowl too much longer. She was briefly tempted to try one, but she was fond of her fingers.

The door he had chosen led to an empty room. This room had two doors and she tilted her head back, staring at the ceiling trying to visualise the size of the building.

Beaumont barrelled through one and she abandoned her calculations, scrambling after him. This Beaumont was certainly a far cry from the one she had met so far. She liked him. The recklessness, however, was going to get them into trouble. He did have the bowl to defend himself with. She just wasn't sure if he would think to use it. Not if meant spilling his plums.

"Who are you?" On the other side of the door, a tall man, and even taller woman, greeted them. Overly muscly with devices in their hands.

All signs pointed to trouble.

Ancilla grabbed Beaumont, bowl and all, dragging him through a door, locking it behind her. The door shook as large bodies connected with it.

They ended up in another room full of boxes being prepped for shipping. She dragged a few in front of the door. With no time to investigate, she grabbed a handful of a box's contents—*quill wipers? why would they have boxes of quill wipers?*—and shoved it in her inner waistcoat pocket.

She wrapped her arm around Beaumont's waist, dragging him through a door which sent them back outside again.

Beaumont doubled over, spewing dark red pulpy juice over the step. It left a gruesome scene. Perhaps the thugs chasing them would think them dead.

{ 16 }

Hoadley Takes All

Lavina Hoadley, Inspector
Noxrath Gendarmerie
Great Espya

Having followed a suspect into the back room and being introduced as his lucky charm I had expected something a bit more...well, interesting. Instead, time slowed. We sat, watching them play what had to be the lengthiest card game that I had ever had the misfortune of witnessing. I swallowed a yawn, the cracks of boredom starting to show.

Perry glanced at me. "It's a fascinating game, isn't it?"

I shrugged, which for some reason he found amusing. I had already examined all the players and none of it screamed anything more than the usual degenerate gambler. The woman on my right took a bit too much interest in my leg but I shifted, draping as much of my wrap across it as I could. Not that there was anything alluring about my thick britches, but it made me feel more comfortable to have a bit of extra material between my skin and her gaze.

The rest of the room was decked out similarly to the main foyer with dark brown woods and purple velvets. A little less embracing of the club's name might have made it a bit easier on the eyes. Servers, dressed like the server upstairs, in different shades of purple, with a service design in their waistcoats, kept offering me drinks, but I waved them away. I had already drunk more tonight than I did most months and the last thing I wanted to do was lose my head.

"Yes, fascinating," I responded. He turned back to me, laughing and I grimaced. There had been a considerable delay in my response.

"I do hope you aren't bored," he said, peering at me.

"I am actually." I sighed. My eyebrows drew together. *Why had I said that? It was not useful to the investigation.* "I'm afraid I don't have it in me tonight to sit here and pretend to care about this." Apparently, my mouth was running its own race tonight. I was always upfront. But not at the cost of the investigation. I found myself standing, addressing the room. "You're all a bunch of fools for wasting so much of your short life on this. Go create something instead."

I needed to get out of here.

Perry's eyebrows raised but he was still entertained and smiled at me. *Why?* The others not so much.

The woman who had been eyeing my leg spat at me. "Who—"

"I would remind you that she is *my* guest." Perry frowned at them.

"A guest who wants to know what the real game is." I glared at them. Any filter I might have had, absent. Though to be fair my filter was never very strong.

Perry smirked. "The game, Inspector..." he began, grin widening in tandem with my eyes. "The game is art, wealth and pneuma."

"Pneuma?" I frowned. How was that part of the game? And it appeared our undercover attempt was wasted. "And what's that got to do with Cuthbert and the money three nights ago?"

At the mention of Cuthbert's name Perry's friendliness disappeared. One of the larger servers took a step towards me.

It hadn't been what I had meant to say but my mouth was choosing its own adventure tonight.

Perry rose to his feet coming to stand directly in front of me.

I scanned the room. Two doors, one leading away from the main gambling hall with its watcher on the other side.

"Cuthbert..." Perry kept just out of arms reach. "Cuthbert was an expensive mistake."

"Expensive? Cuthbert? Well, he can afford to be can't he?" I blinked. At that point, I had no idea what I was going to say next. I shifted my weight towards the door closest to me.

"Can he?" growled Perry, his eyes narrowing.

"What?" I stared at them all blankly. "He had the money for you, right? To cover his losses?"

Perry's nostrils flared. "He was meant to lose."

Meant to lose? Ah, a way of passing on the money without any trail. Clever.

"Nothing to do with me." I waved my hand. "I don't gamble, like you losers."

This was deteriorating quickly. *Hoadley stop talking!*

One of the larger servers lunged forward, grabbing at my arm, but I dove towards the closest door, slamming it shut behind me, legging it.

I was in a narrow corridor with a few other doors. I chose one at random and ducked into it. A small empty room. Well except for the bed, charming. I opened another door, this time into a small mudroom. The exit. I had wanted to explore more but the sound of doors being wrenched open was getting closer. I opened the door in front of me, taking a step to freedom.

A step that didn't land.

I remember blinking. The night sky above me was obscured by too many lights from the surrounding buildings. My wet fingers struggled to detach from the ground. I brought up my hand, discovering it covered in blood.

"Argh." I sat up, to find myself in a sea of red, with a sore leg but no obvious injuries. Beaumont cradled a bowl with blood smeared across his face and Ancilla stood next to him, bouncing on her toes.

"Are you alright?" she asked.

"What the pipe's going on?"

"We've all been drugged. It's all very exciting. Beaumont's sent a beckon for assistance, a while ago actually, but we haven't seen or heard them arrive. He also ate a large bowl of plums and is now throwing it up."

"Plums?" I raised my hand closer, and the heady aroma of plum juice mixed with bile hit my nose. "Oh, for pipe's sake."

I wanted to gag but fortunately, I was too angry to do so. I forced myself to put my hands back in the mess and manoeuvred to my feet, every inch of my body ached.

Crashing in the building filtered through the door I was next to.

"Pipes," I flicked my hands trying to get the regurgitated juice off them. "Can you get him moving?" I asked.

Beaumont was kneeling on the ground cradling his bowl and occasionally wrenching his guts out.

Ancilla stared down at him. "I can try, where are we going?"

"Somewhere not here." I hopped over to a wall and leaned against it, grateful to be out of Beaumont's sick. The first port of call was to find safety and somehow not leave a trail of dark red pointing in our direction.

"We need a steamer. We need to get out of here."

Ancilla stopped fiddling with the door and put an arm around Beaumont, groaning as she dragged him to his feet. Beaumont was not a small man, but apparently, Ancilla was, significantly, fitter than she appeared. The level of fitness I would expect to see in a professional artist perhaps.

Thumps slammed into the door but it didn't open.

"I jammed the hinges," she said.

"What?" I couldn't help myself from glancing back at the door.

Thump, thump, thump.

"People always forget about the hinges when securing a door. A jammed hinge, and that door is going nowhere." She giggled.

I grunted and stepped up to Beaumont's other side, taking some of his weight. I would like to have it noted that he was much heavier than he appeared, even with an empty stomach.

We made it to the corner, but Ancilla jerked Beaumont's body to a halt before we stepped out onto the street in front of the building's front entrance.

"They'll be watching."

I hated to admit it, but she was right.

"Fine, but we need a steamer, and we need to get out of here."

"You don't think the gendarmerie are going to turn up?"

I did not have faith in my own people to come to a distress call late at night on the southside. Maybe I was wrong, but I never had been a gambler.

"I'm not counting on it." A steamer parked in a laneway across the main street caught my attention. "Have you got him?"

Beaumont took some of his own weight, but his eyes were unfocused. I suppose the combination of the drug and the nausea would be enough to throw even the most seasoned of inspectors off.

"I think so."

I trusted that she had the situation in hand and grabbed a wooden slat, using it to hobble across the road. My body angled to capture the shadows. The driver had tilted his chair back and his eyes were closed. I wasn't sure why he was napping here. Booked for a client later? I rapped my knuckles on the edge of the steamer.

He didn't move.

Again, I rapped them, this time with a bit more force.

He still didn't move.

I started up a rhythm. It wasn't too loud certainly not enough to disturb or alert anyone nearby. But for the person in the steamer, it would quickly become apparent that I was not going away.

He groaned and turned his head in my direction and opened his eyes.

"What do you want?"

"I need a ride."

"I'm not working right now." He closed his eyes again, but I wasn't having any of it. I started up my rhythmic tapping on the metal of his door. He opened his eyes again. "Are you trying to be the most annoying person in the world?"

"Nope, it comes naturally. We urgently need a ride. Our friend is not feeling well and is in need of some assistance."

"There is no way I'm putting a barfing fool in my steamer."

I agreed with him. It was not something I would want to do either. But needs must. So far, we had been talking through the veil pulled down from the cloth top of his steamer. I reached out, ripped it away and turned on the signal in my waistcoat. His eyes widened, staring at me with a mixture of fear and suspicion.

"Ah, is that the way it is."

"I'm afraid I am going to have to insist on either your help or the loan of your steamer." I smiled to take the sting out of it.

He spat only narrowly missing me. My eyes narrowed. He had been lucky.

"Get in then."

I chose to sit up the front next to him and directed him to the laneway.

The emptiness of the laneway entrance mocked me.

Ancilla's voice floated through the night, obscured by rough laughter. "I'll take you down..."

I swore, making out two overly large watchers dragging Ancilla and Beaumont deeper into the laneway.

"If you leave," I said. "I'll track you down." The driver's eyes were wide as he stared at me. "You don't want me to track you down, I promise."

I jumped out, limping after them. The watchers were significantly taller than me and it required a bit of a jump, which piping hurt, but I was able to bring my slat of wood up into the jaw of one as he turned towards me. Beaumont kicked out at the knee of the other and as she stumbled, I flipped the slat, slamming it down on the back of her head. Ancilla grabbed Beaumont as he stumbled.

"Move now," I said. I gestured toward the steamer, and we piled in. I took the front seat again. "To The Way. Now!"

The steamer driver hid his face as we pulled away, heading up the street in a sprint.

I sniffed. "Tell them I forced you to do it."

"I'm not sure that is going to fly with these peeps."

"I'll give you a note."

He snorted but sped up.

We pulled into the Way and pretty much fell out of the steamer to be met by the guards responding to our call. I would be submitting a complaint. I doubted they would do anything about it though.

Covered in plums and bile, now was not the time to worry about it though.

"I need to shower." Beaumont stood there, his elegant clothes hanging limply from his body.

"What's going on here?" Alfred, the largest busybody in the joint came hustling out, squawking and fussing over Beaumont. No one cared that Ancilla and I were a mess.

"We were drugged," said Ancilla, in a tone that I would describe as perky. If the drug lowered inhibitions, this Ancilla was having the adventure of a lifetime.

"And Prime Inspector Beaumont threw up plums on us." I wanted that on record. I turned to Ancilla. "We could take this show on the road."

She laughed, gaily. "This is the best night ever." She glanced around eagerly at the guards milling around. "Can we go and arrest people now?"

I had been short-changed the side effects of the drug as well.

"Some of us have to complete paperwork," I said.

Her eyes widened. "Ooo paperwork, is that where we write up our adventures?"

"No one is going anywhere until we have a doctor check you out," said Alfred.

I don't know what I found more perplexing. That he had the right to issue orders. Or that others, some even more senior than him, followed them.

"Why do they listen to you?" I asked, frowning watching them all scurry.

Alfred just tutted. "Inside the lot of you."

We cleaned up, including putting on some clean clothes much to everyone's relief. Mine and Beaumont's came from the spares we kept here at the Way, as any decent inspector would, but I had no idea where Ancilla's oversized striped outfit came from.

"Here you go." Alfred handed me a cup.

"What is this?" I examined it, finding it full of a purple, odourless liquid.

"The antidote." His annoyingly patient expression, the same one he used to deal with the chaos of the night, was directed at me.

"The antidote to what?" I sniffed at it again, hoping to catch a bit of the odour.

"To the drug," he held up his hand, "which is a mixture of alcohol and opium. Best drink it fast."

I hesitated but there was no doubt something was interfering with my mind, so I knocked it back, gagging slightly at the sweet taste.

Ancilla was already smacking her lips. "Tasty."

"Beaumont?" I asked.

"They must have double-dosed him, he was hit pretty hard, but he'll recover." Alfred handed Ancilla a glass of water. "Most likely a drink, something to disguise the bitter taste."

I tried to remember what the whisky had tasted like, but I was ashamed to say I hadn't been paying much attention.

"What do we do now?" asked Ancilla, her eyes bright. She did not look like someone who had been drugged and then re-drugged to balance her out.

I scowled, asking Alfred, "Are you sure the antidote is working?".

He examined Ancilla, his expression uncomfortably intense.

"Alfred, you with us?" I asked.

He shook himself, clearing his throat. "My apologies, Inspector. I..." he said as he glanced at me. "Yes, the antidote is working."

He was right. This time I managed to not say what I was thinking. For which I was grateful. Alfred was well-liked, and I had learnt quickly that people didn't like it when I called him a fool.

"Then thank you, Alfred. I can take it from here."

He stood there staring at Ancilla who was up, tottering around, opening drawers, and picking up anything not locked down.

"Zer Walstrand..." my voice was plaintive.

She laughed and plonked down in a chair near me, gazing at me expectantly. *Great.*

I turned to Alfred, who was still standing there staring at her.

"Where's Prime Inspector Beaumont?" I asked.

He jerked around to me. "He's been escorted home, inspector. The doctor said he just needs to sleep it off and he should be none the worse for wear tomorrow."

My eyebrows pinched together, but I smoothed it out and nodded. Ancilla's gaze danced between us.

"Thank you, Alfred."

He didn't move.

"That'll be all."

"Yes, zer."

The small waiting room next to the Inspectors' pen, a place usually reserved for family and visitors, not suspects, wasn't where I would normally conduct an interrogation, but it would have to do.

"If Beaumont is out," Ancilla glanced around the room again. "Where do we go next?"

"You go home."

"What am I looking for there?"

"A place to stay out of it."

She scowled at me, cheerful expression finally extinguished. "This is just as much my case as it is yours."

This case? This case that my entire career was pivoting on? No. "That is incorrect."

Ancilla breathed in through her nose. "You know you're

lucky I like you." She sat back in her chair, narrowing her eyes.

"I'm not here to be liked. I'm here to solve a murder." I examined her, mirroring her narrowed eyes. "Which would be a lot easier if you shared with me whatever it is you are holding back."

We stared at each other for a while, but she broke first by yawning. I smothered a smirk.

"Any chance of something to drink?"

I ignored that. Alfred had given her plenty of options.

"Let's start with Cuthbert."

Ancilla frowned. "I'll not help you convict my brother."

"So, you don't care who killed Overton?" I sat back, folding my arms across my chest. It was time to take control of this conversation again.

"Of course, I do."

"But you don't want to see them convicted?"

We all have biases, the important thing is to be open to discovering them. And it was time that Ancilla faced hers.

"Yes, but—"

"Only if they aren't your family." I sat up in my seat, leaning forward. "I'll remind you, Zer Walstrand that a man is dead. I'll also remind you that you have not submitted a credible reason for being at the Purple Door last night."

Ancilla shifted in her seat.

"Do you know who Perry was and why he drugged us?"

She blinked.

"No, I don't." She stood, shuffling around the room, her body appearing to be still sore and stiff. "I know nothing about what Cuthbert was into." She stopped, staring at me. "Which was why I was at the Purple Door tonight."

"And did you find anything?"

"No. Before I could, two annoying inspectors showed up." She flicked me an amused glance. "Though..." She waddled over to the piles of clothes. One was mine, I would have to ask if they needed to be taken away for testing, and one was hers. Her pile was also covered in bile-infused plum juice.

I joined her. The pile included her waistcoat and britches, which had magically escaped the red purge, her coat and waterfall wrap taking the most of it. I picked it up, feeling a familiar weight to them.

"I wouldn't have picked you as someone who would choose such an industrial fabric," I said.

She grinned. "It's mine."

I tried not to roll my eyes. "Yes, I know. "

She chuckled. "No need to get grumpy. I'm not stating the obvious. I mean the fabric, it's my invention." She glanced down at the pile that included my dirty clothes, her smile widening. "I hope it's living up to your stringent expectations."

"It's not terrible, stiff, but..."

"Lasts forever though."

Something I appreciated. "You're surprising, Zer Walstrand."

"I thought we agreed on Ancilla?"

"It gave you ideas."

She just chuckled again, shaking her head. She turned

back to her waistcoat and drew out a quill wiper from its pocket. It was all rather anticlimactic, really.

"I already have a quill wiper," I said.

In truth, I had several, but I had always found them extremely useful to have around. After all, they could wipe more than just quills and the best ones, they could stop almost any spill from staining.

"From boxes, being prepped for shipping, at the Purple Door."

"Boxes?" I frowned, taking the wiper from her.

She rolled her eyes at me. "Perhaps I might be more qualified to examine it?" she asked.

I turned it over in my hands, feeling its fabric, its weight. It was reinforced with some kind of mechanism.

"It's definitely enhanced." I peered at it, trying to work out what was different about it compared to my normal ones.

Ancilla huffed, snatching it out of my hands.

"Let me see what it does." She activated it by placing her fingers on touchpoints embroidered into the cloth, probably put there for people who couldn't even work a quill wiper properly without guidance. Lacking a quill, she wiped against the edge of the table. She paled, and she flung it across the room. The whites of her eyes flashed at me. "How? That's impossible."

"Since whatever just happened, happened, that's a false statement."

She glared at me. My interpretation of the expression was exasperation.

"It, it took from me."

"You mean it needed pneuma to operate? Why would anyone make a quill wiper that needed pneuma—"

"No, I didn't use my pneuma. It took it from me."

"That's not possible," I said.

We stared at each other and then down at the quill wiper on the floor.

There was no real reason for something like that to be invented. And to be sold to the public, disguised as a piece of stationery, that was just rude.

"But it doesn't make sense. If the wiper stores it, how do they collect it?" Ancilla asked.

"Are you sure? You only held it for a second. Maybe you imagined it?"

"You try it then." She stood there with her arms crossed in front of her.

I strode over, picked it up, placed my fingers in the touchpoints, and wiped the edge of the table. It was subtle. But there was a pull, a drag on my pneuma, a moment of tiredness. If I had been full of energy, busy and focused, it wouldn't have registered.

Ancilla took it from me, turning it over in her hands.

"A harvester." She breathed. "You hear rumours, but I never thought, I never thought, that they would actually be real."

"Let's say they are," I said, ignoring the irritated glance she flung my way, "as you asked, even if it stores it, how can they use it?"

Ancilla slumped down in a chair. "I'm sorry, I—this changes everything. I wonder if that means..."

I sat across from her, forcing myself to be silent and not pepper her with questions. One puzzle at a time.

She lifted her gaze from the table and stared directly at me. "I...Marcellus might be alive."

"Alive?" I leant forward, staring at her.

"You're very intense, you know." Ancilla flashed half a grin.

I forced myself to sit back. "I've seen Overton's body, I can assure you, he was not alive."

"The thing is..." she exhaled heavily. "The thing is...it might be Fred."

I must admit, I blinked.

"Who *the pipes* is Fred?"

"A server at the Purple Door, he has a similar build and aspirations of being an actor." Ancilla's eyes dropped. "Marcellus hired Fred to impersonate him."

I closed my eyes and took a breath, before opening my eyes again to find Ancilla was gazing at me, concern, tiredness and amusement all mixed together. It wasn't a good look for her.

"What?" An edge in my tone.

Ancilla pushed back her chair, creaking to her feet, and attempted to pace.

"You see...the thing is..." She swung towards me. "Marcellus hasn't been himself." She took another turn around the room.

"Why?"

"The bill, the changes in the legislation, his last chance...and he wasn't what he was."

"Just spit it out Ancilla."

She sent an amused glance my way. She dropped back into her chair, leaning forward with all the intensity she had accused me of.

"When artists get older, they get stronger. The more pneuma you can channel, the easier and easier it gets, so even if your body becomes less fit, it all balances out." She sat back. "But not with Marcellus. When I first started working with him, he could do things in between sips of tea, things that would make me sweat and tremble. But now, now anytime he used the illuminier, he was the one trembling. And what was he if he wasn't an artist anymore? It was his whole identity."

"So where does this Fred fit into it?"

"Marcellus was panicking. The drinking didn't help. And then he did something he referred to as foolish. At the time, I didn't know what, but I knew it went terribly wrong and he said he needed to fix it. Now, it is obvious it was investing with Cuthbert, but I didn't know that then. And he was afraid, afraid of doing the demonstration."

"Had his art degraded that much?"

Ancilla frowned. "I think he could have done it, but it would have been with visible effort." She stared at the table. "He could no longer do it without the shaking and the sweating that beginners show, and he was worried...about what people would say."

"But the presentation went ahead." I frowned. "Is this Fred an artist?"

Ancilla's cheeks darkened. She cleared her throat. "The demo was me." She spoke in a rush. "I've been practising, helping Marcellus when he got tired."

I had been right, the stiffness in her movements had been from more than testing.

"Back to my original question. Who *the pipes* is Fred?" I tilted my head, staring at her. "And are there four of him?"

Ancilla snorted and rolled her eyes. "Marcellus was both a genius and a fool. When you meet Fred—"

"I want to."

"You'll see why Marcellus thought he had a chance. But he was still concerned that people would guess it wasn't him, especially Felicia, so Fred was instructed to keep moving any time she came near him."

I had so many questions, I wasn't sure where to start. "How—"

"How was he moving around?"

That hadn't been the question I was going to ask. "Sure." I tried to stifle the annoyance of us not having this very important information from the beginning.

"The Atwater's house has a huge number of stairs and service tunnels in it. Fred was particularly fond of the service tunnels." She rolled her eyes. "He zipped around in them for the whole three days he was with me."

"Three days?" I straightened, snapping forward. "Was that the last time you saw Overton?"

"Yes." Her body drooped. "But he, he's alive I know it.

I thought...I really thought he would be at Purple Door tonight."

I had a moment of hesitation. To take someone's hope away was no small thing. But I was an inspector. And the truth was nothing to be hidden from. "It was Marcellus Overton's body in the library."

She blinked, her eyes moistening. "Are you sure?"

Dr Morten hadn't confirmed it yet, but if Marcellus hadn't been seen for three days and we had a three-day-old corpse, it didn't leave too much room for doubt.

I nodded. "Yes."

She slumped, gazing down at her clasped hands. "I didn't think Felicia would be fooled by someone else's body, but..."

"I need the details of this...Fred. Name, address. And I need it now."

She sat back, her arms crossed and her amiable, patient mask in place. People underestimated her. I suspected the killer had as well.

"They should have killed you too."

Ancilla blinked. "Thanks?"

"I mean it, you are a witness, you aren't a fool, why keep you alive?"

"My charming personality?"

I shook my head and mirrored her. "I'll have to leave a guard with you."

She scowled. "I want to come with you."

My expression was strained, my body rigid, and I couldn't relax. "Absolutely not."

Ancilla let a small smile slip out. "You don't hide much, do you?"

I sniffed. "I need to investigate these service tunnels and see if what you say is true, talk to this Fred and..." I tapped my fingers on the table.

"And?" She tilted her head, watching me.

"That character Perry," I said. "Something he mentioned..."

Ancilla leaned further forward across the desk. "Let me come with you."

"No." My lips thinned.

"How will you know what to look for without me?"

I glared at her. "I'll manage."

She threw herself back in her seat and her arms up in the air. "You're impossible."

It was my turn to let a smile slip.

"How about a compromise?"

She blinked. "The great Inspector Hoadley compromising?"

I liked the great.

"Let me do the searching tonight and I'll come around first thing in the morning with questions for you."

Ancilla flashed a huge, unexpected smile. "I'm not exactly sure how that's a compromise, but fine." She tapped her fingers on the table.

The introduction of Fred was interesting, and we needed to know more about him, but I doubted he was anything more than a pawn in this. If he existed at all.

I still wasn't sure how Ancilla was involved with this. Still, we had a corpse that died three days before it was discovered, and her explanation was the first one to sound slightly plausible. Which just went to show how improbable this entire case was becoming.

"Fine." I rose to my feet, frowning down at her. "Don't go back to the Atwaters until after I visit in the morning."

She rolled her eyes. "I will not sit around waiting, Inspector. I'll expect you before nine. Otherwise, I'll be at work at the Atwaters."

I nodded. I hated waiting, too.

Ancilla rose, shuffling over to me. "Here." She handed me her pocket watch that she had somehow managed to hold on to. "So you won't be late."

"There isn't some hidden device that allows you to follow me, or something is it?"

Ancilla cleared her throat. "Just a few seconds of sound." She pressed the watch back in my hand. "Be careful Lavina Hoadley. I don't have a sense of all the players in this yet."

It had been a long time since I had had a friend and it made sense that I would meet one who was a suspect in a murder, and illegally modified devices.

"Thank you, Ancilla Walstrand." I looked down at the watch, wondering if I would regret keeping a modified device on me. "I will, I promise."

I had a guard escort her home.

Something was going down at Atwater Place, and I had until nine o'clock to stop it.

Breaking or Breaking Free?

Ancilla was hungry.

She had washed again when she got home and was restless despite the later hour. And the fish wraps seemed a long time ago. She stepped into the quiet hallway and tiptoed towards food.

The kitchen, the largest room in the house, had a high vaulted ceiling with air vents to draw out the smoke of cooking mishaps. The huge, compartmentalised cooking device she had invented early in her teens sat in the centre. Ernest had, surprisingly, supported her patenting it in her name, probably with the expectation that they could make something of it, but it hadn't taken off. Calling it the food juggler had probably decreased its marketability.

Whatever she had been doped with had worn off, and

instead of being ready for the next adventure, now she was tired, hungry, and grumpy.

She stomped over to the food juggler. After all the kerfuffle, the only thing she had to show for it was an aversion to plums.

She threw eggs, bread and sausages into different compartments of her invention. A myriad of gas-powered arms waved, stoking up the hot coals and shifting the food around. It was sometimes random, and the cooking could be uneven, but it left her free to make some coffee.

The coffee machine was her friend. Was everyone's friend. Every time she used it, she was grateful to whatever government official had the foresight to buy it outright from the inventor. The result, the people could purchase coffee devices, free from inventor compensation, and everyone in parliament being re-elected that year.

She picked up her fresh cup of coffee, the plate of food now assembled, and carried them over to the large table in the middle of the kitchen. With a fork, Ancilla shovelled some eggs into her watering mouth.

"Ancilla," said Ernest, entering the kitchen.

She hunched a bit more, shoving another overfilled fork into her mouth, chewing as her cheeks ballooned out. Her gaze stayed lowered. "Hmi."

Pipes it. Why could he not be out, just this once?

He frowned down on her. "This has all turned out to be extremely distressing."

Ancilla wasn't exactly sure what Ernest was distressed about, Marcellus' death or Cuthbert's eminent incarceration.

"Mmhow...mmso?" Ancilla loaded up another forkful.

"Did you know that the minister of the patent office actually called me into her office yesterday?"

Ancilla shook her head.

"She did." Ernest sat, his fingers drumming the table and glared at her.

Ancilla tracked the tempo of his fingers, frustrated but not angry would be her guess.

"What did she want?" asked Ancilla. She didn't really care, but Ernest needed to talk.

"You don't want to know."

Ancilla shrugged. It was true unless it affected her. And even then, she was willing to take the hit if it meant not listening to him go on about his missed opportunities.

"Hmmm." Ancilla took another overly large mouthful of food.

Ernest's lips thinned.

"She wanted to know how I was caught up in the murder of Overton." Ernest's fingers started tapping louder. "She basically accused me of killing him. Wanted to know intimate details of what happened. The cheek. I have been with the organisation for over thirty years, and this is how they treat me? Like I'm dirt."

"Terrible," mumbled Ancilla, ignoring Ernest's gaze as she muffled herself with food.

He turned his head away but didn't leave. "We need to talk about what you are going to do now Overton's dead."

Ancilla used her fork to pick up everything on her plate and shoved it in for one last hurrah.

"Mmwphmm."

Ernest flicked a glance her way, shuddered and stared at the wall, scowling.

"I don't know what you said and, to be honest, I don't want to know." He got up and made himself a coffee while Ancilla chewed. She had quite a lot of food in her mouth, so it took a while. Ernest returned to his seat with a cup of coffee in his hand.

"Where were you tonight?"

Ancilla swallowed the last of her food, gazing at her plate, hoping to find more on it.

Ernest stared at her and the drumming of his fingers, with their nails cut short and the minimum amount of jewellery needed to be socially acceptable, picked up speed.

Odd that he was fully dressed as well. What had he been up to?

"Tonight?"

"Yes, I went to talk to you and the door was locked. I knocked." He peered at her. "Loudly. You're not that heavy a sleeper."

Ancilla mentally scanned her room. She had checked the door and she couldn't remember any evidence of it being broken into.

"It has been a massive couple of days." Ancilla sipped her coffee to flush the last of the food out of her mouth.

"And here you're fully dressed." The rhythm under Ernest's fingers a crescendo. "Where were you, Ancilla?"

Ancilla and Ernest stared at each other.

"Where was I?" She plonked her cup down. "Where was

I after months of working nonstop, culminating with my mentor's death? I was passed out, exhausted. That's where I was."

His lips thinned. "Why couldn't I get into your room? Why are you dressed? Eating breakfast just after midnight?"

That was *a bit* awkward to explain.

"In case you haven't noticed, Melody and Cuthbert lack a certain...respect for boundaries. I didn't want to deal with their drama."

"Hmmm." His eyes narrow, his gaze slashing across her face. "I don't like it."

Ancilla stood up.

"Where are you going?" asked Ernest.

"Work."

"What work? It's after midnight and your employer's dead." Ernest rose, towering over her, his arms crossed.

"The Atwaters are my employers and with Marcellus gone...the demonstration still needs to be done...I need to practise."

Ernest sneered. "They'll never give you that." He leant forward, resting one hand on the table staring at her, disgust oozing from him. "Gifted with a spanner, you're no artist—"

"How can—" Ancilla opened her throat to take in a breath.

"Give up using the illuminier, you don't have what it takes," said Ernest, his lips thin.

"You might be right." She rose on shaky legs and stumbled to the door. "But I'm more of an artist than you'll ever be."

She scrambled back up to her room, reinforcing the hinge

from the inside. To be safe. And crumpled onto the edge of her bed,

What a mess.

The canopy over Ancilla's bed was not worth the hours of attention she gave it. She closed her eyes, trying to force herself to sleep, but not even the quilt's soft warmth comforted her.

Waiting, always waiting.

For what? Hoadley? And before that Marcellus?

Hoadley would discover the murderer and she would be unemployable, stuck here, in this house, forever.

Or she could find what was hers.

She threw back the covers and rolled out of bed.

Time to shine.

She had faithfully followed the rules, written and unwritten, her whole life. Every day a slog.

And yet, the one time she stepped outside the lines, this is what she got. Death and mayhem.

Her jaw tightened.

A quick change into her hardiest outfit and her hand rested on the doorknob. It chilled her fingers. She breathed in deeply.

She had this.

The swish of her shoes against the rug echoed through the silent house. She pulled the door closed behind her and engaged the lock.

Click.

Her body stilled, and she paused, listening. Blood drumming in her ears drowned everything out.

She rolled her feet, flexing her ankle and took her time. Each foot was placed at the edge of the stair closest to the wall. She didn't rush.

Down the stairs and through the kitchen to the back door she was once more in the garden. Only the living room and her bedroom had a view of it and a quick glance showed both windows had their curtains drawn. Still, she kept her movements fluid, keeping close to the statues, any movement blending in with the natural sounds of the night.

Until the garden gate closed soundlessly behind her.

She exhaled heavily and grinned. Perhaps she had missed her calling? She might be suited to a life of crime.

She imagined Hoadley rolling her eyes and shook her head. There would be no rewards for tonight's work if she didn't stay focused.

A fog with the Noxrath metallic aftertaste blanketed the street, and with the waxing moon set, it left only the streetlamps to illuminate the haze.

Their street was empty, except for one steamer idling. Two people sat in the back. She assumed they were returning from a late night out, but they didn't seem to be in any hurry to exit so she headed to the end of the street where a food cart did a night shift.

She paused at the corner. The question was, would Marcellus have left her reward, his schematic, at his workroom at Atwater Place? Or his flat?

The flat. He would not risk any new invention falling into Felicia's hands.

Ancilla's stomach churned at not telling Hoadley about Fred earlier, wasting time waiting for Marcellus to contact her.

The worst part of it all was that everything had gone well. They had navigated the demonstration with only her noticing that the table and chairs were a bit less solid than Marcellus would have made them. Everyone, assuming Marcellus was tired, understood that he didn't want to interact, and Felicia was too busy accepting praise for the illuminier to talk to them.

Until Melody took over the stage. Ancilla had turned to warn Fred, but he smiled.

"Don't worry, Marcellus planned for this." And with that, he had disappeared.

She had been so busy she hadn't seen him leave and come back again. If she knew what they planned—she would have —she would have—in truth she didn't know what she would have done.

Of course, Melody had tracked him down, but returned saying Marcellus was impossible. Ancilla giddy, thinking they pulled it off, had ridden on a high for the rest of the night.

Then the dead body.

But she never once thought Marcellus killed Fred.

Marcellus, the real Marcellus had been planning to return after the party was over, and she assumed he had heard about the body and hid.

She had been right. The food cart was open. She turned and headed down the street toward the sizzling. The spices chased away the metal edge to the fog and she joined the loose crowd gathered in front of it.

With Marcellus dead, there was a lot for Felicia to forgive her for. Not the least, lying for three days, putting her demonstration at risk, and potentially getting her lover killed.

She hated that her father was right, though for different reasons than he imagined but her employment was at risk. She needed that schematic.

She scanned the people who were waiting, trying to work out which one might be a driver on a break.

The clank of an engine spun her around to see a steamer pulling up. Before the driver could turn off her engine Ancilla pounced, negotiating, bribing, with the promise of enough money for several snacks. Her case was helped when the couple from the other steamer on her street joined the crowd, making the wait even longer.

The driver grunted her consent and Ancilla jumped in and was whisked away.

The food cart and the residential neighbourhoods with their well-lit streets disappeared, and the steamer soon entered the more semi-industrial areas with their deeper shadows and pulled up next to Marcellus' flat.

After overpaying the driver, she once more found herself on the street. The fog was worse here, infused with the damp musty odour of the swamps and the nearby dirigible yards.

She scurried up to Marcellus' front door and reached out to unlock it. Her fingers never connecting.

The door swung inward to reveal a middle-aged man with smooth skin and a complete absence of hair on the top of his head.

"Ancilla."

She stared at him her eyes wide. She had never seen him without a wig before.

"Freddy?"

"It's about time." He stepped back gesturing her in. "I have other jobs to get to you know. Not that this one doesn't pay well but I can't sit around waiting—"

"He's dead." She closed the door behind her. She had been thinking Fred was the one who had been killed. Horrible of course, but to be fair the only thing they had in common was Marcellus' deception.

"Dead?" Freddy took a few steps back, sitting on the arm of the nearest armchair. "Who, Marcellus?"

"Yes." She closed her eyes and took a breath. It was the first time she had admitted it out loud. The reality hit her harder than she expected. She forced her eyes open. There would be time to grieve later. "When did you last see him?"

"A few days ago." He shrugged. "I promised to stay here until he came back."

Freddy rose.

"What did he say?" Ancilla glanced around the room. The signs of it being lived in, that had given her so much hope, now mocked her. "When you last saw him?"

Freddy glowered at her. "Oh, you know, remember to say that, go here, do that." His eyes narrowed. "Do the gendarmerie know about me?" Freddy crossed his arms. "I don't want to get involved."

Now that was a question wasn't it? Exactly how deeply was he involved?

"We're all involved." She started moving around the flat, picking up pieces of papers and opening drawers.

"What're you doing?" He turned his head to track her movements.

She huffed. "I need to find something Marcellus left me."

Freddy's face shifted into a sneer.

"Oh that little schematic, the one that was going to make you rich?"

She peered at him, her stomach sinking.

"What do you know about it?"

Why would Marcellus share it with him of all people?

"I know it doesn't exist." He snorted. "As if light can be used to soften fabric." His arms uncrossed, and he shifted his weight forward.

"Doesn't exist?" She tried to blink, her dry eyeballs sticking. She scrubbed at them to force her body to produce liquid.

Freddy's mouth twisted giving his chuckle a hard edge.

"He told me how he convinced you to play along. Warned me not to let you search his place." Freddy moved between her and the door. "Seems he was right not to trust you."

Not trust her? She had risked everything for him. And now here she was stuck in this flat with a what? A suspect? But then why would Fred kill Marcellus and stick around? But he had to know more than he was letting on. She needed to tell Hoadley. Ancilla slammed the drawer in front of her closed, spun and shoved past him.

Freddy grabbed at her arm. "Where do you think you're going." His fingers tightened, digging painfully into her flesh.

"There's nothing for me here, I'm leaving." Ancilla dipped her free hand into a pocket.

"And straight to the gendarmerie." Freddy scowled. "To put the blame on me most likely."

Her arm burned. "If you didn't kill him, why would you care?" she asked and wrenched at her arm.

His grip tightened, and his nails cut deeper into her skin. "Who said I didn't?"

Beaumont wakes up

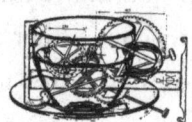

Beaumont closed Hoadley's jotter. Atwater Place. He needed to be there. It was still a few hours until nine, so at least he knew where Ancilla Walstrand was. He picked up Hoadley's words and lay them in her satchel, resealing it.

He made one of the guards drive him and ignoring the front stairs, he entered via the side gate and dodged the occasional moving tentacle and exchanged grim nods with the guards scattered around. By the time he reached Gordon, his head was continuously bobbing.

"Beaumont."

Just seeing Prime Inspector Hortense Gordon dressed smartly, ready for the day, made him feel old, tired. He was proud of her promotion. She was young and sharp. Their work together on the Windlass case had resulted in her being encouraged to take the prime exam earlier than expected and unsurprisingly, to him at least, she was doing a decent job of it.

"Gordon." Beaumont let his eyes drop to the body at her feet. A shattered breath escaped him, and he closed his eyes.

But it didn't make the image of the woman, sprawled out on the ground, her neck broken and her clothes with the myriad of rips in them, disappear.

He forced his eyes open to take in Doctor Morten crouching over her.

"Beaumont..." Gordon reached up, laying her hand on his shoulder. "You don't have to be here, you know that, right? I know I'm not you but..."

"Thank you, Gordon. But this is linked to Overton's death." He pushed at the muscles in his jaw, though no amount of massage was going to get the blood flowing. He swallowed trying to relax his throat. "The real question is, with all the strangeness going on...do you think you can handle working with me again?" Beaumont gave a decent shot at a smile. Her expression suggested he should have tried harder.

She slapped his shoulder but turned her attention to the body on the ground.

Beaumont stared at the sky. "What have you found so far?"

Gordon squatted down and picked up the edge of the torn waistcoat. "She was searched. Thoroughly." Gordon handed over a small pocket watch to him. "This was all we found on her. I've brought in extra guards to comb the area."

He gripped the watch in his hand, lowering himself to a crouch next to Dr Morten. He had to blink the water out of his eyes. He held onto the watch but did not let himself reach out and touch Hoadley. Somehow the thought of touching her would mean this wasn't all just a bad dream.

"Dr Morten, any preliminary findings?"

"I'll know more back at the lab, but I think we are looking at the same killer."

"Why do you say that?" He gazed down at Hoadley's shoulder, letting his eyes focus on a cut made by something sharp.

"It's hard to see out here, but I think it highly likely she died from a lack of oxygen." Morten packed her equipment away.

"But her neck's broken," said Gordon.

"As I said I need to look at this more back in the lab." Morten stood, the knuckles on her hand holding the bag, white. " But I think that was post-mortem."

"Why would someone break her neck after she died?" Gordon, as always was unable to stand still, rose and paced, careful to avoid the marked-out crime scene.

"Slashed and kicked her too," said Morten.

Beaumont forced himself to examine Hoadley's body. "All that damage was post-mortem?"

"Yes." The doctor shuffled back, away from the body.

"They didn't find what they were looking for," said Beaumont.

Gordon nodded. "They were pretty pissed off about it, too."

"This is Hoadley." Beaumont couldn't stop his hand from reaching out. His hand lowered, resting on her shoulder. It was real. She was gone. "She would have saved evidence." He had to believe she did not die for nothing.

Gordon shrugged. "We don't even know if there was evidence."

"Oh, there was." Beaumont gazed down at Hoadley's grazed cheekbone. "She was intense, but she was smart." He pushed himself to his feet. "She found something, I'm sure of it."

"So where is it?" asked Gordon.

Beaumont wrapped his hand around the back of his neck and squeezed.

"It's going to be a long day."

But he would spend a hundred days just like it if that is what it took to find Hoadley's killer.

"Another one, for you," said Gordon. "How long since you last slept?"

Doctor Morten peered at Beaumont, her forehead creasing. "Got some impressive bloodshot eyes going on there Beaumont."

"Indeed." He scanned the Gove full of inspectors. "Do we know where the tracks start?"

"Yes." Gordon strode off towards the house.

"Tabitha, if we could make sure she is treated with respect?"

Morten nodded. "I'll look after her, Barnaby."

He gazed down at his partner's twisted body, swallowed down his fury and turned, catching up with Gordon, matching his stride with hers.

The image of Hoadley's body lying on the ground joining

the crowd of dead in the back of his mind, whispering their disappointment in him.

Gordon picked up a small decorative box. "Which room did she spend the most time in?"

"The drawing room. Long enough to find the hidden desk." Beaumont frowned. "She was also in the room next door and conservatory with Ancilla for a while. And the ballroom and gallery."

Gordon put down the box and shot a stare at Beaumont. "Ancilla huh?"

Beaumont's cheekbones darkened. "Zer Ancilla Walstrand, she is, was, the assistant to Marcellus Overton."

"I know who she is. A very accomplished woman."

Beaumont moved to a chair and crouched next to it running his hands over the frame.

"Hmm."

"Sense of humour too."

"How would you know?"

"Met her once. At an exhibition."

Beaumont paused, flicking a glance at Gordon.

"Firstly, what were you doing at an exhibition and secondly why were you talking to people. You know that you aren't very skilled at it."

Gordon's usually expressive face seemed stiff as she tried to smile at him. "I'm cultured you know. Now don't snort. Fine, Gary was. He wanted to see this exhibit and we were standing in front of this amazing installation, like moving water but you could see all the creatures that lived in it, anyway there was this woman standing, on her own and we started talking. I liked her."

"That woman you liked is currently a suspect in two murders."

"I could, at a pinch, imagine her killing her boss, but Hoadley?" Gordon scanned the room. "If she did hide it in the house, I don't think it's here."

Beaumont brown crinkled. "Gary was? Did he die?"

"He's still alive."

"Good to know." Beaumont glanced at her. "Sorry."

"Happens."

Beaumont groaned, his knees clicking as he stood up. "You're right. She wouldn't have had time to get to know the library."

Gordon headed towards the door leading to the gallery. "Let's see what's through here then."

Beaumont stood in the middle of the gallery. A sizeable room with one side highlighting the atrium, a large stand clock dominating another wall, and every other section covered in shelves, filled with hundreds of devices, each with its own nooks and crannies.

Beaumont exhaled, loudly. "We've got to be smart about this."

"Right smart." Gordon prodded the wall behind some shelves.

"That's your first thought, check the walls?" He carefully picked up an early version of a waste device, trying to work out work out if it had any hiding spaces without damaging it.

"No that is what inspectors are for. But we can make some educated guesses before we hand it over." Gordon touched a section of panelling and started to follow it around the room. Beaumont left her to it, examining the large clock dominating the wall. Surely it offered opportunities for hiding things.

"Atwater Place does have some interesting architecture I'll admit, but I'm not sure that it is worthy of the gendarmerie's attention."

Beaumont grimaced. Did Alistair have nothing better to do with his day?

"Zer Atwater, we meet again."

"You *are* in my house Prime Inspector."

"Your house?" asked Gordon, her words reverberating around the room and Alistair's eyes widened. He took in her lime green striped gendarmerie waistcoat and matching bright green eyes and straightened.

"Yes..." he glanced at Beaumont.

"Prime Inspector Gordon allow me to introduce Zer Alistair Atwater." Beaumont waved a hand between them.

"Two Prime Inspectors on a case? Well with the death of poor Inspector Hoadley..." He frowned. "It has all gotten rather serious, hasn't it? Not that it wasn't before...but..." He bowed in her direction. "Yes, the house is in the Atwater family name."

"Zer Atwater." Gordon had reached him and held out her hand.

Beaumont tried not to frown at Gordon's overly warm

smile. He took in Alistair's friendly face under the flop of overdone dark hair and long body draped in orange pinstripe.

Hoadley, Ancilla and now Gordon.

He couldn't see it himself.

Alistair held Gordon's hand, not immediately letting it go. "What exactly are you searching for?" he asked.

Beaumont cleared his throat and Gordon detached her hand. "We believe something of Hoadley's might be in the building, so we're looking for it.

Beaumont would have preferred to not tell him anything, but he supposed some things couldn't be avoided.

"From the way you are prodding the walls I'm assuming you aren't expecting it to be left on top of a shelf."

"Hoadley was the soul of discretion," said Beaumont his throat tight.

Unfortunately, so much discretion she didn't think she could tell anyone where she was going. No this wasn't her fault. This was his fault for not finishing this case sooner and the killer's fault for taking her life. "If she did leave something behind, I'm sure she would have put it somewhere safe."

"Hmm," Alistair stroked his chin. "From here it appears more like a treasure hunt."

Gordon's laugh peeled out, too loud and too merrily considering Hoadley was still out there in the cold. Beaumont pulled out his jotter, turning it over in his hands, giving him something to stare at.

"You're right, Zer Atwater—"

"Alistair."

"Alistair." Gordon smiled at him. "While there might not be any golden doubloons at the end, since this is, as you have clarified, your house, any suggestions on where we might search?"

Alistair scanned the room.

"Not here. A very nice room but it is a public room. Visible through the glass. My guess would be the library or conservatory." Alistair frowned at them. "This is about Marcellus, isn't it? His death started all of this."

"Yes, zer Atwater, I think we can safely say that," said Beaumont. He tried not to roll his eyes, channelling Hoadley, and her annoyance at repeating the obvious. He liked to think she would appreciate living in his memory that way.

"You were very curious about where he was and who saw him."

Beaumont nodded. "Yes, a natural part of the investigation."

A master painter like Alistair should have a better grasp of shade.

"Alistair," said Gordon, "You mentioned the library." She tilted her head, examining him. "Are there any secret compartments or places where someone could hide something?"

"In a book I would think." He flashed her an attempt at a charming smile.

"Thank you, Zer, we wouldn't have thought of that." Beaumont's voice was dry.

"You grew up in this house, right?" asked Gordon.

"Yes, I had that privilege. Though it wasn't like this then." Beaumont dropped his hands from the clock he had been examining, giving Alistair his full attention. "What do you mean?"

"It was a home back then. Normal rooms etc. I mean the conservatory has always been there but about a decade ago Mother had it completely redone and had the atrium built. It was a massive project but well." He gestured towards the glass wall and the atrium beyond. "It was quite the engineering feat."

"I would like to see all the access points between the floors."

Alistair laughed. "There are a few. Mother put them in wherever she could fit them."

They followed Alistair out of the ballroom and turned left towards a large staircase leading upstairs.

"He's married," Beaumont whispered to Gordon.

"I know." She shrugged, giving Beaumont a small grin.

Beaumont's lips thinned.

"Oh relax." She slapped him on the back. "I would never do anything to risk the investigation." She bounded up the stairs to join Alistair at the top.

"This is the main one staircase," said Alistair, peering down his nose at Beaumont as he started to climb. "It's usually used by the staff and if we want to move pieces of furniture around."

"How many other stairwells are there?"

Alistair shrugged. "I'm not sure. Six? Squeezed into the corners. There used to be only one, the large staircase at the back. You had to walk the length of the house to get to it. Mother decided to make sure she never had to do that again."

"Great," said Beaumont.

He imagined all the different hiding places that Hoadley could have found in this rabbit warren. She must have left behind something. Why else would her body be searched and so much anger taken out on it? But what would her final thoughts have been?

"Sensible," said Gordon.

Alistair smiled at her. "Perhaps I can give you a tour sometime?"

Beaumont firmly gripped the ornate banister as he climbed. When he reached the second level, overlooking the atrium, he forced his fingers to release, stepping forward. Glass on one side and walls covered in moving murals on the other, didn't help.

Alistair examined him. "I'm assuming you'll want to see Marcellus' rooms first."

"Is there a stairwell from his room to downstairs?" Beaumont asked.

"Not directly, but there is a small spiral staircase in the spare room next to him that leads to the gallery."

"Sounds worth checking out," said Gordon and Alistair smiled at her again.

Beaumont's stomach rolled. He knew Gordon was just compartmentalising, but Hoadley deserved their full attention.

Alistair pushed open the first door and Beaumont forced himself to step casually into Marcellus' room. His hands finally relaxing now there was a nice steady wall between him and the glass outside. His brain refused to treat something transparent as a wall.

Beaumont examined the room, immediately seeing why everyone had referred to it as a workshop. There was a day bed on one side but the rest of it was full of worktables and parts, and the main feature was a massive blank wall, perfect for practising light art installations. The wall itself was currently white with a lever on the side, and a dial of colour markings next to it. Some normal, others a metallic shade. His fingers itched.

Gordon kicked one of the metal pieces on the ground. "I know he was a brilliant illuminator, but was he the full package? An inventor as well?"

Alistair picked up the piece of metal and carefully placed it on the workbench. Beaumont hated to think what Gordon had just kicked and was grateful that Felicia wasn't in the room.

"Yes he usually left the building of devices to others, but it didn't mean he couldn't and, to give him credit, he was excellent at taking the base model and tweaking it to give amazing results."

Gordon went up to what had to be the illuminier. It was rather disappointing, a box, with a gramophone on one side and lots of small tubes on the other. She started prodding it and Alistair swallowed a moan. Probably torn between his desire to save the device and not appear fussy.

"Leave the device alone Gordon," said Beaumont. Alistair shot him a glance that Beaumont interpreted as grateful.

"I'm assuming this is the illuminier we've heard so much about?"

"Yes." Alistair stroked it gently, his face wistful. "It is an amazing feat, to be able bend light like this. I just wish..."

"Can you show us what it does?" Gordon asked, sidling up close to Alistair and gazing down at the illuminier.

Alistair's cheekbones were highlighted by a dark tinge. "Unfortunately my mastery of light is limited."

Beaumont forced his gaze to stay on the illuminier. Ancilla could test it. What did that say about Alistair? What exactly was he hiding?

Gordon frowned. "Shame, I'd offer to try, but pneuma's never been my forte." She flicked a glance at Beaumont. "You've got a bit though. Why don't you see if it is working?"

Beaumont cleared his throat. "I doubt—"

"Could be important to the case." She tapped her lips. "Has anyone tried to turn it on since Overton's death?" She widened her eyes and stared at Beaumont. "What if that's the reason he died?"

Beaumont frowned. "We can bring someone in—"

"Or it might be nothing." She shrugged. "The High Protector won't be happy if we waste time testing it when it isn't relevant." She smiled up at Alistair. "Are you sure you can't just..." she spun her finger in a circle above the illuminier.

Alistair gave an uncomfortable smile. "I would if I could."

"Well, it will have to be Beaumont then."

"I really—"

"Nothing fancy, just turn it on, so we can see if anyone has tampered with it." She grinned. "I'll make sure it is documented how the amazing Prime Inspector Barnaby Beaumont was able to test it."

He hated that the prop to his ego worked. If the assistant Ancilla could turn it on, then surely he could. He had opened her diary pages after all. What did that say about Alistair Atwater the master painter though?

He stepped forward.

"Here." Alistair pointed at five finger impressions on each side of the device. "Put your fingers here, and then let the pneuma flow."

Beaumont regretted even considering this idea, his hands trembling as they settled into the grooves. The metal hummed, creating a suction, ground his hands in it and then the pneuma flowed. More pneuma than he had ever experienced before.

"Woh," said Gordon.

Beaumont had closed his eyes and forced them open. A chair and table now existed. Painted in light, but real. Faint and see-through true, but more real than he could ever have imagined. He tried to remove his hands, but they stayed gripped in the flow.

"Impressive Prime Inspector," drawled Alistair. He reached out, grabbing Beaumont's wrists and ripping them off the device. "Best be careful."

Beaumont's arm flopped down to his side as the room was bathed in darkness.

"Awww." Gordon frowned at them. "That was amazing. No wonder everyone is going crazy about it. How does it do that?"

Alistair stared at Beaumont for a moment before turning to Gordon with a bow. "I fear Prime Inspector, that conversation will have to wait until we both have time to sit down and enjoy it."

"Well count me in." She glanced at the illuminier again. "And let me know when the next demonstration is."

"I'll send you an invite personally." Alistair smiled, warmly, at her.

Beaumont practised getting his arms to move again. His whole body suddenly filled with lead.

"You said there wasn't a stairwell in this room?" asked Gordon.

Beaumont could almost see her clicking back into work mode.

The guards, and some inspectors, had already examined the workshop and from what he had read it was exactly what it appeared to be.

"Yes, it's in the next room." Alistair opened the door and gestured for them to exit.

Despite it being the last thing, he wanted to do, Beaumont headed out onto the glass hallway.

He glanced to the left. More glass.

"Where?"

Alistair stepped past him. Beaumont instinctively shuffled sideways to give him more room, briefly pushing up against the glass.

The world exploded with diamonds and leaves.

He would like to say that life flashed passed his eyes but all he could think about was if he was going to go this was a pretty place to do it. That was until a branch of the tree snapped across his back. He howled.

The panel of glass remnants continued their fall to the floor of the atrium.

The tree, large enough to catch him, left him bent backwards across a branch, spasming. He tried to relax his muscles, but fear of falling further only tightened them.

"Beaumont." Gordon leant out to peer down at him. "You alright?"

Beaumont tried to draw in breath without moving his body.

"No," he took another shallow breath, "in a bit of bother really."

He could make out Alistair standing behind Gordon and had a momentary panic that he was about to push her and finish the job on both of them.

"Pipe it." Alistair leaned out as well.

"Perhaps, Zer Atwater, Prime Inspector Gordon, one of you could organise some assistance?" asked Beaumont.

Beaumont closed his eyes and tried to breathe. He had always made an effort to keep his muscle tone to the requisite levels, but he regretted, for a moment, not being as diligent as Gordon.

If she had fallen, she would have engaged her stomach muscles and lifted herself up. All the while keeping her whole weight balanced on her pinkie.

The branch reverberated, and he opened his eyes, swivelling his head to see a ladder appear next to him. Okay so he was somehow meant to get himself to that without falling off, was he?

"You alright to get down now Beaumont?" asked Gordon. The gurgle of laughter dancing between the tones of concern made his lips twist.

"Yes, Gordon I'm fine."

"Never seen anyone get stuck lying across a branch before."

"Yes thank you, Gordon."

"Reminds me of those poor turtles that accidentally fall on their backs. Waving their little legs around."

"Gordon."

"Just making an observation."

Although his back protested every move, he rolled, carefully, onto his side. Attempting to muffle his groans as he inched his way to safety. The ladder pushed back from the branch as he slid up to it, but he grabbed it, holding it firmly against the branch and forcing himself to swing his leg over. One step at a time. But it was only when his feet touched the ground he started breathing again.

"Anyway..." Beaumont carefully turned, no sudden movements, gazing up at the now glass free wall and then at the broken bits of glass scattered around the base of the tree, his gaze connecting with the tired one of Felicia Atwater. Her silver hair was still tightly pulled back. Perhaps a physical representation of her attempting to control the one thing she could during this time of chaos.

"Please accept our sincere apologies Prime Inspector Beaumont." She frowned and tapped her walking stick against the floor. "That glass should be able to hold the weight of a hundred people. I can assure you that we'll have it tested—"

"If you don't mind, Zer Atwater, it might be best if our people examined it." Perhaps someone not ready for his partnership with Hoadley to end? Or had it been intended for someone else? "Gordon, I also want all the other panes of glass tested and safety barriers put up to avoid any other unfortunate accidents."

Gordon nodded, disappearing to find a messenger.

Felicia's eyes narrowed. "Do you think it was deliberate?" she asked.

"That the glass outside of Overton's room was potentially tampered with?" Beaumont frowned as he examined the tree. Like him, it was unlikely that anyone would die if they fell. "With Overton's murder..."

Felicia's eyebrows raised. "You think it was meant for Overton?" She frowned following Beaumont's gaze to the tree.

"Potentially, though I'm not sure for what purpose." Beaumont frowned and stared at the empty hole outside Overton's room. "Did he stop there? To gaze down at the tree or the sky above."

Felicia's face stiffened. "Yes."

Alistair shook his head. "Probably not lately though."

"True, we have been so busy..." her head dropped forward. "We haven't really taken time for breaks." She swallowed. "But he used to sometimes take a moment, especially at night, to stare at the sky."

"Right." Beaumont frowned, he wasn't sure if that helped

him or not. "Have you had any work done on this glass recently? Or any renovations on the home?"

Felicia's eyes widened and she exchanged a glance with Alistair. "A couple of weeks ago. We had a burst pipe in one of the bathrooms upstairs."

"What caused the pipe to burst?"

"I don't know. I put it down to one of those things," said Felicia.

"I'll need the details of who you used."

Gordon practically skipped back into the room.

"Gordon, work was carried out two weeks ago. Would you be willing to track down who did that?"

"Anything for you Beaumont." She patted his shoulder.

Beaumont grimaced, a sharp pain rippling through his back.

Gordon's sharp eyes narrowed. "You alright?" she asked.

Beaumont nodded. "My back is...objecting to the treatment it has received."

Gordon frowned. "Perhaps you should go to the medic. All jokes aside you did take quite a fall."

Beaumont creaked from side to side. It hurt, but no more than normal. If history had taught him anything tomorrow was going to be the bad day. Right now he needed to keep moving if he wanted to be of any use to Hoadley.

"It'll be fine. I'm more concerned about the glass. Wondering if it's possible that the person who killed him wasn't the same person who weakened the glass."

"Two killers and two deaths?" Gordon gave a whistle. "Things are getting interesting."

Felicia, Alistair and Beaumont turned towards her, and she blushed. "Sorry."

"You'll have to forgive my colleague," said Beaumont. "But I can assure you that we are both committed to finding out who killed Marcellus Overton."

Felicia's face sagged. "To be honest it is all a bit much." She blinked. "And with that blasted bill." She glared at the broken glass. "Did you know they asked me to sing to open parliament on the day that they're..."

Alistair wrapped his arms around her shoulders. "Come on, Mother," said Alistair. "Let's leave them to it."

"Yes, yes I think I will if you don't mind."

The dark circles under her eyes highlighted the emptiness in them. He just wasn't sure he would call it grief. Rather a deep tiredness at the weight of it all pulling her down.

"Prime Inspector." A guard rushed over to them, a note clutched in her hand. "You asked to be told when she arrived. She's here and she wants to see you."

Beaumont trudged along the hallway, his gait getting slower and slower the closer he came to the large door of the High Protector's office. He stood there breathing in through his nose, his gaze tracing the vine of scrolls, representing the knowledge of the past, to the centre cog in the door. He reached out, touching it. The door swung inwards.

He entered the office and as soon as he passed the threshold, the door shut.

Click.

Lock engaged. The High Protector Cadwell put down a

letter she was reading, and her gaze landed on him with a punch.

"Prime Inspector Beaumont. Thank you for coming in so early."

"I've been here since I heard, High Protector."

"I see." She frowned at him. "How're you doing?"

"I'm..." He swallowed. "I'm not great. I haven't been...I should've..."

"The only person to blame for this is the person or persons who killed her." She leaned back in her chair. A masterpiece of design made of metal and red velvet that was both aesthetically pleasing, much more than his own which was more metal than velvet, and functionally comfortable.

Beaumont's back protested as he settled into a much more basic seat across from her. "Maybe, but..."

"The message I received said her body was found at the Atwater's residence."

"Amongst the statues, near the external gate. One of the kraken sculptures had a loose tentacle and a mechanic was scheduled to come in and fix it first thing. He found her."

One of Cadwell's eyebrows rose. "And if the mechanic hadn't been there?"

"I don't know..." Beaumont brushed at his face. He hated to think of Hoadley lying there, unknown. "It's not an area the family use that often."

Cadwell leaned forward, resting her elbows on the desk, her hands clasped in front of her. "Why were the guards removed from Atwater Place?"

Beaumont's throat tightened. "Zer Atwater requested it zer and forensics had finished…"

Cadwell's face was grim but she nodded. "Very well, but why was she there on her own?"

He examined her face, trying to find blame. He took a deep breath.

"I don't know High Protector. We had a rough night. I—I was too out of it to…"

Cadwell hummed. "You were drugged. Alfred told me about the state you were in. He said that the drug made Inspector Hoadley and Zer Ancilla Walstrand, reckless."

Beaumont nodded glumly. "I don't know about Hoadley, I don't remember much of her last night, but Ancilla, Zer Walstrand, was, over-excited."

Cadwell grunted. "What lead was Hoadley following?"

Beaumont ran his fingers through his hair. "She was highly suspicious of the Walstrands and she was determined to find out about Cuthbert's link to all of this. And there was a thug, Perry."

"But she ended up at Atwater Place?"

"A recessed desk, it and other recesses, the house is riddled with them, have been searched. Nothing of interest." Beaumont glanced down at his hands. "Her notes were comprehensive—"

"You've read them?" Cadwell raised one eyebrow.

"When the message said she had been killed. I…I felt it might offer us some insight."

Cadwell exhaled. "Quite right. We would have had to read them eventually though I suspect she would have preferred it not to be you." She tapped the edges of a pile of papers on her desk, lining them up. "Did you find anything?"

Beaumont's brow furrowed. In truth he wasn't sure, but he doubted that was what she wanted to hear. "Hoadley carefully captured the conversations with the witnesses she was privy to, her text is a valuable resource."

"All very nice." Cadwell waved her hand. "But does it give any insight into what she did last night?"

"From reading it was clear she wanted to investigate the illuminier device and other devices Overton was using."

"At the Atwater's or his flat?"

"I..." Beaumont lifted his eyes from the carpet where they had been resting and stared at her. "The Atwaters. There were only a few hours left in the night and if she was found just after dawn..."

Cadwell tilted her head, examining him. "Do you want to do this? Or do you want to transfer it all to Prime Inspector Gordon?"

Beaumont stood, pacing to the large window that overlooked the centre of the Way. It had been a long time since he had joined the team in the open courtyard at its centre, which the gendarmerie had filled with a collection of tables and chairs broken up by large pot plants and leftover decorations from some squad celebration.

"I already told her I would stay on. I agree they are linked." He swallowed, "But I don't know if I have the heart to..." Beaumont rested his hand against the glass enjoying the chill of the outside trying to break through.

The High Protector's chair squeaked as she rose, joining

him at the window. "I hope that this tragedy doesn't influence your decision Beaumont."

"My decision?"

"To stay or leave the gendarmerie."

Beaumont blinked, turning towards her. He had written his resignation letter hundreds of times over the last year, but he hadn't been aware that the High Protector knew about it.

"Zer?"

"No need to pretend with me Beaumont. This work is hard to do forever, and you've had some pretty intense cases, especially the last one..."

"Yes, zer."

"People gossip Beaumont, accept it."

"I have, zer." Though their gossip added to the weight.

Cadwell scowled. "We need people like you Beaumont."

Beaumont shrugged. "No one's indispensable, zer." *Necessary* people filled graveyards. Every time he passed one, he found he was less and less concerned with being one. Of the indispensables that is. He was quite happy not being one of the people on the ground.

"True, but you have an excellent mind for these things."

"Thank you, zer." He wasn't sure what that said about him, and his mind.

Cadwell glowered at him. "I want you on this case Beaumont. If it's thrown you for a loop, look after yourself first and all that. But the truth is..." Cadwell's lips thinned, and she peered at him. "I don't want some fool nabbed for this because they have "arrest me" painted all over them while the person who killed one of our own goes free."

"Hortense Gordon is a valuable investigator."

"Yes, she is. But from what I hear, this case is an absolute nightmare with confusing facts all over the place. Not to mention the Atwaters are involved and an Administrator from the patent office. If this came into the office right now there is only one person, I would assign it to, and that's you."

Beaumont grunted. "I'm not sure your faith in me is justified."

"Don't be modest. We all have our strengths." She returned to her chair, settling back, her fingers clasped across her front, examining him. "The truth is Prime Inspector Gordon is a better gendarmerie than you, and don't you forget it. But you...excel at the...nuanced ones. And this has nuance written all over it."

Beaumont ran his hand over his face. "According to Hoadley's notes, there might have been an impersonator on the night, and The lab thinks Overton died three days before." He took her lead and resumed his seat in the visitor's chair, hiding his wince as something in his back pulled tight.

Cadwell threw her arms in the air. "That's what I'm talking about. The newspapers couldn't make up this stuff. I told Prime Inspector Gordon that it was likely that the investigations would be combined with you leading it."

"And what did she say to that?"

"What do you think she said? She told me my idea was brilliant and that she would help in any way she could." Cadwell peered intently at him. "*She* isn't a fool."

Beaumont surprised himself with a chuckle, but it faded quickly. "We spoke and yes, I'll work with her on this."

Cadwell nodded, sitting further back in her chair.

Beaumont cleared his throat. "Who are the Walstrands? I understand that Ernest is an Administrator but is there a mother? Are they connected to a family?" Beaumont hated that he had to ask. He should have already assigned someone to investigate their background.

Cadwell examined him, a slightly amused expression on her face. "Getting me to do your research for you now?" she waved off his objections, "The Walstrands..."

Beaumont waited. Sometimes Cadwell needed a moment to get her thoughts together before launching in.

"The mother, she's gone. Left about fifteen years ago now."

"Is she still alive?" asked Beaumont.

"We believe so. She's the youngest daughter of a very influential family from Muffleward. I understand that they keep track of her."

"And Ernest? Has he searched for her too?"

Cadwell shrugged. "If he did, he stopped a long time ago. From what I could find, when she took off, leaving him alone with three teenage kids, her family did right by them with some financial assistance, but relations were never warm." Cadwell clasped her hands over her stomach. "As soon as the kids' schooling finished, Ernest got a job at the Patent Office and relocated to Noxrath."

"And what does the patent office have to say about him?"

And all the children still lived at home. A tight-knit

family? Brought together by the mother's abandonment? Or a controlling father?

"He's extremely detail-oriented. I think the quality of work is held in high regard. He's had a number of promotions since being here." Cadwell frowned.

"But?"

"There was an implication that he wasn't well-liked."

"In what way?"

Cadwell shrugged. "Just reading between the lines. Despite being promoted, he's never been in charge of any people."

Trusted with secrets but not people. Perhaps the patent office leaders had better instincts than he gave them credit for.

"What exactly does he do there?"

"He assesses similar patents and the appeals to decisions."

Beaumont tapped his lip. "Could that be where Cuthbert is getting the 'prototypes' he's trying to sell? He doesn't strike me as someone who's an inventor himself. Though the sister could be making them."

Cadwell shot a sharp glance at him.

"Perhaps, though the senior leaders had a lot of faith in Ernest's integrity. Which sister are we talking about?"

"Ancilla, the one at the Purple Door last night."

"Best bring her back in." She examined him. "You care for Hoadley. I'll issue the notice to pick her up."

"Yes, zer." Beaumont rose, his throat closing shut. And that was that. Hoadley had joined the endless loop of death and cases that apparently only he could solve. An invisible force strangling him. He forced his fingers to stay relaxed at his sides and shuffled to the door, hearing the click of it unlocking.

He refused an offer of a lift back to Atwater Place. He needed to be outside. Needed a moment, and if he didn't keep moving his back would seize up.

Wrapped up in his coat and scarf and his hat firmly secured to his head he set off for the Atwaters. The bracing wind, a welcome relief after the artificial heat of the Way. He didn't mind being warm but why it also had to be stuffy was beyond him.

Every step helped.

It was too early for much foot traffic, but the sky was a bright silver. Yeast mixed with coffee twisted through the air drawing him towards the open cafes and bakeries.

He bought himself a coffee. Not his usual fare but his brain needed all the help it could get today.

He gulped down the hot liquid as he went, imagining it sloshing through his veins, activating his brain.

The protesters outside the patent office were sharing coffee and snacks before taking their positions. As the date of the bill being read in parliament approached, he doubted it would stay that way for long, but for now both sides were amicable, happy being heard.

Gordon had asked him the other day what he thought about it all. He wasn't sure. Each generation of the Families kept upping the price of medical devices, pushing some medical services out of people's reach. The government couldn't own it all. Would they want them to anyway?

The only thing he was sure of? No one was going to be happy.

Wide stairs and the enormous façade of Atwater Place came into view, along with the guards once more allocated to protect the evidence and the residence.

If they hadn't pulled the guards out of Atwater Place yesterday, if if if. The word swirled, drowning his mind, any peace gained from his walk whisked away.

He climbed the front stairs, his guts clenching, reminding him why he didn't drink coffee.

"Zer." One of the guards on the door greeted him.

Beaumont nodded back.

"Where's Prime Inspector Gordon?"

"In the library, zer."

He gave the guard a nod, ignored the library doorway and headed into the atrium. The tree was beautiful in the winter daylight, its muted green touched with a silver tinge. His legs stretched out and he strode forward pushing through the glass doors. He glanced up at the tree but didn't slow down, pressing through the doors on the other side.

"Prime Inspector."

Between him and the door to the washroom, which he had become intimately familiar with yesterday, was Alistair Atwater.

"Zer Atwater." He nodded respectfully at him but knowing that release was nearby had turned up the pressure on his bowels, the intensity making Beaumont's eyes water. He stepped around him.

"What's this I hear about Marcellus being dead before the party?"

Beaumont almost at the washroom door, spun back around. *Don't react you fool.*

"I'm sorry?"

"Marcellus, I heard he died a few days before he was discovered. How's that possible?"

"Indeed," he said, face stiff. "Can I ask, zer, where you heard this information?"

Alistair frowned. "From some techs talking while waiting for their coffee."

"And they mentioned Marcellus?"

"No, not specifically, but how many other illuminators are the subject of a murder enquiry?"

Rage whipped through him. Weak from tiredness and guilt Beaumont struggled to contain his frustration. Alistair's eyes widened and Beaumont drew in air through his nose forcing himself to calm down.

"It's true then?"

Beaumont's lips thinned. "As I am sure you are aware I can't share details of the investigation with you."

"Perhaps then I should ask around? See if anyone, the press, the Walstrands, see if they have heard anything?"

Beaumont didn't like being blackmailed. He moistened his mouth.

"There are some...anomalies with the tests. The lab techs believe that this confuses the time of death. This has not been verified by the doctor and it is something we are investigating."

Alistair's eyebrows drew together. "And you'll tell me if it is?"

"Zer Atwater—"

Alistair held up his hand and exhaled heavily.

"Fine, fine. But I would appreciate any information you can share."

"I'm hoping, Zer Atwater, that the next bit of information I share with you will be of the arrest of Overton and Inspector Hoadley's killer."

Alistair flushed. "Yes, right of course. Sorry for your loss. Always hard to lose one of your team."

"Indeed," said Beaumont, the pressure inside him building again. "If you don't mind?"

"Yes, yes. Of course."

Beaumont strode into the washroom, locking the door behind him. The last thing he wanted was anyone else interrupting him. As the internal pressure reduced below, the tension in his neck and shoulder rose. What a mess.

He washed his hands and splashed some water on his face, staring at the deep caves under his bloodshot eyes.

As long as Hoadley's killer was out there, rest would have to wait.

Ancilla Fights

It had taken a cog up the nose and a sharp kick to the knee before Ancilla had been able to escape Freddy.

Once on the street, she saw a large couple getting out of a steamer, but she ducked into the narrow alley that led into the Treadways a few blocks away, rather than risk going to strangers for help.

The alley was so narrow that she pushed against its sides to help her along. Freddy wouldn't be far behind, and she needed to be in the safety of the Treadways before he found her.

Her breathing drowned out any noise, but she didn't waste time looking behind her and focused on moving as fast as possible. At the end of the alley, she slowed her pace to match that of the tide of people grabbing a quick break-fast before starting work, forcing her lungs to slow down and swallowing her gasps. A food cart that used a steam lift to carry its clients to a rooftop that was decorated with metal flowers and plants caught her eye. Last time she was here it had served a decent bacon bunty. It also gave her an excellent view of the street.

Despite the pale silver of early light and the icy winter's morning, the workers at the dirigible yards and manufacturing warehouses were out getting their breakfast. At any other time, she would have had some of her invention cards. These were the customers for her fabrics after all. But instead, she pulled her coat closely around her and tilted her hat, protecting herself from the unwanted gazes, and the cold. A coffee, and a bacon bunty, there was no reason to go hungry, allowed her to blend in, and the steam of the coffee warmed her face. The familiarity of its fumes made her feel, for a moment, that everything was going to be okay.

She sat there for an hour, watching the sun come up, scanning the street for Freddy. He did not show.

Freddy killed Marcellus? It just didn't make sense. She was starting to get some glances as the morning crowds built up, so she took the lift down and hailed a steamer.

There was nothing for it, she needed to get back to the Way and find Hoadley, now.

But the traffic made it slow going.

"The last time I saw it this busy was when the patent office was doing their best patents of the year parade. Do you remember that?" said the driver.

"Yes, it was an enjoyable parade." She smiled awkwardly at him.

"A great parade. But the problem with parades..." he adjusted one of the mirrors so he could see her more clearly. "The problem with parades is that they have to block off some of the streets. Always causes mayhem."

She poked at her temples. Right now, her head was full of information and its implications, and she just wanted to sit there and feel overwhelmed by it.

"Yes, true. But nice that people get to celebrate don't you think?" she mumbled. The only beneficial thing about the parade was that Ernest was usually involved, and he often took Cuthbert and Melody with him giving her a rare moment of privacy.

"Yeah, well I don't think they are celebrating today," said the driver.

"No, I suppose not." Ancilla gazed at the arms and elbows shoving each other that filled her view.

"The whole thing is more trouble than it's worth if you ask me." The driver twisted around trying to peer into the throng of people.

Ancilla was not sure exactly what he was looking for. "Really?" She could have smacked herself.

"I suppose it makes sense." He peered at her in his mirror. "Though I don't know why some of the Families are supporting it. I mean what's in it for them?"

"I don't know. I suppose I just assumed they thought it was the right thing to do." She shrugged, holding her hands out wide palms up.

"Right thing? The Families? All they have to do is release

their designs to the market. No need to make a song and dance about it with bills and all that."

"I suppose not." Ancilla stared at him, her head tiling. But she really didn't care, all she wanted to do was hand over the problem of Freddy to Hoadley.

"Also, what I would like to know..." he hit the horn as a steamer changed lanes in front of him. "Is what the government gets out of it too."

"I don't think they get anything."

"Not directly, but there will be something. Problem is we won't know until the next bill comes through."

"Another reason to clog up the roads." Ancilla gave a little laugh, but the driver didn't join in, so it faded into awkward silence.

"What's your business with the Way?" he asked.

"The Way?"

"That's where we are going aren't we?"

"Er...yes that's right," she mumbled.

He examined her. "You don't seem like the kind of person who'd be getting into trouble."

"I have something I have to give them."

"I hope they reimburse you for this ride." He moved over a lane but immediately came to a stop. People overflowed the footpath into the street, trapping the steamers. "Not that you are going to get there anytime soon."

"No."

The steamer door flung open. Hands grabbed Ancilla, dragging her from the steamer.

"Hey, let her go." The driver scrambled out.

Fingers dug into her arm as they dragged her, keeping her off balance, the driver disappearing behind the sea of people. There were two of them. One had his arm under her shoulders, forcing her face into his chest, smothering her. The mixture of stale sweet and spices suggested it had been a while since he was home. The other clamped her arm around Ancilla's waist, lifting her up so only the tips of her toes dragged against the ground.

She twisted, managing to wrench her head free.

"Guards." She had never trained to be a singer, but she threw as much pneuma as she could into the sound. It didn't act the same way as light, but she managed to amplify it enough to hear herself over the noise.

"Shut her up you fool."

"You shut her up."

A hand tried to grab hold of her head, to press it against the chest. She twisted her head free again.

"Guards." She got a bit more volume this time.

"Pipe it."

One of them squeezed her head. The other one crowded close, hiding the move from any curious gazes in the crowd.

Ancilla twisted her upper body, following the direction of the vice around her head, and the grip on her waist slipped, causing her feet to jolt against the ground. But with her head firmly pressed against the chest she wasn't free and clear yet.

On the upside her hands were.

She jabbed in the general direction of someone's kidneys and the grip around her head loosened.

A pair of hands grabbed at her from behind, but she kicked backward connecting with something soft and she dropped into a crouch. Not the most defensible of positions but enough to give her a much-needed second to get her bearings.

A large woman and man spun towards her, looming over her with matching snarls on their faces.

The back of her brain clicked. The couple in the steamer. But why follow her?

Get away first, investigate second.

She pushed up and sideways into the thick of the crowd and legged it. People swore at her, elbows connected with her head, but soon she had enough people between them to confuse the issue.

Ancilla focused on being small and invisible. Something that she had spent her whole life practising.

The beginning of Clearwater Way was visible at the end of the crowd.

She hurried towards it. The crowd thinned at the edges, reducing her cover even as she got close to freedom. She pushed through and stepped onto the Way.

A hand thumped down on her arm, hitting the same bruised flesh that everyone was so fond of all of a sudden. She winced and raised her gaze to the two people in front of her.

"You, come with us."

{ 20 }

Death's Confusion

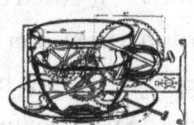

Beaumont needed to speak with Dr Morten. His instincts had been wrong once before. What if they were again? And once again someone died because of his blindness.

Pipe it.

He went to find Gordon in the library. She was standing in the middle, staring at some pages.

"You found it?" he asked.

She shook her head. "Latest pathology reports. I think we need to talk to our Dr Morten."

Beaumont nodded. "How?" Beaumont's lips disappeared. "How could she not know that the body was more than a few hours old?"

More time wasted. People would report him for loitering between Atwater Place and the Way by the time this was over.

"Everyone makes mistakes, we can't talk." Gordon trotted along next to him.

He grunted and kept moving.

Gordon groaned. "When are you going to forgive yourself for that? He wasn't even a suspect—"

"We should have seen it." Beaumont hunched his shoulders but didn't slow down.

"Why? We aren't all-powerful. We followed the evidence."

"To the wrong person." He focused on lengthening his gait.

"Temporarily." Gordon threw her hands in the air, increasing her trot to keep up. "We got him in the end."

"Not before another death." Beaumont closed his eyes. "Before more kids died."

"And who knows how many more saved."

"Now Hoadley's killed because I've been dithering on this case—"

"Has it even been forty-eight hours?"

Beaumont did not respond and focused on extending his stride as much as possible forcing the only slightly shorter Gordon to move up to a bit of a jog.

He probably should have taken a steamer, but the walk had allowed him to calm down. He paused in front of the mortuary and took a few deep breaths.

Beaumont stared at Gordon. She stared back.

"You might be right," he said.

"I usually am." Gordon shrugged.

Beaumont shook his head. "But that doesn't explain a doctor not being able to tell the difference between an hour-old and three-day-old corpse."

He pulled the door open but was forced to step aside to let the latest tour group out. They seemed to be almost hourly these days.

The morgue gave the light an unnatural tinge during the day, giving death a harsher edge, sharpened by the compounds soaking the air.

Beaumont headed to the autopsy room. He rested his hand against the door.

"You don't have to go in," said Gordon. "I can ask her the questions."

Beaumont wished he could, he wished he could walk away from this but the inevitable knock on his door advising him of another death turned his hand.

Keeping his eyes high he stepped through, the visible huff of his breath the only sound.

Ping.

Other than the machine.

What the pipes?

"Could she be finished already?" Beaumont asked.

"No way," said Gordon.

"Pipe it." He spun from the room, strode down the corridor and pulled open the door to Dr Morten's office.

He would like to think he loomed in the doorway, but that was hard to carry off in a morgue where everything was scarier than he was.

"Prime Inspector." Dr Morten glanced up. "And Prime Inspector." She frowned. "A bit confusing to have you two working together, isn't it?"

"Anything from Hoadley's autopsy?" asked Beaumont. He tried to stop his lip from curling up in a sneer.

Dr Morten dropped the paper in her hand and sat back lacing her fingers together across her stomach.

"No, I was still working on the report from the last corpse you gave me."

His sneer slipped through.

"I'm sorry to be adding to your busy schedule."

"I always know I am going to be busy when you are on the case Beaumont."

Gordon's hand on his shoulder was the only reason he didn't lose control.

Dr Morten smiled.

"Now we have the pleasantries out of the way what brings you both here with such energy?"

Gordon stepped forward and shuffled between them. "We have a query about the time of death of Marcellus Overton."

Dr Morten nodded. "My report will reflect my initial assessment. Asphyxiation, and death within two to three hours of it being reported."

"What about the lab report?" asked Beaumont. He stepped further into the room.

"Lab report?"

"The one that indicated he might have died a few days before," said Gordon, stepping in next to him.

"Are you questioning my judgement Prime Inspectors?"

"We're concerned the facts don't add up Doctor," said Gordon, her smile sharp.

Doctor Morten rolled her eyes. "You're all fools. The lab

work is inconclusive, and I sincerely doubt Timothy could find anything unless it was handed to him, outlined, in bold."

"They found markers in the blood that said Overton was killed almost three days before he was reported dead," said Beaumont. His fingers wrapped around the back of his neck as he contemplated his friend.

"And how many witnesses told you that they saw Overton that night?" she asked.

Beaumont contemplated on whether to tell her about Fred or not.

"Witnesses are notoriously unreliable as you know." Gordon gave her a fake smile. "We had thirty people swear that they saw someone throw a chair through a window and it was only because there was a guard on the street who saw what really happened that the man wasn't convicted. So forgive me if I don't trust a witness as far as I can throw them." Gordon peered down at her. "What I do like is lab results."

"My report stands." Morten sat back, her fingers woven together and resting across her stomach.

The chemicals were softer in here but right now it didn't make it any easier to breathe.

"Have you sent your report in yet?" asked Beaumont. Was it about losing face?

"No."

"You could revisit it without anyone—"

"I'm not changing my report to please you Barnaby Beaumont." She creaked up to standing. "Now if you'll excuse me, I have to autopsy the latest corpse you have brought me."

"No." Gordon glared at her.

"I'm sorry?"

"I'm still listed as the Prime Inspector on that case, and I believe that you have a conflict of interest so I will be organising Hoadley's body to be removed from here and taken to the next available morgue."

"That's hours away and will only delay your investigation. On what grounds?"

"You worked with Hoadley didn't you?"

"I met her once."

"I believe that you formed an attachment to her. Especially as she was the colleague of your friend Barnaby Beaumont."

Dr Morten growled.

"That's ridiculous."

"But within my rights. If you'll excuse me, I have a body to organise." Gordon spun around but squeezed Beaumont's shoulder as she left. "Don't get arrested." Was breathed into Beaumont's ear and then she was gone.

Neither Dr Morten nor Beaumont moved.

"Why?"

"Why what?"

"Why are you filing a report you know isn't correct?" asked Beaumont.

"It's correct."

"You know this is wrong." Beaumont shook his head. The pain in his back billowed up into his head, the floor beckoned but he stayed on his feet. "What, or more importantly who are you protecting?"

He found Gordon standing guard over Hoadley's body.

"Has she been tampered with?"

"No, I don't think so. I did a quick check, and her clothes all seem to be in the same condition as when I sent her off with them."

Beaumont's hand hovered above Hoadley's shoulder. A whisper away from touching.

"She wasn't easy," said Beaumont.

"No."

"But she cared."

"Yes," said Gordon, gazing at Hoadley's face, no more peaceful in death than it had been in life.

"She asked to work with me." Beaumont frowned. That still puzzled him.

"Are you surprised?"

Beaumont blinked, glancing up at Gordon. "You know why?"

"Your solving of the Windlass Case."

He didn't feel brilliant, especially since he hadn't solved it fast enough to save the children.

"Not brilliant enough."

Gordon huffed. "This again? It was horrible, wrong, but there was nothing we could have done to save them, when are you going to realise that?"

"If I had realised—"

"What? That automatons in the neighbour's house were dead children powered by goodness knows what? How silly of you not to realise that straight away."

Beaumont glared at her. "We don't know they were dead. If—"

"Barnaby, their brains were killed as part of the process those monsters put them through. You saw the report, you know that." She exhaled heavily, shaking her head. "How many times do we have to have this conversation?"

"Do you really believe that those two noobs would have had the skill and ability to do that level of biomechanical work on their own?" His lips thinned. "Because if you do then perhaps the promotion was premature after all."

He snapped his mouth shut, wishing he could have caught the words and reeled them back in.

The breath hissed out of her, as if he had physically punched her.

"I know you're hurting, and I know Hoadley's death has hit you hard, so I am going to forget you said that."

"Steamer is ready, zer." Dalley stood awkwardly in the doorway.

"Stay with her," Beaumont growled.

"Yes, zer."

Dalley gazed at Hoadley's body, her chin dropping into her chest.

"Is there someone we have to notify?" asked Gordon.

Beaumont exhaled heavily. "No." He rubbed his face, ignoring the slight wetness around his eyes. "Her parents were run over by a steamer whose engine blew."

"And there's no one else? No friends, no extended family."

Beaumont's shoulders slumped. "Nothing in her file."

Beaumont and Gordon watched as she was taken away.

Off to another town whose cold hands would only care about the puzzle she presented.

He liked to think she would have appreciated that.

"Prime Inspector Beaumont." A guard ran into the room.

"What?" He frowned at the guard. Was it too much to have a moment, a moment to think, to give Hoadley's memory the respect it deserved?

"You and Prime Inspector Gordon are needed urgently, zer."

"Why?" asked Gordon, her eyes bright.

"Cuthbert Walstrand, he's being extradited."

"Why are they taking Cuthbert?" Beaumont asked the guard, his head spinning.

"Smuggling, zer, the case is being run by Blagwallow. They followed it here and found the Purple Door full of devices with unregistered modifications."

"Pipe it." Beaumont had a vague memory of boxes, but he had been too far gone to open them.

Gordon frowned. "Modified? How?"

"I don't know, zer. I only know they have Cuthbert at the Way and they are filing the paperwork to move him today."

"*Pipe it.* Come on Gordon."

Beaumont strode from the morgue and hurried back to the Way. He was greeted by the sight of Cuthbert being led out in manacles towards a long-distance travel steamer.

"Stop, wait." Beaumont sped up, ignoring the pain shooting through his back. "He's a suspect in a murder."

The guards paused and a man with an inspector's insignia on his waistcoat glanced at him.

"Do you have any proof of that?"

"We're gathering evidence in regards to two murders," growled Beaumont. "Which trumps a minor fraud charge or whatever it is you think you are going to charge him with."

Of average height with a sharp, intelligent face, the Blagwallow inspector stood straight and stared at him.

"There isn't anything minor about it. Cuthbert Walstrand has been tagged as the head of a major counterfeiting ring. I'm not letting him out of my sight."

"Cuthbert?" asked Beaumont his voice rising sharply. Unless Cuthbert was the most brilliant actor in the world, he sincerely doubted he was capable of coordinating his wardrobe let alone a large organised criminal enterprise.

"Hey," said Cuthbert, "I've got skills."

Beaumont glared at him, and Cuthbert laughed, shrugging. Cuthbert leant against the steamer, his feet crossed. If it wasn't for his hands restrained by reinforced manacles, he might have been going to a party.

Beaumont examined him. "Skills at annoying the wrong people."

Cuthbert winced. "We grasp to luck it dissolves, we grasp to love it dies, we grasp to life it decays, we grasp our whisky and it's okay." His shoulder lifted.

"There's no whisky where you're going," said Beaumont. He turned to the other inspector. "He's obviously—"

"You think that him saying oops must be a mistake, is

going to replace the hard work done by my team in tracking him down you're seriously mistaken," said the inspector.

Beaumont scowled.

"You aren't taking that man away. Guards, make sure Cuthbert doesn't move while the inspector and I visit the High Protector."

The inspector stared at the sky and sighed but followed him into the Way.

The air left Beaumont's lungs, hissing between his teeth. He slammed down on his heel with every step, the pain travelling up his spine, fuelling him.

Storming into the High Protector's office was not a smart move, but he was long past caring what it would do for his career. In fact, if she threw him out all the better. He could wash his hands of this mess and then use them to paint a beach scene while Wilhelmina wrote her next brilliant novel next to him. He might even become the painter his parents had always dreamed he would be, rather than the broken wreck he was now.

High Protector Cadwell sat, hands clasped in front of her, relaxed in her chair, facing the door.

"I have to say Beaumont, your angry walk is almost as effective as knocking," she gave a slight smile. "I am pretty sure the whole building's a shake." She turned to the inspector who kept pace next to him. "Inspector Logan, I take it that your collection has been interrupted?"

"You knew?" asked Beaumont. "But I told you that he was a key person in this case."

"Enough to tie him directly to Overton's or Hoadley's

deaths?" She sat there, in her large comfy chair with faint amusement on her face.

Which did nothing to calm him down.

"Overton died the night he gave Cuthbert all his money." Beaumont's voice rose. "Who stole it rather than give it to the criminals—"

"Alleged..." Cadwell's voice was soft.

Beaumont grunted. "...criminals at the Purple Door. If Inspector Logan wants to investigate illegal modifications I have a list of names I could suggest over Cuthbert Walstrand's."

"Prime Inspector Beaumont." The High Protector stood, her arms relaxed at her sides and her back straight. "Do you have anything that would allow you to hold Cuthbert Walstrand in custody?"

Beaumont tried to breathe in through his nose and engage his brain, but all he wanted to do was throw things.

"No."

"Then Inspector Logan, proceed with your arrest."

Logan threw him a sympathetic glance and Beaumont forced himself to nod at him.

Logan left, and the High Protector sent a note advising of the release of the suspect to Blagwallow's custody. To avoid any confusion, she said.

She sat down, this time inviting Beaumont to sit as well. He dropped into the chair with a huff, wincing as he jolted his back.

"The investigation isn't going well then?"

Beaumont tried to bring himself back into professional form.

"It's a complex case."

"Simplify it for me." She leaned back in the chair.

"Despite what Dr Morten says, Overton died three days before the party. Hoadley's notes suggest he hired someone to impersonate him while he dealt with the money situation with Cuthbert."

"Another layer of confusion." Her fingers drummed on her stomach. "Do we know who this person was?"

"Yes, Hoadley's notes identify him as a Fred Bramble."

"Who knew about this?"

Beaumont exhaled. "Ancilla Walstrand."

"Hmm." Cadwell's brow wrinkled, and her fingers continued to drum. "Maybe the whole family is more involved than we have given them credit for."

Beaumont scratched his cheek. Ancilla was involved, or at the very least keeping pertinent information back from him. But to kill two people?

"It doesn't seem to fit..."

"Sadly Beaumont, people are always surprising us in new and unpleasant ways." Cadwell sat forward. "Hoadley talked to her just before she died, didn't she?"

With a grim expression, Beaumont nodded. "Yes, High Protector."

"I'll allocate more resources to bringing her in and hold her for formal questioning. This is no longer a polite chat." Cadwell adjusted her waistcoat and straightened. "Atwater

Place is also starting to make noise about all the guards tramping through it."

Beaumont cleared his throat. "But surely they understand with another death?"

Cadwell waved her hand. "Never mind that. I will deal with the Atwaters. You focus on the case at hand and leave the politics to me."

Beaumont's eyebrows raised. The High Protector rarely got involved in cases these days, preferring a lighter touch.

She dismissed him and he left to find a guard standing outside with a copy of the order of Cuthbert's extraction in his hand.

Hopefully, he would have better luck keeping hold of the other Walstrands.

Beaumont threw Cuthbert's extradition papers on his desk and took a few turns around the room. He needed to focus, and he needed to get himself under control. Despite the pep talk with the High Protector, he couldn't let go of the fact Cuthbert was gone.

His door slammed open.

"Where are they?"

"What?" Beaumont prided himself on his witty responses and he was glad to hear that he still had it.

"Where are my children?"

A twinge of concern around the visibility of capillaries in Ernest Walstrand's face, and the emphasised veins in his forehead and neck helped Beaumont keep his responses civilised.

"What all of them? How would I know?"

Though not necessarily helpful.

"I have it on authority that Cuthbert has been arrested." Ernest slammed the door behind him trapping Beaumont.

Beaumont's pacing had left him standing in front of his desk, bringing him within striking distance. He shifted his weight forward onto the balls of his feet.

"Cuthbert Walstrand has been arrested and removed from Noxrath by the Blagwallow gendarmerie in connection with unregistered modifications of devices."

"That's ridiculous." Ernest stared up at the ceiling before returning his gaze to Beaumont. "I want him released this instant."

"He's no longer under the guard of the Way, Zer Walstrand. I'm afraid there is nothing I can do." Beaumont wouldn't have done anything anyway, but he had to admit having Cuthbert in another jurisdiction had some unexpected benefits. Not that he would tell Inspector Logan or the High Protector that.

"And who exactly does have control of this situation?" Ernest leant forward and the red in his face deepened.

"Inspector Logan is the person you need to contact." Beaumont squashed down a flair of guilt.

Ernest hissed and stepped forward. "I know you had something to do with this Beaumont. I have seen you watching us. I want you to know that I won't forget this, forget how you have treated my family."

Ernest spun around and put his hand on the door.

"You said your family? Are Melody and Ancilla in trouble as well?"

Ernest peered over his shoulder at Beaumont. "Not unless you've arrested Melody for standing next to my steamer?"

"Not that I am aware of."

Ernest snorted and opened the door.

"And Ancilla?" Beaumont asked, "Is she also looking after your steamer?"

Ernest stepped through the door but turned back and glared.

"I don't know where the fool is." He scowled. "No doubt she is off somewhere shoving her face with food."

Beaumont couldn't really see anything wrong with that.

"Is everything alright here?" asked Gordon.

Beaumont peered past Ernest to see her leaning against Hoadley's desk.

"No everything is not alright you incompetent fool." Ernest stormed through the office and Beaumont and Gordon followed. More to ensure that he left than out of any particular interest.

In a petty move, Ernest knocked over a couple of statues on the way out. Beaumont suppressed his desire to arrest him for property damage.

"What a gasser," whispered Gordon.

Beaumont hummed agreement.

Outside they found Melody sitting on the front of the steamer eating an ice cream which she had purchased off one of the food carts set up near the Way. Beaumont had always found ice cream in winter a strange choice, but to each their own.

"Get off," said Ernest his voice ripping across the court-yard.

Melody rolled her eyes but slid off.

Ernest stormed around to the driver's side of the steamer but paused before opening the door.

"Get rid of that ridiculous ice cream, you aren't eating that in the steamer."

Melody put one hand on the door and let the ice cream drop to the ground with the other. It landed with a splat and Beaumont took some pleasure in the fact it hit the outside of the steamer and Melody's boots before she disappeared.

They drove off and the ice cream lay there, now nothing more than splattered trash, just like his investigation.

{ 21 }

Trapped

Ancilla tried to focus on the positive side. She was at the Way. What she had spent the last two hours trying to achieve.

The shackles put a damper on the sitting and sharing information with Hoadley over some tea or coffee that she imagined.

"Do you understand that you are being held on suspicion of a connection with the murder of Marcellus Overton?" The inspector sitting across from her didn't seem that bright. Not compared with Hoadley anyway.

Where was Hoadley? Probably out at the Atwaters causing trouble. Someone had to let her know that she was here.

"I need to speak with Inspector Hoadley or if she is not available Prime Inspector Beaumont." So far that was all she had said and that was all she was going to say.

The inspector leaned forward. "You'll speak to me."

"I need to speak with Inspector Hoad—"

He stormed out of the room slamming the door closed. Temper temper.

Her mouth was tacky, but she didn't want to risk having to go another round of foolish questions, so she sat there, staring at the wall trying, to get her thoughts together.

The door creaked open to reveal a tall woman robed in official attire. Her hair had grey streaks and laugh lines striped her face.

"There you are." Her eyes narrowed. "I owe Alfred an apology." She reached forward, taking Ancilla's hand, and releasing the manacles.

"Ow." Ancilla cradled her stinging wrist. "I would like to talk to Inspector Hoadley."

"I'm afraid she's not available." The woman took a chair opposite Ancilla, dropping the manacles on the table.

"Then Prime Inspector Beaumont."

Ancilla stared at the manacles, rubbing her wrist. The last thing she wanted was for them to be put back on.

"Nor is he. But perhaps I can help." She examined Ancilla.

"And who exactly are you?" Ancilla tilted her head as she took her in. The eyes indicated a depth of understanding that reached beyond this small puzzle.

"Oh, allow me to introduce myself." She leaned back in her chair. "I'm High Protector Diana Cadwell."

She smiled and Ancilla blinked.

"The High Protector?"

"Yes. I can assure you that anything you can tell Hoadley or Beaumont you can tell me."

Ancilla shifted in her seat. "How do I know you will share it with them?" She blushed at her intrepidness in talking back to the High Protector but at this point, she had already made so many bad decisions what was one more.

"Why wouldn't I?"

"I don't know, but then I don't know you or whatever you are mixed up in." Ancilla gulped. This really was so much easier with Hoadley. You always knew where you stood with her.

"Would it make you feel better to know that it will always be on the opposite side of your father?"

Ancilla rubbed her forehead. "I'm not sure that that is actually helpful, however, I take your meaning." Her hand dropped back into her lap.

"Excellent. What do the inspectors need to know?"

She explained about Fred, though it turned out the High Protector already knew that part. Ancilla should have guessed that Hoadley would document their conversation.

The High Protector was however interested in Fred being in Marcellus' flat and in the abduction attempts.

"And they were the same people outside your house?"

"Yes, I..." Ancilla gripped the back of her neck. "Yes, I think so. Yes."

"Hmmm..." Cadwell sat back in her chair observing Ancilla. "I don't know how much you know, or to be honest how much I should tell you." She frowned, the grooves on her face deepening. "There have been a few developments that you may not be aware of."

The High Inspector sat there staring at Ancilla.

"What kind of developments?" asked Ancilla.

The High Protector straightened, her face smoothing out, without losing any of its grimness. "Firstly, your brother Cuthbert has been arrested."

Ancilla's body heated up. Despite everything she didn't dislike Cuthbert, and a small part of her hoped he would escape his foolishness.

"For what?"

"Unregistered modifications."

Ancilla swallowed. "You said firstly."

"Yes..." the grimness in the High Protector's face deepened. "Inspector Hoadley has been killed."

Dizziness struck Ancilla. The blood in her head rushed down into her body, attempting to ground her but instead making it hard to think.

Perhaps the High Protector was lying. Some sort of twisted attempt to get a confession from her. Ancilla examined the High Protector's face but found nothing but grief.

How was this possible? Why didn't she insist on staying with her last night? Where was she that she was so alone that no one could help her?

"Where?"

"Atwater Place, in the grove of statues near the garden gate."

"Why?" Her throat spasmed.

"Pursuing a line of inquiry."

Ancilla controlled the snarl that threatened to rip across her face. She wanted Hoadley here. Now.

"I..." Ancilla blinked.

Every single one of her next steps required Hoadley to be alive, to be willing to talk and listen to her. Everyone else was just going to dismiss her as a nobody or as a suspect, and she wasn't sure which was worse.

"It's a great tragedy. The whole gendarmerie is in shock."

They should be burning with guilt. She hadn't been blind to how they treated Hoadley.

"Sure."

The High Protector examined her. "I can see that this is a bit of a shock to you as well, perhaps more so than your brother's arrest."

"Hoadley was worth a thousand Cuthberts."

She might have only known her a couple of days, but she recognised a kinship, an analytical mind similar to her own. She tried not to think of the thousands of conversations that they would never have.

"Yes." The High Protector tilted her head examining Ancilla. "Yes, she was." She stood and stared down at her. "I can see you need a little time. I will pass on your information to the Prime Inspector, but I'm sure he will have more questions."

Ancilla didn't move. She sat there staring at the wall, barely noticing the High Protector leave.

One Clue at a Time

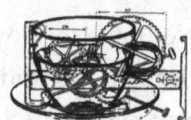

Beaumont needed to get back to Atwater Place.

"What's going on?" asked Gordon. She swerved the steamer, narrowly avoiding a pedestrian running to join the crowds on the other side of the street.

"The bill? The protests?" Beaumont slumped in his seat. He hadn't wanted to take a steamer, but time was of the essence and he had foolishly thought it would be faster.

"I thought that was over?" asked Gordon.

At least she had offered to drive. He needed a moment to think.

Beaumont shook his head. "How you've survived this long in life I don't know."

She grinned. "I don't need to keep on top of stuff, that's what you're for."

He grunted. "It isn't over yet. Tomorrow's the big day, and the crowds are getting restless."

"What's this one about?"

Beaumont banged his head on the back of his seat.

"How?" he groaned. "The lifespan of the patent limit? To only last the lifetime of the inventor?"

"What happens after that?"

"It becomes free for people to use and modify without paying inventor compensation."

"What to anyone? Not even the government."

"Not even the government," he said.

"That's crazy. Why would the Families agree to that?" Gordon hit the breaks to avoid hitting a suddenly stationary steamer in front of her.

"A lot haven't." Beaumont shifted so he had a better grip on inside of the steamer. "They are probably funding these protests, however the ones that do are holding firm and have the majority of the people on their side."

"But why would *any* Family support something that is going to give them less money?"

"Perhaps because it is the right thing to do?" Beaumont shrugged.

Gordon snorted. "How you can still be an idealist. Nah, there's definitely something in it for them."

"Which sums up the crux of the argument between the two sides."

Gordon shook her head and changed lanes but as soon as she did, the one she joined ground to a halt.

"Pipe it." She banged the steering wheel. "We'd get there faster walking to the Atwaters than staying in this."

Beaumont nodded. "Park and walk from here?"

"Rightio." Gordon swung the steamer down the next street and muscled into a park with some moves that had Beaumont tightening his grip. She glanced at him and grinned. "Come on, it wasn't that close."

"If you scratch it, the report's yours."

"Love a long report." Gordon jumped out of the steamer and bounced on her toes while Beaumont dragged himself out.

"You are a very strange person, I just want you to know that," he said.

"Strange is great right?" She grinned at him.

"Sure." His lips twisted up, even the edges of his eyes crinkling.

They wove through slow-moving steamers to a footpath and a restaurant came into view. Beaumont's stomach growled.

"It has to be already made and something you can eat while walking," said Gordon.

He hadn't been planning on stopping anyway. The servers at the restaurant remembered Beaumont from his last visit, and soon both Gordon and Beaumont left carrying small bags of toasted goodness.

She opened her bag and took a bite. "It's good." She finished it. "Eat and walk if you are going to be slow about it.

He followed her, paying more attention to his food than their direction.

"Wait no," he said but it was too late. She turned the corner, and he followed her right into the crowds outside the patent's office. Someone knocked the bag, and the other half of his food onto the ground. "No," he cried, as it skidded away, kicked by several feet.

"Pipe it, you weren't joking." Gordon took a few steps back and joined him.

He glared at her.

"I lost my bag."

"What?"

"It still had half the toasted cheese in it." It was ridiculous he knew but he wanted to howl his disappointment but was jostled and instead focused on staying on his feet.

"Seriously? I think we have bigger problems." She frowned at the crowd in front of them. "I think we should go back—"

Two bodies locked in battle slammed into them and it took all of Beaumont's and Gordon's strength to remain standing.

"Pipe it," Beaumont grabbed at one of them and tried to pull them apart.

Gordon, seeing Beaumont had the woman, grabbed the man, holding his arms. Beaumont's grasp slipped and the woman got a couple more hits into the man, before he could get control of her again.

"Why are you helping her? She's the one who's crazy," cried the guy in Gordon's arms.

"We're not helping anyone, zer. We're trying to break up the fight. Are you hurt?"

"It'd take more than that." He tried to puff his chest, but it was difficult with his arms pulled tight behind him.

Beaumont continued to struggle with the woman who twisted and turned trying to get free.

"Stop. Stop it. I need you to—" she landed an elbow directly on his sternum but he managed to keep a hold, even as he gasped for air.

A couple of guards came crashing through the crowd.

"Guards, these two—"

"Prime Inspector, we've got this." The guard, who Beaumont vaguely recognised from the Way took the woman from his grasp and the other took Gordon's. "We've been chasing them through the crowd, zer. They've been causing all sorts of trouble."

Beaumont appreciated the assist but would have preferred the guard to have kept a firm hold on the woman's elbows. She flipped one up and out and it smashed into his nose.

"Pipe it." He clamped down, trying to stop it gushing blood.

"Sorry, zer." The guard took a firmer hold. "Shall I book her?"

"Yeph."

"On it, zer." The guards dragged their two fighters out of the crowd and around the corner, and hopefully to separate cells.

"You alright," asked Gordon.

Beaumont glared at her.

"Whad yod thing?"

"Okay okay a medic first, get that bleeding under control and then..."

"Dod dime."

"No time?" She pulled him out of the crowd, using the path cleared by those who had wanted to watch the fight, and back around the corner. "You're no use like that."

"Dab."

Gordon frowned at him for a bit and then her eyes widened. "The lab..." she gazed around, "are you sure you don't want the hospice, or for me to send for a mobile medic? Okay, okay...no need to get upset, let's see if the lab has enough stuff to patch you up."

Beaumont glared at her as they trotted along the back streets.

Timothy, back on duty, started laughing when he saw Beaumont's face. "Not so pretty now huh?" Despite the laughter, Timothy grabbed a first aid kit and directed Beaumont to take a seat. "Not broken, but you've a gusher." He cleaned and packed it up. "In the pursuit of a suspect heh?"

"The crowds," said Gordon who had wandered over to the shelf of skulls with their bone tattoos and picked one up.

"Er if you could put that down?" asked Timothy with a quick glance over.

"What is it?" She turned it over in her hand.

"It's a mapping of trauma."

"Pretty." she put it back down and Timothy's shoulders relaxed.

"Dank dou," said Beaumont.

Timothy laughed. "We can't have you running around

sounding like that in the middle of a murder investigation. Give me a sec."

Beaumont closed his eyes and rested his head against the wall next to him. This was all happening because he didn't take time to stop for food.

"It wasn't because I made you get a takeaway."

He opened his eyes to narrow slits and found Gordon staring at him in exasperation.

"Sorry," his cheeks heated. He forgot how well she knew him sometimes.

Timothy came back into the room holding the biggest needle Beaumont had ever seen. He should have gone to the hospice.

"That's one gigantic needle," said Gordon getting up and walking over to Timothy to examine it. "What's it for?"

"Dr Morten invented it. It reduces swelling and bleeding and will allow Beaumont to talk normally again." Timothy took the casing off the needle itself and drew a green liquid into it.

Beaumont's eyes widened.

"Is it safe?" asked Gordon. "It doesn't look safe."

"It's perfectly fine. We use it all the time." Timonthy approached Beaumont, the needle held aloft.

"On what?" Gordon peered at the needle, her eyes narrow. "I didn't think you, or Dr Morten for that matter, got live people here?"

Timothy blushed slightly and Beaumont pushed himself back in his chair.

"Technically we haven't used it on a live person ourselves,

but the medics use it all the time. It is the same stuff." As he got closer to Beaumont, and the comically large needle loomed.

"I'm glad it's not me." Gordon took a seat next to Beaumont, presumably to get a front row view of the action. "Do you see that needle Beaumont? It's huge."

"Des dank dou Gordon."

Timothy stepped up close to Beaumont and the needle hovered above his eye.

"Where dou going do pud dad ding?"

"Where am I going to put it?" Beaumont was pretty sure that Timothy smirked a bit. "It needs to go near the site of the wound. I'm going to inject a bit into the soft part of your cheek near your nose."

"Doo big."

"Big? Yes, well the truth is the medics would probably use a smaller needle but this is all we have sorry."

Beaumont closed his eyes and tried to think of something, anything except the pressure from the needle pushing into his skin.

"You should see this. The needle is so huge that as it pushes through the skin its making this massive hole." Gordon's voice was high and bright. "Will it scar?"

Beaumont wanted to open his eyes but he was too afraid to move and make it worse.

"It should heal fine. This stuff is great. If she had registered it in her name she might have made a fortune." Timothy pushed the needle in a bit deeper and Beaumont worked at not moving, by this point he wasn't even breathing. "Seals the wound, helps it heal, all without the inflammation response of the system. A game changer."

"Beaumont it's a shame you're missing this, he's pumping in that whole needle full of green liquid into your face. It must feel so uncomfortable." Vibrations from Gordon jumping around travelled up his chair. Meanwhile the pressure in his face was going to explode. "Who did register it then?"

"Apparently the Government had this one."

"Hmm, I'm not sure I like this new fact about Government being able to own patents."

Gordon's voice was overly close, and Beaumont could imagine her peering at the needle where it entered his skin. He shivered.

"It's been like that for over a decade now," said Timonthy, his voice dry.

"Still, where will it all lead?"

Beaumont didn't really care about anything but what the green liquid was going to do to him.

"Okay I am going to remove it now." Timothy's voice was soft and soothing. Or perhaps it was just because he was saying the exact words Beaumont wanted to hear.

"Beaumont, you wouldn't believe how deep that needle went in."

The warmed-up metal slid out of his skin.

"Almost there."

Something wet and hot slid down his face.

"You're bleeding," said Gordon.

"Is id oud?" he asked, his lips barely moving.

"Yes, let me clean you up," said Timothy.

A wet cloth was dragged across his face and the packing around his nose was slowly removed.

Beaumont opened his eyes and turned his head to glare at Gordon.

"You're the most unhelpful person. If I'm ever in the hospice, please don't visit me."

"Aww look at that, you have your t's back." Gordon thumped Timothy on the shoulder. "Way to go lab man."

"Er thanks?" Timothy disposed of the needle and then came back to join them. "The crowds are rough, are they?"

Beaumont carefully nodded. He touched the plaster that was still across his nose. Despite the horror of the needle he was glad he would not be walking around with a pad shoved up each nostril.

"Yes, and it will no doubt get rougher before tomorrow. But in the meantime, our problem is the murder of Marcellus Overton, and our Inspector Lavinia Hoadley."

"Yeah," Timothy huffed. He rubbed the back of his hand across his forehead, his eyes squinting. "I was actually glad to see you." He shook out his arms and glanced at them. "I've some more of the lab work back."

"What?" Gordon bounced. "Why didn't you send it to the Way?"

"Because I just got it and then you turned up?"

Beaumont scanned the lab, realising that there was only Timothy. "Where is everyone."

"After pulling two double shifts, we decided to be silly and let them go home and rest." He rolled his eyes. "Because we have this whole crazy don't hurt people thing."

"Everyone should have that thing," said Gordon. Then she frowned. "Though then I would be out of a job, which I love...this is very confusing."

"Focus Gordon." Beaumont carefully touched his nose, smoothing down the edge of the plaster. "We need to get to the Atwaters."

"Hmm, well you would probably be best off going the long way round." Timothy tilted his head. "No point driving, the traffic has gone crazy as well."

"Yes thank you Timothy that is very helpful," said Beaumont.

"Hey," Timothy held up his hands and took a step back. "Just trying to be helpful. How's the nose by the way?"

Beaumont had the grace to blush and mumble an apology. "Anyway, what were the results on Hoadley?"

Timothy sat on the edge of a stool, his leg starting to swing. "It's probably no surprise that we found the same unidentified substance in Hoadley."

"Could she have fought against it?"

Timothy shrugged. "Without knowing more...I can't say."

"Do you have any idea what it is?" asked Beaumont.

Timothy shook his head. "We think it's botanical, some sort of hybrid plant probably. Too many to identify it exactly but..." he jumped up and hurried to the back of the lab.

Beaumont went to rub his face but dropped his hand before he hurt himself. Though whatever Timothy injected him with had reduced the pain considerably.

Timothy came back with a small tube in his hand.

"Here," he said handing it to Beaumont.

Beaumont took it turning it over in his hands. "Is this for my nose?"

Timothy rolled his eyes. "Not everything is about you Beaumont, no that's an antidote."

Gordon pinched the tube out of Beaumont's hand, opening the lid and sniffing it.

"It smells like moss."

"Don't do that." Timothy took it back from her with a frown. "It is designed to naturalise the botanical agents of a similar family type as the one we think was used. You have to eat it though."

Beaumont stared at him. "Eat it."

"Yes, it is, mostly harmless. But it needs to be put under the tongue in order to be absorbed rapidly enough." He handed it back to Beaumont, who slipped it into one of his pockets.

"Thanks."

"Now we have stopped sharing tubes of moss can we get back to finding what Hoadley died trying to save??" Gordon's foot started tapping.

If Hoadley had been standing next to him he would have been feeling her judging gaze on him about now. He attempted to push himself to his feet. His head swam for a second before settling.

"You alright?" asked Gordon.

He probably would have been a bit more moved by her concern if she had slowed down to hear the answer.

Frying Pan, Fire

The clock on the wall ticked and its hands shifted to nine o'clock.

Ancilla tried to create saliva but all she managed was a thicker glue, her gums and tongue squelching when she opened and closed her mouth.

Ancilla's eyes burned, but her body didn't have enough liquid to create tears. An intelligent and passionate person in a sea of self-interest and apathy, Hoadley had shone. Perhaps this was all a mistake?

No, there was no way she could imagine the desert that was this room. Its air old, full of the stale sweat of scared people. Its walls bare except for the clock. So much grey. Grey walls, grey table, grey chairs, even a grey clock. Did they have it specially made? Found an artist who used steel rather than brass and bronze? Just to make sure that all hope was leeched from the room?

Ancilla stood stretching her arms above her head. She was on her own. That much was obvious.

She was almost glad Cuthbert had been arrested. His self-destructive path only had one end. If she had known how to heal him, how to help him let go of thinking he needed to shine bright so his mother, and father, would see him, or that they even mattered, she would have. But she couldn't, and now the wait was over.

She wasn't sure how deep Ernest was in it. But she knew, in her very core, that if Cuthbert was involved, it was Ernest who had gotten him there.

If they asked her directly, what would she say?

Ancilla dropped into the chair, cradling her suddenly heavy head in her arms on the table in front of her.

"Ancilla."

She lifted her head and straightened, her eyes widening. "Al-is-stair, wh-at, are you do-ing here?"

His gaze softened. She hated the pity behind his gaze. It was always there but today it was more pronounced.

"I came as soon as I heard you were arrested."

"How?"

"Necket told me she overheard one of the guards say that Ancilla Walstrand was locked up. Are they looking after you?"

"Thirsty." If she was going to be cast in the role of victim, she might as well get some water out of it.

"Guards." Alistair strode back to the door and knocked on it sharply. "Guards."

It was opened on the other side and Ancilla could make out a man in a gendarmerie uniform. He was a solid man, the type that made you careful not to make any sudden moves.

"Everything okay, zer?"

The guard's face struggled to move into a concerned expression, but she gave him points for effort.

"When was the last time Ancilla had something to drink?"

The guard's eyes widened, and he swallowed. "Err..."

"I want water brought in here immediately."

Alistair waved him away and the guard disappeared.

Alistair took a seat next to her.

"Thanks," she whispered.

"How long have you been here?"

Ancilla shook her head and raised her hands.

"I'm—"

"They're the criminals."

The guard reappeared carrying a tray with a jug of water, a glass, two cups of tea and biscuits. Warmth for Alistair flowed through Ancilla.

Ancilla reached for the jug. If Alistair hadn't been there she would have drunk straight out of it but instead she poured water into a glass, emptied it, refilled it and drank a second glass in between breaths.

"Thank you," she said, with a stronger tone and less gluggy sound effects.

The guard nodded and retreated from the room. The guilt on his face might have been wistful thinking on her part.

Alistair picked up one of the cups of tea and sat back in his chair, somehow making it appear comfortable.

"Do you know what this is all about?" he asked.

Ancilla shook her head. "I mean I know it is about what happened to Overton and Hoadley. But I don't know why I am here."

"I'm sure it is a misunderstanding." He stared at the blank wall, his smile fading away. "But the most important thing is to get you out of here."

"I'm hoping once Beaumont is back that..." She stared at the cup of tea in her hand.

The door to the room crashed open. "Zer Atwater, you need to leave, zer." Two guards stood in the doorway their jaws set.

The blood left Ancilla's face.

"I'm not going anywhere." Alistair stood. "She has the right to have a person with her."

"I'm afraid that's no longer the case, zer."

Ancilla swayed in her chair.

Alistair scowled. "Don't say anything." He examined Ancilla, concern creasing his face. "Ask them on what grounds and remember what your rights are."

Ancilla nodded, but having never been in this situation before she actually had no idea what her options were. A slight buzzing started in her ears.

Alistair left and the door slammed shut.

Click.

A bolt sliding into place. But here it was on the outside of the door. She wanted to be back in her bedroom, safe, with her door secure. Ancilla swallowed and practiced breathing in and out.

With Cuthbert, and most likely Ernest involved, it would make sense that they would look to her as well, that was all.

What would Hoadley do? She would stay calm and pay attention.

Ancilla contemplated the tray. It was going to be a long day and she was going to need her wits about her.

She had eaten all the sweet biscuits and was finishing her tea when a guard opened the door to reveal the High Protector. Seeing the tea, the High Protector asked for a fresh pot and a cup for herself.

They stared at each other.

Once the new teapot and cup had arrived and fresh tea poured, Cadwell finally spoke.

"Ancilla Walstrand, you have shared the story of a man called Fred Gilbert Bramble who was hired to impersonate Marcellus Overton on the launch party of the latest Atwater prototype. You admit supporting this charade by working the device and pretending it was Marcellus who was there, is that correct?"

Ancilla nodded. "Yes, that's correct."

"Very well. On the information that you provided the gendarmerie visited Marcellus Overton's residence. On entering they discovered Zer Fred Gilbert Bramble's body."

Ancilla's teacup landed on the table with a clatter.

"Freddy's dead?"

"Yes."

Ancilla's eyes went so wide the skin around them stretched taut.

"Who killed him?" Ancilla wanted to hit herself on her forehead. Of course, they think she did it. She was probably the last person to see him alive.

The High Protector glared at Ancilla, her face bleak. "At this time, we believe it to be you."

"But why would I come here, bring Freddy to your attention so you could discover his body?"

"You didn't come here voluntarily."

"But I was on my way here. None of you even knew where Freddy was. If I hadn't said anything you would never have discovered the body. Or even if you did you wouldn't know it was connected to me."

"Perhaps you knew we would inevitably link the murders and wanted to get in first?"

"It wasn't me." Ancilla shook her head.

The High Protector rapped her knuckles against the tabletop. "Your brother has already been charged. Is it too much of a stretch for us to assume that you are also involved, and this led to the murder of your co-conspirators?" The High Protector's gaze never left Ancilla's face.

Ancilla could tell that the High Protector Cadwell smiled easily. She suspected Cadwell was someone she would want to share a drink with. Not that she would accept a drink from her right now. Ancilla wasn't sure she would accept a drink from herself right now.

"They might be my family, but it doesn't mean I am the same as them."

"The environment we are brought up in can shape us."

"Everyone has at least two choices, to be the same or the opposite."

"Nothing in between?"

"Possible but harder."

The High Protector snorted. "Indeed, it is." She drummed her fingers on the table. "I'll be honest I never expected to find you as a suspect in a murder enquiry."

"I'm not sure why you expected to find me at all." Ancilla stared at her trying to work out if she had ever met her before. She was significantly older than her and probably even a generation older than Ernest. But there was something familiar about her face. "Those two, the ones who tried to abduct me, they must have followed me from Freddy—"

"I'm sure you would like us to think that." She gave a sharp nod. "Okay here's what we're going to do. No charges, but you're going to stay here, I'll make sure you have food and drink, until Beaumont and Gordon have finished collecting their evidence."

"I want to speak with Prime Inspector Beaumont." She wasn't sure why. The only person she wanted to speak to was Hoadley.

The High Protector smiled sharply. "I'm sure he wants to talk to you as well."

She stood up and knocked on the door. Gazing back at Ancilla, she smiled. "Don't worry those guilty of these crimes will be put away in the end."

And then Ancilla was on her own. She pushed her chair back and paced. Ernest and Melody arrested. Melody wouldn't have done anything. She wouldn't risk her independence on a dubious scheme. After their mother left Melody had as little to do with any of them as possible. She would not be happy about being dragged into this. Ancilla expected she was regretting not *wasting* her money on renting a flat now.

But Ernest. She didn't doubt for a second that he believed he was above the law. He'd always seen the world the way he thought it was *meant* to be usually with him at the top. The promotions made it worse. She was pretty sure he had his sights on the head of patents role. Which is why she was actually surprised that he would be involved in criminal enterprise. It could only risk his ambition. But then maybe not, he might have thought he could have it all. Wealth from stolen prototypes and status from within the patent office. She liked to think he had gradually fallen into it, but she wasn't sure if Ernest had ever done anything unintentionally.

This was it. Years of toil and sacrifice, and it was over before she even got a chance to get started.

Just like Hoadley.

Hoadley's Clue

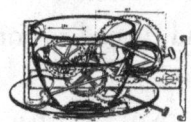

Beaumont stood in the middle of the prototype gallery in Atwater Place.

Vyner turned all the lamps up to full power, but despite the illumination most of the antiquated devices did not have anywhere to hide anything. Nor were they allowed to disassemble them.

"Piece of paper, right?" Gordon asked, picking up an antique and turning it upside down, looking for a hidden compartment.

The number of things that Gordon had broken was something of a legend. He could see the interrogation now.

And exactly why did you let her handle a priceless antique?

"Careful." He scanned the room. "It depends, but yes at least one piece of paper, possibly two."

"What makes you think it was here?"

"This was the last room she was in." Beaumont rubbed the back of his neck. "Drugged, trying to find the perfect spot. She would have taken what she could get."

"What do you think is on it?" Gordon picked up another antique, spinning it in her hands.

"We don't even know if it is a message yet," Beaumont reached over and took it from her, carefully placing it back in its spot, "but knowing Hoadley, I am, of course, expecting the murderer's name to be on it."

Gordon stopped and turned toward Beaumont, her eyes wide. "Really?"

Beaumont snorted. "No." Neither Hoadley, or he were that lucky. The tiredness and constant pain that was his life made his eyes water.

"How's your nose?" asked Gordon.

"My nose?" Beaumont touched the plaster across the top of it. He had received a few looks but no one had had the courage to ask. "What's that got to do with it?"

"I thought you might be in pain which is why you are all grumpy." Gordon shrugged and picked up another priceless Atwater heirloom.

"I'm grumpy because I feel like I am spending hours wandering around, without actually getting closer to catching the killer." And in pain. His back muscles spasmed assent.

"Or killers."

Beaumont hummed. "They're linked. The question is which one do we focus on first?"

"Hoadley of course. She died protecting something." Gordon picked up another priceless antique and prodded it.

Beaumont's breath hitched when she dropped it down with a bang.

She stood in the middle of the room and turned. Over a hundred devices. With the majority of the gendarmerie on crowd control, they were down to the bare bones needed to keep the crime scene secured.

"You knew Hoadley best, how did she think?" asked Gordon.

Beaumont scanned the room.

"She would dismiss the obvious," he nodded at the clock, and Gordon nodded. Mainly because they had both searched it thoroughly.

"Okay not the clock."

They examined the others.

"What about the...or the..." Gordon pointed at some other devices, both of which they had already searched.

Beaumont frowned at them. "She was leaving it for me though, wasn't she?"

"Yes. Where would Hoadley, drugged and pursued, leave something for you?"

Beaumont's eyes fell on an original prototype that he loved so much. It had come a long way. Wide as a dinner plate it would take a strong person two hands to lift.

Background sounds faded. He glided over. How many times had he opened a compartment that allowed you to add more tea. Though with a cup this size it would take an entire bag to fill it. He pressed the drawer in, it clicked, opening, and a letter, creased and imprinted with the metal frame of the plate itself appeared.

"A letter," said Gordon, peering over his shoulder.

He reached out, picking up the edge between his fingers, lifting it gently, careful not to tear it. "Yes, I can see that." Hoadley had died for this.

"It appears Cuthbert isn't the only family member who's been dabbling," said Gordon.

E,

I trust this letter finds you in a position to rectify the situation that C has created.

Ilegal modifications of devices are occurring and I refuse to believe it is without your knowledge. F is also clearly involved considering what I just saw at the PD. It is sad to see that she has sunk so low.

Regardless, I expect you to return the funds that C has stolen from me and use your position to resolve this situation. If you do, I will leave without notifiying the authorities of your and F's illegal activity.

If my funds are not returned tomorrow, I will see to it that your daughter is the one who does the demonstration, not me and my next communication with you will be in person and in public.

MO

"Makes more sense than Cuthbert being the ringleader," said Beaumont, picking up the letter and reading it again.

"But why? Why would a senior patent officer risk his career?" asked Gordon.

"That bill is making everyone crazy," said Beaumont.

"I wonder about the modification racket that Inspector Logan is chasing." She frowned. "It would make it much easier for them to run if they had an official in the patent office to assist them."

He nodded, his mind caught up in the implications of the letter.

"F, Felicia Atwater or Florence Necket?" he asked.

"Probably both." Gordon clapped her hands. "Right, I'm going to find Vyner, and some guards, and collect all the papers in the house."

Beaumont blinked, glancing at her. "Do we have authority—"

"Got it as soon as Hoadley's body was discovered."

At least the investigation was now being conducted in a way Hoadley would have approved of. Beaumont swallowed and nodded.

Gordon left to hand out orders.

He stood at the glass doors leading out to the garden. He unlocked them, allowing the cool afternoon air in. What had it been like in the early hours of the morning? Alone. Stumbling.

He wished, with every fibre of his being, that she had waited, for him, a guard, anyone. Or would there have been different dead bodies? Better his than hers.

Beaumont carefully sealed the letter in his vest. The special pocket was also water and fireproof, something that was made publicly known, after a few unfortunate *accidents* to inspectors returning to the Way with critical information.

Gordon's enthusiastic tread heralded her return.

"I've arrested Vyner."

Beaumont blinked. "What? Why?"

"The little weasel was showing me his rooms and his writing station. All looking above board right." She paced, waving her hands. "But you know that I can't exit a room without checking the light fittings." She stopped and turned toward him.

He chuckled. "In which you have never found anything, ever."

Gordon touched her nose. "Until now."

"Seriously?"

"Stuck to the metal base was a series of small jotters." She windmilled her arms. "I kid you not."

"I don't suppose the jotters talk about the modification of devices?"

Gordon shrugged. "No, but they did keep very accurate records of all the *extra* money that Vyner had been receiving and who from."

"We knew he was blackmailing Overton." Beaumont closed and locked the door and turned towards her.

"But we didn't know that he received small sums from Ernest Walstrand and a *very* healthy supplemented income from the Purple Door now did we?"

Beaumont's eyes widened. "No, no we did not. How much are we talking?"

"Double what he makes as a house manager here." Gordon

crossed her arms and leant against the side of a cabinet of priceless antiques.

"They would expect a lot for that kind of money."

The cabinet clinked.

"Yes, they would. Including the removal of anyone getting in their way," said Gordon.

"Pipe it." Beaumont stood and paced the room. "Are you thinking he's the killer?"

"If he was ordered to do it...sure."

"By who?" Beaumont's fingers snagged in the knots in his hair.

"Now that's the question." Gordon pushed off the cabinet sending it swaying. "Our beloved Ernest Walstrand and someone who I am assuming is high up at the Purple Door. Know anyone who frequents it?"

Beaumont shuffled over and stabilised the cabinet, glaring at Gordon. "Ancilla Walstrand."

"I thought she was there with you?"

"No she was already there."

"Now that's interesting," murmured Gordon, tapping her cheek.

Beaumont frowned. He didn't see it. "What did she have to gain?" Sure, she wasn't the mouse they had all, except for Hoadley, cast her as, unless the mouse was wearing armour and equipped with a flamethrower, but he also didn't get a sense of avarice or need for power.

"Even if it got her out of that house? Living with Ernest can't be a picnic."

Beaumont grimaced. "Maybe."

"When people are trapped...they do stupid things."

He lifted his gaze to the sky, hoping for inspiration to strike. "Do we know where she is?"

"Locked up and awaiting our pleasure. I asked that they bring Melody back in too. I want to talk to the whole family."

"The father as well." Beaumont turned to her with a slight smile on his face.

Gordon's eyebrows raised.

"Do we have enough?"

Beaumont tapped the letter in his pocket. "Between this and Vyner's notes about payments...we definitely have enough to bring him in for formal questioning."

"Let's go pick him up." She rubbed her hands together. "A high-level Patent Office official. I am not sure if this is going to be good or bad for my career." She frowned. "You should do the arrest. You still don't care about your career going down the gurgler, do you?"

Beaumont snorted. "No and fine. But you take the lead in getting us through the crowd."

"Deal." Gordon practically bounced from the room.

Beaumont touched his vest pocket. He could only hope he could get the justice Hoadley deserved.

The crowd outside the Patent Office had tripled in size, and the debate raged on, but the Guards had managed to put up some barriers at the entrance of the building if anyone was brave enough to get to them.

He shook his head and pushed the political dispute out

of his mind and focused on what he was here to do. Arrest Ernest Walstrand. Something that was going to give him more pleasure to do than it had any reason to.

"Move people." Gordon strode ahead of him.

Despite the heightened energy of the crowd, they gave way to her unquestioned belief that they would let her through. They gave him a few suspicious glances but left the gap open long enough for him to keep close behind her. He glanced back, the path disappeared.

A wall of guards stood along the barriers outside the Patent Office doors. Once nodded through, they found themselves in a sea of calm. The cool of the stone, impossible to heat in winter, caused the air to fog in front of his face.

Gordon glanced around. "Okay, Beaumont. I got you in, let's bring this home."

He rolled his eyes. She could be so dramatic at times.

"You do know I'm going to arrest a man sitting in his office? This isn't going to be that exciting."

"I believe in old Ernest."

Beaumont gave a nod to one of the Guards as they passed through. "I sincerely hope not."

They had to ask the receptionist the way, but he pointed up a set of stairs and to an office on the right.

"Thanks," he said. The receptionist blinked but nodded.

The stairs, hard and cold and longer than he was used to, caused a slight huff of air to escape his lips on reaching the top.

"Need a moment to catch your breath there, gramps?"

Beaumont frowned at Gordon. "Did you want to do this?"

Gordon held up her hands. "Have pity on my future."

Beaumont shook his head and moved to the door on the right. He pushed through into a large office with an amazing view over the park outside. Somewhat ruined today by the crowds flowing through it.

Ernest Walstrand was in his element. A high-backed black chair framed him, his hands resting on its oversized arms, behind the largest desk Beaumont had ever seen. It was also the cleanest with not a single piece of paper on it. What exactly did he do here?

"Ernest Walstrand," Beaumont made sure he stayed near the door so his voice carried into the hallway. If he was going to do this, he was going to do it right. "You're required to come in for questioning and are being treated as a suspicious person in relation to the murder of Marcellus Overton, and Inspector Lavina Hoadley and in relation to illegal modifications along with Cuthbert Walstrand and Reginald Vyner."

He sat there, impervious, sneering, until Vyner's name was mentioned.

"I'm not going anywhere." Ernest fingers struggled to grip the wide arms of the chair, dimpling the soft fabric covering it.

"This is not a request." Beaumont stepped further into the room allowing Gordon and the couple of Guards she had tapped to be seen.

"Your career is going to be mud after this. Coming here, to my place of work. I'll ruin you." Ernest stood up, tugging at his waistcoat, glaring at them.

"You'll have to do that down at the Way." Beaumont stepped to the side and gestured at the door. Ernest's head was held high as he marched through the building. Beaumont imagined a slight tremor in his hands though.

Ernest refused to engage with them. There was only one way out and that was through the front door. The crowd, realising that something interesting was happening quietened to watch as he was escorted out.

Beaumont's stomach sank. It was a long walk back to the Way with a suspect.

"This way, Zer Walstrand," Gordon said gesturing down a side lane. Beaumont almost laughed. Leaving their steamer here seemed like a lifetime ago. But there it was. Undamaged and ready to bring the culprit home.

Beaumont opened the back door, controlling himself from giving a jaunty wave. Ernest glared razors at him.

Not trusting Ernest, Beaumont adjusted the steamer, locking the back doors, and kept an eye on him while Gordon drove.

"Your family has been playing fast and loose with the law, Zer Walstrand," said Beaumont. He stretched his legs out and into a relaxed pose but made sure he had a clear view of Ernest through the mirrors.

He didn't respond.

"Of course, it doesn't help with the father abusing his position. What did you do? Find the patent applications from those who couldn't protect themselves if someone made some tweaks to their invention?"

Ernest sat up straight. Rigid.

"When did you bring Cuthbert into the fold?" asked Gordon. "Fairly recently I would imagine. That bill coming in about to muck up your sweet deals, was it?"

Ernest shifted in his seat but otherwise didn't respond.

"What I can't understand is though, why would you use Cuthbert?" Beaumont tsked. "The man has walking disaster all over him."

Ernest didn't say anything, but Beaumont got the sense that he agreed with him.

"For some reason, you decide you needed a bit of distance between yourself and Overton." Beaumont tracked Ernest's movement in the mirror. "Perhaps you no longer trusted Vyner?" Earnest stiffened and Beaumont swallowed a grunt of satisfaction. "I don't blame you. I wouldn't trust him as far as I could throw him. Kept asking for more did he?."

"What surprises me," said Gordon, zipping through the back streets, "is that Ernest here was able to run an entire criminal enterprise of counterfeit prototypes while also holding down a full-time job," said Gordon.

"Hard to be an expert at two things," mused Beaumont.

"He must have been a terrible employee."

Ernest opened his mouth but snapped it shut again and stared out the window.

"It's sad when people take money for work that they don't do, or don't do properly." Gordon shook her head. "This arrest is for the betterment of the Patent Office."

"You are so right Prime Inspector Gordon."

"Thank you, Prime Inspector Beaumont."

The banter between them flowed naturally, winding

Ernest up tighter and tighter and tighter. By the time they pulled into the Way's courtyard he was thinking he might need a medic on standby.

"Here we are, Zer Ernest." Two guards came trotting up to them and they assisted Ernest out. Beaumont waited, leaning against the steamer. Ernest may or may not have killed Hoadley, but he was part of the reason she was dead. "Welcome to the next part of your life."

Ernest growled. Sweat pooled under his arms, staining his shirt. But his thin lips glued together showed he wasn't a complete fool. Though if he trusted Cuthbert with any secrets Beaumont might need to revisit that.

"Show him into an interview room, make sure he is secure," said Gordon.

The guards nodded and hauled him away.

"Do you think we can get him to talk?" she asked.

Beaumont shrugged. "Probably not. I think he's used to feeling angry."

"Shall we let him stew and start on Ancilla or Melody first?"

Beaumont stroked at his chin.

"Let's see how sticky Melody's fingers are."

He wasn't quite up to the disillusionment that an interview with Ancilla would bring.

25

Ancilla's Freedom

The tea and biscuits long gone, along with the light of the day, left nothing but grey empty walls and an uncomfortable chair.

She had tried to close her eyes and tell herself a story, but she had too much adrenaline pumping through her to concentrate.

"Ancilla."

And then Alistair was there smiling at her. With an order from the High Protector for her to be transferred to house arrest at the Atwaters for the remainder of the investigation. Relieved at this evidence of the High Protector's belief in her innocence, she had followed him back to Atwater Place. She had breathed easily for the first time that day and answered his questions about her health, settling into her favourite chair in the small room next to the conservatory.

"Thank you, Alistair," she smiled at him. "I cannot thank you enough."

"Nothing to do with me. Mother organised it all."

"You've both been so kind to me."

"Nonsense. It is ridiculous how you are being treated. Now Mother is here, but upstairs so you should be able to have some quiet."

"Thank you." She smiled at him.

He stopped in the doorway, turning back to Ancilla. "You won't try to leave the house, will you? The guards, the domestics, have instructions that you aren't to leave except in the company of myself, Mother, or the gendarmerie."

She blinked. It hadn't even crossed her mind to try. She was not such a fool.

"No of course not."

"It's just with Vyner being arrested, eyes are on us...not that I can say I'm surprised. Mother and I had discussed a few times about replacing him. But it is so hard to find decent people and we had Necket, so it seemed easier to leave him be. A mistake on our part certainly." He shook his head.

"Do you know what he was arrested for?"

"No, Necket saw him being escorted out but missed the actual event."

Ancilla chuckled. "Poor Necket, she won't forgive herself for that." She picked up the other cup of tea and took a sip.

Alistair smiled at her. "No, I suspect she would have paid to see that one." Alistair gave a small bow. "I have to get back to the warehouse, but I'll be back for dinner."

Alistair's kind face stared back at her. She had never

understood why his wife spent so much time on the mainland. He was pleasant, both in personality and to look at. Not to mention his painting of his mother in song, a masterpiece. She had always thought it sad he didn't paint more. Why Felicia kept him busy with trivial family business rather than honouring the artistry in her family.

"I look forward to it."

Dinner with the Atwaters would be a lot nicer than at the Way.

Apparently, it was not the comfort of the chair that prevented her from resting. After attempting to close her eyes Ancilla had thrown herself out of the chair and paced. The rug under her feet might be softer but it didn't make her mind any stronger.

Hoadley. If Hoadley was here now, what would she do? Would she sit around wallowing? No, she would fight, fight to the very end.

Ancilla wished she had a quill and paper, but she glanced at the various glasses, cups and saucers. Between them, she could make something happen.

It took a few minutes but soon she had the sauces and teacups all organised. The teacups represented her family members, the saucers represented the Atwaters and Necket, and a large glass became Overton with two small glasses representing Freddy and Vyner.

What did she know?

Marcellus was completely obsessed with having a device registered under his own name. Despite his own fame, he had always hated the fact that Felicia was the owner of so many devices that he had worked on.

Ancilla had overheard a number of arguments usually with Felicia pointing out that he made the devices so much better than she ever could and yes the original idea might be someone else's but he took it to the next level. He was never satisfied though. The cost of being great was that he was always pushing himself and others. It made him a brilliant illuminator but not necessarily satisfied with life.

With the bill about to be changed, he might have seen it as his last shot at immortality. A device forever known as his.

Cuthbert was involved. He had always been a fool chasing the easy way to fortune rather than focusing on what he had. He also had a gift with words which he had practiced more in influencing people to help him than in building his skill with poetry. A loss to the world she suspected.

But father. Would he really do it? Was he also chasing immortality?

Ancilla moved his cup over to join the larger glass and Cuthbert's cup.

She paced the room. This was useless, all it was going to tell her was that they were involved. It wasn't going to show her who the murderer was.

Okay, so the question is why did Overton need to die? Cuthbert lost his money. He wouldn't be happy about it. And where did the Purple Door come into it?

Freddy—a witness to Marcellus not being around for the last three days—killed. This meant whoever was running this didn't realise that the gendarmerie already knew that. It also meant that in their mind she was the only other witness. If she had stayed at home, would she have left it alive?

Maybe this was all planned. Those quill wipers, building them took knowledge, skill and planning. How else to collect them? It would have to be a massive endeavour, with resources. Guilty for even thinking it, the first face that flashed into her mind was Alistair. Definitely something he could organise.

The painting he had done of Felicia. Alistair was known as an artist, but that was the only piece of art he had ever displayed. A piece of art recently completed too. What if, what if it wasn't his own pneuma, what if he had worked out a way to drain Marcellus's and use it himself? This wouldn't just be small amounts from people using pen wipers. That painting had taken some serious talent.

Poor Marcellus.

Ancilla swallowed and stretched, feeling the tiredness that still lingered in her muscles. And her? Had they taken from her as well?

What would have happened if she had continued the demonstrations?

Ancilla shuddered. How many artists would have been asked by the Atwaters to use the illuminier?

Meanwhile, Alistair's art would have become critically acclaimed.

Ancilla slumped down in a chair, cradling her head in her hands. No one was going to believe her. She hadn't seen anything but deference from Prime Inspector Beaumont to the Atwaters, and without any kind of proof, other than a wake of dead bodies behind her, why should they.

She closed her eyes and allowed the grief of the loss of someone who had actually seen her, heard her, wash over.

The lights danced.

Ancilla opened her eyes to find the conservatory alight with birds and flowers like she had never seen before. Escaping the recliner, she moved to the entrance of the conservatory.

Its lush greenness was even more vivid than usual, at the centre of the twirl of birds and flowers was the copper device, glowing and Felicia standing next to it, her arms extended, her fingertips brushing its exterior, the outer layer of skin pulsing with light.

Ancilla's mouth dropped open as a large multi-coloured bird flew overhead. Its beak opened but no sound came out.

Ancilla gazed at Felicia.

"How?" Ancilla's gaze dropped to the illuminier on the ground, with three thin copper pipes connecting it to the pulsing copper pot. "An amplifier?"

Felicia's head turned towards her, and her lips turned up.

"That is one way to describe it."

Felicia was, as always, impeccably dressed, exuding a calm demeanour.

Deep down Ancilla never really believed Freddy fooled Felicia.

"Why?" she asked. Foolish question. The only thing she should be focusing on was getting out of this alive.

Felicia usually kept her hair tied back in a tight twist or bun, but today it was out. Longer than Ancilla remembered, reaching just past her shoulders with a soft wave that softened her face. But nothing could soften the rage.

"Betrayal, revenge, a place in history." She shrugged, her gaze never leaving Ancilla's face.

"That's a lot of things," said Ancilla, trying to subtly shift away. "Alistair still around?"

A thin smile spread across Felicia's face. "That pneumaless son of mine? No, he is off playing with his little ventures."

"His painting—"

Felicia smirked. "Don't play the innocent with me. You know exactly where that pneuma came from. How a member of the Atwater family could be so empty..." She gazed around the conservatory. "There's really no point in it all is there?" She glared at Ancilla. "If I hadn't stepped in the Atwaters would have faded from history...now..." She shrugged.

"Now? What will one painting do?"

Felicia waved Ancilla's words away. "I don't care about the painting." She paced the room, never taking her gaze off Ancilla. "But I won't be the Atwater that let the family be forgotten."

"How could anyone forget—"

"What's left after I die? No inventions will be held by the Atwater name once I'm gone, a son who can't even muster enough pneuma to turn on the family crest, and what? An ungrateful country that will distort my creations as soon as my body's cold in the ground."

Ancilla was going to take a guess that Felicia wasn't a fan of the new bill then.

"So why not register them in Alistair's name so it's for his lifetime—"

"Because he can't do the demonstration you fool." Felicia's hiss lashed across the space between them.

Ancilla blinked. Of course, to register a device the listed inventor had to be an artist capable of demonstrating it in front of the Patent Officials.

"So instead of registering Marcellus as an Atwater, your solution was to drain your lover dry?"

Felicia stared, eyes cold and empty. Ancilla's stomach dropped.

"You mean the lover who was leaving me, and for what? A few more coins in his pocket? What did he need that I couldn't provide?"

Ancilla gulped back her response.

"Fair enough." Ancilla swallowed, taking another step back. "But what about the quill wipers? They are going to hurt people who have never done you any harm—"

"Oh," Felicia smirked. "You meant the commemorative quill wipers that I am giving to the Patent Office and Parliament?"

Ancilla just stared at her. That was a lot of artists she was planning to drain.

"But how do you collect it?" Ancilla ran her hand through her hair again. "I just can't work that part out."

It might not have been the most important question at that moment. Asking Felicia not to kill her probably should have been at the top. But it had been a block in her pipes ever since she worked out what they did.

"What do you think our waste devices are for?" Felicia turned towards Ancilla. "You're just like that little cockroach of an inspector, aren't you? A little pest, scurrying around in the walls. Only solution termination."

Ancilla stepped further back, trying to angle herself so that she was closer to the door to the drawing room. There were guards out the front. She just had to get through to the foyer. She breathed in through her nose and centred her weight.

The anger drained from Felicia's face and Ancilla was once more confronted by the head of the Atwater family. Ancilla's pulse, which had already been racing at a decent speed, increased.

"A pity you're not more like your father. Perhaps we could have taken this next adventure together."

Felicia had picked up her walking stick at some point and was a lot closer than Ancilla expected.

"My father?" Ancilla shifted closer to the door. "What does he have to do with it?"

Felicia shook her head. "Children are so disappointing."

Her lips spread in a grin, but with the dead empty eyes, it was all a bit creepy.

Ancilla kept inching towards the door, but Felicia struck. Her cane slammed into Ancilla's legs sending her to the ground and a hard hand smeared a cold gel across her face.

"A little gift from a friend," said Felicia, her voice empty.

Ancilla fell backwards, landing with a thumb on the

ground. Tears gathered in the corners of her eyes as she struggled with the rage pumping through her even as her body fought for oxygen. Felicia relaxed her hold and Ancilla dragged in a breath.

"What was that?"

"Hmm, it is working fast on you."

Ancilla was prodded by the stick in Felicia's hand. She struggled to keep her eyes open but even her eyelids became more and more unresponsive.

"Why kill me..." Ancilla gasped as her lungs took shallower and shallower breaths.

A voice hissed in her ear. "You'll only wish you were dead."

26

Beaumont Brings It Home

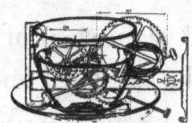

Beaumont entered the room to find Melody Walstrand scowling at the door.

"Zer Walstrand," said Beaumont. He kept his voice low but sharp.

"Prime Inspector," she growled. "Where have you been? I've been here for ages. No water, no tea. I'm thirsty, hungry, need to go to the washroom and have no idea what is happening."

Beaumont blinked.

"Right." He turned towards the door. "Guards, please organise a bathroom break and water and tea to be provided."

"Yes, zer."

"Follow the guard, Zer Walstrand, freshen up...and then we can talk."

"I know my rights." She rose to her feet, her shoulders back and her stare direct.

Beaumont noted that she waddled slightly as she followed the guard and suspected that she really had needed to use the washroom. He was only surprised she hadn't been banging on the door.

Water, tea and some biscuits arrived. Beaumont reminded himself to send a thank you to Alfred, and Melody was escorted back by Gordon.

Her face brightened at the sight of the teapot.

"Oh, marvellous." She sat down and happily poured herself tea, taking a sweet biscuit. Her world apparently once more returned to normal.

"What's all this about?" She nibbled at the biscuit.

"Death and fraud," said Gordon, her face cold. Beaumont wanted to roll his eyes at her for the dramatics but kept his focus on Melody.

"Oh," her eyes widened. "How interesting. I suppose I knew about the death part, with Overton, and that uptight Inspector got done in too didn't she?"

"Yes." Beaumont frowned at her. "Inspector Lavina Hoadley was killed in the course of pursuing her duty."

Melody waved the hand holding the biscuit a fine spray of crumbs wafted through the air. "Of course, terribly tragic. But I don't see why I was manhandled and thrown in here?"

"Your family is implicated in the fraud."

"What Cuthbert? Yes, but you already have him."

"Your father as well."

Her eyes widened. "Father?" She ate a bigger bite of the

biscuit and took a few moments to chew and wash it down with some tea. "I don't see how. There is no way he would risk his position at the Patent Office."

"Even for money? To have a device registered in his name before the bill is passed?"

Melody took another sip of her tea. "That bill, it's driving everyone mad I tell you." She put her teacup down. "Maybe..." her forehead creased with fine hairline tracks. "There has been some extra cash coming in. But..." her fingers tapped on her lips. "It seems like a massive risk."

Beaumont remembered her sitting in front of the household ledgers. He had the family bookkeeper in front of him.

"How long would you say that the extra cash has been coming in?"

She picked up her tea and sipped it. "I don't know if I should talk. I don't want to get father into trouble."

"That ship has sailed. The only question now is if you're joining him on it." Gordon sat back in her chair, hands folded loosely across her stomach.

Melody examined her and then him.

"What do you think I have done?"

"Assisted your father with selling unregistered modifications."

"That does sound like something Cuthbert would get caught up in, but I still don't know why you think I am?"

"Your father needed a go-between he could trust."

"And you think he would trust me? He would be a fool to trust any of us really. And father is many things, but he isn't a fool. Usually."

"Why do say that?"

"Say what?"

"That he wouldn't trust any of you?"

"Cuthbert would be sure to screw it up. High and mighty Ancilla would turn him in and as for me..." she shrugged. "It doesn't sound like something I would find fun."

"And why's that important?"

"I don't waste my time on anything that isn't fun."

"But you like doing the family accounts."

"Numbers are fun."

"Then let's talk numbers," said Gordon, leaning forward. "Any extra, fun, over the last few months?"

"Not the last few months."

"What about years?" asked Gordon her eyes tracking every one of Melody's twitches.

Melody's fingers drummed the table.

Beaumont left to give an order to collect all the ledgers and books from the Walstrand residence.

He returned to the room, feeling Melody's gaze track him as he moved across it, sitting down opposite her.

"How long?" he asked, pouring her another cup of tea.

She cradled it in her hands. "Three, maybe four."

"Isn't that when Ernest last got promoted?" asked Beaumont.

She played with her teacup, taking another sip.

"Yes, I suppose so."

Beaumont exchanged a glance with Gordon. How deep did this go? He made a mental note to check out the details of the promotion.

"And since then, you've seen more money coming in than you expected?" asked Beaumont.

"I assumed father was getting bonuses or something."

"Bonuses? From the Patent Office?" said Beaumont, his voice going high. In all his years of service, he had never received a bonus.

Her eyes dropped and she shrugged.

"Okay, so what did you do?"

She raised her eyes and frowned, puzzled. "With what?"

"When you saw the extra money?"

"Nothing why?"

"You didn't discuss it with your father—"

Melody's eyes had widened. "With father? Goodness no. He wanted me to make sure all the bills were paid. He had given the task to Cuthbert first, but we kept having debtors coming around, and we were getting such a terrible name that I took over. Father wasn't happy about it, but he liked not having creditors at the door."

"..." Beaumont cleared his throat and glanced at the jotter in front of him. "You took over the books? Potentially that extra income could have been there prior?"

She shrugged. "Who knows, Cuthbert was a terrible book-keeper. I really don't know what Father was thinking."

Beaumont had a pretty clear idea. Ernest had gambled that she wouldn't care, rather than not notice.

There was a knock on the door and a guard appeared with a basket filled with small cakes.

"What do we have here?" A waft of sweetness greeted them, and Beaumont's face brightened.

"Butler Necket sent this around for Zer Walstrand. Heard she had been locked up and didn't trust us to feed her."

"And you had to bring them in now?" drawled Gordon.

"She was quite insistent, zer and we felt it was the better course."

"Necket's here? Can I see her?" asked Melody.

Beaumont blinked. "I didn't realise you knew Necket."

"I visit the Atwater's too you know." Melody patted her hair. "Necket has a keen interest in those number games, the ones in the newspaper."

The guard reached into the basket and pulled out a newspaper folded to the puzzle page and Melody's face lit up and she clapped her hands.

"Marvelous." She reached towards it.

"I think we are getting off track, have you checked the basket?" said Gordon.

"Yes, zer, cake and the newspaper."

"Fine put it down and let's get on with this interview."

Melody went to grab the newspaper, but Beaumont was there first.

"I'll need to make sure there aren't any messages here first."

Melody rolled her eyes. "You can't suspect Necket surely? That woman is more loyal to the Atwaters than they deserve."

"Loyalty to a family is not the same as not being involved in illegal activity."

"Cuthbert is right, you are fools."

Gordon sat forward. "The question we're trying to answer is whether you are."

Melody picked up a bit of cake, popping it in her mouth.

Beaumont was trying very hard to not get annoyed.

"Zer Melody Walstrand—"

"He's getting serious," said Melody around a mouthful of cake.

"Zer Melody Walstrand. Unless you can give us any information to the contrary, we are about to charge you with fraud and will be considering charges of involvement in a plan to murder Overton, Inspector Hoadley and Fred Gilbert Bramble."

Melody swallowed the rest of the cake. "Who's Fred Gilbert Bramble?"

"Overton's impersonator," said Gordon.

"Why would Overton need an impersonator?" Melody's head tilted, her gaze flicking between them.

Beaumont imagined throwing the basket of cake across the room. Instead, he picked one up and shoved it into his mouth. He groaned. He hadn't tasted a cake this delicious since he was at the Walstrand.

He used the tea to wash it down.

"Why does this cake taste the same as the one I had at your family home yesterday?"

Melody picked up another small cake and smiled at it.

"Necket and I, well we bake."

"You bake?"

Melody sat up straighter. "Yes, do you have a problem with that?"

"How often do you do this...baking?"

"I am not sure that is any of your business." Melody blushed, slightly.

Beaumont didn't know what it all meant, or if it meant anything. "What about last night? Where were you then."

"It had been a long day. I was tired and to be honest a bit grumpy. Necket had popped round and well one thing led to another and we went and saw a play."

"A play."

"Yes, it's at that new round theatre. The play was something awfully gothic, murder on crow or something like that."

"And what time did you get home?"

"We ended up at this lounge with a live band. All hand-played, no devices. It was interesting. Messy but fun."

"Do you remember the name of this club?"

"The Desmonds."

"I've heard good things about it. Low tech but got a solid vibe. A bit fringe." Gordon leaned forward in her chair.

"It was great." Melody smiled at her.

Beaumont got up again, this time giving directions to have a guard grab Necket and verify Melody's statements. If what she said was true, then she was probably out of the frame for Hoadley's murder at least.

"There's still the matter of"—he cleared his throat—"the fraud."

"I didn't have anything to do with it."

"But you knew something was going on."

"With my father, something was always going on. I was just glad that the company we were keeping in Noxrath was of a higher order. I was never going to make it as a singer with the help of the riffraff he called friends back in Blagwallow."

"And who exactly was this...riffraff?"

Melody yawned. "Is this going to go on much longer? I feel like I have been talking about things I have absolutely no interest in for hours."

Gordon leant forward. "You'll stay here until we are one hundred per cent sure you aren't involved."

"Fine." She picked up a cup of tea and took a sip.

"If you answer our questions..." Beaumont tapped the side of the now cold pot. "We will leave you alone with your puzzle, the rest of the cake and a fresh pot of tea."

Melody flashed a natural, and brilliant smile. Beaumont blinked. He suspected she was even more dangerous when she didn't have her armour up.

"Ask away then." She gestured grandly in their direction.

"The riffraff. What do you remember?"

He stopped at the washroom, too much tea, again. After relieving himself, he cleaned his hands, splashing his face with water trying to wake himself up.

He stared at himself in the mirror and adjusted his waistcoat, turning on the signal. The gendarmerie's pattern shifted and settled strong and clear. There was no mistaking who he worked for, and he found he needed the support of the gendarmerie right now.

Gordon was waiting outside in the hallway.

"Are you ready?" she asked.

"Let's get this over with." He straightened his shoulders and entered the interview room.

The empty room. The air in his lungs hissed out between his teeth. "What the?"

Gordon grabbed the guard who was standing outside the door of the empty room.

"What exactly are you guarding?"

He stared at her blankly.

"The interview room, zer."

Gordon growled. "There doesn't appear to be anyone in the interview room."

"No, zer."

"Why are you guarding it?"

"Because—"

"Where's the person who was in here? Zer Ancilla Walstrand?"

"The Atwaters came and got her, zer."

Beaumont wanted to head-butt him.

Gordon stepped between them.

"I'm assuming you didn't hand her over just because they asked nicely?"

"No, zer."

They stared at him and he stared back.

"Why did you release Ancilla Walstrand to them?" growled Gordon.

"Because the High Protector told me to."

Beaumont glanced at Gordon. She shrugged, as perplexed as he was.

Beaumont blinked. "Exactly how did the High Protector advise you of this?"

"She sent a message, zer. It had her official seal."

"Who handed you the note?" asked Gordon.

"Alistair Atwater, zer."

"And it was him and Felicia Atwater who took Ancilla?"

"Just Alistair Atwater, zer. He said Felicia was waiting outside for her."

Beaumont swore.

"Why would Alistair be involved in the fraud?" asked Gordon.

"It's not the fraud. No this is about Felicia and Overton and the illuminier. *Pipe it.* I can't believe I didn't see it." Beaumont pulled at his hair.

"What?" asked Gordon.

"Come on we need to talk to the High Protector and find out if she actually did release her or whether Alistair organised it," said Beaumont.

"Why would he risk it?" asked Gordon. "And for Ancilla?"

Beaumont trotted into the hallway but halted and glanced back to find Gordon staring at the guard.

"Why are you guarding an empty room?" she asked.

"Because no one told me to stop, zer."

Gordon shook her head. "Consider the order given and check in with the shift supervisor on where you are needed."

The guard nodded gratefully and headed off.

Gordon caught up with him.

Beaumont snorted. "Might need a bit more coaching on decision-making that one."

Gordon hung her head. "Sometimes there's too wide a gap, that not even the best will in the world can span."

They stopped to issue the alert.

"Can someone find out how Alistair Atwater and Ancilla Walstrand left? Was it on foot, in a steamer? A hire steamer? A bike what?"

He wished Alfred was still on shift but a chorus of *yes, zers* came back at him so he had to trust they would.

"Thank you, I'll be with the High Protector."

He stormed through the hallway with Gordon on his heels. His face pulled downwards and when he glanced at Gordon her face was uncharacteristically grim as well.

Beaumont was getting used to not knocking. He found the High Protector standing at her window. Her hands clasped behind her back staring at the sky.

"High Protector," said Beaumont, his voice ricocheting around the room.

Cadwell turned. "Shouldn't you be investigating?"

"Alistair Atwater has taken Ancilla Walstrand from the Way on your authority."

She straightened. "What?"

"He presented a message, with your seal, to the guard that said Ancilla was being released into the Atwater's custody."

Cadwell's face drained of colour.

"We need her back here. Now."

Beaumont blinked. What did she think he was going to be doing? "I've issued an alert."

Cadwell's face aged before him. "Do you know where he would take her?"

"I think he'll make a break for the mainland," said Gordon.

Cadwell nodded, her face grim. "Are we thinking he killed Overton?"

"Why else take Ancilla and run?" asked Beaumont, he paced and pulled at his hair.

"Perhaps they are in it together?" said Gordon, bouncing on her toes.

Both of them hopped up on adrenalin. He needed to calm down.

"Find them and find out," ordered Cadwell.

That was literally what they were going to do. But if it made her feel better to issue the order. Beaumont shook his head at himself. Focus.

Beaumont stopped outside the Way, staring at the guards and steamers coming and going.

"Do we know where we are going?" asked Gordon.

He scowled at her and kicked at the ground.

"If you were the son of a powerful family and escaping with your lover and a revolutionary device that is your link to fame and fortune, and you can avoid the gendarmerie?" asked Gordon.

"First I would head to a country that didn't do extradition."

"Right, so pretty much any country on the mainland."

"How would we leave Noxrath and Espya?" Beaumont rubbed his eyes.

"It will depend on whether my partner in crime was voluntarily joining me or not."

"If voluntary?" He turned to Gordon.

"Travelling as a couple, on our honeymoon? A nice little cruise?"

"And involuntary?"

"Smuggler, or similar. A dirigible and cash payments."

"Okay so we go one way," Beaumont pointed towards the dirigible yards, "And we send the inspectors to the other." He pointed in the general direction of the river.

"Or we split up?"

It made sense for each of them to grab an inspector and go their separate ways.

"No." Beaumont took a breath. A gamble or an educated guess? "Let the inspectors take the cruise angle. We'll take the dirigible yards."

"Still betting she is innocent?"

"What?"

"Here we are, wandering through the airship yards after dark with only a couple of guards for company while the inspectors are visiting luxury cruises."

"So?"

"Are you really going to make me spell it out?"

Beaumont lengthened his stride, Gordon's laugh running behind him.

Damp motor oil settled in his nose. Mount Nox wrapped around the yards, protecting them from any kind of air movement leaving the yards humid and mouldy.

Beaumont wished they had taken a moment or two to think about the inevitable fog and visibility.

Beaumont's gaze flicked around as he searched for the source of the scurrying sound.

"What was that?"

"What do you think it was? Probably a rat." Gordon snickered. "You probably should have changed your shoes."

Beaumont stared down at his favourite boots. When he had put them on he had seen visits to the Atwaters and the Walstrands homes not traipsing through a shipyard.

An engine started up. He exchanged glances with Gordon. While dirigibles did fly at night it wasn't common, especially on winter nights with a heavy layer of fog.

"Where's it coming from?" asked Gordon.

Beaumont shook his head. With the fog distorting the noise, it was impossible to tell.

"We'll have to guess...wait..." A soft glow appeared to his right. The kind of glow that he would expect to see on the torchlight of a ship. "Light."

Gordon broke into a trot heading towards it.

"Careful," hissed Beaumont.

She slowed enough for Beaumont to catch up with her and together they approached the airship. A twenty-seater, if that, a personal pleasure craft really.

"Do the Atwater's have a dirigible?" he asked.

"I didn't see one listed."

"So, he's stealing it then."

"Or borrowing it, they are the kind of people who have friends that do."

"Doubt he had time to ask." Beaumont kept his voice soft and his footsteps gentle as he approached the main entrance.

The door was unlocked, sloppy, so he pushed it open, peering up the stairwell.

Empty, but a light at the top fell into his vision. He gestured at Gordon to follow, and they both carefully climbed the stairs, keeping their backs to the wall. At the top, they found themselves on a small landing, light, from a half-opened door, illuminating the stairs. Gordon went up to it and glanced at him. He took a breath and nodded. She pushed it open, and he rushed through before skidding to a halt.

The pain in his throat made it hard to swallow. She was positioned in an armchair. Her blank gaze stared at them. The illuminier next to her. It wasn't until she did a slow blink that he started to breathe again. They stood there all staring at each other. Beaumont glanced at the illuminier on the table.

"I suppose that answers that question then." His face, grim.

Ancilla's gaze shifted between them. He wanted to shout at her and ask her why she would throw her life away on someone like Alistair Atwater and the dubious success of a stolen prototype.

Gordon snorted. "And opens some others, but first things first. Where's Alistair?"

Ancilla just stared at them. Beaumont scanned the room and pointed at another half-opened door.

"Through to the bridge do you think?" he asked.

"Yeah. How about you watch Zer Walstrand here and I'll get the pilot."

Beaumont nodded. He didn't like splitting up, but Ancilla couldn't be trusted. "Be careful—"

"When am I not careful?" Gordon grinned and ran through the door at full speed. Beaumont gurgled, but she had survived this long so he had to assume she would survive this. Plus he had the problem of Ancilla Walstrand to solve.

He stared down at her and then reached for his restraints.

"Zer Walstrand, you are being arrested on suspicion of fraud and murder. The details of the charges will be explained back at the Way however I need to put you in restraints, and we need to remove you from this ship."

He stepped forward. A slow dreamy smile spread across her face.

"Hmm"

"The gendarmerie, Zer Walstrand."

She blinked at him. He took a step closer but she didn't make any attempt to move or get away. He crouched down next to her. She rolled her head to watch his movements and her smile broadening.

"Zer Walstrand."

"Hmm."

"You are under arrest."

"Hmm," she purred.

He reached out and touched her. Her skin was warm, her arm completely relaxed. He shifted closer, gazing into her eyes.

"Ancilla?"

{ 27 }

Ancilla's Haze

Ancilla floated. Her muscles relaxed and for the first time that she could remember, she wasn't afraid.

She could only do small movements but that was okay. She was comfortable.

It took a few goes but she eventually lifted her eyelids and there was a soft light. Everything was a bit hazy, but she got the impression of a very lush lounge. She liked that. Certainly, the chair she was on was very comfortable. She would happily give anyone interested a recommendation about it.

She opened and closed her eyes a few times and the room came more into focus. Dark woods and burgundies, nice. She even liked the splashes of green from the plants, but she wasn't quite sure why they were there. She rolled her head. Blinking at the illuminier on a large brass table next to her.

Two figures rushed into the room. They needed to slow down. No need to rush through life.

They had identical patterns on their waistcoats. It was a bit gauche of them to wear the same waistcoat at the same time. They seemed nice though. The woman was fidgety, unable to stand still but she liked the man. He was nice and still. He stared at her. It was restful the way he didn't move.

The fidgety one left in a rush. The man removed his hat, tossing it aside.

The man moved closer to her and came into focus. Her gazed drifted over his floppy blond hair. She wished she could lift her hand and touch him. She bet it would feel great. She liked feeling great.

He knelt next to her.

Her head rested against the back of the chair. She let it roll towards him. He was quite close now. He had kind eyes. She smiled, happy to stay there, gazing at him forever.

His lips moved. Soft sounds floated through the air. She liked the sound. She tried to make sounds back her mouth was happy to just rest.

His hand appeared between them. On one of his fingers was a green gel which he pressed against her lips. The pupils of his eyes expanded but he blinked, returning to them to normal. He pushed his finger into her mouth, smearing the gel under her tongue, removing his finger he used it close her jaw.

Her mouth started to feel uncomfortable, so she swallowed but there was no saliva to help push it down.

"I have to go and check on Gordon. In a few moments you are going to have a lot more movement. Take it easy and wait here for our return."

She focused on getting rid of the moss flavour in her mouth, but she couldn't help but think he had a nice voice.

He didn't move.

"Water." He disappeared and then came back with a glass of a clear liquid, forcing her to drink some. It helped and she was able to relax again and smiled at him.

"I have to go. The ship is moving, and we need to get control of it if we are going to get out of this. Don't do anything rash okay?" He rested his hand on her knee. She liked that. But then he was gone.

Her lips turn downwards, but she was tired, so she let her eyelids close, ready to float. But instead, her muscles started twitching. She squirmed in the seat stretching her arms and legs, scraping her skin against the fabric of the chair trying to get some relief from the feeling of ants running through her skin.

It intensified, until she slid off the chair, rolling around on the floor her arms and legs flailing about. She kicked one chair, but it was her foot that gave way and her eyes watered while she tried to work out what was going on.

The combination with the vibrations in the floor and a sense of acceleration only had one answer, she was on a dirigible.

The End of the Matter

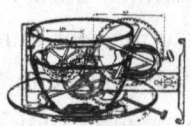

One of the major frustrations with being gagged was that Beaumont could not swear out loud.

What a disaster. He should have stayed with Ancilla. Instead, here he was, bound, and now they both had gags glued on. Thanks Gordon.

He shifted, trying to peer at Felicia standing at the wheel and calmly navigating the Noxrath air space.

Felicia Atwater. She had been a suspect, of course. They all had been. But if he had been asked to make a bet at the beginning of this, he would have put long odds on her. In fact he would have put Alistair Atwater ahead of her by a mile.

Throwing it all away just because she didn't get to keep it forever.

She turned, feeling his gaze.

"I don't know why my little plant extract isn't working

on you and your friend there." Felicia's glare took in Gordon who was flopping around wasting her energy trying to get free. "But whatever it is, it's not going to save you."

He pushed at the expertly tied ropes around his wrists and ankles. She might be right. The only question he had was why he wasn't dead already.

"You're probably wondering why you aren't dead already." She made a few more adjustments at the helm of the airship. "Let's just call you insurance until I get out of Espya airspace." Grunting satisfaction, her hands let go of the wheel and she stepped down from the helm. "Though I am not sure what use you will be to me after that."

He felt guilty about Gordon dying. And to be honest he wasn't that happy about his own imminent death either. Or Hoadley's killer, and there was no doubt in his mind that she was the one who had killed her, off free to galivant around the mainland.

Ancilla ran into the room. He tried to shout a warning, but she threw herself forward, tackling Felicia. Felicia spun out of the way, pulling out the stick that had been their undoing.

At first glance, a simple walking stick, and such a common sight, he hadn't seen it anymore.

The stick connected with skin and created a charge. A weapon that had not appeared on any list he had seen and was either unregistered or illegal. Either way it had been unexpected.

"Everyone's awake today," Felicia snarled, striking out at Ancilla, who jumped out of reach, but not before a spark jumped from the stick to her clothes, giving off a faint burning smell.

"Felicia, think of your Family name, of everything you have built," said Ancilla, treading carefully just out of reach.

"Everyone, my country, my lover, my son, have all betrayed me, and my ancestors, after lifetimes of nothing but service."

"Service?" Ancilla blinked at her. "You call having every possible advantage in this life service?"

Felicia dove forward, slamming her walking stick down on Ancilla's shoulder.

The burning smell grew stronger, but Ancilla leaned into it grabbing Felicia's arm, pulling her forward, and off balance. The force of it threw Felicia down and her stick flipped from her hand bouncing across the floor to land four body lengths from him.

Ancilla threw herself on top of Felicia and pulled out wires from her pockets using them to bind her.

"I should have killed you first." Felicia kicked at her, but Ancilla sat on the back of her legs and Felicia flailed about.

"You're just lucky that Hoadley would want you arrested, otherwise you'd already be dead." Ancilla picked up Felicia's head and slammed it into the ground.

Beaumont's eyes widened and he thrashed around, trying to get Ancilla's attention before the situation escalated. She glanced over at him, sighed and shuffled over.

"This is going to hurt." She smiled.

Without even a moment for him to think about what she

meant, the gag was ripped off taking half the skin of his face with it.

"Pipe it."

"It will sting a bit," said Ancilla as she pulled out a small tool form her pocket and used it to break open his restraints. "But it settles down sooner than you think, five minutes at most."

He was grateful to know that his face fire was going to burn out soon.

"My legs."

"Yes, I'll get to them I just need to ... got it."

Beaumont massaged his wrists as she attacked the restraints on his feet.

Sharp thumps brought their attention to Gordon. She now had hold of the stick but due to her own restraints she had to hold it in her hand behind her.

"I'd better..."

"Yes."

Ancilla double checked Felicia was still groggy, and bound, before heading over to release Gordon.

Rip.

"*Pipe it*, that stings like a gasser," moaned Gordon.

"How are you?" asked Beaumont.

"Besides my face being on fire, frustrated and annoyed with my own stupidity at being overpowered by an old woman and having to be saved by a mouse. I'm fine," she snarled.

Ancilla released Gordon's restraints and Gordon shoved

herself to her feet rubbing her wrists and shaking out her legs.

"Who is the mouse?" asked Ancilla with a frown on her face.

"You are," said Gordon.

"The important question is, who's going to fly the ship? Because I am pretty sure those buildings aren't going dodge themselves."

Ancilla scrambled up to the wheel and with a practised move unlocked it, gently steering it on a course between buildings.

"You know how to fly this thing?" asked Beaumont.

"Of course, she does," said Gordon glaring at him. "We aren't hitting any buildings are we?"

"I'm trying to ascertain whether we need assistance in getting this ship down," Beaumont growled. He flushed as he glanced at Ancilla. "No disrespect to your flying skills, Zer Walstrand."

"None taken, but I once spent six months testing dirigibles so hopefully I remember enough to get it down."

"Great," he huffed, relaxing.

Ancilla glanced at him, with a small smile. "It's been a while though."

"Didn't see that one coming," said Gordon.

Beaumont turned to her. "You didn't see the partner of the victim as the murderer?" Conveniently forgetting his own dismissing of Felicia as a suspect. "Didn't I teach you anything?"

Gordon laughed. "In most cases yes – but in this one – well I thought it would be more interesting."

"People are always interesting."

"Not when they do the same stupid shit every day."

"It is new to each of them."

Gordon laughed again and held up her hands in surrender.

Beaumont glanced around. Not many guards. Everyone was busy with crowd control and the haul they had brought in. Between the fraud and the murder, they had picked up almost ten criminals.

"I heard Perry is kicking hard to be released," said Gordon

"We know he was a main distributor. The question is, will we have enough to hold him?" he rubbed the back of his neck. "Hoadley's notes and Ancilla's statement should be enough to try at least."

"She didn't deserve to die," mumbled Gordon.

"No." He exhaled. The memorial service was delayed a week so that everyone could attend.

"Are you staying?" She glanced sideways at him.

Beaumont's fingers dove into his hair, catching on more knots and curls. Did he want to? Did he want to spend his time doing this kind of work?

"Maybe."

A messenger sped into the room, clocked them, and shoved a note into his hands before running off to deliver her next message.

He turned it over in his hands noting the High Protector's seal. Cracking it open he read the note.

Gordon peered over his shoulder. "Well?"

"She wants to see me."

"I hope you stay." Gordon lifted her gaze, staring at him. "There's good work here to be done."

He nodded and went to discuss his fate.

He passed through the open double doors to find Cadwell standing at her window.

"Close them, will you?" she asked.

He turned back only to find her assistant had beaten him to it. The lock clicked. He turned to the High Protector.

She turned from the window and gestured for him to take a seat. Settling into her own chair she picked up a piece of paper on her desk.

"It appears that Zer Perry is not happy with his arrest."

Beaumont's eyebrows raised. Hoadley would have been pleased.

"Most people aren't." He snorted. "Happy being arrested that is."

Cadwell laughed. "True, but he has escalated to a formal complaint around illegal arrests and harassment and such."

Beaumont shrugged. "There's a report on my desk saying his pneuma was all over the stolen prototypes."

Because of Hoadley. She had the foresight to leave a series of instructions with Alfred for the day shift to carry out. He just wished she had followed her own advice and left the rest of the investigation for the day.

"He's saying he didn't know."

"I have another report that says that despite considerable effort to hide it he is the owner of the Purple Door and the two who attempted to abduct Ancilla Walstrand are employed by him."

"Are they now? Do we have a warrant out for them?"

"They are in custody." A smile creased her face. "We also have some evidence that he owns the vehicles used to transport the prototypes between Blagwallow and Noxrath." Cadwell put the paper down. "I'll let him know we won't be progressing his complaint."

He remembered the debrief after the Windlass case. Everyone congratulated themselves for capturing the killers. Forgetting the small cold bodies in the morgue. How quickly the world moves on. In the end, what did it all matter? Would anyone even remember he existed if he left?

"Is there anything else?"

"Is there anything else?" She grunted. "A few things yes."

Beaumont sat up straighter. "Zer."

"Ancilla Walstrand. Are we comfortable that she wasn't involved in this?"

"Yes, zer." Beaumont kept his hands relaxed in his lap. "She did hide that Fred Bramble was impersonating Overton on the night of the launch, at the request of Overton. But other than that, there doesn't appear to be any reason to suspect her, zer."

Hoadley had, rightly, suspected there was more to her than met the eye, but from her notes he could tell she trusted her.

"And the fact she saved your lives doesn't hurt."

"No, zer."

Cadwell frowned. "With her father and brother locked

up and Felicia Atwater also charged with the murders of Overton and Hoadley—"

"Not Fred Bramble?"

"The evidence suggests that it was the two Purple Door employees who abducted Ancilla and killed Fred."

"On Perry's orders?"

"Or Felicia's." She frowned. "A highly unnecessary death, but apparently someone felt his silence could not be bought."

"Have we connected Perry to Felicia Atwater?" asked Beaumont, his eyebrows rising.

One of the secrets that Felicia was prepared to kill to protect and for what? To be remembered? He could only hope the Way remembered Hoadley long after Felicia, Ernest and Perry were forgotten. But he doubted it.

"Not firmly, but yes she was the brains behind the pneuma harvester modifications and had assisted with the production."

"What about the numbing potion?"

Cadwell's brows drew together. "I've allocated a couple of inspectors, but unless Felicia has a lab that I am not aware of she had help."

"What do you want me to do with Alistair Atwater?"

The High Protector drummed her fingers on the desk. "A tricky business. Felicia's guilt means all the assets are seized. There is no evidence he was involved, and from what I understand he has joined his wife on the mainland. For now, not our problem." She leaned forward, resting her elbows on the desk, staring at him over steepled fingers. "Unless you plan to follow him?"

Beaumont leaned back.

"I have another postcard from Wilhelmina on my desk."

"You'd be bored within a week."

"I'd like to find that out for myself."

And heal. Be away from here, away from this.

She glared at him. "Or..." she laced her fingers in front of her. "You could stay here, but in an...advisory capacity."

"Advisory?"

"Move between departments, help out on the tricky cases."

"And when there are no tricky cases?"

"There are plenty of unregistered prototypes to chase, and with a pneuma harvester out there... I suspect you will be able to take your pick...Specialist Inspector Barnaby Beaumont."

His eyebrows ran up his forehead.

She waved her hand. "If I can't make up a title then what's the point of being the High Protector."

He huffed. It sounded okay in theory, but he suspected that it would end up with him dealing with political stuff.

"And it won't be all political stuff," she smiled. "I've already got a team for that."

He tested the tightness of the muscles in his face. For the first time in a long time, his fingers pressed in without pain. What did he have to lose?

"I don't want to work on my own."

Her eyebrows raised. "Very well I can—"

"I want the Hoadley's of the world. The puzzle solvers."

"And how many of these do you want?" She sat back examining him.

"I'll find them."

She glanced at him, an amused expression on her face.

"So that's a yes then?"

He rubbed the back of his neck and gave a shallow nod. "I'll give it a go."

"Please," she grunted. "Don't overwhelm me with your gratitude."

{ 29 }

Family's End

Ancilla wanted to go home and to bed. It had taken hours to finish her statement and she was exhausted. Now it was dawn, again, and she needed a bath. And a change of clothes and something to eat. First, however, she needed to see Ernest.

When she had asked, they had originally said no but she had escalated her request to the High Protector and had gotten a special dispensation to be able to see him with a guard present. She didn't want to be alone with him anyway.

They had taken his work clothes and he was now dressed in loose britches and shirt with a custodial waistcoat that not only clearly showed he was in custody but was alarmed if he tried to take it off or leave the Way. His face was red and at least one vein was throbbing. His fingers were drumming like a hummingbird on a table.

"Father."

He sneered. "I don't suppose you are going to make yourself useful?"

"Would you have told me?"

He stared at the wall.

"Or would you have just sat there and watched me be drained dry?"

He glared at her. "I told you not to play the artist."

"And that was you protecting me? What about Cuthbert? He is going to spend most of his years in prison."

"Maybe it'll improve his poetry."

"He wouldn't be in this mess if it wasn't for you."

His face went redder, but he snarled. "That little shit wouldn't be anything if it wasn't for me."

Pity he hadn't tried to resist arrest a little. Gordon and Beaumont might have been able to rough him up a little.

She glared at him, the tips of her fingers numb. "I doubt I will see you again."

"Everything you are, I paid for," he spat.

She gazed at him. A deflated spider whose web had been ripped apart.

"Maybe that's true." She nodded at the guard, and he opened the door. "But I get to choose what I do with it."

She left, tuning out the shouted words that followed.

The world, highlighted by a bright sun streaking through called to her. With the fog dispersed even the steel edge to Noxrath's air was lighter than normal. It was a long walk back to their house, but she couldn't stand being trapped even in an open-topped steamer, so she meandered.

It wasn't long before she left the Way behind and her steps took her past the empty patent office. She stopped and stared. A lone stroller holding a placard passed her.

"Where is everyone? I thought today was..."

The placard holder stopped and stared at her like she was from a foreign world. "They called the ballot in the final session last night."

"Did the bill pass?"

"Of course, it did, never any doubt. But no one's stopping to ask why so many Families supported it, did they? Who knows what they've got planned." His face was grim. "But we'll be watching." He stomped off.

She stared after him and then back at the Patent Office.

A new era. For good or evil, only time would tell.

Sugar and butter-infused steam from the chimney of a food cart caught her attention.

A small bag of pastry goodness later, she stopped at the intersection of the street leading to Atwater Place. She turned away, following an alternative route through one of the central parks.

People were out and about now. Young couples sharing a stolen moment over coffee, older friends enjoying the rare sunny winter day and the artists stretching their legs before a day of practice.

The streets got busier until she was just one of the crowd, her cloak of averageness once more engaged, giving her freedom. But the need for a wash forced her footsteps towards her familiar cage.

The vault was locked, the stairs rolled back. She shook her head and walked around to the back gate.

The octopus was still on its journey for freedom. Its second tentacle was further through, and she gave it a tap.

"You've got this."

She let herself in the back door.

The house wasn't empty.

"Ancilla."

She blinked, her head tilting as she took in Roger holding a box.

"Roger." She glanced at the box, but she didn't care. "I hope what's happening with us isn't affecting you?"

He shook his head. "No, no, not at all." He gave a rueful smile. "The Hawkes Family is glad I left when I did though." He glanced down at the box in his hand. "I left in a bit of a rush so just came back to get some of my things."

Ancilla nodded.

"Of course." She smiled. "I hope that one day I am reading about you being Noxrath's most famous poet."

He rubbed the back of his neck, smiling. "Well, I'm a long way off that."

They stared at each other. Ancilla awkwardly broadened her smile.

"Well, it's been a long night I'm just..." She pointed past him towards a stairwell that led up to her room.

"Right, of course." Roger stepped to the side and Ancilla gave him another awkward smile as she passed.

"Good luck with it all," she said.

She made it to the doorway.

"I told Titus Hawkes, he's their metal artist, I told him about the juggler." Roger's words stumbled over each other.

Ancilla spun around. "The juggler?"

Roger blushed. "Yeah, well, I love that thing and it's probably what kept me here all these years." He shrugged. "It's a brilliant piece of work."

"Okay." Ancilla patted her head, but instead of her hair, her hand landed on her hat. She pulled it off, her turn to blush.

"He was interested, very interested. He said that if you didn't get arrested to come and see him."

"See him."

"See him." Roger enunciated it slowly, a soft, concerned look washing across his face. "For production and distribution."

"The juggler?"

He smiled. "Yes, the juggler." He shook his head. "Get some sleep. I'll leave a note for you for tomorrow."

She blinked at him and nodded, stumbling up towards her room. She detoured past Melody's bedroom door to find it already open and her room cleared out. The reality of it made her sigh.

Perhaps she should follow suit. Leave this place and start afresh.

But first sleep. A quick wash wicked away tension from her bones. And not before long, she was crawling into bed, pulling her quilt over her and letting exhaustion take her under.

The precipice of afternoon and evening granted her room a soft glow when she resurfaced.

She needed to talk to Melody. Fortunately, guards were gossips. She splashed water on her face and dressed, braving the world once more. This time she found a steamer to take her to the flat near the Treadways.

Her hand paused over the locking mechanism, but she pulled it back and knocked.

It opened to reveal Necket who immediately blushed on seeing Ancilla.

"Zer Walstrand—"

"Ancilla, please." She smiled at Necket. "I think we are long past formalities, don't you?"

Necket smiled. "Yes, I suppose so. Please..."

She stepped out of the doorway giving enough space for Ancilla to walk through. She found Melody sitting in the middle of the floor surrounded by ledgers. She peered up, blinking.

The flat had been cleared of Marcellus' things and given a good clean.

"Do you need a place to stay?" asked Melody.

Ancilla's face softened.

Who knew—

"Cause you can't stay here we don't have room."

The world kept on turning.

"I'm staying at the house in Villiside."

Melody's eyebrows raised. "Why you would want to remain trapped there I don't know."

Ancilla's face was still but inside she suppressed a wince.

"That's one way to look at it." She gazed down at the ledgers surrounding her sister. "What are you doing?"

"Trying to find the money."

"Money? The gendarmerie has frozen all of Dad's—"

"Our mother's money, money that wouldn't be caught up in the freeze and that we might be able to live off until we can access his accounts or sell the house."

Ancilla shot a glance at Necket who had winced, gazing at Melody in sympathy.

Ancilla cleared her throat. "I'm not sure how long that is going to take Melody." Ancilla was pretty sure it was never, but she didn't want to completely crush her. And she wasn't sure she wanted to sell the house. "Do you have enough for now?"

"Melody has picked up some bookkeeping work in the neighbourhood," said Necket.

"What since yesterday?" Ancilla asked.

"No of course not," snapped Melody, making a note on another ledger.

"Er..." Ancilla glanced at Necket.

"She already had a few that she helped, for a small fee. Word of mouth has gotten around and now she has more time she had taken on more. It isn't much but enough to help."

"And what about you?"

Necket smiled. "The Atwater Foundation contacted me, gave me this flat, and asked me to be the government liaison in the first instance."

"I'm glad they are taking care of you," said Ancilla,

turning back to Melody who was once more lost in her ledgers. She stared at her sister for a moment, but Melody didn't look up. With a shrug, Ancilla shuffled back towards the door with Necket following her. "You and my sister huh?"

Necket's cheeks darkened. "Yes, I know you might think I am too old..."

"I think you're a saint." Ancilla shook her head. "Are you sure? I mean if she gets comfortable, and you don't charge her rent, she probably won't leave."

"I'm counting on it."

Ancilla laughed. "I don't know whether to say congratulations or commiserations but if it is what you want..."

"It is."

"Then I hope you're both very happy."

With her sense of duty appeased—and considering that enough of a success for the day—she returned to the empty house, bathed again, and crawled back into her bed.

It was dark when she woke up. She probably would have slept all the way through to the next day except her stomach was making its emptiness known. She stretched and after a bathroom visit, dressed.

The kitchen was empty of even the most basic foods, so she headed out. It was a little too late for most of the restaurants and after a few closed kitchens, she was directed to a small place on the next block which promised some amazing dishes and was open all night.

It was easy to find. Wafts of spices, caramelised meats and vegetables floated enticingly through the air. Her mouth watered and she had to swallow a few times, so she didn't walk in dribbling.

"Can I help you, zer?"

"Yes, A table for one."

"Of course, right this way."

She followed the server past the foyer area into a large room overcrowded with chairs and tables. She could imagine it was normally full but with it being so late only every second one was filled which meant she had a clear view of Beaumont at a table of four. He had a banquet of bowls filled to the brim with richly coloured dishes, rice, vegetables and sauces.

It sickened her that he could have such an appetite while Hoadley was lying cold in the morgue.

Beaumont glanced up as she approached, his mouth full of food. He chewed.

"Prime Inspector—"

"Actually," he took another bite of his food, talking around it, "it's Specialist Inspector now."

So, he'd gotten a promotion out of her death as well. "What's a specialist inspector?"

"Basically, he sticks his nose in other people's cases."

And makes a mess of them. She glared down at him. His chewing slowed down until he swallowed and placed his cutlery back on the table.

"Will you join me?" he asked.

"I'm just here for some food." She turned away, but the scraping of a chair being pushed back made her pause.

"I…"-a heavy exhale-"If I could go back and do things differently I would."

She swallowed and turned back to him.

"She was worth ten of you."

"I would have swapped places with her in an instant." He stared at her. "Please, you don't have to eat alone."

She gazed down at the table and back up to him.

"We've saved each other's lives…" he smiled at her. "Surely that deserves at least one shared meal?"

She took a seat. A server appeared and she ordered a bowl of something warm and healthy.

"Excellent choice," said Beaumont beaming at her.

She recoiled and his smile slid away, his eyes dropping to the food in front of him.

"It isn't fair," said Ancilla. Her eyes heated, the exhaustion of the last few days crashing down on her.

Beaumont sat back, his face grim. "No, it's not."

"She shouldn't have been alone."

"No." He spread his hands out, his face drooping.

"Why was she?"

Beaumont stared at her, opening and closing his mouth.

"None of you had her back."

"Your dinner," a server placed the meals in front of them and Ancilla focused on the food. Easier that way.

After she had finished her meal, she rose from the table and stared down at him. "Good night Specialist Inspector Beaumont." She left.

"Ancilla."

It probably wasn't a surprise that he followed her. What

was he going to do? Sit at the table and stare at his empty plate?

Still, she was ready for this to be over. She glared up at him. "I'm that way." She pointed down the street.

"I'm that way too," he said.

What witty conversationalists.

"Oh."

"Would you be kind enough to escort me home?"

Ancilla glanced at him in surprise. "Me?"

"My small abode is closer than your house. And it appears after the events of the day that it is I that need your protection." He smiled at her as he said it.

What were they going to do walk awkwardly a few steps apart? "Of course, happy to be of service." She took a step, so she was between him and the road. "Full protection mode engaged."

He grinned at her, and her heart beat a little faster. They strolled in companionable silence.

"This is me." He stopped in front of an elegant building. Its beautiful sweeping archways were a testament to modern design.

"I shall consider my duty completed again."

He raised an eyebrow. "Your duty?"

"To get you home safe."

He smiled. "I appreciated the backup."

She peered at the façade but couldn't see anyone's lights. It was very early.

"Good night or should I say good morning, Specialist Inspector Beaumont."

"Good morning, Zer Walstrand." He gave a small bow and turned to walk into his building but swung back. "Oh, I think this may be yours."

He held out the pocket watch. She stared at it and then up at him.

"How?" she asked.

"Hoadley..." He sighed and stared down at his toes. "She had it on her."

She let him drop it into her hands and tucked it into her waistcoat pocket.

"Thank you." She squeezed the pocket watch. "It has been a wild ride these last few days..." she gazed at him. "I'm sorry I blamed you for Hoadley's death. I want you to know that the only person to blame is Felicia and her unwillingness to accept the future." She adjusted her hat, giving a soft chuckle. "Now you're a Specialist Inspector, our paths won't be crossing—"

"Zer Walstrand," he shook his head. "I'd thought better of your observational skills than that." He flashed a fully charming smile at her and disappeared into his tenement.

She blinked, stared at the entrance to his building and a small smile flicked up.

She pulled the pocket watch back out and the cog on the side scraped against her skin. She pressed it in and a voice beyond the grave whispered through the night.

Morten.

{ 30 }

Epilogue

 From the desk of Ancilla Walstrand

This morning Felicia Atwater was executed for the deaths of Marcellus Overton and Lavina Hoadley. But it can never be made right. Not really.

I have been investigating, discretely, Dr Morten and I think she has started creating the pneuma drains again, this time with a twist. I hate that it even exists. I haven't told Barnaby. I should have. But all I had was a whispered name. Would he have even believed me?

I am fully healed now, I can feel my core is solid, but I can't do light art anymore. Perhaps just a mental block, but I am back to metal.

The octopus has pushed open its cage some more and has a third tentacle out now. I thought it would take years for it to break free, but now it's got a grip it seems to be accelerating its escape. I am going to create an underwater world of metal sculptures for it, a home for when it fully escapes.

Roger followed through and my juggler is being developed and distributed by the Hawkes Family. They have enough preorders for a full year's production.

I am now officially financially independent. Which is a good thing as they have seized all of Ernest's accounts. I thought they would take the house too, but rumour has it that the High Protector stepped in. I don't know why, and I don't like that I owe her a favour. But still, I have a home.

The Hawkes are also using my fabric for tablecloths and chair coverings. Apparently, the restaurants are clamouring for a fabric that can survive clients and can be customised in colour and design.

No one wants it for clothing yet though. Only a select few hardy souls, Hoadley and I included. I still can't believe Hoadley's gone. I keep expecting her to storm in demanding justice. Despite it all, I'll use the fabric for my outfit for Melody and Necket's registration ceremony. I don't know what Melody did to score Florence Necket, but I am happy for them. To reduce the risk of some hideous overly bright on-sale fabric ruining Florence's day, I gifted Meldoy a registration outfit in a flattering soft green.

Florence sent me a heartfelt thank you. I had better get changed. Barnaby found out that Florence included one of her cakes with the thank you message and was probably already on his way.

Hopefully the cake will soften the blow when I reveal exactly what Tabitha Morten has been up to.

HARRIE BLAKE

harrieblake.com

**Enter the draw for a free advance
copy of the next release.**